KEEPING MISERY
COMPANY

KEEPING MISERY COMPANY

MICHELLE LARKS

URBAN
CHRISTIAN

www.urbanchristianonline.net

Urban Books, LLC
78 East Industry Court
Deer Park, NY 11729

Keeping Misery Company ©copyright 2007 Michelle Larks

ISBN 13: 978-1-60162-877-0
ISBN 10: 1-60162-877-3

First Trade Paperback Printing November 2007
First Mass Paperback Printing April 2010
Printed in the United States of America

10 9 8 7 6 5 4 3 2 1

*This is a work of fiction. Any references or similarities to actual
events, real people, living, or dead, or to real locales are intended to
give the novel a sense of reality. Any similarity in other names,
characters, places, and incidents is entirely coincidental.*

Distributed by Kensington Corp.
Submit Wholesale Orders to:
Kensington Publishing Corp.
C/O Penguin Group (USA) Inc.
Attention: Order Processing
405 Murray Hill Parkway
East Rutherford, NJ 07073-2316
Phone: 1-800-526-0275
Fax: 1-800-227-9604

Dedication

This book is dedicated to Donna Reese, Cheryl Katherine Walsh, Anita Peterson, and Rhonda Bogan, four women who were very instrumental in helping establish my writing career. I would also like to dedicate *Keeping Misery Company* to my Sisters in Christ, Kelley Hicks, and Reverend Joan Ewing. Thank you for allowing me to talk to you and bounce ideas off you when we shared lunch at the Golden Corral Restaurant in 2005.

Last but not least, this book is dedicated to the memory of my brother, Roland Harris Jr. I'm going to miss you, but I know we'll meet in the sweet by and by.

Acknowledgments

As always, I must give my thanks to my heavenly Father above. Thank you for the many blessings You have bestowed upon me as I continue on my journey of life.

To mothers, Mary, Jean, and Bertha, stepmother Carol, and my dads, Macio, (deceased) Isadore Jr., and father-in-law, George. Without all of you, there wouldn't be a Michelle.

And my daughters, Mikeisha and Genesse, I love you.

To all my sisters; Patrice, Sabrina, Katherine (deceased), Adrienne, Donna, Catherine, and Rolanda. To my sisters-in-law, Angela, Patricia, Franshun, Kimberlyn, Toscha and Jacqueline. My brothers; Jackie, Marcus, Isadore III (deceased), Roland, (deceased) Darryl, Wayne, Michael, and Rodney. My brothers-in-law, Stephen, Michael, and Shedrick. My nieces and nephews; Maverick (deceased), Rasheema, Tyrone, Tashawn, Josh, Donald, Terrence, Damiko, Dominique, Michael M., Bryant, Ceora, Alexis, Kathleen, Michae, Stephanie, Nicole, Jordan, Isadora IV, Kapricia, Angelina, Atrecia, Shedrick Jr., Sheena, Michael H., Darryl, Kemo, Joshua, Jamarha, Jacoby, Jericho, Jeremy, Angela, Jasmine, Diontay, Kyrie, including the newest, twins, Nichole, and Nicolas. And to my grand nieces and nephews; Keon, Rae Nicole,

Adora, Jalin, and William. Big Sis and Auntie Chelle loves all of you, our present and future.

Special kudos to Joylynn Jossel, my editor at Urban Christian Books, thank you for the opportunity to allow me to spread the word. Also, heartfelt appreciation to my agent, Tee C. Royal and my VOA, Denise Glessner.

To the churches and ministers, who during my lifetime, has nurtured my spiritual diet; Good Shepherd Community Church, Haven of Rest Baptist Church, and Friendship United Methodist Church.

I'd like to express my gratitude to my sister/ girlfriends who've listened and encouraged me as I rambled on about my stories; Cynthia L., Cynthia D., Herlinda, Nancy, Eveline, Joyce, Mary, and Liz. Also thanks to several authors who have lent me a helping hand along the way; Francine Yates, Barbara Keaton, Sheila Peele-Miller, Sheila Goss, Elaine Overton, Valerie Coleman, Margie Gosa-Shivers, and Kendra Norman-Bellamy. Oops, I can't forget to thank Mary Bell, Reverend Vivian Carter, Patrick McFowler, Zelda Robinson, and Glenn Murray for your solid encouragement.

I'd like to thank the bookstores that allowed me to sign in your establishments and stocked my books on your shelves. The libraries who invited me to participate in your author events and all the book clubs that invited me to your book club discussion, I had a blast. And to those book clubs that reviewed my books, my co-workers, friends, and the people in my community, Bolingbrook, as well as people who have invited me to participate in your events helping me to get the word out, I appreciate you more than you can know.

Much love to the readers who have supported my endeavors since I wrote my first book. Where would I be without your generous support? It is greatly appreciated.

To my husband, Fredrick, I love you and thank you for all of your unwavering support and love.

Chapter One

Ruth Wilcox's eyelids snapped open like a shade on a window. She stretched, then turned to her left side and peeped at the silver and black clock radio that sat on the nightstand on the righthand side of the bed. The bright red LED segued into eight o'clock A.M.

Darn it; I meant to get up earlier, she thought as she sat up abruptly, yawned and rubbed her eyes.

"Danny!" Ruth yelled her husband's name, short for Daniel, in a raspy, just-got-up-in-the-morning voice. She rose from the bed and walked down the gray, carpeted hallway to the spare bedroom only to find it empty.

Daniel had already left for work. The man of the house was employed as a supervisor for the Chicago Transit Authority. Earlier that morning, one of his employees had called him on his cell phone and informed him that he was ill and wouldn't be at work that day. Daniel would have to drive the No. 6 Jeffrey bus in place of his sick employee.

Ruth stood in the doorway with her hands on her wide hips. The ends of her hair stood tousled over her head like a bird's nest. Her eyes swept over the orderly room. Daniel had opened the red mini blinds before he left for work, allowing an *anemic* ray of sunlight to flood the white painted room. A red and white-checkered comforter draped the corners of the bed neatly.

His black and green plaid, worn, slippers sat side-by-side at the bottom of the bed. A corner of the navy blue border wallpaper was peeling and laid limply away from the wall.

Ruth looked inside the room apprehensively, as if she expected her husband to suddenly appear out of thin air, and ask her what she was doing in his room. Danny's personality included a private streak and he'd told Ruth many times that he hated for her to snoop through his things.

She walked over to the closet, opened the door, turned on the light, and riffled through the pockets of the clothing he had worn the day before.

She found a book of matches from the bar that Daniel and his brother, Fred, frequented. Ruth removed a scrap of paper with a woman's name and telephone number scratched untidily upon it. She held the paper away from her face and squinted at it. Her lips poked out angrily. Then she crushed the paper, stomped out of the closet, and walked across the room to the trashcan and dropped the offending items unceremoniously inside of it.

As a bolt of pain shot up Ruth's leg, she scrambled out of the room and back down the hall into the pink and black tiled bathroom that adjoined the master bedroom; her room. She stood in front of the door-length mirror and pulled her yellow and green faded, cotton nightgown over her head.

Her dark eyes traveled the length of her body as she critically assessed it. Her face flushed rosily and her eyes dropped in dismay at the sight of her nakedness.

Why did I let myself go like this? she wondered as her gaze fell to her pouched stomach. Ruth gathered a portion of the round flesh between her fingers. "More than an inch," she said to herself. She sucked in her belly. Her eyes dropped to the patch of gray and black pubic hair. Her upper arms and thighs were flabby. Her salt and pepper hair, which stopped just below her ears, was in desperate need of a rinse and perm.

She lifted a lock of her limp hair, dropped it, and blew a strand out of her face. Her plump, brown sugar-colored face crumpled as a tear trickled down her right cheek. *God, I look a mess. I need to lose at least twenty pounds.* She then examined her legs. *But at least my legs still look good. I don't have varicose veins or anything.* Her pear shaped breasts were no match for gravity though. *That's what I get for breast-feeding the kids.*

Ruth's career since marrying Daniel Wilcox, Senior, nearly thirty-five years ago, was that of a stay-at-home mother. Her primary job was to raise her son, Daniel, Jr., nicknamed DJ, and daughters, Sarah and Naomi.

She sighed heavily, because somewhere along the way, she had carelessly abandoned her role as a loving wife.

Ruth turned away from the mirror and stepped into the steamy shower. Hot, gushing water washed away her tears, but not her thoughts as her mind wandered to her husband, who she was estranged from in her own house.

Daniel had moved to the spare bedroom two years ago when Ms. Menopause came knocking on Ruth's door; and she was still an unwelcome visitor. Ruth experienced many of the physical discomforts of middle-aged women—night sweats, hot flashes and weight gain. Her sex drive had also tapered to almost naught.

The last few times she and Daniel had relations, as Ruth calls lovemaking, it was painful. The area between her legs ached when they were done, and her breasts were sore for days. They had come perilously close to divorce when the mood swings kicked in. Daniel jokingly began calling her Ruthie, his nickname for her alter ego.

Ruth was an active member of the Baptist church she belonged to and volunteered for many committees. She was the church secretary and occupied a desk outside her father's *maple-paneled office*, Reverend Isaiah Clayton, who was the pastor, three days a week. Initially Ruth worked without pay, but as the membership rolls swelled, the church decided to pay her a salary.

But somewhere between raising children and church activities, Ruth lost sight of being Mrs. Daniel Wilcox and the oversight had severely damaged her marriage.

After Ruth showered, she dressed in a black pleated skirt and a white peter pan-collared blouse. She hastily brushed her hair into her usual mushroom hairdo, the same style she's worn since high school.

She patted her hair one last time and walked down the hall to her red and yellow kitchen. White curtains with strawberry appliqués hung brightly at the kitchen window. Red canisters gleamed on the black and white faux marble counter. A red floor mat lay in front of the kitchen sink.

She put a pot of coffee on the stove to brew. Before long, the strong aroma filled the kitchen. The telephone jangled, breaking the silence.

"Hello," Ruth answered.

"What's up, Mama?" Naomi's voice boomed loudly in Ruth's ear.

Ruth clicked on the speaker button of the white cordless Bell South telephone and set it on the table while she turned down the stove burner. "Nothing, baby girl. How are you doing? Shouldn't you be in class or something?"

"Naw, I have forty-five minutes to spare before my first class."

"And you're up already? I remember when I had to call you at least four times before you'd get out of the bed in the morning." Ruth and Naomi chuckled at the memory.

"That was then, this is now. Although, I have been late to class a couple of times," Naomi confessed, feeling slightly chastened.

"I hope you aren't failing any classes, Naomi Wilcox. 'Cause your father will hit the roof," Ruth said, sitting down at the kitchen table. "You know he was adamantly against you going away to college anyway. It took me three months to convince him to let you go to SIU."

Naomi, the youngest Wilcox child, was a freshman at Southern Illinois University in Carbondale, Illinois. Daniel felt spending money on a college education for her was a waste of time and money. Her grades and belligerent attitude towards him when she entered her teen years was tantamount to throwing away his hard earned money as far as he was concerned.

The youngest member of the Wilcox family's adjustment to college had been difficult. Naomi had few friends, so she and Ruth talked on the telephone at least twice a day. Daniel felt that was one time too many, which added another bone of contention between the couple and drove his point home that his wife puts their children's needs over his.

Naomi was a pretty, plump, honey-colored young woman with shapely legs like her mother's. Her hips were widely rounded and her waist small. She wore micro braid extensions in her dark wavy hair and had a standing appointment for a pedicure twice a month.

Ruth would sneak and send Naomi money without Daniel's knowledge. She spoiled the couple's youngest child rotten, and hasn't been able to cut the imaginary apron strings. Her rearing of Naomi produced a sometimes lazy, immature girl, but Ruth wasn't worried about her daughter's character. She attributed the traits to her daughter being a teenager, and assumed that in time Naomi would outgrow her character flaws. Daniel, of course, begged to differ.

Ruth took a cup out of the cabinet and poured herself a cup of coffee and sipped it while she and

Naomi talked. Ruth and Naomi chatted a few minutes longer on the phone before Ruth brought their conversation to an end. She didn't want to give her daughter an excuse for being late to class.

After Ruth finished her conversation with Naomi, she sat thoughtfully at the kitchen table. Her chin was propped on her left hand as she listlessly stirred the remaining coffee inside her cup. Under the fluorescent lights in the ceiling, the white and silver appliances sparkled brightly.

Ruth became upset as she sat and thought about finding the name and number in Daniel's room. She tried to pinpoint exactly when they had arrived at the godforsaken place they now inhabited. Originally, she thought it happened at the onset of menopause. But as her mind wandered back in time, she knew their difficulties began as far back as when Naomi was born.

They had disagreed about bringing another child into the world. Ruth overruled Daniel's wishes, and the wedge between them deepened as time elapsed. With many concessions on her part, they still managed to function as a family unit.

After Naomi became thirteen years old, Daniel felt Ruth should loosen the apron strings a bit. He proclaimed that the time had come for the two of them to spend more time together, but Ruth staunchly disagreed. Naomi was experiencing self-esteem issues regarding her weight, and Ruth felt it was her job as a mother to help her child work through her problems.

That caused another wall of distance to rise up between wife and husband. Then menopause struck, their lovemaking decreased, and Daniel moved into the spare bedroom. Ruth wasn't sure how to bridge the gap between them and return to the other side.

Daniel began spending more time out of the house with his single brother, Fred. And when Daniel did manage to stay home, his body was planted downstairs in the den in front of the television, which was always tuned to a sporting event.

Ruth uneasily noted the change in her husband's behavior. But instead of talking to him about her fears, she didn't say anything, and hoped the problems they experienced would just go away.

Lately, Daniel had been coming home later and later. When she asked about his activities, he'd just say he was hanging out with the fellows. If he was messing around, and the thought did cross her mind a time or two, she was one hundred percent sure that he'd never leave her and break up the family unit.

I know what I'll do. Ruth snapped her fingers. *I'll call Dr. Jackson and make an appointment. Maybe she'll prescribe hormone replacement therapy regiment Umm hum, that's what I need to do.* She traced circles on the kitchen table. *And I'm definitely going to call Eunice and have her do something to my hair.*

She put two slices of bread in the toaster and reached inside the refrigerator for the container of butter. Ruth had just sat the tub on the table when the telephone rang again.

"Hello, Sarah. How are you?" she asked, after seeing her oldest daughter's number on the caller ID.

"Fine, Mama. And you?" Sarah replied.

"I'm doing fine. How's your day going so far?"

"Not too bad."

The Wilcox's oldest child was employed as a customer service representative for ComED Electricity Company. She'd been employed there since she had graduated from high school. In addition to working, Sarah opted to attend a junior college part time. She was an attractive looking, shapely, kind, outgoing woman. Naomi was slightly jealous of her older sibling, because she felt Sarah possessed many of the traits she yearned to have herself.

"What do you have planned for today?" Sarah asked her mother.

"I'm due at the church at eleven o'clock to help prepare for the senior citizens luncheon. And that's about it," Ruth replied as she set her plate and cup on the counter.

"How's Daddy? I guess he's at work."

"Yes, he is. I didn't get a chance to see him before he left, so I guess he's okay."

Sarah informed Ruth, "today is report card pickup day at school and I plan to leave work early to get the kid's cards."

"I'm sure their grades are fine. You make sure education and good grades are priorities for your children. They know that and I'm sure they'll be fine," Ruth assured her daughter.

Sarah was divorced, and the mother of eight-year-old Joshua, and six-year-old Magdalene, whom the family called Maggie for short. Sarah's ex-husband, Brian, was sometimes lax about paying his child support stipends on time. Brian's indifference, or reluctance to pay the money in a timely fashion, would often leave Daniel picking up the slack, which was usually around the children's birthdays and holidays.

"Mama, my break is almost over. I'll talk to you later." Sarah informed her mother.

"Okay dear, have a blessed day," Ruth said to Sarah, and placed the phone receiver back into the cradle. Ruth finished eating the toast and replenished her coffee. After she finished her meal, Ruth washed and dried the dishes, put them back inside the cabinet and then she headed out to church.

At ten-thirty, Ruth arrived at Jubilee Temple Baptist Church. She wiped the sheen of perspiration from her face, and rolled up her sleeves. She donned an apron as she prepared plates of food in the hot church kitchen. After the elderly were fed, Ruth decided to make a detour on her way home to visit her best friend, Alice. She always seemed to know what to say to make her feel better.

Chapter Two

As Ruth drove west on 87th Street, she passed a Bally's location and Women's Workout World. A mental picture of herself huffing and puffing as she worked out on a treadmill caused her to break out in a hot flash. She laughed aloud. *Maybe I should sign up at one of those places and try to lose some weight. Then maybe I won't find women's phone numbers in my husband's pants pockets.*

Before long, Ruth was parking her beige Cadillac STS in front of Alice's dark brown, brick bungalow on Michigan Avenue in the Chatham community, not far from her own home. She rang the doorbell and her friend opened the door.

"Hey Ruth, how are you doing today? What's new?" Alice's plump, caramel face was wreathed in a smile.

"Oh, fair to middling, I'd say," Ruth said glumly as she stood outside the door like her feet were glued to the step.

Alice grabbed Ruth's arm and tugged gently. "Well, don't just stand there, come on inside."

The friends walked through Alice's brown brick Georgian-styled home to the rear of the house to the sun parlor and sat together cozily and gabbed. Yolanda Adams sang softly from the stereo.

Ruth's best friend was a virtuoso pianist. She'd instructed some of the most promising music students in the Chicago area, regardless of their economic backgrounds. Her husband, Martin, had been employed as a financial planner, and he'd left her more than economically comfortable when he passed away several years ago.

"I'm thinking about surprising Daniel and making travel arrangements for us to go on a cruise over the Christmas holidays," Ruth confessed as she smoothed the hem of her skirt.

"Hmmm," Alice said, nodding her head, "that sounds like a good idea in theory. But you and I know Daniel doesn't like surprises. Why are you going to go through all that trouble for something that may blow up in your face? Oh, I get it, it's for your anniversary, right?"

"Our anniversary is coming up on December thirty-first. But I have to admit, I have ulterior motives, Allie. I woke up this morning and looked at myself in the bathroom mirror, and I swear I wavered between screaming and throwing up. It's time for me to make some changes in my life. Daniel and I have grown apart, and I need to do something, anything, to put back the oomph in our marriage."

Alice, clad in a brown sweat suit and scuffed

white tennis shoes, listened to her friend skeptically. She wore a caring expression on her face.

Alice and Ruth had been best friends since first grade. It was now 1998, and the women's relationship had withstood the test of time. They shared their innermost secrets with one another.

"He's not messing around again, is he?" Alice asked, matter-of-factly. She looked away from Ruth and down at her tangerine-colored fingernails, which were in need of a manicure.

Ruth rubbed the skin between her eyes and sighed. "He could be. I just know that something isn't right. I found another telephone number in his pants pocket." Tears sprang in her eyes.

Alice reached over and patted Ruth's arm. "That in and of itself doesn't mean anything. We both know Daniel's a flirt, and that he's still a good-looking man. With the shortage of men these days, I'm sure all kinds of women throw themselves at him," she said, trying to reassure her friend.

Ruth sniffed and wiped her nose with the back of her hand. Alice got up, walked into the bathroom, and returned with a tissue.

Alice, like Ruth's family, was prominent in the Chicago ministry. Her late grandfather was an evangelist, and founder of their family church. Her brother, Luke, took over the reins of the church ten years ago when their father retired from his ministerial duties.

When Martin, passed away, outsiders were informed that his death was the result of a rare type of cancer. As his condition worsened and after consulting with Martin, Alice placed her husband in a nursing home the last few months of his life where he died. Caring for Martin had become too onerous for Alice to handle alone. Only a select few, not even her closest relatives, were aware of the fact that he had died from AIDS-related complications. Martin was bi-sexual and had succumbed to the lure of the forbidden fruit.

Since the couple wasn't blessed with any offspring, Alice felt Ruth's children, her godchildren, especially Naomi, were her own.

"I don't know what to do. I feel so helpless," Ruth confessed. The corners of her mouth drooped despondently. "When I woke up this morning, Daniel was gone. There was a time when he'd wake me up and kiss me before he left for work. He doesn't now, and half the time, I don't know where he goes after work." Ruth was too ashamed to meet Alice's eyes.

"You don't expect your marriage to be like it was when you got married, do you?" Alice asked, kindly. Her hands were clasped together as she leaned forward in her seat.

"I don't know what I expect anymore. Half the time, we're like two ships passing in the night. The passion has gone out of our marriage. It's my fault mostly. Because of menopause, my body hurts when we have relations, so we rarely have sex." Ruth bit back a sob.

"Maybe you should see a gynecologist?"

"I'm thinking about it." Ruth crinkled her nose. "But you know I hate putting drugs in my body.

"Do you remember when we married how our mothers told us if we didn't see to our husbands' needs, someone else would?" Alice asked Ruth.

Ruth nodded. "Yeah, but I don't remember either one of them telling us what to do during our middle ages, especially during menopause."

"Luckily, I didn't have that problem with Martin. By the time menopause hit, we were a couple in name only."

"We were so innocent back then," Ruth sighed. "If your mother hadn't talked to us about the birds and the bees back then, I wouldn't have known what to expect on my wedding day. Even she couldn't prepare me for the likes of Daniel. And Queen didn't even make an effort to talk to me."

Ruth and Alice's mothers were a contrast in looks and personality. Queen Esther, Ruth's mother, barely talked to her daughter, unless she was correcting her on proper church etiquette. She was short, standing only five foot, two inches tall. Her complexion was almond and her chest was puffy like a bird, a nicely rounded behind, and shapely legs; even at age seventy-four. She wore her thick, bluish gray hair coiled in a French twist. The first lady of the church was always dressed in a style befitting her elite status.

Queen was utterly consumed with her role as the minister's wife, second chief in command of the Temple. She considered her maternal duties completed when Ruth married Daniel against her better judgment.

Precious, Alice's mother, tried to prepare the young women for the male species, but omitted telling the young ladies how to cope with a husband with strong sexual drives, and Ruth was ashamed to talk to Precious after her marriage to Daniel. She was afraid something was deficient with her sexual make up. Prior to the birth of their children, Daniel expected to make love with his wife at least two or three times a day. Ruth thought that after a couple had relations, usually at night with the lights off, that it was sufficient until the next night.

Before the children were born, Ruth sometimes had to literally fend off his advances in the bedroom. She never admitted it, but she was glad when she had her monthlies; at least then she'd get a break from the action.

Alice stood and pulled a brown leaf off one of her potted plants sitting on the windowsill, giving Ruth time to compose herself.

"Maybe you and Daniel should talk to Bishop, or go to couples therapy or something?" Alice suggested.

"Oh no, I couldn't do that." Ruth's face took on a look of consternation. She waved her hand dismissively. "I can't talk to my father about my marital problems."

Alice stood and placed her hands on her hips. "I guess you're right. But I thought since he counsels members of his congregation about almost anything, you could talk to him." She paused and chose her words carefully, "Ruth, do you really think a cruise will fix what's wrong with your marriage?" Alice asked curiously.

"I don't know," Ruth sighed, twisting a lock of her hair in her fingers. "But it certainly won't hurt to try, along with me losing twenty pounds and doing something to my hair." She self-consciously patted her head.

To soothe Daniel's demands over the years, Ruth

promised him that after the children were grown and out the house, she'd devout her time solely to his creature comforts. Naomi's first semester at college was coming to an end, and Ruth had yet to make good on her pledge.

To those on the outside looking in, especially the members of the Temple, the first daughter of the church's lineage was impeccable. She should have been guaranteed a one-way ticket to heaven.

Ruth was the daughter, granddaughter, and great-granddaughter of The Church of God and Christ Ministers. Her sires were fiery, pulpit-thumping pastors in the tradition of Southern Baptist ministers.

When Ruth's father, Reverend Isaiah Clayton, Jr., took over the ministerial reins from his father, he had already attracted a following in the Chicago area. The church membership swelled to over five thousand. Reverend Clayton conducted three Sunday services, along with outreach programs and other religious activities during the week.

Reverend Clayton and Queen Esther are the parents of two children, Ruth and her older brother, Ezra, the black sheep of the family.

Ruth attended a Christian elementary school and an all girls' catholic high school. To her surprise, her father had suggested she enroll at Malcolm X Junior College for her post high school education. He felt her attending a non-Christian college would round her out as a person. And during her commute to school was when Ruth first laid eyes on the man who was to become her husband, Daniel Wilcox. And the rest, as the say, is history.

Chapter Three

During Ruth's first year of college at Malcolm X, she met Daniel, who'd just started working for CTA Public Transportation. It was pure kismet that brought the unlikely couple together.

Nearly a year after riding Daniel's bus to school, eighteen-year-old Ruth approached her father, who was affectionately called Bishop by family members, as he sat in the den of their home, working on his Sunday sermon.

Ruth was deliriously in love and wanted her parents to meet Daniel. She sailed into the den as if she were floating on air. She wore a long, pink bathrobe. Pink curlers crisscrossed her head, and she wore pink bunny slippers on her feet.

"Daddy, can I talk to you about something, if you aren't too busy?" Ruth's voice trailed off uncertainly.

"I always have time for you, baby girl. Come on in and have a seat. What's on your mind?" Bishop pushed the papers he'd been working on neatly to the side and gave his daughter his undivided attention.

"Daddy, I've met *him*, the man I love and want to marry." She sat on the brown and yellow Naugahyde sofa across from his desk. Her eyes twinkled like stars.

Bishop looked at Ruth shocked. His eyes widened like nickels. He held up his hand. "Whoa there. Who is this fellow? Where did you meet him?"

Ruth smiled joyously and clasped her hands to her chest. "His name is Daniel Wilcox. I ride his bus every morning to school. Even if I'm running a little late, he'll wait on me. Daddy, he's the nicest man I've ever met."

"Hmm, do you mean he's a bus driver?" Bishop's left eyebrow rose doubtfully.

"What's wrong with him being a bus driver? They make good money. I mean, I don't know how much money Danny makes, but I assume he makes a lot. He's so nice, Daddy."

"He hasn't tried to get fresh with you, has he?" Bishop frowned, clenching his hands together.

Ruth blushed. "Of course not. Danny is a perfect gentleman. He's asked me to go out with him lots of times, but I know you and Mama won't give me the okay until you meet him first. So I want to invite him to dinner Sunday. Please, Daddy?"

A lump rose up in Bishop's throat. He had never seen his daughter look so lovely before despite her attire. Love had softened her features, her face glowed. His intuition told him that his baby girl thinks she's in love. And he wasn't quite sure if he was ready to deal with losing her. He felt a keen sense of frustration, because he knew his daughter could do better than a bus driver.

"Is he a Christian, Ruth?"

Bishop had higher aspirations for his daughter. He secretly hoped she would marry a minister, ensuring that the church ministry would be passed on to a male family member.

Ruth re-rolled a curler that had slipped loose before answering. "Well, kind of," she replied, evasively.

"There's no half-stepping when it comes to the Lord. You know that. Is he or isn't he a Christian?"

Ruth looked cornered. She put her hands in the pocket of her robe and crossed her fingers. "He believes in God, Daddy. Daniel just isn't a practicing Christian."

"You know whomever you marry has an obligation like all of our family to elevate God and the teachings of the Lord."

Ruth nodded. "We've talked about the Temple, Daddy. Danny understands my role as first daughter of the church, and he promises to support me."

Bishop flinched when Ruth said the name *Danny*. Her voice rose an octave higher, and her eyes became dreamy when she said Daniel's name. He sat against the back of his chair.

"Life was much simpler back in my day. The young people in my circle only associated with other minister's families. No one had to explain roles or anything like that. Everyone knew what was expected of them," Bishop sighed.

"That was years ago," Ruth said softly, peering at her father intently. "Times have changed. Plus you and Mama are from the south, and everybody knew everybody in the town you're from anyway. I know if you and Mama give Danny a chance, you'll adore him. All I ask is a chance. Please, Daddy?"

Bishop didn't have it in him to deny his daughter anything her heart desired. "Talk to your Mother about inviting this Danny to dinner next Sunday," he said, grudgingly. "And ask her to schedule dinner around three o'clock. I promised Reverend Rawlins I'd try to make it to his church for their revival service later that evening."

"Thank you, Daddy," Ruth squealed. She jumped from the sofa and rushed to her father, hugging his neck. "I promise that you and Mama will love Daniel."

Ruth walked down the hallway to her parent's bedroom. Queen Esther stood in the mint green and ecru colored room, removing outfits from the closet to take to the cleaners. "I'm going to take these to Brother Smith in the morning," She pointed to the mound of clothing on the bed. "Do you have anything that needs cleaning? I can take them with me?" Queen Esther didn't miss the ecstatic look on her daughter's face.

"Momma, I talked to Daddy and he says it's okay with him if I invite a friend over for dinner Sunday," Ruth informed her mother. She sat down on the side of the maple four-post bed.

"Did he now? And who would that be? Alice is away at school." Queen Esther checked the pockets of her beige suit jacket.

"I met a boy, and I'd like you and Daddy to meet him." Ruth followed the clothing on the bed.

"Who is the young man? Someone from church?" Queen Esther asked hopefully. She paused and gave Ruth her undivided attention.

"Not exactly." Ruth explained to her mother how she met Daniel.

Queen Esther worked hard to keep her expression neutral as she listened to Ruth speak. A feeling of dread filled her body. *Just wait until I talk to Bishop. What was he thinking? Telling Ruth that it's okay to invite a bus driver to our house!* She thought as she tried to suppress a frown that threatened to cover her face. Bishop had the final say so in the Clayton household, so Queen Esther had no choice but to consent to Ruth's request for Daniel's dinner invitation. The older woman nodded and then continued her chore as Ruth glided on air out of the room and back to her own bedroom.

When Ruth saw Daniel on the bus the following day, she told him about her plans for him to meet her family. Daniel eagerly accepted Ruth's invitation to dinner. When he arrived at the Clayton house, he was dressed to the nines, or so he thought. But Bishop was unimpressed with the young man's appearance. Daniel wore a dark sharkskin suit and alligator shoes. Bishop dismissed his daughter's suitor as flashy and uncouth. He frowned upon sharkskin suits as much as he did pantsuits for women.

The visit proved to be disastrous. The atmosphere was heavy and oppressive. Conversation was slow because Daniel felt intimidated by Bishop. He sighed with relief when Queen announced dinner was ready. She had prepared a huge meal like she was cooking for the deacon board.

Ruth felt anxious, and she sensed her parents weren't impressed with her suitor. Queen Esther looked down on people who used slang terminology, and Daniel, in his nervousness, couldn't seem to speak a smidgen of proper English.

To Bishop's dismay, Daniel began eating before the meal was blessed. And from there, the evening snowballed downhill like an avalanche.

Queen's most prized possession, an Irish linen tablecloth, which was a family heirloom from her great-grandmother and had been passed down to her, was draped across the large mahogany dining room table. Daniel accidentally spilled gravy on it as he ladled a spoonful onto his potatoes. He dabbed at the spot with his napkin, which only made the stain worse.

Queen jumped out of her seat like she was surrounded by a swarm of bees. "Please, just leave it." She rushed into the kitchen and returned a box of baking soda and proceeded to clean the dark stain.

After she returned to her seat, she picked up her fork, pointed it at Daniel and asked, "Where is your family from young man?"

"From here. I mean I grew up in Chicago."

"What part? Where did you go to church?" Queen interrogated Daniel like a police detective interrogating a suspect.

He started squirming in his seat. "I, uh, didn't go to church much growing up. Mostly only on Christmas and Easter."

Bishop pursed his lips together and frowned at Ruth critically as he put a piece of roast turkey on his plate.

"Danny was raised in Stateway Gardens," Ruth added. "I think it's admirable that he and his brother were able to make it out of the projects and make something of themselves." Her eyes shone as she smiled at Daniel, encouragingly.

Shortly after dessert was served and eaten, Daniel pushed the cake plate away, wiped his mouth with a linen napkin, and stood.

"Uh, it's been a blast meeting you folks," he nodded at Bishop and Queen Esther, "but I really gotta go now. I have some bidness to take care of."

Queen stood, and with a deadpan expression on her face, began stacking the dishes. "It was interesting meeting you, Daniel"

"Same here," Bishop intoned, halfheartedly.

Ruth rose from her seat and walked with Daniel to the foyer. "I know dinner was a little bit awkward. But give my folks a chance, things can only get better from here."

Daniel put his hat on his head and stroked Ruth's cheek. He shrugged his shoulders. "I don't know about that baby, I don't think your folks cared for me. Today definitely wasn't one of my finest hours. I'll see you tomorrow. Dinner was, I don't know, different." He opened the door and went out.

After closing and locking the front door, Ruth returned to the dining room, looking miserable.

Queen shook her head from side to side and informed her daughter, "He's not suitable, Ruth. Find someone else." She finished clearing the dishes off the dining room table.

Ruth held back tears of dismay as she went

into the kitchen and placed dishes in the dishwasher. She turned the appliance on and went into the den to talk to Bishop. He gently informed Ruth he didn't think Daniel was the right man for her.

"Baby girl, that young man seems too worldly for you. Why don't you go to the Baptist convention with your mother and I this spring? I'm sure you'll meet a slew of eligible young ministers there."

But Ruth, much to Bishop's surprise, refused to back down. She squared her shoulders and raised her chin a notch. "Daddy, I'm going to continue to see Daniel. I told you I love him." And that's exactly what she did.

Chapter Four

When Daniel had returned home after the dinner with Ruth and her parents, he was in a foul mood. He threw his coat on the chair in the living room of the two-bedroom apartment he and Fred shared, and then Daniel went into the kitchen to fix himself a drink. He returned to the living room and flopped down on the red faux leather couch.

Being with Ruth's parents that afternoon filled the young man with self-doubt. He knew Ruth was the woman for him, because he figured he could mold her into the perfect wife. But he felt diminished being around her parents, like he didn't matter.

Thoughts of Daniel's childhood crept into his mind. His mother died of a drug overdose when he was ten years old. He and Fred's father was incarcerated for life in a federal prison located in downstate Illinois for murder, so he was unable to play an active role in his sons' lives.

The brothers' maternal grandmother had raised them after their mother passed. Gertrude Lamont was a big-boned, no-nonsense woman, who sipped whiskey daily from a Mason jar. After she became entwined in a liquor haze, she would remind her grandsons the only reason she allowed them to stay with her was because of the stipend the city paid her.

There was little love or sustenance in Gertie's house. Fred had fond memories of his mother, whereas Daniel's recollections were mostly blank.

When their mother, Linda Wilcox, wasn't high, which was the case most of the time, she became repentant and showered her boys with love and affection.

Daniel had only experienced unconditional love from one person his entire life, his brother, Fred. Until he met Ruth, his motto for dealing with women was, *hit it and quit it*. But the quiet love and attentiveness of Ruth had crept into his heart.

Sometimes circumstances occur in life, which benefit other family members down the road. And a situation that worked in Ruth's and Daniel's favor was the fact that the Claytons were estranged from their oldest child and heir apparent Ezra. The couple decided they couldn't alienate the only child they had left. So when Ruth openly declared her intentions regarding Daniel, Bishop and Queen had no other option but to accept their daughter's choice. Bishop asked Ruth to at least wait until she finished school before she married Daniel.

They even tried to encourage her to attend a university outside of Chicago, in hopes of putting distance between their daughter and her beau, but Ruth stood her ground. She and Daniel were joined in holy matrimony on June 29, 1972.

Queen, always mindful of doing the right thing for the congregation, put together a lavish ceremony for her only daughter. Bishop reluctantly married his daughter to a young man he was sure would break her heart.

One of Bishop's biggest regrets was that the church wouldn't be passed on to a male family member. He doubted if Sarah's son, Joshua, would follow the family heritage. The boy was too consumed by sports like his father, especially basketball.

Bishop was brought up in a patriarchal structure and it never occurred to him that his female family members might have an interest, or were even qualified, to carry on the family tradition. And in his many years of guiding the church, he never deviated from his stance.

Chapter Five

Daniel had been employed by CTA for more than three decades, and he was looking forward to retirement once Naomi finished college.

Monday evening Daniel pulled his double-sized bus into the designated stall, Number 6A in the CTA garage, and shut off the engine. He hopped down the last step of the bus and strutted towards the building with pep in his step. It was three o'clock in the afternoon, the end of the first shift.

Daniel was of medium height, and a handsome, honey complexioned man that stood five feet, ten inches tall and had a muscular body from working out. He had set up a gym in the basement of his and Ruth's home. His six-pack wasn't as toned as it used to be when he and Ruth first married, but his midsection was relatively firm.

Daniel's arms were rock hard from years of steering buses. His appearance suggested he was ten years younger than his fifty-eight years, whereas

Ruth, at fifty-five looked much older than her age. Back in the day, Daniel had a reputation as a notorious player. He was a fastidious dresser, and kept up with the latest fashion trends.

When his hairline began receding, and when he found more gray hairs on his head than he cared to count, Daniel shaved his head and grew a salt and pepper colored goatee beard.

Ruth had a fit when he went to the shopping mall and returned home with his left ear pierced. Later he sported a small diamond earring stud in it. She didn't speak to him for nearly a week; she simply rolled her eyes every time she saw the "bling bling".

He clicked on his cell phone and checked his messages. Ruth had called and left him a message a couple of hours ago. But his eyes lit up as he listened to his second message. The number was a very familiar number and belonged to Lenora Johnson.

Afterward, he punched in a phone number and said, "Hey, lady, I'm on the way to the bar. I'll see you in about half an hour."

When Lenora answered his call, she said, "that's twenty-nine minutes too long for my taste. I need to see me some Daniel now," the young woman pronounced in a sexy tone of voice.

Daniel threw his head back and roared with laughter as he listened to Lenora's raunchy response. "Danny need to see him some Nora too."

"Danny, although it's frigid outside, I'm burning inside. I need you to work your magic on my body and douse the flame that's engulfing that special *part* of my body. What can you do for me,

Boo? Do you feel you're up to the task of cooling me off?" She made half-cooing and shivering noises over the telephone and sang a few off key bars of the James Brown song, "Body Heat."

"Well, I'm not a fireman or nothing," Daniel joked, but I do have a hose on me, and I'll see what I can do to help my fair damsel in distress. You know first hand that my mouth-to-mouth resuscitation technique is excellent too. Keep the home fires burning baby, I'm on the way."

After he completed his call to Lenora, Daniel quickly dialed his home number and left a message on the answering machine, informing Ruth to have dinner without him because he'd be home late. He felt relieved that she wasn't home to take the call personally and he didn't have to play twenty questions.

Daniel chewed the fat with a couple of co-workers as he changed clothes in the locker room. Then he donned a pair of blue jeans and a Bear's sweatshirt, his jacket, and walked outside the bus barn to his car.

The November temperature had dropped and it was chilly outside. Daniel shivered as he zipped up his brown bomber leather jacket. He started his pride and joy, a black convertible Mustang, complete with black leather interior. He had ordered the car from the factory with all the bells and whistles. He changed the radio station to WGCI 107.5 and hummed to the music, as he pulled onto 79th Street and headed east.

Daniel paused at a red light and his thoughts flitted between Lenora and Ruth. He'd come to the conclusion that he loved his wife, but wasn't in love with her. Between raising the children and church, she never seemed to make time for him. But if Bishop said jump, she would ask how high. Daniel resented his father-in-law's interference in his marriage and for his influence over Ruth that he was never able to break.

When Daniel had first met Ruth and they began talking earnestly, she'd stand at the front of the bus near his seat, clutching the pole at the top of the bus with her schoolbooks tucked under her other arm. Ruth was barely out of high school, but something about the shy schoolgirl tugged his heartstrings. He perceived that the plain looking young woman possessed goodness and inner beauty.

Daniel thought Ruth was average looking, and to him, her being plain was a plus because he didn't have to worry about other men hitting on her.

Daniel's brother had schooled him during Ruth and Daniel's courtship on the benefits of marrying a church girl, citing church girls were faithful and knew how to take care of a man. "Not to mention they were freaks in the bedroom," Fred had told Daniel as he smacked his lips.

Sadly, that adage didn't prove to be true with Daniel and Ruth's relationship. When he complained to his brother, Fred point blank told him, "I told you to get with a church gal, not a minister's daughter. That's where you screwed up, boy."

Daniel had hoped to mold Ruth into the wife he wanted her to be. Like many men of the past generation, he wanted his cake and to eat it too. He wanted to be the center of Ruth's universe and for her to wait on him hand and foot. He didn't take into consideration the frequent demands the church, and then the children, would take of her.

The first ten years of their marriage he attended church services regularly, always at his wife's side. But then his appearances started to dwindle. Ruth made her concerns about his no-shows known, which only irritated Daniel. He felt she was a nag, constantly harping on his disappearing acts.

Daniel had strayed during the marriage on more than one occasion, but he'd never been tempted to leave Ruth until he met Lenora, the woman whom which he was on the way to put her fire out.

A half an hour later, Daniel sat on a black barstool near the entrance of Monty's House Of Spirits, a bar located on the southeast side of Chicago, near Rainbow Beach, nursing a drink. His head swayed to the music from the jukebox. He kept glancing at his watch, waiting anxiously for Lenora to arrive.

The red M on the picture window had long since burned out on the blinking red neon sign in the window of Monty's Bar. It was only four o'clock, so the evening crowd hadn't arrived yet.

Betty Wright wailed from the jukebox about her first lover; How she loved him and wasn't too proud to show it. The bartender wiped a damp spot on the bar. He paused for a moment and asked Daniel, "While I'm here, do you want another drink?"

"Yeah, bring me another Crown Royal and coke." He pushed the change from a twenty-dollar bill toward the man. Daniel's cell phone rang. "Hello?" he said, answering the call.

"Hi, honey. I just walked into the house and listened to your message. I stopped by to see Alice while I was out," Ruth explained. "Where are you?"

"Over on the east side, at a bar. I'm waiting on Fred."

"How long are you're going to be out? I was hoping we could go out to dinner tonight."

"Ruthie, you should've said something to me earlier. Fred and I will probably end up at his house to watch Monday night football after we leave here. The Bears and Vikings are playing." He turned up the glass and swallowed a large gulp of the drink the bartender had set in front of him a minute before. He nodded to the bartender to bring him another refill.

"I tried to catch you before you left this morning, but I overslept. So what time will you be home?" Ruth asked cheerfully, masking her pain.

Daniel felt a feather light kiss on the back of his neck. The scent of *Tresor* perfume announced the person lurking behind him. He spun around and winked at Lenora. She was dressed jauntily in a matching brown bomber jacket that matched Daniel's, blue jeans, and a brown and beige Shetland wool sweater. A beige and brown tasseled cap covered her head. She wore matching mittens on her hands.

"Hey, I gotta run. Fred just walked in. I won't be out too late." He closed the phone without waiting for Ruth to reply.

The dial tone signaled Daniel had hung up. Ruth's eyes brimmed with tears. She clicked the phone off and placed it in the charger, which sat on the kitchen counter. Her face was downcast and tears streamed from her eyes. She could have been the model of a portrait entitled *Despair*.

How am I going to fix whatever's wrong with our marriage if Daniel won't give me a chance and come home? Maybe I'll go by Sarah's house and spend some time with her while I wait on him. No, she's at school. Ruth shook her head and stood indecisively in the middle of the kitchen, briskly rubbing her upper arms. *What am I going to do?*

Daniel could care less what Ruth was going to do with herself as he and Lenora moved to a cozy red leather booth. She clutched his arm tightly as she snuggled next to him. Lenora was thirty-five, only a few years older than Sarah.

Lenora owned her own bookkeeping firm, servicing small minority companies. She also owned a condo in Evergreen Park and worked from home.

In Daniel's way of thinking, Lenora possessed all the qualities Ruth didn't. His young mistress was vivacious, beautiful, and full of life. Pleasing him had been her number one priority since the onset of their affair.

Lenora's complexion was a creamy café-au-lait. Her shape was curved like an hourglass, and she wore her brownish red hair in a blunt cut with copper red streaks. Her eyes were light brown and slanted. Her lips were thick, which Daniel described as one hundred percent kissable.

The pair met a few years ago at a Bulls game Daniel had attended with Fred and Lenora with her sister, Felicia.

The four avid b-ball fans sat in the same section of the stadium. Daniel couldn't keep his eyes off the young enthusiastic woman with the red Bulls cap covering her head and wearing the number 23 jersey. Lenora thrust her fisted hand in the air and chanted defense loudly along with the crowd.

Later, Daniel discovered that Lenora was just as crazy about football. He salivated with delight when he learned that she could even follow the game.

He had tried many times to entice Ruth to share his love of sports, but when she watched games with him, she became bored and asked too many questions. He was aghast when she exclaimed touchdown after Michael Jordan, his tongue wagging, dunked the basketball.

"It's a dunk, Ruth. Touchdowns are done in football, not basketball," Daniel had groaned in exasperation.

Lenora leaned over and kissed Daniel on the cheek. She tenderly wiped the smudge of lipstick off his face. "How long can you stay out tonight, boo? Do we have time to go to dinner?"

"I can't stay out too long, maybe a few hours or so. I'll be right back." Daniel walked over to the jukebox and slipped a dollar into the slot for two songs. He selected, "The Thrill Is Gone," by B. B. King for himself, and, "Let's Get It On," by Marvin Gaye for Lenora. When he returned to the table, Lenora had called the bartender over and ordered drinks.

"You aren't trying to tell me something are you? Because those songs are definitely contradictions to each other," Lenora commented with a twinkle in her eyes, although her high voice trembled with a tinge of tension.

Daniel leaned over and kissed her ruby red lips. "Of course not," he protested. "I played the first song for me and Ruth. It describes the state of my marriage. And the second is what I always want to do when I think of you. I better not stay out too late this evening. Ruth sounded like she has some issues, and I don't feel like dealing with her tonight." He looked down and clasped his hands together on the table.

Lenora looked away surreptitiously, then she sipped from a bottle of Coors beer. What could she say? She'd fallen in love with Daniel even though she knew he was married. She was content with the relationship for the time being. But she felt her biological clock was ticking, and she wanted to have at least one child before she turned forty.

Daniel didn't know that she had attended a Sunday service at the Temple a year ago to check out the competition. She was shocked when she laid eyes on *the wife*, as she called Ruth in a falsetto voice. She felt Daniel's mate was plain looking and frumpy, and that she looked more like his mother than his wife.

Hours elapsed, and soon the small bar was overflowing with bodies. A few couples danced on the miniscule dance area, stepping Chicago style to an old Kool and the Gang tune.

The bar patrons endlessly consumed beer and salted peanuts while the jukebox churned out tunes non-stop. Daniel glanced at his watch and saw that it was almost nine o'clock. He knew it was time for him to head home. If luck were on his side, Ruth would already be in bed, fast asleep.

He leaned over and nuzzled the side of Lenora's neck. "Hey baby, it's that time. I gotta go home."

Lenora's catlike eyes glinted with displeasure. "It seems like whenever we're in the middle of having a good time, you announce you gotta leave. Can't you stay just a little while longer?"

Daniel grabbed her hand and shrugged helplessly. "Come on, Nora, don't be that way. You know if I had my way, we'd stay here till the joint closes and then go to your place. But I'm not in the mood to listen to Ruth's whining about where I been, and how come I stayed out so late."

Lenora opened her mouth as if she was going to reply, then she shut it. She playfully punched Daniel's shoulder. "I'm going to let you slide this one time, Boo, but mark my words, the next time we get together, you're not going to get away so easily."

He smiled at her, looked up, and motioned for the waitress to come over to the table so he could settle the bill. The young lady was flirting with a customer at another table, so Daniel pulled another crumpled twenty-dollar bill out of his pocket, laid it on the table, and helped Lenora put her jacket on. They then exited the bar.

Daniel drove her home. Lenora had taken a bus to the bar, since the bus barn wasn't very far from the bar. He would have gone out of his way to pick up Lenora since she lived west of the city, but the couple would have lost precious quality time. During the ride, snow began falling lightly. Lenora tried unsuccessfully to lure Daniel into coming to her apartment and staying just a little while. When Daniel pulled in front of Lenora's building, her tongue was wreaking havoc on his ear. He reluctantly removed her arms from around his neck and promised to meet her Friday after work. She reached over and unlocked the car door and got out.

"I'll call you tomorrow. I might just work half a day," he shouted to her retreating body.

She stopped mid-step as she walked on the concrete path leading to her building. She turned and waved good-bye before walking inside the double glass doors of her apartment building.

Daniel shifted the car into drive and then drove off. During his ride home, traffic was light. The streets were mostly deserted since the temperature had dipped down into the teens. A few teenaged boys congregated on a corner with hoodies on their heads, wearing sagging jeans with high topped, untied gym shoes. They blew on their hands as their bodies vibrated from the hawk that was outside in Chicago full force.

Before long, he arrived home and parked his Mustang in the two-car garage located behind the bungalow where he and Ruth resided. As he walked toward the back door, he shook his head regretfully, realizing he'd probably have to shovel snow in the morning before he went to work since the snow was now falling heavier.

After setting the burglar alarm on the keypad in the kitchen next to the back door, Daniel walked down the hallway off the kitchen to his room. He sat on the bed and removed his shoes and socks.

The first floor of the dark brick bungalow consisted of three bedrooms and one and half baths, off the hallway to the left of the large eat-in kitchen. There was an entryway to the living room off the right side of the kitchen. The living room was L-shaped and attached to the dining room. From the backdoor in the kitchen, one could see to the front door. The basement in the house was finished and so was the attic.

Ruth, aware of every reverberation of the old house, heard Daniel tread outside her closed bedroom door. She was clad in a worn, navy colored terry robe with curlers in her head and cold cream on her face. She rose from the bed and walked into Daniel's bedroom. He looked at her wearily, taking in her appearance, comparing her to Lenora.

Ruth sat hesitantly on the edge of his bed. "How was your day?" she asked.

Daniel stifled a yawn. "Tiring. I'm too old to deal with rush hour traffic. Thank God I only have to do it when I can't find a replacement driver." He walked over to his closet and removed a pair of pajama bottoms. "What did you do today?"

Ruth perked up, because initially she had felt an invisible aura of hostility when she walked into the room.

"I went to visit Alice today and I talked to Sarah and Naomi. Joshua and Maggie got their report cards today. Sarah said their grades were good."

Daniel nodded as he removed his clothes. He was only half-listening to his wife speak. Their conversations were always the same subjects; the children, church, or Alice.

As Ruth sat on the bed, she began fidgeting. She

watched Daniel undress and admired his body. *It's not fair*, she thought, bitterly. *How come Daniel has managed to defy Father Time, while Mother Nature has been so cruel to me?* She self-consciously tightened the belt of her robe.

"I think I'll call DJ and Chelsea tomorrow morning," she added. "I haven't talked to them in a couple of weeks."

Their son and daughter-in-law were soldiers, officers in the United States Army, and stationed in Germany. They were the parents of four-year old Daniel, III.

"That sounds like a good idea. When you talk to them, tell them I said hello," Daniel remarked as he put on a T-shirt. "Do you want anything else, Ruth? I'm kind of beat." He sat stiffly near the head of the bed and yawned.

Her checks reddened with humiliation, like she'd been stung by a bee. She felt like he was dismissing her. She stood awkwardly.

"I'd like us to go out to dinner tomorrow, or one day this week after you get off work. That is, if you don't have other plans?" Her eyes bore into his pleadingly.

Daniel felt a pang of remorse at how troubled Ruth looked. "Sure, dinner will be fine. I'll come straight home tomorrow." *Good, now that will free me up to see Lenora Friday*, he thought to himself.

Ruth's spirits soared, and she moved toward Daniel as if to hug him. Instead, she stepped backwards out the room.

"Have a good night, dear," she said to him.

"Yeah, you too," Daniel murmured, as he stretched out comfortably in the bed . . . alone.

Chapter Six

Daniel worked late Tuesday and Wednesday evening, so he and Ruth's dinner date had to be postponed until Thursday evening.

Thursday morning, Ruth awakened around nine o'clock. After showering and dressing in a denim skirt and a white angora sweater, she headed to the kitchen to prepare herself some breakfast. She turned the thirteen-inch television to Channel 7 and caught the last twenty minutes of the *Oprah Winfrey Show*.

After she finished eating, she washed dishes and cleaned the house. She hummed as she worked. Her mouth was curved into a smile the entire morning. Knowing she had a date with her husband later that day suffused her body with a warm, fuzzy glow.

Ruth called her physician, Dr. Jackson's office and made an appointment for next week to discuss hormone replacement therapy. When she finished with the call, she dialed Eunice's telephone number, her hairstylist and a member of the Temple. Ruth begged the stylist to please squeeze her in that afternoon. Eunice instructed her to come over immediately because her next appointment wasn't for another half hour.

After she hung up the telephone, Ruth hurriedly put on her coat, left the house, got inside her car, and sped to the shop.

When Ruth arrived at the shop, Eunice greeted her and told her to have a seat in her styling chair. Eunice was a pencil thin, bronze colored, energetic woman. She was dressed in red cords, and a black smock atop of a red and black stripped sweater. Eunice combed out her hair, and asked her, "What do you want done today?"

Ruth looked at her image in the mirror and sighed, "I want the works. How about a whole new body? I'm kidding. I want a rinse, manicure and pedicure."

As Eunice massaged Ruth's scalp, she paused with her right eyebrow arched in the air. "What's the occasion?"

"There's no special occasion, I'm just celebrating life." Ruth smiled. "I feel like being pampered, and what better place than at your shop?"

Three hours later, Ruth's appearance changed drastically for the better. Eunice had talked her client into getting a sleek bob haircut. Her hands and feet were painted a delicate coral pink. Eunice opened her bottom drawer and pulled out a makeup bag. She waxed Ruth's face and chin. Then she applied light makeup across her face and lined her lips.

When Eunice finished working her magic on

Ruth, she spun the chair around for Ruth to face the mirror. When Ruth spied her reflection, her hands flew to the sides of her face.

Eunice smiled approvingly. "Wow! You look good, Sister."

"I don't think I've looked this attractive since my wedding day," Ruth exclaimed as she patted her hair. "Thank you for the makeover, and for the good job you did styling my hair. I swear I feel fantastic, like I won a million bucks in the lottery or something."

Eunice grinned. "Well, I must admit, you certainly don't look like the same woman that walked in here. Way to go, Ruth."

"Thanks, Eunice. It's going to take time for me to get used to this short hairdo."

Eunice reached inside her drawer and pulled out a turquoise silk scarf. She laid the thin scrap of material gently across Ruth's head, then looped the ends loosely around Ruth's head. "I'm not gonna mess up your hair. I just want to give you an idea of how to wrap your hair at night."

Ruth silently watched Eunice's motions in the oversized lightened mirror over her workstation. Her hands shook slightly after she took the scarf from Eunice and clumsily tried to duplicate the stylist's instructions.

"I think I have the hang of it now. If not, I'm sure Sarah will come by the house and help me out."

After paying the bill, she presented Eunice and the manicurist, with generous tips.

Ruth drove west on 83rd Street. She decided to splurge and buy herself a new outfit. She turned into the parking lot of a clothing boutique. She went in and tried on several dresses, but what eventually caught her eye was a black and silver, double-breasted pantsuit hanging on a rack.

Bishop frowned upon women wearing pants. He felt women wearing trousers made them appear too masculine. Queen Esther didn't own a single pair of pants.

Desperate times call for desperate measures. I have a marriage to preserve. Forgive me, Daddy. Ruth looked at the price tag on the suit, which cost a little more than she had planned to spend. The owner made a great sales pitch and ended up talking Ruth into buying a pair of black pumps and a matching handbag also in addition to a surprise for Daniel later that night.

Ruth stopped at McDonald's and bought a salad for lunch, then headed home to eat and take a nap.

Four hours later, Daniel walked through the front door. As he headed to his bedroom, he did a double take when he passed Ruth's room.

"You look nice," he stammered. "What are we celebrating?"

Ruth paused. She was spraying Estee Lauder perfume over her body. "Thank you. Can't a husband and wife enjoy dinner out once in a while?"

"Sure. But I thought we were just going up the street to Pepi's, the Mexican restaurant, or someplace like that. Since you're so dressed up, where do you want to go?" Daniel leaned against the doorway, looking puzzled.

"I made a reservation at the Signature Room, which is on the 95th floor of the John Hancock

Building," Ruth responded, as she finger combed the sides of her hair.

"Hmmm." Daniel's eyes narrowed as he stroked his beard. "Give me a minute to take a shower and change clothes."

An hour later, he had changed into a dark colored suit and pewter gray shirt.

The couple exited the house. Daniel opened and closed the door when Ruth entered the car. He got inside the vehicle, started it up and drove to the Dan Ryan Expressway, where he drove north. Ruth leaned over to change the radio dial to a gospel station.

"Will you please leave the radio alone? I'm listening to that song," Daniel said, clearly annoyed. He hated for his wife to change the station when they rode in his car, especially if a song he liked was playing.

Ruth sat back against the edge of the seat. Her lips tightened then relaxed. "I talked to DJ today. He and Chelsea are doing fine. They're trying to get reassigned to a base close to Illinois. But with the fighting going on in the Middle East, he thinks there's a possibility one of them may have to go over there."

"That wouldn't be so good, not with them having a child and all," Daniel replied as he sped up and changed to the next lane.

He snapped his fingers and hummed the lyrics to the Commodore's song, "Brickhouse." Visions of Lenora swaying to the beat of the music danced in his head. Silence fell between the couple.

Daniel's cell phone rang. He looked at the Caller

ID and then answered it. "What's up, Bro? I'm cool, what's happening with you?" he said, talking to Fred.

Ruth glanced over at her husband and then outside the car window. She opened her purse and took out a tube of lipstick. She added a light coating to her lips.

"I'm headed to the Phase II lounge. I wanted to know if you wanted to hang out with me for a few hours." Fred said from the other end.

"Naw, not tonight," Daniel replied, glancing over at Ruth. "I'm headed downtown as we speak. Ruth and I have a dinner date." He put on his blinker and moved to the right lane. "I'm almost at my exit. Later, dude."

Fifteen minutes later, Daniel was driving north along Michigan Avenue, trying to find a parking space.

"We're supposed to be at the restaurant like now." Ruth tapped the face of her wristwatch. "Our reservations are in ten minutes."

"I didn't plan on shelling out extra bucks for valet parking, but I guess I have no choice now." Daniel made a quick left turn into the parking garage, after circling the block unsuccessfully a few times for a parking space.

After handing his keychain to the red uniformed attendant, Daniel warned the young man, "Be careful with my ride." He and Ruth strolled quickly to the elevator. Silence stood between them as they rode up to the 95th floor.

"Good evening, sir and madam," the Maitre'd greeted them as they walked to the waiting area. "Do you have a reservation?"

Ruth nodded. "Yes, our last name is Wilcox."

He checked the leather bound reservation list and then closed it. "Right this way." He led them to a table near the window. "Enjoy your meal. Your waiter will be with you shortly."

The Chicago skyline loomed magnificently outside. A Chinese vase, overflowing with pink tea roses, entwined with baby breaths sat in the middle of the table.

Daniel spread the white, crisply ironed napkin in his lap. He looked up to find their waiter standing next to the table holding two menus.

"Hello, my name is Solomon. I'll be your waiter this evening. Can I bring you the wine list?"

"No," Daniel answered tersely, loosening his tie. "Just bring me a Cognac. My wife will have an iced tea."

"I'll be right back with your drinks," he said. Solomon returned minutes later carrying the drinks on a small tray. He placed them on the table. "Are you ready to order?"

Ruth leaned forward in her chair. "Give us a few more minutes." She looked at her husband, reproachfully.

Solomon stuck the order pad in his pocket. "I'll return in a few minutes."

Daniel looked at his wife innocently and shrugged his shoulders. "What?"

"Do you always have to drink hard liquor? It would've been nice if you had ordered a bottle of wine for us."

"Ruth, lay off, please. If you wanted wine, all you had to do was say so."

Daniel snapped his fingers to get Solomon's attention. When he returned to the table, Daniel asked him if he'd bring them the wine list.

"Forget it. I've changed my mind," Ruth said. She picked up the menu again. "What are you going to have? I think I'll have the swordfish."

"I'ma get a big, well done T-bone steak," he said as he closed the menu and placed it on the side of the table. "Are you sure we aren't here to celebrate something? You have to admit, we don't usually do this kind of stuff; go to a five-star restaurant for dinner on a week night."

Solomon returned with a basket of warm bread, took their orders, and then left the couple alone.

"Well, to be honest, I have a surprise for you." Ruth's voice trembled.

"What is it?" Daniel asked, staring at his wife curiously.

Ruth reached into her purse and pulled out a pair of tickets for a five-day Bahamas cruise in December. She handed them to Daniel.

"Nice," he said, in a non-committal tone of voice. He passed the tickets back to her.

"You could show a little more enthusiasm," Ruth said uneasily, as she stared at Daniel defiantly.

"Maybe I would have if you had discussed this with me before you made the reservations," Daniel said. He tore off a hunk of warm Italian bread from the red and white checkered linen covered loaf.

"I wanted to surprise you. When you bought the Mustang, you didn't bother to discuss it with me first," Ruth replied, nearly in tears.

He passed her the breadbasket. "Oh, I'm definitely surprised, Ruth." He slathered butter on the slice of bread. "I'm just not sure about the timing. Won't Naomi be home in December? How will she get back to school after Christmas break?"

Ruth set the tickets beside her plate. She looked upset. "In case you've forgotten, Daniel, Naomi is eighteen, and she's more than capable of taking the train back to Carbondale. If the weather isn't too bad, I'm sure Sarah or Alice would drive her back to school."

Daniel knew her feelings were hurt. He pulled the collar of his shirt away from his neck, knowing he was in for a long night.

Ruth looked at Daniel as she set the glass of water on the table. "Isn't that your cell phone ringing?"

Daniel pulled the phone out of his jacket pocket and scanned the caller ID. "That call was from one of the guys from work. I'll call him later," he said. Daniel struggled to keep a smile off his face. The caller ID had displayed Lenora's number.

Ruth shook her head from side-to-side, eying her spouse critically. "You need to put a stop to your office calling after work hours. This is our time, not CTA's."

"Ruth, you know as the yard supervisor, I have to be available to my men after hours. It's probably Willis calling to let tell me that Michael is still sick and that he'll be off again tomorrow. I'll have to take his shift again."

The waiter brought their food to the table. Ruth closed her eyes and blessed the repast. They ate and didn't speak much during dinner. Daniel kept checking his watch impatiently, like he had another appointment.

After sharing a slice of strawberry shortcake for dessert, Daniel removed his credit card from his wallet while Ruth made a trip to the ladies room.

Daniel watched her return to the dining area, and stood as she returned to the table. "Let's go," he said.

Ruth tried to make idle chatter during the ride back down to the ground floor and as they waited on the valet to bring the car around.

Once they were settled in the car, Ruth brought up the cruise again. "Danny, you didn't say anything about the cruise during dinner, don't you want to go? You're always complaining about how we don't spend enough time together. This cruise would be a perfect opportunity for us to get away and relax."

"I don't know, Ruth. If we go out of town, won't that take away from the time you and Naomi have during the holidays?"

Daniel kept his eyes on the road. He felt ambushed, and if dinner was any indication of the state of their marriage, how could he and Ruth endure a week with just each other's company?

"I'll talk to Sarah, maybe Naomi can stay with her those few days."

"Let me think about it," Daniel said elusively as he pulled up in front of their house.

"Why aren't you parking in the garage?" Ruth asked. "Are you going somewhere?"

"It's still early, only eight o'clock. I think I'll run by the job and see what that call was about."

Ruth opened the car door. "You can't call from the house?" Her voice rose, pleadingly.

"Yeah, I guess I could, but I'd rather go on in. I won't be gone long, no more than an hour."

"I really wish you would call from the house. I'd really like to spend some time with you," Ruth begged as she got out the car.

Daniel shook his head regretfully and watched his wife walk into the house. Her shoulders were slumped and her head bowed down. She didn't wave good-bye to Daniel.

Once Ruth was inside the house, she walked to her bedroom. She looked at the black negligee lying on the bed that she'd purchased earlier that day, while she was out shopping. That was Daniel's gift for later that night. Ruth snatched the flimsy material off the bed and stuffed it inside her top dresser drawer. She then sat on the side of the bed and removed her new shoes, which pinched her toes.

She smoothed her hair back on her head and rebuked herself for not talking to Daniel about their marriage as she had planned. Maybe if she had followed her plan, he would be home with her now instead of God knows where.

Ruth's stomach fluttered. She felt unsettled about Daniel's reaction to the trip. Her gut feeling told her he didn't want to go to the Bahamas, and that he was trying, in his own clumsy way, to spare her feelings. *I wonder where Daniel really is.*

Chapter Seven

Lenora sat on her leopard skinned sofa, comfortably dressed in an oversized T-shirt, which stopped midway at her thighs. Reading glasses were perched on the edge of her nose, and she was writing figures on an accounting pad. When she finished her calculations, she entered the data into her laptop computer.

The end of the month and quarter was rapidly approaching, and her clients expected their financial statements no later than the second of the month.

Her hands were poised above the keyboard, and a black mechanical pencil was stuck between her lips. She listened to Jill Scott sing, "Golden," as she worked. Her cell phone sounded, breaking her concentration.

"Hello," Lenora said, answering her phone.

"What's up? What you doing over the weekend?" Lenora's younger sister Felicia asked. The caramel-complexioned young woman, a few shades darker than her sister, pulled a black hair clip out of her hair and massaged her scalp. Though Lenora and Felicia resembled each other, the young Johnson sister was a less sexy, more wholesome version of her older sister. She was medium height and weight, and Felicia wore her sandy brown hair in an upsweep style, usually a French twist.

"I don't have anything planned. You know I try to keep my weekends free in case Daniel can make time for me."

"You've been kicking it with him for awhile," Felicia remarked nonchalantly. "Where do you see the relationship going?" She didn't really approve of Lenora dating an older married man.

"It's hard to tell," Lenora admitted, sighing heavily. "When Daniel and I started hanging out, he was pretty adamant about how he wasn't ever going to leave his wife. But lately, he's been playing what I call the What If game."

"What the heck is the 'What If game'?" Felicia asked. "I don't think I've ever heard that one before." She sipped from a glass of Arbor Mist White Zinfandel wine. She set the glass on the floor next to the chair she was slouched in.

"You know, what if we lived together, how would we pay bills? Do I want to continue living in my condo in Evergreen, or move back to the city? Things like that," Lenora said, waving her hand in the air.

"Hmm. It sounds like you whipped it on him real good," Felicia chuckled. "Daniel's a nice man and all, but I don't think I could get with a man old enough to be my Daddy. Ugh, that's disgusting. Is he flabby like Daddy?"

Lenora took a sip of her tea. When she heard Felicia's question, she sputtered and the liquid spewed everywhere. She quickly snatched the papers from the table.

"Girl, please, Daniel is definitely not flabby, he's youthful for his age. His body is tight, thank you. You can quote me on that." She walked into the kitchen and pulled some paper towels off the holder.

"I don't know, Lenora, your being with a man that old seems obscene in a perverted way," Felicia commented after she leaned over and picked her glass of wine up off the floor. "You don't have a father fixation or something?"

When Daniel had introduced himself to the sisters at the Bulls game, Felicia thought he looked okay for an old guy, but his game was weak. She was taken aback when her sister pressed her telephone number into his hand.

"Chile, please," Lenora laughed as she balled up the paper towels. "Daniel is my boo. Trust me, there ain't nothing about, or on him, that reminds me of Daddy."

Felicia shared the latest family gossip with Lenora and the sisters made plans to go the mall over the weekend, if Daniel couldn't get away from his wife.

Lenora pressed the disconnect button on her cell phone and dropped it on the couch. She picked it up and thought about calling Daniel. Usually she waited on him to call her, but she hadn't talked to him since earlier that morning. Maybe he was home watching the basketball game. She dialed his cell phone number. The phone rang five times before going to his voice mail. She sighed heavily into the phone without leaving a message. She continued working, knowing he would call her when he had the opportunity.

Daniel turned the key in the lock, twisted the door handle, and walked softly into Lenora's apartment. He had impulsively decided to go to her condo and surprise her. She had given him a key to her secured condominium apartment a year ago.

By the time he arrived though, she lay asleep, curled up on the sofa. One of her arms was flung over her face, and she snored noisily. The financial statement she had been working on earlier had slipped from her hand and lie on the black shag-carpeted floor.

Daniel tiptoed to the couch, knelt down, and kissed Lenora's lips. Her eyes opened sleepily, but when she saw Daniel's face, she looked pleasantly surprised. Her lips widened into a smile.

"Danny, what are you doing here? I expected a call from you right about now." She glanced at her watch as she sat up, then she eyed his body from head to toe. "Where have you been, to a funeral or something?"

He slid onto the sofa beside her. "I had an urge to see you." His nose wrinkled distastefully. "I had dinner with Ruth, and the evening was a disaster. I felt like I was choking." He removed his tie and dropped it into his jacket pocket.

Lenora grasped his hand and made comforting

noises. "Do you want a drink?" She ran her hand through her hair, suspecting it was mess.

"No, I'm good. If I didn't know any better, tonight I would've suspected Ruthie was trying to flirt with me," Daniel groused.

Lenora cleared her throat. "She's your wife, Daniel. I'm sure she gets the hots for you like I do." She squeezed his hand. *Men are so dense sometimes. What does he expect me to say about Ruth?*

"She blew me away by making travel reservations to the Bahamas in December, a few days after Christmas. She had told me earlier this week she wanted to go out to dinner. I thought she was going to rag about our marriage, and instead, she wants us to go away on a trip."

"Do you want to go with her?" Lenora asked in a neutral tone of voice, masking the tension that fluttered in her abdomen.

Daniel hesitated before he replied. "Truthfully, I don't know if I can stand being in a cabin with her for a week." He felt torn.

Daniel had gotten used to Ruth going to church, which enabled him to come and go as he pleased, allowing him to spend at least a few hours with Lenora on Sundays. But he realized on another level, he was hurting two women. He had strong feelings for both his wife and mistress.

"I think Ruth's idea is a good one. You know how cold it gets here in Chicago during the winter." Lenora walked to the bar and poured herself a glass of wine from a crystal carafe.

Daniel watched her buttocks sway from side to side. *Damn, she's fine, and so different from Ruth. If I could come home to that every night and hit it, that would be pure bliss.* Lenora hadn't expressed any interest in becoming his wife, but sometimes it became hard for him to leave her and go home to his empty bed.

Lenora sat down carefully on the sofa, turned up the wine goblet, and drank greedily. Daniel reached over, caressed her firm thigh, and pulled her close to him. His groin tightened attentively when she leaned against his chest.

He reached under her T-shirt and caressed her chest, moving his hands to her breasts. "Who do these belong to?" He leaned down and kissed the tender orbs of flesh.

She moaned. "They're yours, Daddy, all yours." She turned toward him and gently nipped his lips.

Their breathing became labored, and the temperature in the room became muggy. Lenora unzipped Daniel's pants and began to massage him. He took her hands in his and gently pushed her away from him. He stood and fastened his clothes.

"As much as I regret leaving you so abruptly like this, I've got to go home." He looked at his watch. "It's getting late. Give me a rain check and we'll finish our business tomorrow." He grabbed her head between his hands and kissed her lips roughly. "I think I'll leave work early tomorrow and meet you for lunch."

She flung her arms around Daniel's neck. "You know you're wrong for leaving your baby high and dry. But sure, you know where to find me tomorrow. And, boo, lunch is on me," she said, walking him to the door.

Lenora planted her body in front of the door. "One more kiss," she moaned.

The two embraced, and it took all of Daniel's willpower not to stay at the apartment. Lenora's hot body squirmed in his arms. He wanted to tear her clothes away off her frame and ravish her on the floor.

He groaned with longing and felt along the sides of her curvaceous body one more time. "I've got to go," he said regretfully to Lenora, as he fixed his clothing, which had become twisted from the couple's desire. "I'll call you in the morning while I'm on my way to work."

Lenora moistened her finger and ran it across Daniel's lips. "You do that. I'll be waiting on your call." She leaned in and seared Daniel's lips with her own.

As Daniel walked to his car, he glanced up at Lenora's window. She waved good-bye to him. *I wish I could stay, I don't want to go home*, he thought to himself as he got inside his car.

He revved the engine, burning rubber, trying to expend jittery energy. *There's going to be hell to pay when I get home. Ruth is going to have a hissy fit.*

Lenora followed Daniel's taillights, and watched him make a right turn at the corner. She tugged the cord on the lamp, and went to her bedroom with a smug pleased look on her face. *I know how to handle my business. Daniel will be back for more. Now deal with that, Mrs. Wife.*

Chapter Eight

When a couple of hours elapsed, and Daniel still hadn't returned home, Ruth became frantic with worry. After the credits started rolling at the end of the *Tonight Show*, she went into the kitchen to prepare a cup of pekoe tea.

The mailman had delivered the latest issue of *Ladies Home Journal* earlier that day. Ruth was aimlessly flipping through the pages of the magazine when she heard the front door open and close. Daniel walked into the kitchen. He swore under his breath and frowned when he found Ruth waiting up for him. He knew he'd have to listen to her complaints about his coming home late.

Daniel transformed his expression to a pleasant one, smiled and said, "You're still up? I thought you would've gone to bed by now."

Ruth folded her arms across her chest. Her lips compressed into a thin line. "Where have you been, Danny?"

"I lost track of time while I was at the office. Then later I stopped at a bar and had a drink with some of the fellas." He turned and walked out the kitchen toward his bedroom.

"I'm talking to you, Danny. Don't leave the room; at least give me the courtesy of hearing me out!" Ruth yelled.

He took off his jacket and walked back into the kitchen. "What's the problem, Ruth? I didn't think I had to account for my time like a child. Excuse me." His voice deepened sarcastically when he said, "excuse me."

"I was worried. You said you'd only be gone for an hour, and instead, you've been gone for over three hours. You could've called me."

"Look, I'm sorry. I didn't think about calling you. I have to get up in a few hours, so can we continue this conversation later?"

Ruth blinked back tears. She knew her husband wasn't being honest about where he'd been. She shot him a look of disgust and stalked down the hallway to her bedroom, slamming the door behind her.

After Daniel undressed, he lay in the bed with his hands clasped behind his head. *Maybe I need to make some changes in my life. Perhaps it's time for me to leave. I'm not going to tolerate Ruth talking to me like I'm one of the children. Yes, I'm definitely leaving early tomorrow.* He fell asleep dreaming about Lenora and how the T-shirt she'd worn showed him proof positive of what he was missing on a nightly basis.

* * *

Three days a week, Mondays, Wednesdays, and Fridays, Ruth worked at the church. On Friday morning, snow was falling lightly, and she debated staying home. But she knew her father depended on her assistance, so she dressed and fixed herself a pot of coffee. The temple was located fifteen minutes from her house. Before long, she was parking her car in the nearly deserted parking lot and was sitting at her desk working on the bulletin for Sunday's service.

She answered the ringing telephone, "Praise the Lord, good morning. You reached Jubilee Temple Church. How may I help you?" Ruth paused. "Oh, hi Alice. How are you?" she asked despondently.

"I'm good and nosy. I wanted to know how your dinner with Daniel was last night. I bet he was surprised when you showed him the travel arrangements."

"Dinner was great. You know the Signature Room has good food. And yes, you could say he was surprised," Ruth replied, vaguely.

"I wanted to let you know that Naomi can stay with me while you're out of town. I'll make sure she gets back to school. If the weather is mild, then Sarah and I will drive her to Carbondale. If not, I'll make sure she catches the train."

"Thanks, Allie, I appreciate it. Look, can I call you back? I'm in the middle of doing the programs for Sunday. I'll call you tonight."

Okay, I'll talk to you later."

Sometimes sharing all your innermost secrets with your best friend wasn't a good thing. And now Ruth regretted sharing her plans about the cruise with Alice in the first place. She turned her attention back to the computer monitor and corrected a misspelled name. The intercom on her phone buzzed.

"Ruthie, can you come to my office for a minute?" Bishop buzzed his daughter from the intercom on his desk.

"Sure, Daddy, give me a minute." Ruth grabbed a pen and pad off her desk and walked into her father's domain.

Queen Esther had decorated the airy, maplewood room. The floor was covered with brown carpeting. Bishop's desk was massive, and matching bookcases filled with theology books and many versions of the Bible lined the wall. A brown corduroy sofa rested on one wall. Two wingback chairs were positioned in front of the desk.

He peered up at his daughter over the top of his glasses after she walked into the room. She sat down in one of the chairs in front of his desk.

"Your hair looks nice," he remarked and removed his glasses and punched the bridge of his nose.

Ruth self-consciously pushed a lock of hair back off her forehead. "Thanks. What can I do for you?" She uncapped the pen and laid the pad on her lap.

"I'd like to read you a portion of my text for Sunday's morning service and get your opinion of it. Tell me what you think."

Ruth always gave her father constructive feedback, critiquing his sermons, but her heart wasn't in the chore this morning. She was still hurt by Daniel's blatant disregard of her feelings last night.

When Bishop finished reading, he looked at Ruth for comments. She was gazing sadly out the window behind his desk as if she hadn't heard a word he said.

"Ruthie, earth to Ruthie! How was that?"

"It sounded fine, Daddy."

"What's wrong, child?" Bishop asked, kindly.

He didn't miss the dark circles under his daughter's eyes, which suggested she'd had a sleepless night; and her eyes were dim, like someone had turned off a light switch inside her retinas.

"Nothing. I just felt a little tired when I got up this morning."

"Well, why didn't you say something? I could've asked Patricia to come in. Do you feel like staying? If not, I'll call her and you can go home."

"Thanks, Daddy. I think I'll go home."

Ruth returned to her desk and decided to continue to work on the Sunday bulletin until Patricia arrived. She re-opened the Microsoft Word document, and typed without interruption until Patricia taped her on the shoulder to announce her presence.

After the women chitchatted for a couple of minutes, Ruth said, "I've finished with pages one and two. You can pick up at page three." She handed Patricia a couple of pieces of paper.

"Is there anything else you need me to do?" she asked Ruth. She set the papers on the desk, walked to the coffee pot, and poured herself a cup of the brew.

"If you have time, could you do one other task? Some checks came in the mail today, and I need you to record the totals in the ledger." Ruth reached into the bottom drawer and removed a burgundy binder and ten checks. "Put the checks in the safe when you're done."

The church wasn't located very far from the bus yard, so Ruth decided to surprise Daniel and meet him for lunch. Maybe she could articulate the misgivings she was feeling, and they could repair the chaos their marriage had become mired in.

Before going to Daniel's job, Ruth made a detour to Dominick's grocery store located a mile from the church. She stopped by the deli section and purchased potato salad, coleslaw, ham, roast beef, condiments, and a loaf of bread. She walked into the CTA building half an hour later.

When she arrived at Daniel's office, the door was closed and locked.

"Hi, Ruth," Edward Lewis, one of Daniel's co-workers greeted her.

"Hello, Ed. Do you know where Daniel is? I wanted to surprise him with lunch." Ruth lifted up the brown bag.

Edward looked uncomfortable. "Uh, I'm not sure where Daniel is right now. Maybe he went to lunch already."

"If you don't mind, I'll wait a few minutes for him."

"That's fine. How are the children?" Edward replied, obviously relieved.

They caught up on current events for a few minutes, and then Edward returned to work. Ruth took her cell phone out her purse and called Daniel. He didn't answer. She was clicking off the phone when Simon, another one of his coworkers, walked over to greet her.

"Hello, Mrs. Wilcox. How are you doing? I think Daniel has left for the day. I overheard him say something about he wasn't feeling well."

Ruth looked embarrassed. She felt a hot flash erupting, rising from her toes to her head. "Thanks for telling me, Simon. He probably tried to call me earlier and I missed the call. It was nice seeing you again."

As she walked back to her car, Ruth's face darkened with anger. She unceremoniously dumped the bag containing the food in a garbage can outside the building. When she got inside the car, she tried calling Daniel again, to no avail. Her intuition told her he was with another woman. She laid her head on the steering wheel and cried.

Chapter Nine

When Daniel arrived at Lenora's place for lunch, he deliberately left his cell phone, which was powered off, locked in the trunk of his car. After nearly sampling her goods the night before, he didn't want any interruptions during his time with his lady today. In addition to owning a cell phone, Daniel carried a pager, and only Lenora and Fred were privy to the number. He didn't want to blur the lines between wife and mistress. So far, he assumed he had successfully kept Ruth in the dark regarding his secret life.

Daniel stopped at a floral shop a couple of miles south of Lenora's house and purchased a bouquet of her favorite flowers, mums and lilies. When he arrived at her condo, he pressed the doorbell to her apartment as he stood outside a glass door separating him from the lobby area. Even though he used a key last night to enter her apartment, doing so wasn't his usual M.O. Plus he wasn't able to surprise her too often, so when the opportunity presented itself like it did the night before, he took advantage of it.

"Who is it?" Lenora asked. She spoke in an indecipherable accent on the intercom as she pressed a button to see who was downstairs in the lobby through a security camera.

"Ya man," Daniel answered. The buzzer sounded, he pulled the door open, and bounded up the stairs.

When Lenora opened the door she looked amazing, dressed in a form fitting, red and white floral silk kimono. Daniel's eyes lit up appreciatively as his gaze traveled the length of her body. Her fingernails and toenails were painted blood red. Rice powder was dusted over her face. Her lips glowed cherry red, and her eyes were heavily made-up with a mascara pencil. Daniel's body quivered as he handed her the flowers. Chills racked his body like he had a fever.

"Well, looka here, looka here." Daniel stepped back and looked at the gold apartment number on the door. "Am I in the right place? If I'm not, Lawd, have mercy."

Lenora grabbed his arm and pulled him inside. She bowed, shut the door, and said, faking an Asian accent, "Of course you're in the right place, mister. Welcome to Lenora's Garden of Beauty. My aim is to please you. Sit back and enjoy as I make your every fantasy come true."

She led him to a stack of pillows on the living room floor. The mini blinds were drawn, and red rays of light glowed from the floor lamp.

She had decorated the room to resemble a Japanese boudoir and restaurant. Appetizers steamed from trays on top of the bar, and Lenora had placed scented candles on the end tables. Their delicate jasmine scent perfumed the air. A bottle of Dom Perignon and two crystal goblets chilled inside a silver cooler. Daniel felt like he had stepped into the love land.

Lenora helped him out of his clothing and into a burgundy and gold robe. She handed Daniel the bottle of champagne. He popped the cork and poured the bubbly liquor into the crystal goblets.

"I want you to make yourself at home," she cooed as she bent over Daniel, affording him a view of her delicious behind. He wondered, *how is she going to sit down wearing that dress?* Leonora stood up and walked into the kitchen.

She returned carrying warm towels. She washed his hands and feet. He watched, fascinated as her body seemed to contort and slither to the floor like a cobra. She hand fed her man egg rolls, stuffed crab cakes, and other mouth-watering delicacies.

"Nora, baby, I can't believe you're sitting in that dress or whatever it is. You look good, baby, real good; good enough to eat," Daniel effusively complimented her.

"Thank you, kind sir. This geisha girl definitely takes tips." She stood and bowed submissively to him.

Following the meal, Daniel and Lenora sipped more champagne. She turned on her CD boom box with a remote control unit. Daniel's favorite group of all time, Earth, Wind and Fire, crooned, serenading the couple. Lenora stood and beckoned for him to join her. They danced sensuously to the melody of "Love's Holiday."

As Daniel held Lenora in his arms, he felt the ties that held her outfit together. Using his teeth, he bent slightly and unfastened them. When the kimono dropped to the floor, she was totally nude underneath.

Lenora, in turn, untied the belt to his robe, and slid it off his body. He easily lifted her up in his arms and carried her to the pillows on the floor, where he proceeded to finish his business from the night before.

Chapter Ten

Ruth's mouth twitched uncontrollably, and she became visibly distraught when Daniel didn't return her phone calls. She sat in the bus yard parking lot for a half hour waiting for her husband to call her back. She then drove aimlessly around the neighborhood for a couple of hours, brushing away tears that slipped down her cheeks before she finally decided to go home. The battery in her cell phone had long since died from the numerous attempts to call her husband.

As soon as she walked in the house, the tears that had trickled down her cheeks like a leaky faucet during her drive home, scalded her eyes and flooded down her cheeks like a geyser. She checked the answering machine. There was one message from Naomi. Ruth walked into her bedroom and collapsed face down on the bed like a stack of children's building blocks and cried herself to sleep.

Around seven o'clock that evening, she stirred and looked at the clock.

"Danny?" she called frantically, but there was only silence. She rose and walked through the darkened house.

Four hours later, Ruth sat at the kitchen table motionlessly. Her lips sagged, and her eyes flickered as she glanced at the telephone expectantly. She wondered if Daniel had become ill, or if he had been involved in an accident.

Her mind shied away from the possibility, like a skittish colt, that he was with another woman. The thought punctured her heart with tiny pinpricks. During the couple's almost thirty years of marriage, Daniel had never stayed out all night. She tried calling his cell phone for the millionth time, and once again, was routed to voice mail.

She paced the length of the kitchen, then stopped in front of the sink and clasped her hands in front of her body. *Where can he be? Is he all right? My God, he could be dead and I wouldn't even know.* She looked up. *Lord, what should I do? Wherever he is, please don't let anything bad happen to my husband.* Her mouth moved soundlessly in prayer.

Ruth stood and walked into the living room. The fluorescent light from the kitchen cast an eerie shadow in the front room. She stood beside the maroon drapes and peered out the delicate, pink lacy sheer curtains. There wasn't any movement on the darkened street. When she was driving home earlier, snow had begun coming down. Now an inch or two had accumulated on the streets.

She walked back into the kitchen, flipped off

the light switch and went into her bedroom. Ruth lay across the bed fully clothed.

Before she dozed off after eleven o'clock that evening, her last conscious thought was that she was going to call Fred if Daniel didn't return home within the next couple of hours. Now here it was two o'clock in the morning when the sound of the back door closing awakened Ruth. She glanced at the clock.

To her surprise, Daniel didn't bother to turn on the kitchen light to announce his arrival as he usually did when he came home after darkness had fallen. She listened to his light footsteps from the kitchen to the hallway, as if he were tiptoeing down the hallway to his room.

A bolt of anger, like an arrow, pierced Ruth's heart. She jumped from the bed and sped out into the hallway. She flipped on the light switch, and glared daggers at her husband. Daniel walked cautiously around the corner into the hallway; he looked up and saw Ruth facing him with her arms folded across her chest and her mouth tightened in battle mode. His footsteps faltered. He sighed and continued walking toward Ruth and his bedroom.

As he passed by Ruth, the odor of raw sex floated from his body and singed her nostrils. He opened his mouth, trying to gather his thoughts, but his brain stuttered in shock seeing her up and out of bed so early in the morning. He silently berated himself for oversleeping at Lenora's house and not taking time to shower. As he drove home, he had hoped that Ruth would be asleep.

She recoiled away from her husband like she had walked up on a rattlesnake. Her nose rose in the air like Samantha Stevens on the television show *Bewitched*. Ruth's face crumpled like a dented car fender, tears springing into her eyes. She reared back, her hand flew up, and she slapped Daniel so hard he fell up against the wall. She raised her hand to slap him again, but he caught her hand in his before she could do it. She raised her other hand and scratched his cheek.

"Ruth, have you lost your mind? What's wrong with you?" Daniel snarled. He held her writhing body in his arms.

"Don't ask me something as stupid as *what's wrong with me*," Ruth's voice rose hysterically, "when you have the nerve to walk into our house, the home we raised our children in, stinking of another woman!" Ruth shouted at the top of her lungs. Her hair was mused and her face was contorted with fury. "Leave! Get out of here now!" She pushed Daniel away.

He held his hands up in surrender and smirked cruelly at Ruth. "Be careful what you ask for, Ruthie. I'm out of here. Call me when you come to your senses." He marched quickly to the kitchen and let himself out the back door. The door banged loudly.

Ruth turned around and walked slowly back to her room, holding her abdomen, doubled over with grief. She sat on the edge of the bed and covered her face with her hands. Her body shook uncontrollably as tears rained down her face.

Chapter Eleven

After Ruth lost her mind, Daniel revved the Mustang's engine loudly and drove around the corner to the front of the house. He pulled the car in front of his residence and shifted the car into park. Daniel stared at the one story reddish brick bungalow surrounded by a gray chain link fence.

Ruth kept the couple's beautiful antique furnished home with artisan woodwork, immaculate. Daniel paid for a landscaping service to keep the lawns mowed and in tiptop condition.

In the corner of the living room sat Ruth's pride and joy, a white Baby Grand piano.

A melancholy feeling coursed through Daniel's veins. *This could be the last time I call this house home,* he thought to himself.

He rubbed his eyes tiredly. Daniel realized that Ruth would be upset with him for staying out all night, but it wasn't like she was giving it up to him. He had his needs, and he had honestly counted on her Christian forgiveness. Lenora's sexcapades, and the three bottles of champagne they consumed, had worn him out. Plus driving the huge bus the past few days had taken a toll on his energy level, and somehow he'd lost track of time.

He opened the glove compartment and riffled through the inside. He pulled out a cigarette from Fred's stash. The older Wilcox brother kept a pack inside the car for when he was hung over and he didn't have the energy to go to the store. Daniel lit the Newport. The clock on the dashboard read two forty-five A.M. He'd planned on going to work early and catching up on overdue paperwork. Daniel pulled his cell phone from his pocket and left a message on his supervisor's voice mail, informing him that he'd be in later that day.

He exhaled a plume of smoke as he contemplated where to spend the remainder of the night. His small head urged him to go back to Lenora's house so he could lose himself in her willing flesh. But his big head told him to go to Fred's house until Ruth cooled off. He glanced at his house as he inched down the street.

When Daniel arrived at Fred's apartment he let himself inside with his spare key. He walked in and sat down heavily on the black leather couch. The place was a mess. There were two half empty glasses of Cognac sitting on the wooden oak cocktail table. One glass bore the imprint of a dark lipstick stain. Newport and Virginia Slims cigarette butts overfilled the red plastic ashtray that lay in the middle of the table. Daniel assumed that his big brother was entertaining female company. He could hear the sounds of smooth jazz coming from behind Fred's closed bedroom door.

Daniel leaned back against the couch and spied a black lace bra stuck between the couch cushions. With a distasteful expression on his face, he gingerly picked up the material and dropped it on the side of the sofa.

He pulled off his shoes and lay on the couch, his forehead furrowing with lines. He yawned, turned over, and immediately fell sleep.

When he awakened three hours later, Fred sat at the kitchen table. The room was adjacent to the living room, and he stared at his brother with a bemused expression on his face. He sipped from a cup of coffee and turned the page of the *Sun-Times* Newspaper, which lay spread before him.

Fred was a redbone color, a shade lighter in complexion than his younger brother. He was tall and lanky, resembling their deceased mother. His wavy black and gray hair was pulled back into a rubber-banded ponytail. His face looked worn, and his nose was hooked. Fred's large hands were calloused from years of operating a printing press machine for *the Sun-Times* Newspaper.

Fred was and still is a master player. He had been married and divorced three times. Out of those marriages he became the father of two children, a daughter and son. Unfortunately, his relationship with his children was nonexistent due to his incessant bickering with his exes over child support money.

He turned up the cup of coffee and drained it before looking at Daniel and asking, "What happened to your face? It looks like a tiger by the name of Lenora clawed you. Did she get tired of sharing you with Ruth?" He lit up a Newport cigarette and exhaled a puff of smoke.

Daniel touched the side of his face. The reddened wounds throbbed. "Naw, Lenora didn't do this, Ruth did."

Fred peered narrowly at him. "What's up, bro? You can't keep your women in check?" He set the empty cup on the table. "How did Ruth find out about Lenora?"

Initially, Daniel looked ashamed, but his expression became defiant as he told his brother what transpired the previous night and that morning. Fred listened, nodding and shaking his head as he spoke.

When Daniel finished his tale, Fred said, "Bro, I thought I taught you better. You didn't play your hand correctly at all. So you overslept, big deal. All you had to do was shower before you went home and deal with being MIA. Why complicate the situation by not showering? Do you want your marriage to end?" He wagged his finger at Daniel.

"Honestly, I thought Ruth was asleep," Daniel replied. "You could've knocked me over with a feather when I saw her standing in the hallway still up, ready to jump on me. She asked me to leave and I did. As far as my marriage is concerned, yeah, maybe it's over. I think it's been over for a long time." Daniel looked pensive.

"So, what are you going to do?" Fred asked his brother as he stood and stuck his wallet and keys in his pocket. "No, tell me later. Look man, I gotta run and earn that paper," he said, getting ready to go to work.

Daniel rubbed his chin. "I don't know what I'ma do. Until Ruth cools off, maybe I could stay here with you for a while, if you don't mind. I can sleep on the couch."

"Just don't get in my way, little brother. I can't have you messing up my mack," Fred joked as he went out the front door. "I'll holla at you later." He closed the door behind him.

Daniel walked into the kitchen. He shook the coffee pot to see if there was any java left. No luck. He opened the refrigerator door and stale odors greeted him from the dingy appliance. A container of ossified Popeye's chicken and a couple bottles of beer sat forlornly on the middle rack. His nose twitched in the air. *Oh well, I might as well go to McDonald's.* He left the apartment in search of nourishment.

Chapter Twelve

Brring, brring. The sound of the telephone ringing awakened Ruth. She sat up rapidly and looked at the caller ID. Alice's telephone number was displayed. Ruth fell listlessly back onto the bed. Her head pounded with pain and her wrinkled hands trembled slightly. She closed her eyes and massaged the area between her eyes. She let the call go to voice mail.

The house felt unnaturally quiet. Ruth sensed Daniel hadn't returned home, as he had promised. When the events of the following night came flooding back into her mind, she felt betrayed that her husband of more than thirty plus years hadn't bothered to call and beg for her forgiveness. Her heart thudded erratically as the scent of Daniel's body last night invaded her psyche.

She felt panicky and her breathing became shallow. She breathed noisily through her mouth and began hyperventilating. *Maybe I was too hasty. I should've given Danny a chance to explain what hap-*

pened. Her eyes glittered with tears. She dropped her head. *What could he really say anyway? I know I smelled another woman on my husband. Daniel cheated on me. How could he do this to me?*

Her being was filled with conflicting emotions. Ruth reached over and unplugged the telephone jack, then turned over wearily and fell back asleep.

A week had elapsed, and Ruth hadn't talked to her husband. She was too proud to call him and Daniel still hadn't returned home or called his wife. Ruth's emotions vacillated between anger and fright. The fact that Daniel hadn't even tried to make amends rocked Ruth's world to the very core. She became depressed. Her spirits plummeted abruptly, like an elevator careening out of control.

She hadn't enlightened her family or friends about her and Daniel's impromptu separation, because she assumed he would've returned home by now. The past Sunday was the first time she'd missed church services in years.

Like a thief in the night, Ruth called Bishop's office a little after midnight and left a message on his answering machine stating she was ill and wouldn't be attending church service. Before she hung up, Ruth added that she planned to stay home from work for a few days. She left messages for Sarah, Alice, and Naomi when she knew they wouldn't be home, telling them the same story.

After spending most of Sunday indulging herself in a pity party and ignoring the telephone that rang off and on during the day, Ruth rose from the bed Monday morning and walked into the bathroom. Dark markings, like half moons, circled her lifeless eyes. Ruth looked at her reflection, bewildered, as if she was trying to identify whom the harried looking woman in the mirror was.

Her body erupted into spasms of hot flashes and Ruth sank to the floor. The cold tile was soothing to her warm flesh. A light sheen of perspiration coated her forehead as she rested her arms along the side of the toilet. The straps of her gown hung limply off her shoulders.

She looked upward, and said in a hoarse voice, "Lord, why me? Haven't I been a good and faithful servant? I've done everything you've requested of me according to your Word. Most of the time I've tried to be a good wife to Daniel. Why is this happening to me?" Teardrops sprinkled her arms. Ruth looked at the doorway and Bishop's immeasurable girth loomed before her. Ruth, immersed in her personal pain, hadn't heard the front door open and close from the bathroom.

She knew her father must have let himself in with the key she had given him, against Daniel's wishes, when they purchased the house. In Daniel's opinion, Alice having a spare key for emergencies was sufficient enough.

Bishop looked down at Ruth sadly and walked into the tiny bathroom. He helped his daughter up from the floor and led her to the bedroom.

He sat in the chair adjacent to the bed wearing a dark shirt and a white clerical collar. His massive shoulders and arms strained against the seams of his black and white tweed jacket.

As Bishop listened to Ruth's sobs, his hands

grasped the Bible so tightly that his knuckles whitened. His heart was filled with anguish. Finally, the storm passed, and Ruth lay in the bed, softly weeping and hiccupping in intervals.

Bishop cleared his throat, and asked in his soft baritone voice, "What's wrong, Ruth?"

Ruth looked away from her father. "Lord, help me, Daddy. Daniel has left me."

Bishop shook his head in disbelief. "I don't believe it. Why would Daniel leave you after all this time? You two have been married for nearly thirty-five years. I don't understand."

Ruth snorted. "Another woman, what else? Isn't that what happens to older wives after we put in the time?"

He peered at her narrowly. "You know better. I've been with your Mother all my life, and other men in the church have stayed with their wives."

"Daniel and I aren't by any stretch of the imagination you and Mother," Ruth nearly screamed. She tried to get her emotions under control. Her voice dropped as she said, "This is a different era."

"Regardless of what chapter of time this is, marriage vows remain the same. You promised to love and obey your husband when you married. That never changes."

Ruth's chin lifted defensively. "I didn't promise to share my husband, Daddy, and I'm not going to."

"Are you sure Daniel is having an affair?"

"As sure as the sky is blue," she moaned. "I know my husband. And this isn't the first time he's cheated on me. This is the first time he slipped up and got caught. In the past, I've ignored the warning signs that he was messing around, but I know in my heart he has committed adultery before." Ruth's face was suffused with red blotches.

"If you're so sure that Daniel has been committing adultery, then what made him leave you this time?" Bishop asked, seriously.

"I asked him to leave and he did. He disrespected me by staying out all night, then tried to sneak in the house reeking of another woman. He didn't even bother to hide it. I won't stand for that, Daddy," Ruth whispered.

"You know God tests us, Ruthie. He puts obstacles in our path to see how we cope with them. Only you know how much you can take, and your threshold for pain. But I urge you as your Father and minister to give yourself time to heal and then to talk to Daniel. Don't throw your marriage down the drain because of your husband's foolishness."

Ruth ran her hand over her head. "I can't promise that, Daddy. I can't promise anything."

The tears she thought had long dried up flowed down her face again. Bishop felt torn, not sure if he had helped his child or not. When he met Daniel, he found the young man's character flawed, and had perceived the shortcomings would present a threat to his daughter's happiness. His prediction took years, but now the chickens had come home to roost.

Bishop felt helpless with the situation at hand. He thought, *I should be doing something to comfort my daughter.*

He glanced down at his watch, "it's nearly lunch time, would you like me to fix you breakfast? I bet you haven't eaten yet. Let me warn you that although I'm not the best cook in the world, I can still put a simple meal together. I bet you haven't been eating properly, have you?" He stood and laid the Bible on the chair.

Ruth shook her head grimly from side to side. "No, not really. I don't have an appetite along with a husband." Ruth's eyes watered. She swallowed and rubbed her eyes.

"Well, at least let me make us some coffee. Go get dressed, by then it should be ready. Then we can talk more about what you want to do."

"You don't have to fuss over me, Daddy. Really, I'll be okay. I'm sure you have other things you could be doing instead of being here with me." Ruth stood up.

"I'm not going to take no for an answer. I'll see you in the kitchen shortly." Bishop walked out the room, and down the hallway to the kitchen. The first thing he did was put on a pot for coffee.

As he stood at the stove scrambling eggs, and waiting for the coffee to brew while Ruth dressed, Bishop wondered if he was doing the right thing. Perhaps he should have called Queen Esther and asked her to come over and join them.

After they finished the meal, Bishop read Bible scriptures to Ruth, trying to console his daughter. She listened to her father's words half-heartedly, her heart felt too burdened with grief.

Several hours later, Bishop put on his coat and prepared to leave Ruth's house. He picked his fedora hat up off the cocktail table as he and Ruth walked to the front door.

"I'll call you later today and see how you're

doing, Ruth. Don't isolate yourself from friends and family. In times of trouble, you have the Lord and your family to lean on. You don't need to go through this trying time alone."

Ruth didn't look as pale and sad as she did when Bishop first arrived. Her arms were clasped across her chest. She said in a quivering voice, "I just need time alone to figure out what I want to do. I'll be okay, just give me time."

Bishop rubbed her shoulders comfortingly. "I know you have a lot on your mind. But I feel you didn't give your husband a chance to express how he feels about a separation, Ruth. You just reacted to the situation. Maybe your marriage can be saved."

"I disagree, Daddy. Considering Daniel hasn't called or returned home, speaks volumes of what he wants," Ruth responded sadly. "Sometimes you just can't fix what's broken. It might just be time for me and Daniel to move on with our lives."

Bishop shook his head from side to side and replied carefully. "Have you forgotten with God all things are possible? Talk to our father, meditate and pray, Ruth. The Lord will show you the way."

Ruth nodded. "I will, Bishop. I promise I will."

After her father departed, Ruth returned to the bedroom, sat on the rocking chair, and opened her Bible, the one her grandfather presented her with when she was baptized.

Ruth's spirit had lifted a bit due to Bishop's visit. Still she wondered how Daniel was faring, and if he had someone to comfort him. Or if he even needed comforting?

Chapter Thirteen

Daniel sat in his office at work, with his feet up on his desk, speaking on the telephone to Lenora.

"I have some free time today. What are you doing later? Why don't I pick you up at seven o'clock and we go out to dinner?". he asked her.

"You're taking me to dinner and it's not my birthday?" Lenora quipped, scratching the side of her head. "What's up?"

"I have some news I want to share with you," Daniel answered. "Since Red Lobster is your favorite restaurant, how 'bout I pick you up at six-thirty for dinner. That is, if you're available." He teased her with a grin on his face. Daniel sat upright in his chair.

"Sure. I mean I don't have any plans," Lenora lied. She'd actually made plans to visit her family that evening. "I'll see you later." She made kissing sounds.

"Okay, baby. I have another call." Daniel noticed the red button on the phone was flashing, indicating he had a new voice mail message.

He entered his voice mail code and listened to Bishop's request they talk as soon as possible. His father-in-law went on to add that he'd just left Ruth and she was in a bad way. He cajoled his son-in-law into calling him.

Daniel's face clouded with annoyance as he listened to his father-in-law's message. *How dare Ruth confide our problems to her father?* Then after further thought, he had to admit to himself, he knew there was a possibility she might've talked to Bishop. Daniel clasped his hands behind his head and leaned back in the chair.

While Daniel was becoming acclimated to his new surroundings at Fred's house, he hadn't seen Lenora. Instead, he talked to her on the telephone, claiming he needed to spend time with Ruth. In reality he was waiting for the scratches on his face to heal. He hadn't told Lenora that he and Ruth were separated. He planned to break the news to her this evening. He decided not to contact Bishop just yet, and to call Ruth next week to set up a meeting. He picked up a pile of papers and began reading them.

Even though he'd only been staying with Fred for a short time, Daniel had forgotten how much of a slob his brother could be. The apartment stayed in a constant state of disarray. He had gone grocery shopping a few days ago, and Fred had already eaten most of the food. Daniel knew it wouldn't do any good to talk to his brother about the situation. That is, unless he planned to stay

with him indefinitely. And he knew living with
Fred wouldn't work out, because he was too used
to being taken care of by Ruth and he liked his
surrounding and belongings in a certain order.

Daniel contemplated moving in with Lenora,
and a beaming smile appeared on his face as he
imagined living with his lady permanently. But
he felt it would be politically incorrect; his being
married to a minister's daughter and living with
another woman, unless he was legally separated
or divorced. A shiver ran up his spine just thinking of divorce.

Daniel and Lenora shared dinner at Red Lobster on 95th Street in Oak Lawn that evening. They
munched on mozzarella sticks, Lenora sipped a
strawberry daiquiri from a tall frosted glass, and
Daniel guzzled his usual drink, Crown Royal and
coke. The waitress had already taken their dinner
orders. Lenora ordered the ultimate feast, and
Daniel, the shrimp scampi.

"So, how did you manage to get out tonight? I
thought Ruth had you on lockdown, since I haven't
seen you in almost a couple of weeks." Lenora
counted on her fingers. She pointed to her watch.
"And it's after seven o'clock, past your curfew for
us to meet. You're usually home by this time," she
kidded him. During the course of the couple's
relationship, thought not often, Daniel would distance himself from Lenora, so Ruth wouldn't suspect he was cheating. Lenora assumed her not
seeing Daniel over the past week was one of the
times.

Daniel took a sip of whiskey before announcing, "Ruth threw me out."

Lenora's mouth dropped. "Ruth threw you out? I don't believe it. When?"

Daniel sighed then lifted his glass, looking for the waitress. He then looked at Lenora, who gazed adoringly at him like he was Jesus Christ arisen from the dead. Her eyes shone with joy and her lips widened prettily in a huge grin.

"She sent me packing the night I overslept at your place. She hadn't gone to bed, as I assumed she had. She was steaming mad. She didn't ask any questions, she just assumed I had been with another woman. After physically attacking me, she asked me to leave."

"So you've been where for the past few weeks?" Lenora asked, noticing for the first time, the light scratch marks on his face. She leaned over and kissed them. "My poor boo, let Nora make you feel better." Her tongue lightly flickered over his face.

"I've been living with Fred. But I'm not sure how long that's going to last at this point. My brother takes sloppiness to a whole new level," Daniel complained. He kissed Lenora's lips.

"Daniel, why didn't you tell me when she first threw you out? My feelings are hurt." Lenora pouted. She folded her arms across her chest. "I can't believe you didn't share something so momentous with me. I thought we were like this," Lenora crossed two fingers together. "You were wrong for not sharing the news with me, Boo."

"I didn't intend to slight you, babe," Daniel apologized, copping a feel on her thigh. "But this hasn't been an easy time for me. I needed time alone to decide what I'm going to do. Trust me, my first thought was to come to you. But with Ruth being a minister's daughter and all, I've got to take it slow and show her and the children some respect."

Lenora dipped a cheese stick into the thick red sauce. She yearned to ask him a million questions, but her mind told her to follow his lead and be patient.

"So, have you talked to Ruth since she put you out?" she asked airily, waving the food in the air.

"No. I know she's waiting on me to call, begging her to let me come back. But I've come to the realization that I don't want to go home. I can't make any promises right now, babe, but I hope as far as our relationship is concerned, we can bump things up a notch in the future." Daniel looked into her face.

Lenora dropped the cheese stick onto her plate. "Are you crazy? Of course I'm game. I'd like nothing more than to spend the rest of my life with you. Daniel, you don't know how hard I've prayed that we could be together one day. I don't like sharing my boo with anyone, especially with your wife. Do you see us getting married one day?"

Daniel cringed. He looked uncomfortable upon hearing the word *marriage*. He hadn't really given any serious thought to marrying her, not yet. But if that's what it took to keep this beautiful, young energetic woman by his side, so be it. He might have to hedge things a bit in the beginning.

He grabbed her hand and said, "Nora, I'm not even divorced yet. Let's take things slow. I still haven't talked to Ruth about a divorce yet."

"Oh, my God," Lenora gushed, clasping her hands together. "Wait until I tell Felicia. Daniel, you have to meet my family. I'm so happy that I could burst. Thank you Daniel. I love you, boo." She rained kisses upon his face. She didn't care who stared at them. The moment she had hoped for had come. Daniel finally wanted a commitment from her.

"Just think, we can go out on dates all the time like a regular couple. Not that it bothered me that we couldn't before. Still, it will be great having our relationship out in the open."

Daniel interrupted her, holding his hand up. "Not just yet, Nora. Until I get things squared away with Ruth, we still have to keep our relationship on the down low. But not as low as before." He laughed aloud at his own joke.

Lenora grabbed his hand and kissed it. "I know what you mean. I just never thought I'd hear you say you wanted to move our relationship to the next level. Never in my wildest dreams did I think Ruth would find out about us and you two would split." She leaned over and kissed Daniel's cheek. "Well, keep in mind, my door is open for you twenty-four seven, and you can stay with me if you want."

"There's no place I'd rather be than sharing your house, your bed, and enjoying your body." Daniel leered at her. "But all things in time. We'll eventually get there, Nora."

The waitress returned with a platter containing their entrees. Lenora spread her napkin in her lap and Daniel did the same. She picked up her fork and began eating.

A tiny voice in Daniel's head warned him. *Don't move so fast until you've settled things with Ruth. Have you forgotten you have children to consider, and that you'll probably have to pay child support for Naomi? You know the kids are going to be disappointed about the split, and they're going to take Ruth's side. They are closer to Ruth than you.* For a hot second, Daniel wished life could just go back to the way they were before he overslept at Lenora's house.

But, on the other hand, Ruth didn't satisfy his sexual needs, nor did she make him the center of her life. Sex played a big part in his life. He couldn't be expected to stop enjoying the physical side of love just because his wife didn't want to play. His children were all grown up and now he wanted to play.

Suddenly Daniel thought about the fact that children had never come up between he and Lenora. He made a mental note to ask Lenora if she planned on having children. He hoped she didn't want any. *Been there and done that.* Maybe he could talk her into getting her tubes tied. *Hmm, now that's an idea*, he thought.

Chapter Fourteen

The day after Bishop's visit, Ruth decided to finally retreat from her bedroom, removing the chains of her self-imposed exile. The linens on the bed were wrinkled and slightly musty. After she showered and dressed, Ruth rinsed out the coffeemaker, put a fresh filter in the pot, and spooned beans into the compartment. She sat at the table lethargically with her hand resting on her right cheek, contemplating her day. *The first thing I need to do is change the linen on the bed and do laundry,* she thought to herself.

To keep Sarah and Alice at bay while she pulled herself together, Ruth kept the deadbolt lock fastened on the front and back doors. She forgot to engage the locks after Bishop left her house. Ruth managed to keep her conversations with Naomi to a minimum, saying she had been feeling ill.

After she drank two cups of the strong dark liquid, Ruth returned to her bedroom and stripped the bed of the linens. She put a clean, Downy fresh-smelling set on the bed. When that chore was completed, she went into the bathroom and removed soiled clothing from the hamper. She sat on the side of the bed sorting them into neat piles.

She was downstairs in the basement putting a load of clothes in the dryer when she heard footsteps upstairs. Her heart rate accelerated and her mouth went desert dry. As she wondered if Daniel was upstairs, she saw Sarah coming down the wooden stairway.

"What are you doing here?" Ruth looked at her daughter warily after she shut the dryer.

Sarah ran to her mother and hugged her tightly to her body while Ruth stood with her arms dangling at her sides limply. Tears gushed down Sarah's face. "Mom, I haven't talked to you in over a week. I came by to check on you, and make sure you're all right."

Ruth grumbled, irritated. "As you can see, I'm fine." The doorbell rang.

Sarah said, "I'll get it." She returned upstairs.

When Ruth went back upstairs and walked into the kitchen, Alice and Sarah were standing in the middle of the room whispering. Alice eyed her friend compassionately. She walked over to Ruth and embraced her friend's body tightly.

"What brings you here?" Ruth asked after Alice sat at the table. Ruth's body rested against the counter and her already dim mood darkened at the unexpected appearance of her daughter and Alice. She knew they had come over to see about her because they cared, but Ruth wasn't sure she was ready to talk about the separation. And the fact that Alice and Sarah came to her house without calling first caused Ruth to feel like she'd been blindsided.

"I'm hurt that you'd even ask that question," Alice replied, removing a scarf from around her neck. "You're in pain, and as your best friend, I want to do whatever I can do to help you."

"Why don't I warm up the coffee?" Sarah suggested. She turned the coffeemaker on.

Ruth walked to the table and sat in a chair. Sarah stood at the stove and looked around the room critically. Dishes were stacked haphazardly in the sink, the floor looked dingy and in need of cleaning. Crumbs, like dust mites, rested on the usually immaculate countertop.

It was obvious to Sarah that her mother hadn't cleaned the house recently, and her stomach tumbled. She felt like the world as she knew it had been upended. Sarah self-consciously sat down at the table. Her left hand was tucked under her chin.

"Bishop told me that you and Daddy are having problems," Sarah said. "When you didn't return my calls, I became worried. I came over a couple of times, but you didn't answer the door. At first, I was going to use my key and come in. Then, on the other hand, I wanted to give you your space. After so many days went by and you didn't answer the door, I decided to take my chances and just come in. Like Aunt Alice, I want to do what I can to help. I was just so concerned about you." She lowered her eyes, embarrassed.

As Ruth opened her mouth to speak, tears fell from her eyes. "I don't quite know what to say to you or anyone else. This situation between your Daddy and me is personal, and not up for discussion. I'm not ready to share any details yet. I wish Bishop hadn't said anything. I would've told you what happened eventually."

Alice felt as upset as Ruth. It was obvious her friend was suffering. She stood and walked over to Ruth and embraced her. "I'm so sorry," she choked out.

Sarah brushed a tear from her eye and shook her head sadly. She noticed the coffee was boiling. She stood and removed cups from the cabinet and poured coffee into them.

The women didn't speak for a time. Ruth rubbed her hands on the warm coffee mug while Alice aimlessly stirred sugar into her cup.

Sarah put on a brave face. "Mom, what are you going to do? Where's Daddy?"

Daniel wasn't in the habit of calling his children on the telephone to talk. Usually he spoke to them when Ruth called them or they called her.

Ruth shook her head. "Your guess is as good as mine. I don't know where your father is staying. I suspect he's with Fred. As to what I'm going to do, I'm still trying to figure that out." She rubbed the side of her face, feeling humiliated.

"Why did Daddy leave?" Sarah asked with the directness of a youth. She set her mug on the table after taking a sip.

"Let's get something straight," Ruth said, waving her hand in the air. "I asked your father to leave, he didn't leave me." She covered her face with her hands.

Alice frowned and tsked at Sarah. Then she

grabbed Ruth's hand and held it tightly in her own. "Have you talked to Daniel since he's been gone?"

"No," Ruth gulped. "I can't believe he hasn't called me. I don't know what I'm going to do yet. After all these years of listening to and counseling women at church on this very subject, how ironic I find myself in the same predicament. Sometimes I feel helpless, then mad. I can't control getting old any more than I can control Daniel's actions. I've tried my best to live my life right and do the things God expects from me. I've tried to be a good wife to Daniel, a Christian woman, and raise my children correctly. And what do I get in return? A slap in the face." She looked mournfully at Alice and Sarah.

Ruth continued. "I know Queen Esther will want to come over here with her minions from the Mother's Board to pray for me. Mother will also give me her lecture on how I'm obligated to work things out with my husband. It's too bad Queen and I don't share a close relationship. It would be nice to have a mother to comfort me right now. I haven't talked to Mother—although she has called—because I know all she would say is how I'm Bishop's daughter, and I have to set an example for the church members. But you know what? At the end of the day, I'm a child of God like everyone else.

"When my outreach committee counsels our downtrodden sisters, as we smugly call them, we tell them what we think they should do to be good Christian wives, and pray because God will help them through their trials. But you know, what we tell them isn't enough. Those words are meaningless and can't begin to soothe the sorrow I feel in my heart that I've failed. Bishop and Queen Esther's daughter couldn't get it right, so how can I expect other women to?" Ruth dropped her head on the table and sobbed quietly.

Tears dripped from Sarah's eyes.

Alice hugged her friend's shoulders and said, "Ruth, I'm so sorry about what has happened. But know this, you don't have to go through this situation alone. Let me and Sarah stay and do what we can to help you."

"But it's not your problem or Sarah's," Ruth blubbered helplessly. "It's mine and Daniel's. Lord, I don't know what to do."

After about ten minutes of crying, Ruth finally calmed down. "I'm a little tired, I think I'll go to my room and lie down a bit." Her eyes were swollen. Without meeting Alice and Sarah's eyes, she walked slowly to her bedroom.

Alice looked at Sarah and shook her head sadly. "I think one of us should spend the night with her. I can stay, I don't have any plans this evening."

"I don't either," Sarah answered despondently. "I didn't realize Mama was in such a bad state. I don't think it would hurt if both of us stayed with her. I'm going to call Brian and see if he can keep the kids overnight."

"Ruth has been there for so many people, myself included," Alice said, nodding. "Now that she needs help, I'll be here as long as she needs me. You said she was washing clothes when I arrived, so I'm going downstairs to finish doing the laundry."

Sarah stood, walked over to the wall phone, and picked up the receiver to call Brian. "I'm going to call Brian now. Mama needs us. I'm going to stay as long as she needs me, even if I have to bring the children here."

"Me too," Alice vowed. She opened the basement door and walked down the staircase as Sarah said hello to Brian.

Chapter Fifteen

A week later, after missing her first Sunday in a row for years, Ruth decided to go to church services at the temple after Alice promised she'd go with her. Ruth felt her best friend's presence would help keep the gossips at bay. Alice was the designated driver, and was en route to the Wilcox house.

Ruth stood in the middle of her bedroom indecisively. She really didn't feel up to going to church. She felt self-conscious, like there was a big "S" carved in her forehead, proclaiming she and Daniel were separated.

Thanksgiving was next week, and for the first time since she and Daniel had married, Ruth didn't feel like preparing a big meal for the family. She wanted to be left alone.

She had finally talked to Naomi and Daniel, Jr. about the marital split. Naomi would be arriving home from school on Monday and Daniel, Jr. was working feverishly to get leave to come home for

Thanksgiving. He promised to be home for Christmas, if his plans fell through for Thanksgiving.

In preparation for church, Ruth began to dress in a lilac and yellow floral rayon dress. She cinched a matching belt about her waist. She walked to the closet and pulled out a dark purple felt hat with a black flower tacked across the front. The doorbell chimed, indicating Alice had arrived.

When she opened the door, Alice looked at her friend from head to toe. "It's cold outside. Are you sure you're dressed warm enough?" Alice wore a silver fox coat with a matching hat pulled over her head.

"Let me get my jacket, then I'll be ready to go. The cold weather isn't a big deal for me. Mother Nature had given me my own personal defense mechanism. Hot flashes," Ruth added as she opened the closet door. She put on a black jacket, then a black wool coat. She locked the door behind them when they left.

"Have you talked to Daniel yet?" Alice asked after they were inside the car and she was pulling away from the curb.

"No, I haven't. If I don't hear from him today, then I'm going to call him at work and suggest we meet soon."

Ruth turned her head and looked out the side window. The past few weeks had taken on a surreal quality. She could hardly believe all the issues confronting her.

Daniel had made her a statistic—no, correction—if she was honest with herself, she had made herself one; a minister's daughter on the verge of divorce, all because of her cheating husband. *Sometimes I wish I could flip a switch, forgive Daniel, and welcome him back home.*

When Ruth and Alice walked into the sanctuary, the congregation was singing the last verse of the morning hymn, "A Closer Walk With Thee." Ruth felt paranoid, like the usher was staring at her pitifully, when she handed her the church bulletin.

Alice was headed to Ruth's usual seat in the second row, center pew, behind Queen Esther. Instead, Ruth tugged the back of her friend's coat to indicate she wanted to sit closer to the back row. Alice looked at her questioningly. Ruth mouthed plaintively, "Please?" Alice knew then that today's service was going to be a long one.

The wooden pews in the sanctuary gleamed. Bishop wasn't lax on the upkeep of the church. He kept his crew replenished with newly paroled young men from his prison ministry. The ex-felons polished the seats on a weekly basis. Baskets of roses, carnations, and greenery were placed around the altar.

Reverend Newman, one of the assistant pastors, rose from his seat and walked to the podium to lead the congregation in prayer. As the service progressed, the choir sang, "He's Able, What A Friend We Have In Jesus," and, "Jesus Can Work It Out." The colossal choir's voices soared as they repeated the refrain to "Jesus Can Work It Out." Ruth's eyes dripped tears as she listened to the beautiful voices. The words helped quell her fractured soul.

Bishop, clad in a black robe that was trimmed in gold along the shoulders, rose from his seat to deliver the morning sermon. He laid his Bible and papers on top of the podium. Then he adjusted the microphone.

His voice thundered. "Let the church say Amen!" He smiled benevolently at his flock. "Please open your Bibles to Ephesians, Chapter 4, Verses thirty-one through thirty-Two." Bishop intoned, " 'Let all bitterness, and wrath, and anger, and clamor, and evil speaking, be put away from you, with all malice.' "

The theme of Bishop's text that morning, not surprising to his daughter, was forgiveness. Ruth cringed in her seat. Queen Esther glanced back at her daughter after shouting several hardy Amens. Ruth wished she could just leave. Her legs twitched as if they had a mind of their own.

Every time Ruth fidgeted in her seat, it seemed Bishop paused speaking and looked in her direction. Ruth settled down in her seat and began to listen to the words her father spoke. "'And be ye kind one to another, tenderhearted, forgiving one another, even as God for Christ's sake hath forgiven you.' "

Ruth closed her eyes and listened to her father's words. Then peace, like a river, flooded her soul. Though her heart was still heavy, she realized she was at home, her spiritual home. Ideas ricocheted through her mind as to what she should do about the state of her marriage.

Thirty minutes later, Bishop opened the doors of the church to invite those visitors without a church home to join the temple. Before Reverend Newman could raise his hand and begin the benediction, Ruth fled the sanctuary. Alice trailed behind her.

They walked toward the ladies room when Mother Edna Campbell, a member of the Mother's Board, and Queen Esther's best friend, spotted the women with her eagle eyes. She grabbed Ruth in a bear hug. Her white uniform was immaculately pressed. Her skinny legs were encased in skintoned hosiery, and her feet in white orthopedic shoes. Mother Campbell's bifocals sat crookedly on her narrow nose.

She clasped her hands together and said, "Ruth Ann, I want you to know you're in the entire Mother's Board's prayers."

Ruth felt alarmed. Sweat trickled down the sides of her face. She looked helplessly at Alice and murmured quietly, "Thank you, Mother Campbell."

Alice, not one to disappoint a friend in need, looked at her watch and stated decisively, "Ruth, it's time for us to go. We have an appointment. Mother Campbell, we'll see you another time." She steered Ruth away. "Do you need to stop and talk to your folks?" she asked Ruth. She spied Queen Esther, dressed to the nines in a royal blue two-pieced skirt suit with matching blue pumps on her feet and a midnight blue feathered hat on her head. She was headed their way. Her Bible was tucked under her arm and her purse dangled from the other.

Ruth sullenly nodded at her mother. She whispered to Alice, "I guess that answers your question."

Queen Esther handed Alice her Bible and

engulfed Ruth in her arms. Then she took a step backward and looked at her daughter critically. "Ruth, you look peaked. You've got to take care of yourself, no matter what Daniel has done. Someone needs to take you shopping. That outfit is so outdated."

A few members of the church standing nearby turned to eavesdrop on the conversation. Ruth noticed the curious stares thrown her way. She felt mortified, and whispered softly through clenched teeth, "Mother, I'm fine."

"My poor child. What are you doing Wednesday night? I can gather a group of the women from the Mother's Board and meet at your house. We need to pray for you, Ruthie. Our Heavenly Father will see you through this trying time."

Sarah and her children walked over to where Ruth and Queen Esther were standing. Ruth shot her daughter a thankful look. Queen Esther, mindful of her great grandchildren's presence, dropped her conversation with her daughter. Ruth chatted with Sarah and her grandchildren for a while. Soon, Ruth and Alice made a graceful exit and headed out of the church.

After the two women entered the car and fastened their seatbelts, Ruth and Alice decided to go to Evergreen Park and have lunch at the Applebees Restaurant. Following the meal after the drive to Ruth's house, Alice put the car in park and turned to her friend. "Do you want company? I can stay with you. I don't have anything to do except go over lesson plans for my students for tomorrow. But I can do that from here if you want me to spend time with you. I know it wasn't easy being at church today."

"You're right about that," Ruth said, smiling weakly. "If you hadn't rescued me, I'd probably still be in Queen's clutches. Mother Campbell would have insisted we go back into the sanctuary so the Mother's Board could pray for my soul." The friends chuckled, picturing the scene.

"I can see Mother Campbell putting her Bible on your forehead, asking the Lord to cast out the divorce demon," Alice laughed.

Ruth laughed until tears spilled over her cheeks. She wiped her face and patted her friend's hand. "Ally, thanks for everything. I appreciate all you've done." She unlocked the car door. "Now go home and relax; I'll be fine. I'll call you if I start feeling lonely." She got out the car.

Alice tooted her horn as she drove away.

Ruth went inside the house where she quickly changed clothes and put on a pot of water to boil for tea. After pouring herself a cup of tea, she sat in the living room wearing a blue floral quilted robe and blue slippers on her feet. Gospel music flowed from the CD player. She sipped the tea and then closed her eyes and meditated.

After she opened her eyes, Ruth removed her Bible from the cocktail table. The book was opened to her favorite scripture, the 121st Psalm. "I will lift up mine eyes to the hills, from whence cometh my help. My help cometh from the Lord, which made heaven and earth."

Suddenly, Ruth heard the front door lock turn. She looked up and saw Daniel. He was wearing a black leather coat and a matching cap sat on his head.

"How are you?" she asked. Her eyes searched his face hungrily.

"Fine," Daniel answered, tersely. He removed his coat and cap, laid them on the back of the couch and sat down.

He noted the anguish on Ruth's face. She stared at him dispassionately. Her face looked lined and older to him.

"How are you doing, Ruth?" he asked.

She scrutinized Daniel as he stared back warily at his wife. She was amazed that he appeared unscathed by their spur-of-the-moment separation. He looked positively peaceful to her, like his life was carefree as a bowl of cherries. Her lips trembled uncontrollably as she recalled the other woman's scent on him the morning he left. *Perhaps*, she thought, *she's the reason for his seemingly peace of mind.*

"I'm making it," she replied nervously as she laid her arm on the side of the sofa.

He sensed Ruth wasn't going to make this meeting easy for him. In his heart and mind, he had already severed the marriage. Talking to her was merely a formality.

"How are the kids? Have you spoken to them about our separation yet?"

"They know you're gone," Ruth replied, dryly. "I haven't given them any details."

"I'd like to talk to them myself, if you don't mind," he requested. "We need to talk about what we're going to do and finalize our plans."

"What are you saying, Daniel?" Ruth's voice

quivered. "Are you saying you want a divorce?"
Her heart beat *rat-a-tat*, as if signaling a death knell.

He licked his lips and said, "Yeah, Ruth, I want
a divorce."

She felt like her heart was shredding to tiny
pieces. She snapped her fingers. "Just like that?
You just waltz in here and make your announcement, like it's no big deal. What about what I
want? What about our children?" She tried to
keep the hurt out of her quavering voice.

Daniel pursed his lips and shook his head regretfully. "Ruth, I still care about you. I always
will. You're the mother of my children." He
closed his eyes as if recalling the words he'd re-
hearsed. "The truth is, we haven't shared a real
marriage in the true sense of the word for a long
time. Our interests are different. You're content
with going to church and the family. And I want
more." He hesitated and looked at his wife. "I still
want to go out and have a good time. We're both
older now and the kids are grown. Who knows
how much time we have left on this earth. Why
shouldn't we enjoy our older age as much as we
did when we were younger?"

Ruth's hands shook slightly. She crossed and
uncrossed her legs. "We took vows, Daniel; Until
death do us part. Doesn't that mean anything to
you?"

He wiped his perspiring brow with his hand.
"Things haven't sat right with me since Naomi
was born. I feel like you let your father and mother
dictate how our marriage should be. I went along
for the sake of appearances. I've had enough of
Bishop, Queen, and most of all, the almighty

temple. Ruthie, enough is enough, it's over." He stared around the room, much like he had outside the house the night he left.

Pictures of the children were lovingly placed about the room. Prom and graduation and wedding pictures were encased in silver and gold frames. Shots of the grandchildren, the precious third generation, smiled in their birthday suits, lying on their tummies atop pink and blue blankets. The room held so many memories, commemorating many years.

Ruth looked traumatized, as if her best friend had been killed right before her eyes. She knew from past experience that Daniel wasn't going to change his mind. A part of her wished she hadn't said anything that night and forced his hand. Maybe he would still be home with her today.

"Danny, I know I haven't been as attentive to you as you'd like, but I love you. You're the only man I've ever loved my entire life. Can't we work on our issues and see a counselor? I want our life back. I love you, Danny, please don't leave me." Tears rushed down her eyes, and her nose started running. Her body felt hot as if she had a high temperature.

"Ruthie, I don't want to try and fix something that's been broken for a long time. I care about you, but no, I don't want to stay married," he replied, adamantly.

"Why, Danny, because of the other woman?" Ruth's voice sounded catty, but she couldn't stop herself from asking that question. Daniel's face became blurred because of the tears that momentarily blinded her eyes.

Daniel hesitated and looked at a spot beyond Ruth. He couldn't meet her gaze. "Naw, Ruthie, this is something I want to do for me."

She felt like a dagger had been thrust deep into her heart. She sensed Daniel was lying about the other woman. *He must really care for her*, Ruth thought.

He suggested that she initiate the divorce proceedings. "Whatever you want, Ruthie, the house whatever, it's yours. I'll buy you out."

Her voice broke. "I'll talk to my lawyer after the holidays," she said.

Daniel had borrowed a few of Fred's shirts and he'd gone shopping to replenish his wardrobe. He felt it would keep confusion at a minimum until he talked to Ruth. He stood and held his cap in his hands awkwardly. "I'll come over one day when you're at work and get my things. I'll also call the kids this week and talk to them. When will Naomi be home?"

"Monday." Ruth stood and followed Daniel to the door. "Aren't you forgetting something?" she asked as tears trickled down her face.

He looked back at her quizzically. "Like what?"

She held out her shaking hand. "Your keys to the house."

He pulled his Ford emblem key ring out of his jacket pocket. His hands shook slightly as he removed the house keys from the ring and handed them to her. The look she gave him was one of pure desolation. He felt a brief tinge of sorrow, but bid her a hasty retreat nonetheless.

The key chain slipped from Ruth's hand onto the floor as she stood at the window. She watched

her husband of nearly thirty-five years saunter
out her life.

She heard Daniel's car door slam and felt in-
credulous that he never looked back. She pushed
a tear from the corner of her eye as she walked
into the kitchen to call her father and inform him
that her marriage was officially over.

Chapter Sixteen

A week later, Ruth, Sarah, Naomi, and DJ, along with his wife, Chelsea, were gathered around the dining room table. The family's mood was sulky. Remnants of the Thanksgiving meal lay on plates and serving trays. Ruth stood and began clearing the table.

The Wilcox family usually shared the holidays with their extended family, Bishop, Queen Esther, Fred, and Alice. But this year, Ruth decided to partake in the holiday repast with just her immediate family. Bishop and Queen Esther weren't happy with her decision. Ruth's mother felt like their daughter was pushing her parent's away. The empty seats Bishop and Queen usually occupied, and Daniel's vacant seat at the head of the table, were loud reminders of how drastically the Wilcox's life had changed.

After the meal, DJ put the *Shrek* CD into the DVD player for the children to watch. Daniel and Ruth's three grandchildren, Joshua, Maggie and

Daniel, III, sat atop of a blanket on the floor of the den. They stared wide-eyed at the big screen television. Laughter rang from the room, and spoons tinkled merrily as they scooped spoonfuls of chocolate ice cream into their mouths.

The adults were in the dining room discussing the demise of their parent's marriage.

"Dad is wrong, plain and simple," DJ grumbled. He thumped the table with his finger. A goblet clattered in place.

Chelsea patted his hand. "Honey, you need to calm down," she admonished her husband.

"Chelsea," he roared, pounding on the table, "my parents are getting a divorce!" He wore a dazed expression as he glanced at each woman, as if to say, *what is this world coming to*?

Naomi looked distressed. She lowered her head as her mouth trembled. Her eyes were bright with unshed tears. Though she wasn't as close to her father as Sarah, she sensed Daniel's leaving was somehow her fault. She watched Ruth remove bowls and trays of meat from the table.

"Mommy, do you need any help?" she asked.

Ruth sighed. She used the back of her hand to brush a lock of hair off her forehead. "No, stay where you are. I'll clean up."

Sarah sensed Ruth kept herself busy to keep her mind off Daniel's defection. She jumped up from the table and went into the kitchen, where she rinsed the china and loaded the dishwasher.

"Mommy, you were up all night preparing the meal. Why don't you go sit down and rest? I'll take care of things in here," Sarah said.

The doorbell chimed.

DJ stood and muttered as he walked to the door, "I hope that isn't Dad. I know he doesn't have the nerve to show his face here this evening." He opened the door and Bishop and Queen Esther stood at the entrance.

The children ran from the den to greet their great-grandparents. Bishop's eyes homed in on his daughter. He thought she looked tired.

After he and Queen Esther exchanged greetings with the children, Bishop walked over to Ruth. "I know you told us you wanted to be with the children. We just couldn't stay away." He patted her arm.

Ruth smiled grimly. "I made potato pies. Would you and Mother like some with coffee?"

Bishop rubbed his rotund stomach and smiled. "Of course! I love your potato pie."

"Thanks. Just a small piece for me," Queen answered. "I'm watching my weight. How is everyone doing? Baby DJ has grown so much since the last time we saw him."

"We're doing fine. And you're right, that boy is growing like a weed," Chelsea answered.

Sarah added, "Bishop, why don't you and Queen have a seat? I'll fix the pie and coffee."

Naomi went into the kitchen to help her big sister with the refreshments. They returned to the dining room a few minutes later with pie, plates, and a carafe of coffee. Everyone was seated at the table. Naomi handed a pie tin to Bishop, while Sarah poured cups of coffee and took them to her grandfather and grandmother.

Bishop cut a slice of pie, then looked at Ruth

and asked, "How's it going? Have you spoken to an attorney yet? What are you going to do?"

She gritted her teeth. "I talked to an attorney that Alice recommended, and I have an appointment with her next week. I'm going to go ahead and start divorce proceedings."

Queen Esther whined, "Can't you try to work things out?" She wore a pained expression on her face. "How will it look to the members of the church? Our daughter getting a divorce?"

"Mother," Ruth complained petulantly, "this is my life you're discussing, not yours or Daddy's, nor the church's. I'm doing my best to move on. I hope you and Daddy will support me and let me work things out my way."

"Sure we will," Bishop answered, as he shot a warning glance at his wife.

Queen Esther opened her mouth to speak and then snapped it shut. But she couldn't resist adding, "Well, I hope you have a competent lawyer. You should use our lawyer and take everything you can get from that ungrateful sinner."

"The situation isn't about being vindictive," Ruth replied. She wiped her shiny forehead with a napkin. Her body felt hot, like she'd been ignited with a flame.

"I agree with Grandmother," DJ interjected. "Dad should be made to pay. Don't let him just walk away from his responsibilities. Make him take care of you for the rest of your life." He was devastated by his father's callous treatment of his mother.

The children didn't know Daniel had left their mother for another woman. Daniel and his son were scheduled to meet Friday evening after Daniel got off work, where he was certain to get the whole truth.

"This is Ruth's cross to bear, and she must deal with it as she sees fit," Bishop proclaimed as he sat his cup of coffee on the table. "She'll do the right thing."

Ruth flashed her father a feeble, but grateful smile. *Thank God someone has faith in my judgment.*

DJ again voiced his displeasure. "I still don't think you should let Dad walk away like nothing has happened. My God, he's torn this family apart."

"Son, let's talk in the other room," Bishop requested to his grandson. The men walked over and stood by the piano. "I know it's a difficult time for you—the situation with your parents—but you're going to have to step aside and trust them to work their issues out."

"I hear you, Bishop. I know what you're saying, but they're my parents for God's sake. How can I not be involved?"

"In my day, we called it staying out of grown folks business, and some things never change. Your Mother will do what's right for everyone."

DJ's eyebrows rose skeptically. "And what about my Dad? He's never made life easy for anyone. I hate seeing my mother hurt like this."

Bishop nodded his head. "Trust me, we all do. But we all have to put our feelings aside, and let Ruth and Daniel work it out."

DJ shook his head from side to side. "I don't know that I can do that, Bishop."

"You're going to have to try very hard, and

every time you get an urge to interject your opinion, call me. I promised Ruth we'd give her space to work out her issues," his tone became stern, "and we're going to do just that. Do you understand me, DJ?"

"I'll try, sir." DJ said, grudgingly.

Ruth was considering asking Sarah to move in with her, and she planned to talk to her about it after meeting with the lawyer. Sarah resided in a three-bedroom apartment in the South Shore area. The building was going to be converted to condominiums next year, and Ruth was sure Sarah was worried about moving since she couldn't afford the down payment.

Ruth had originally planned to talk to Bishop and Daniel about loaning Sarah the money, but with latest turn of events, Sarah moving in with her would be a win-win situation for mother and daughter.

Several hours later, Bishop and Queen Esther departed. DJ and Chelsea laid on the sofa bed and watched television in the basement. Daniel III, and Joshua lay on the sofa bed in the living room watching another movie. Maggie lay on the bed in her mother's old bedroom reading a book.

Naomi sat on the floor in her bedroom, chatting on the telephone with one of her high school girlfriends. Sarah sat on her mother's bed and talked as Ruth wrapped her hair.

Ruth, standing at the mirror to her dresser, tucking the ends of the scarf, said, "Thanks for all your help today, Sarah. I think everything went well."

Sarah covered her mouth, yawning. Then she

said, "Yes, the day turned out nice. You appear to be adjusting better to life without Daddy." She leaned back on her elbow.

"Everyday is a new adventure," Ruth remarked, matter-of-factly. "I don't know how well I've adjusted. When all of this was going on, I forgot I was a child of God. I forgot to have faith. I've been reading my Bible and praying for God to give me strength to get through this trying time. Who knows? Maybe all of this is for the best." She smiled at Sarah.

"To let Grandma tell it, you and Daddy divorcing is the worst thing to happen in the world. After my divorce of course," she said.

Ruth spread cold cream on her face and looked at Sarah through the mirror. Mother and daughter laughed aloud.

"I want to talk to you about an idea that's been buzzing around my head. I hadn't planned on saying anything about it until after I talked to the lawyer. But now seems like as good a time as any. And you don't have to give me an answer right away." She paused. "I'm one hundred percent sure Daniel and I will end up in divorce court, and I'd love for you and the children to move here with me so that I can help you with them. I've been lonely living here alone, and maybe you and the children being here will ease some of my pain."

Sarah's eyes expanded with pleasure, like a child's. She clasped her knees. "Sure, Mama, I'll definitely think about it." She smiled.

It hadn't been easy for Sarah to make ends meet, and if she moved in with Ruth, that would ease her financial burden considerably. She stood up and stretched, then she walked over to her mother.

"I'm tired." She patted Ruth's hair. "I'll see you in the morning. I'm glad I decided to spend the night here. I'm too tired to go home."

"Goodnight, and get some rest. I'll see you in the morning. I love you, Sarah." Ruth smiled at her daughter.

Sarah murmured, "Good night, sleep tight. I love you too, Mama. And remember, you're not alone."

Ruth decided to look in on Naomi, who was still yakking on the telephone. She gestured she was going to bed and would see her in the morning.

Chapter Seventeen

Daniel knew the minute he and Lenora stepped inside the foyer of her parent's overheated apartment on Thanksgiving afternoon that he wasn't dining with a typical middle class family.

Jamal, the youngest of Lenora's twin brothers, opened the door. He stood unmoving in the middle of the doorway with his arms folded across his chest and stared menacingly at Daniel.

"What's up, old G?" he asked with a smirk on his face.

"My name is Mr. Wilcox," Daniel replied, forcefully.

He scowled at the young man dressed in blue jeans that sagged so low over his waist, that Daniel was afraid they were going to fall off his bottom any moment. He wore a white wifebeater, although the temperature outdoors was frigid. Colorful tattoos decorated Jamal's upper arms, and his head was covered by a blue doorag.

122   *Michelle Larks*

Hmm, let's see, no doubt he's a gang banger in the making, Daniel thought.

"Aw man, I'm just messin' wit'cha. Stop trippin'. Yo, Mom and Dad, Lenora's here with her old man." Jamal moved inside the apartment away from the doorway.

A naked little boy, who appeared to be two years old, streaked out of the adjoining room. He stopped in his tracks in front of Daniel and Lenora, looking for an opening to run out of the apartment. Daniel stood in front of the boy to block him from going outside. The little boy's hair was half braided, and the loose locks stood up on his head like a Mr. T Mohawk haircut. He looked up at Daniel, frowned, and then urinated on Daniel's leather pants.

"Oops," Lenora said, bending over and scooping the child up in her arms. She held him away from her body. "Kente, bad boy," she said, scolding her nephew, who giggled at his Aunt. "LaQuita, come here and get your child! Why isn't he dressed?" she yelled.

A teenaged girl ran to the door. She looked to be around sixteen or seventeen years old, and she was dressed in black jeans and a white, tight cowl neck sweater.

"Sorry," she mumbled, "I was just gettin' ready to dress him. Come on, Tay Tay."

"Danny, this is my youngest sister, LaQuita, and her son, Kente." She gestured toward the pair.

"Pleased to meet cha," LaQuita replied. Her eyes were downcast. "Sorry 'bout Tay Tay's accident. He ain't potty trained too good." Kente twisted in his mother's arms, trying to get down. "I'ma go finish gettin' him dressed." She shrugged in Lenora's direction as she walked down the hallway.

Lenora led Daniel to the bathroom. "I'm sorry about that," she whispered. "Sometimes my family takes a little getting used to. But they aren't that bad once you get to know them."

"Is that so?" Daniel responded, lifting his eyebrow skeptically. "What else is in store for me?"

She shook her head. "Truthfully, there's no telling."

"I know whatever it is, it won't top Kente's baptism," Daniel said, trying to joke. "I paid three hundred dollars for those pants, I hope the stain comes out."

While Lenora stood sentry outside the bathroom door, Daniel looked around for a clean towel and couldn't find one. When he bent over and picked a rag up off the floor, roaches scurried into the corners of the room. The afternoon definitely wasn't off to a good start.

When he came out of the bathroom, Lenora took him into the living room and introduced him to the rest of her relatives. Felicia sat on the sofa with a bottle of water in her hand, wearing red suede pants and a gold sweater. She lifted the bottle of water and smiled at Daniel.

"Hey, Daniel, what's up? Welcome to the Johnson family's humble abode," Felicia greeted him.

"I'm doing fine. It's good to see you again, Felicia," he said.

Lenora pointed to an older, rotund version of herself, and said, "Danny, this is my mom, Glenda

Johnson." She wore an apron over a shapeless brown dress, and cloth slippers were on her feet. Her mushroom-styled hair hung limply on her head.

She's not too bad looking, Daniel thought. *She's like a worn out version of Lenora.* Fred's voice popped into his mind, *remember, girls' mamas look like how they're gonna look when they get older.*

"Welcome to our home," Glenda greeted Daniel warmly, thrusting her hand out. She yelled to the twins, "Jamal and Jabari, get your stuff off the couch so Mr. Wilcox can sit down!"

"Please call me Daniel or Danny," he said to Glenda.

"Ain't ya kinda old to be hitting on Nora?" Jabari asked Daniel stepping inside the room. His twin had already given him the 411 on the older man who Lenora brought to dinner.

Daniel ignored the question. Other relatives gathered in the living room, and Lenora proceeded to introduce him to them.

"This is my aunt Deedee. She's Mom's oldest sister," Lenora said, pointing to a woman dressed militantly in army fatigues and lime green high-heeled shoes. Her wiry hair stuck out the side of a matching army-issued cap.

"Are you in the service?" Daniel asked her, trying to make conversation. "My son and daughter-in-law are stationed in Germany."

She looked at him like he was crazy. "No way, I just like the uniforms."

"This is my Aunt Annette, and her husband, Leroy, who we just call Hubby, cause she changes husbands so fast, we can't keep up with their names," Lenora joked. "And these are her children, Kahlil, Kadeesha, Mokeisha and Niyana. And this little fellow is Deron." Deron, who looked to be about five years old, walked over to Lenora and she patted her little cousin's head. When he smiled from ear-to-ear, Daniel noticed his front teeth were missing.

Annette and her five children looked ghetto fabulous in their K-Mart blue light specials. Leroy looked like he was trapped in an eighties time warp. He was dressed in a red striped shirt, and orange and brown plaid trousers. His straight hair was nearly shoulder length, and moistened by jheri-curl juice.

Annette guffawed, snapped her fingers in the air from side to side, and said, "At least no one can say I can't get a man." She grabbed Leroy's arm affectionately.

"But can you keep him?" a tall heavyset man who looked to be around Daniel's age, asked Annette as he walked into the room. He was dressed in a kelly green sweat suit. The shirt was covered with food stains. He stared at Daniel curiously. "I'm Ernest Johnson, Lenora's Daddy. And who are you?"

"Daddy, don't start," Lenora begged her father. "Daniel is a very good friend of mine."

Jabari snickered. "Old friend is more like it." The twin brother's dapped knuckles. The ends of the young man's cornrow braids curled just above his shoulders.

Lenora glared at her brothers and shook her head warningly.

Glenda, DeeDee, and Felicia laughed at the

twins' antics and then went into the kitchen to finish preparing dinner.

"It's nice to meet you, Daniel. Me and Reggie, Felicia's old man, are watching the football game; the Lions and Cowboys. Care to join us?" Ernest asked Daniel.

"Sure," he responded.

Leroy walked over to the boom box that was sitting on the shelf of a sagging wall unit. "I bought some CDs with me. Anybody mind if I put one on? I ain't into no football."

The family groaned aloud and bolted from the room. He put on James Brown's, *Say it Loud*. He grabbed Annette's hand and pulled her up from her seat. They camel-walked across the hardwood floor.

The children went into one of the bedrooms to watch television. Jabari and Jamal went into their bedroom to watch BET videos. LaQuita picked up Kente and took him into the bathroom to finish braiding his hair.

Daniel followed Ernest into a small, paneled, enclosed back porch off the kitchen. An old thirteen-inch, black and white television was perched precariously on a lopsided table. Lenora escaped to the kitchen to help the women.

"You drink man?" Ernest asked Daniel. "This here is my son-in-law, Felicia's husband, Reggie." He motioned to the young man sitting on the couch.

Reggie looked up, nodded at Daniel, then his eyes darted back to the television.

"You want a beer or something?" Ernest asked, popping the cap on a can of Coors.

"Sure, I'll have what you're drinking," Daniel said, after he sat on the lumpy sofa.

"Nora, bring your friend a beer!" Ernest shouted. The men's eyes were glued to the television.

After Lenora brought Daniel's beer to him, she returned to kitchen.

"Before you leave here today, how 'bout me and you have a man-to-man talk? I wanna find out your intentions about my daughter." Ernest slyly cut his eyes at Daniel.

"Sure," Daniel muttered. *What have I gotten myself into?*

Reggie glanced at Daniel sympathetically and then turned his head back to the television. "Did you see that play?" he exclaimed. Reggie was a thin, handsome man. He was a little shorter than Felicia and wore his hair in dreadlocks. Lenora had told him that Reggie was a barber by trade. He and Felicia owned a hair salon that catered to both sexes. Lenora and Felicia co-owned the building that housed the beauty shop.

Dinner was an eye opening experience. The adults gathered round the oak dining room table. Books lay under the legs of the table to align it. The scarred top was laden with food. Two card tables were set up in the living room for the young people.

Glenda fed Kente. Rashon, LaQuita's baby's daddy, rang the doorbell as Ernest hastily blessed the food. The family could hear Rashon and LaQuita arguing noisily in the living room. Kente spit food out of his mouth constantly and Glenda spanked his hands when he began throwing peas at family members.

The Johnson family brought healthy appetites to the table. They put a huge dent in the food. Daniel had to admit the Johnson women could cook, *but not as good as Ruth*.

After dinner, Uncle Leroy continued to entertain the family with old school music, while Ernest and Daniel resumed talking on the back porch.

"So, what do you wanna know about me?" Daniel asked Ernest. He was aware Lenora's father couldn't be too much older than him.

"I wanna know what your plans are 'bout Nora?" Ernest shifted his body on the couch. "She's a good, hardworking girl. I'd hate for some old man to put the moves on her and mess up her life."

"I'm very fond of Lenora," Daniel answered, sitting upright on the couch. He stared into Ernest's eyes. "We're gonna take it slow and see what happens."

"How old are you, Daniel?" he asked. He picked up the remote and changed the channel.

"In my mid-fifties," he said. "Although it's been said I don't look my age."

"Are you aware that you're twice my Noree's age and then some?" Ernest asked with a snide tone in his voice. "Do you have benefits where you work? Is your health good? Me and Glenda would hate for our daughter to be stuck with a sickly old man when she gets to be our age." He noted the look of surprise on Daniel's face. "You did know how old she is, didn't you?"

"Sure I did," he replied, tightly. "Lenora and I don't keep any secrets from each other." But if the truth were known, inwardly he felt embarrassed, like a teenaged boy caught with his pants down.

Ernest sensed Daniel was lying about knowing Lenora's age. He took a sip of beer. *I wish I could be a fly on the wall, and listen to Noree and Daniel's conversation tonight.* He laughed aloud at the look of discomfort on his daughter's boyfriend's face.

"I can assure you, Ernest, that my intentions towards Lenora are pure. I would never do anything intentionally to hurt her."

"You just make sure you keep it that way." Ernest set his can of beer on the table.

When the men finished talking, they returned to the living room in time to catch Leroy putting on a CD, the theme song from *Soul Train*, into the boom box. He insisted everybody take a trip down the line to work off the calories from dinner. Daniel wanted to laugh as he watched Leroy's hair flop on his head while jheri-curl juice flowed through the air.

"Come on Nora and Daniel, shake what God gave you." Leroy snapped his fingers to the beat of the music.

Daniel, laughing, put up his hands in protest. "Not this time, man. I'll catch you next trip."

Leroy made a vee sign with his hand, imitating Don Cornelius. "Remember, it's about, love, peace, and soul. Catch you on the downside." He walked over to Lenora. "It was nice seeing you, baby girl. Daniel, my man, gimme five." He held his palm out.

Daniel slapped his hand and said, "It's time for us to go. I have to work in the morning."

Glenda stood up from the chair she was sitting

in. She said, "Let me wrap up some cake and pie to take with you."

While she went to the kitchen, Lenora retrieved her and Daniel's coats from her parent's bedroom.

When Glenda returned she handed Lenora a brown paper bag. "Don't be a stranger," she said to Daniel. "Come and visit us again."

"I will," he said, solemnly. "Good night everybody."

"I'll call you, Mama," Lenora promised, kissing her mother's cheek.

Glenda pulled Lenora's scarf around her neck. "It's cold out there. Stay warm."

Daniel and Lenora left her parents apartment and walked down the dark deserted street to Daniel's car. She noticed Daniel was unusually quiet during the drive to her condo. Before long the pair stamped their feet on the welcome mat in front of Leonora's door before entering the apartment. Once inside, Daniel made a beeline to the bar in the living room. He poured himself a generous helping of cognac. Lenora hung her navy blue wool coat in the closet. She picked up Daniel's jacket and hung it in the closet also.

"Do you want something to drink?" Daniel asked her. She shook her head no. He walked over to the couch and sat down heavily.

"I guess you didn't have a good time today?" she asked as she sat beside him, looking at him concerned. He wore a dejected expression on his face. "I know my family is a bit much."

"Yeah, you're right about that. What got me was your father's attempt to have a man-to-man talk with me while we watched the game," Daniel snorted.

Lenora walked to the bar and returned with the carafe of cognac. She placed it on the cocktail table.

"It would've been nice if you would've told me your real age before I met your family," Daniel grumbled after he poured more cognac into the snifter.

"I knew if I had told you my age, you might've thought I was too young for you," she admitted. Her brow puckered as she chewed on a split fingernail.

Daniel felt a twinge of unease as he leaned his head on the back of the couch. He closed his eyes.

"Nora, your age is important. Is there anything else you've forgotten to mention, like having any children?" he asked her, sarcastically.

"Of course not," she replied, contritely. She caressed Daniel's hand. "You're the first man I've met in a long time who's caught and held my interest. I just didn't want to spoil things between us." She dropped her head.

"Try to see things my way," he said, sardonically. "Your father telling me you're only twenty-eight years old, well, it kinda took me by surprise."

"I can understand that," she said. "But you warned me time and time again, how you weren't ever going to leave your wife, so I figured I'd enjoy our relationship while it lasted. There was no need for me to rock the boat since we weren't ever going to be together anyway."

"You should've told me, Lenora, right from the beginning." Daniel felt tendrils of fear brush across his neck. He stood up abruptly. "I'm going out for a little while."

"Are you really coming back, Danny? Are you going to stay with me tonight, like you promised?"

He didn't answer her. She watched the door open and shut. Her mouth dropped open. She sat on the sofa for a while, then stood, turned off the lights and retired to her bedroom. She lay on top of the comforter feeling worried. *Was Daniel having second thoughts? Maybe I should've told him that Glenda and Ernest aren't married, and that they've been shacking up ever since Glenda was pregnant with Felicia. No, I better hold off telling him that for now. When Daddy was telling my secrets, he didn't bother to air his own dirty laundry.*

Daniel drove slowly to Fred's house. The day seemed like a scene out of every stereotype movie he'd ever seen. He felt out of synch. He'd never admit it to anyone, but he missed being with his children and brother today. Since day one of Daniel and Ruth's marriage, Fred spent every holiday with his brother's family.

He thought to himself, *maybe I should've stopped by the house to see the kids,* cause when he talked to his son and Sarah earlier, he could hear the hurt in Sarah's voice. The conversation with DJ was strained. He felt his son judged him harshly, and he had a problem with his son's hostile attitude.

When he paused at a stoplight, he punched the steering wheel in frustration. Then he cursed under his breath when his hand began to throb.

Doubts about his relationship gnawed in Daniel's mind while he drove to his brother's apartment and continued as he walked inside the building.

Daniel knocked on Fred's door. His brother looked at him sideways when he opened the door. Daniel walked in and sat on the couch. Fred walked into the kitchen and returned with a fifth of whiskey and two paper cups.

"What's up, little bro? How was dinner with your new folks?" He unscrewed the top on the bottle and poured the brown liquor into the paper cups. Then he handed one of the cups to Daniel.

"What happened in there?" Daniel asked, glancing toward the kitchen. A smoky stench lingered in the air. Scorched fried chicken lay in a skillet, congealed in grease. Two blackened pots sat atop greasy ringed burners, inside of each was seared collard greens and yams.

Fred sheepishly said, "Well, it wasn't Ruth's cooking, but it was better than nothing."

"You couldn't get one of your women to cook for you? Brother you're slipping," Daniel replied.

The brothers laughed and then sat together in companionable silence. They drained their cups of whiskey, and Fred poured more of the amber liquid into their cups.

"Nora lied to me about her age," Daniel sighed. His face was creased with irritation.

"And what's so bad about that? Women always lie about their age."

"Well, in her case it's a big deal. I thought she was a couple of years older than Sarah, and I found out she's more like a few years younger than my oldest kid, and finding out the truth kind of bothers me."

Fred took his time replying. "Who's it a big deal to, Danny? Your wife, father-in-law, or you?"

Daniel shook his head. "To everyone you said, but mostly to me."

"Well, she ain't jail bait. So, what do you care?"

Daniel leaned forward. "If she lied about her age, then whose to say she isn't lying about something else?"

Fred started laughing, and a glint of anger shone in Daniel's eyes. "What does it matter, age is just a number. Anyway, the younger, the better, right?" Fred said.

Daniel shrugged his shoulders. "Do you realize how much flack I'm going to catch from that?"

"Flack from who? You and Ruth are already separated, so what does it matter?"

Daniel sighed and cupped his face with his left hand. "Flack from my children, that's who."

Fred opened his mouth and closed it. "Well, little brother, you'll figure it out."

"You're right," Daniel said.

He got up off the sofa, slipped on his black leather coat and gloves. He left and returned to Lenora's house to spend the night with her as he had promised.

Chapter Eighteen

Monday morning following Thanksgiving, Ruth stood inside her office at the temple. She opened a package of computer paper and placed the sheets inside the tray of the laser printer. When she returned to her desk, she noticed Queen Esther standing in the doorway, holding up a bag from Schlotsky's deli.

"Mother, you startled me. What are you doing here?" Ruth exhaled softly. She knew it was only a matter of time before her mother cornered her so Queen could give her spiel on how Ruth should preserve her marriage.

"I thought it would be nice if we had lunch together." Queen Esther removed her coat and took a Burberry scarf off her meticulously coifed head. She laid the garments on the couch, then she walked to Ruth's desk and began unloading the contents of the bag.

"White or rye?" she asked, removing packets of ham and roast beef from the bag.

"Rye, please." Ruth's eyes traveled downward to her hips. She sighed. Queen watched her daughter with an amused look on her face.

As the women demolished the sandwiches and macaroni salad, Queen Esther spoke in a conciliatory tone. "Ruth, I want you to please consider carefully whether you really want to divorce Daniel or not. We don't need any scandals in the family right now." She wiped a crumb off her chin.

"I'm sorry, Mother, but I had little control over when my husband decided he wanted to screw another woman."

"You'd better watch your mouth, Ruth Ann Wilcox, we're in the Lord's house." Queen Esther's lips tightened, like she'd bitten a piece of bitter fruit.

"God will forgive me. Mother, please allow me to make my decision on my own without any influence from you. I'm over fifty years old, when do I become old enough in your eyesight to live my life the way I see fit?" Ruth's eyes darkened angrily, like a thundercloud.

Queen Esther's hand fluttered to her chest. "There's no need to talk vulgar to me. A few members of City Council have approached your Father about running for Mayor. He has a chance to leave his mark on the community and city at large. What greater honor could he ask for? Bishop should never have agreed to your marrying Daniel. And I told him so in no uncertain terms. I knew that man would bring us down, and sure enough he has," she sniffed. "This isn't the time for another divorce in this family. It could jeopardize your Father's political aspirations."

"That man, as you call him, is your grandchildren's father, and I won't have you talking negatively about him," Ruth murmured calmly, though rancor simmered in her soul. "What about me, Mother, my feelings and how I'm coping with all of this?"

"The Bible says you reap what you sow. Ruth, you made your bed, now lie in it," Queen Esther replied, coldly.

"What, like Ezra made his bed, and you made him lie in it, Mother? God, what disappointments we both must be to you."

"Leave your brother out of this." Queen Esther's voice rose slightly.

"Ezra could be dead or dying at this very minute. You've cut him out of your life and turned your back on him because of his lifestyle. I guess you're not eager to let that piece of news get out to the media either. We wouldn't want anyone to know how the First Lady of Jubilee Temple hasn't seen her oldest child in over thirty years, now would we?"

"That's a low blow, even for you, Ruth." Queen Esther's face paled. She pulled on her coat, and said in a shaky voice, "Trying to talk to you calmly and rationally is an exercise in futility. I've got to run. You go ahead and have it your way. Your father spoiled you rotten and this is a prime example of what happens when you spare the rod."

"Mother, I think your idea to leave now is a good one, before I say something I'll regret." Ruth's chest heaved, and she panted heavily as her body flushed with rage. She felt lightheaded.

Queen Esther shot a harsh look at her daughter before leaving the office. Ruth folded her arms, put her head down on the desk, and cried. Her brother's presence weighed heavily on her mind. Ruth felt ashamed because she hadn't talked to him in nearly a year.

She picked up the telephone and called Alice to ask her to come to the church. Alice arrived twenty-minutes later just as she promised.

"What was so urgent that you needed me come over now? It's starting to snow," Alice said when she walked into the office. She noticed Ruth's swollen eyes. "What's wrong? Did you talk to Daniel?"

Ruth pulled a tissue out of her desk drawer and blew her nose. "Mother just left here. We exchanged words. I said some mean things to her and I hurt her feelings as usual."

"I'm sure whatever she said hurt you equally as well." Alice tried to comfort her friend.

"Ally, Ezra has been lurking in the back of my mind for a couple of weeks. I have a premonition that he's in trouble and needs help. When Mother went on about how selfish I'm being about Daniel and my marriage, I snapped and mentioned my brother. She then hightailed it out of here like wild dogs were on her heels."

"I don't think Queen Esther has ever come to terms with or forgiven Ezra for being gay. You know how pretentious she is." She rubbed Ruth's cold hands.

"I didn't mean to unload on you, Ally. I shouldn't

be dumping all of this on you, especially since Martin and Ezra were lovers. You're the last person I should be running to with my problems." Ruth wiped her runny nose.

"I came to terms regarding Martin's sexuality a long time ago, so I'm fine with all this." Alice clasped Ruth's hand. "Do you have any idea where your brother could be?"

"The last time I talked to him—and that was at the beginning of the year—he said he was staying at a homeless shelter near downtown."

She nodded at Ruth. "When you get off work, let's go downtown to the Pacific Garden Mission and see if we can find him."

"Thank you for being my friend," Ruth said as a tear seeped down her left cheek.

Chapter Nineteen

When Daniel finished his workday, he drove to a café on 79th Street off King Drive to meet DJ. There was an automobile accident on 79th Street near the Dan Ryan Expressway and traffic was backed up, so he was running a few minutes late.

When he finally arrived at the Captain's Table Cafe, DJ was sitting ramrod straight in one of the blue booths near the rear of the building, stirring a cup of coffee. He was dressed in his Lieutenant Colonel Army uniform. Daniel strolled over to his son. DJ stood to greet his father and they shook hands.

Initially, DJ was standoffish toward his father. He didn't make eye contact. He stared at a point behind Daniel's shoulder. He watched women enter the café with their children in tow, wearing bulky down coats, which made them appear twice their normal size. Bus passengers huddled near the door of the restaurant waiting for the #3

King Drive bus to arrive. Cool air snaked into the restaurant as the door opened and closed.

Finally, DJ looked directly into his father's face. Daniel almost wished he hadn't, because myriad emotions were reflected on his son's visage. Daniel was taken aback at the naked loathing in DJ's eyes, as he tried to talk to his son.

"Dad, why don't you refresh my memory and tell me again why you want a divorce? I don't quite remember your reasons. The whole thing seems crazy to me, breaking up our family." DJ enunciated his words clearly.

Daniel was surprised at the venom that erupted from his son's mouth. He stuttered, "Uh yeah, I do want a divorce. Your mother and I have grown apart, our interests are different. Since you and your sisters are grown, now seems like the best time to end this cha . . . I mean marriage."

"You know what, Dad? I hear you, but your reasons sound like a bunch of bull manure to me. I always knew you were selfish, but what you've done to this family takes the cake. Mom has dedicated her life to taking care of you and us children. And now you want to tear the family apart?" He peered at his father through narrowed eyes. "You have to know you're hurting Mom. Don't you love her anymore?"

Daniel felt a heavy weight slide to the middle of his stomach. What could he really say anyway? If he were honest with himself, Ruth hadn't done anything terrible to him. Unfortunately, she just wasn't Lenora. He knew his son wouldn't understand his feelings, and kids usually sided with their mother during breakups.

"There's not another woman involved, is there?" DJ probed, suspiciously.

Daniel dropped his head nearly to his chest. DJ leaned forward in his seat and opened his mouth to protest. Then he closed it. Daniel leaned across the table and placed his hand on his son's arm.

"Son, at least hear me out, please?"

He glared at his father and pressed his lips into a thin slash, and shook off his father's hand from his arm. "For God's sake, Dad, I grew up at the temple listening to gossip about you my entire life, how you messed around with other women. I even got into fights when I was a kid because boys taunted me about you. But I'm telling you, if your real reason for wanting a divorce is another woman, then I'm through with you. Our relationship is terminated; we're done."

Telltale signs of guilt were written all over Daniel's face. He clutched DJ's arm again. "Son, hear me out."

The angry young man pulled forcibly away from his father and stalked out the café. A few people in the café stared at Daniel quizzically when DJ slammed the door shut when he left. Daniel sat heavily in his seat. If he didn't realize it before, he knew now that he was in for a rough ride with his children. Daniel realized out of his three kids, Sarah might be the only one to continue a relationship with him, regardless of his actions.

He had fully expected the children to take their mother's side in the marital rift, and he knew DJ wouldn't have any mercy on him. Still, it cut him to the quick that his son walked away without hearing his side. He rubbed his eyes, left a couple of dollars on the table, and walked out the cafe. *Nora* Baby, I need you. *She'll cheer me up.*

Daniel drove to Lenora's place, and after arriving, the couple sat quietly in her kitchen at the table. Daniel flipped through the pages of *Sports Illustrated*. There was still a sense of awkwardness between them. Daniel still felt a tiny sense of betrayal about her lying to him regarding her age.

Lenora stood at the stove preparing dinner. She hadn't cooked a meal for Daniel before, so she decided to whip something up and impress her man with her culinary skills.

"Danny, why don't you go into the living room. Isn't *Sports Center* on or something? You're making me nervous sitting here staring at me."

Daniel stood up and slid the chair up to the table. He walked over to Lenora and clasped his arms around her back. "Okay. I'm sorry that I'm making you nervous. What are you making to eat?"

"I thought about fixing red beans and rice. Do you like that?"

"Sure, Nora, whatever you make is fine with me." He walked into the living room, picked up the remote, and planted his body on the sofa. His cell phone rang. It was Fred.

"What's up, Dan? What you doing tonight?" Fred asked.

"Nora's cooking dinner. We planned on staying in. Why, what are you doing?"

"One of my coworkers is getting married tomorrow, and a bunch of us are meeting at a Gentleman's Club in Romeoville. Why don't you join us?"

Daniel glanced towards the kitchen. He heard a crash and then heard Lenora cursing loudly.

"Uh, tonight isn't a good night. I don't know about my baby's cooking. I have a feeling that's not one of her strong points. Maybe I should stick around tonight."

"Come on, Daniel, I know you ain't gon' let no young girl lead you around. Boobies and booties are gonna be flowing all over the place. Are you game?"

"I'll pass. Maybe we can do something tomorrow night?" Daniel asked, hopeful. He didn't feel like discussing his love life with Fred, and not doing so was a first for him.

"I don't get you, man. Your nose is so wide open that a horse could trot through it. I know I taught you better than that. Call me tomorrow if it's okay with Miss Nora. You better make sure she'll let you come out. I'll holla at ya tomorrow."

Lenora walked into the room with a glass of wine for him.

He said, "You know I don't drink that stuff; it's for women. Why don't you bring me a beer?" He flipped the television from station to station.

She walked across the room to the bar and sat the glass of wine on it. Then she went back to the kitchen and returned with a chilled bottle of Corona beer.

"How's dinner coming?" he asked after he sat the bottle of beer on the table.

"Daniel, please use a coaster. Dinner is coming along just fine. Do you like ham hocks?"

Even though his doctor had warned him to

watch his pork intake, Daniel didn't want to call attention to his age. He simply said, "Yes, I like pork anything." He turned the channel back to *Sports Center*.

"Well, I'm going back in the kitchen. I'm going to bake cornbread to go with dinner."

"Sounds good. I'ma watch television while you're cooking."

Lenora went back into the kitchen and picked up the telephone to call her mother.

"Hey Ma, it's me, Lenora. I'm making dinner for Daniel."

Glenda laughed. "Nora, you don't know the first thing 'bout cooking. Wha'cha making?"

"Red beans and rice with cornbread and ham hocks," Lenora whispered.

"Baby, will you bring me another beer?" Daniel called, from the living room.

"Give me a minute, boo," she said to Daniel. "Mom, I want to show Daniel I can do everything better than his wife can do. I bought a couple cans of red beans and a box of rice. I'm just not sure what to do with the ham hocks." The meat lay in the sink draining.

The day after Thanksgiving Glenda called to gossip with her daughter about the meal. Lenora revealed to her mother that Daniel was married but separated from his wife and that her mission was to become the next Mrs. Daniel Wilcox.

Glenda didn't approve of Lenora and Daniel's relationship. She and Ernest felt Daniel was too old for their daughter. She warned Lenora that Daniel's wife would always be a part of his life.

But Lenora was stubborn like Daniel, when she made up her mind about something there was almost nothing anyone could do to make her see another point of view. So Glenda and Ernest backed off giving Lenora any advice.

"Okay, I'll help you out this time, but don't make a habit of calling me when you decide you want to top your man's wife. This is what you need to do to fix the hocks. First make sure you clean them good. Then put a pot of water on the stove," Glenda instructed her daughter.

"How much water should I put in the pot?" Lenora asked, reaching in a bottom cabinet for a silver pot.

"Use the biggest pot you have and fill it almost to the top. Then put the hocks in it and let them boil for a couple of hours."

"How will I know when they're done?" Lenora turned on the hot water.

"You'll know cause the meat will be tender. You know what I mean. Two hours should be long enough."

"Thanks, Ma. I'll call you back if I need more instructions."

"Bye, baby. And good luck." They hung up the telephone simultaneously.

Lenora put a three-gallon sized pot full of water on the stove. She turned the burner on high and while the water was heating, she stood at the sink and washed the ham hocks.

Holding the pieces of meat up in front of her and eying the pieces critically, she was satisfied they were clean enough. She walked to the refrigerator and took another bottle of beer out for

Daniel. She then went into the living room and gave him the bottle wrapped in a napkin.

"I meant to ask you, how did your meeting with your son go this afternoon? By the way, when is Ruth going to see a lawyer?"

"We talked a few days ago. She plans on starting the petition after the Christmas holidays."

"Another month? I guess that's not too bad. I can't wait until you're free and I can proudly show the world my man." She leaned over and kissed his lips.

"Do I smell something burning?" he asked, looking towards the kitchen. The smoke detector began buzzing.

"Shoot." Lenora jumped up from the sofa and ran into the kitchen. The room was smoky, and bits of charred rice was smoldering inside a pot on the stove.

She smacked her forehead lightly. *I thought I turned the rice off. I guess I forget.* She put on oven mitts and removed the pot from the stove. She took it to the sink and tried to scrap the rice out of the pot. After unsuccessfully trying to dislodge the gooey mess, she gave up and tossed the pot in the garbage can.

Daniel fell asleep waiting for her to finish cooking. Finally, she walked into the living room looking bedraggled, and announced that dinner was ready. He stood and went into the bathroom where he washed his face and hands.

When he made his way into the kitchen, Lenora had dimmed the lights. He slid into the chair across from her. The table looked appealing. She had gone for a formal look, inappropriately setting the table with her best china and glassware with gold cloth napkins. She went overboard in her zest to impress him.

Daniel murmured grace and picked up his fork. He poked at the lumpy rice and the blackened beans. He put a tiny forkful of rice in his mouth and swallowed, not bothering to chew. He picked up his glass of water and gulped it down.

After the burning pot incident, Lenora had taken a deep breath and boiled another pot of water for the rice. She looked at Daniel forlornly. "I'm sorry, Danny, I guess I overcooked the rice and beans. The cornbread was hard as a brick. I wanted dinner to be perfect, but I don't cook much since I live alone."

Daniel tried slicing the meat from the ham hock bone, but the skin was tough as leather. "Don't worry about it, baby. You have plenty of time to try new recipes on me. Let's just order in and spend the evening right here."

Lenora stood and walked over to him. She had a look of relief on her face. "Thank you, Danny." She kissed him. "I feel better. I'll call and order pizza, but I want you to know dessert is on me," she said, winking at him.

Chapter Twenty

Bishop looked up as Queen Esther walked into the den, carrying a plate of food that she set on the table. He was in the middle of writing a speech for the young adult's musical scheduled for Sunday evening. He noticed his wife's face was drawn and her mouth drooped.

"Thank you, dear. Are you joining me for dinner, or have you already eaten?"

"I'm not hungry." She sat primly on the edge of the chair facing Bishop's desk and crossed her legs. She glanced at the pictures of Ruth's children and grandchildren on the shelf behind him.

Bishop took off his glasses and rubbed his eyes. "What's wrong, Esther?"

"That daughter of yours. Who else?"

"You need to lay off Ruth, Esther. She's going through a tough time. I know she's struggling with her faith, and rightfully so. She's a grown woman, and we have to let her figure out what she wants to do with her life and husband." He wiped his glasses with a tissue and put them back on his face.

"Why do you always take her side over mine, Bishop? I only have her best interest at heart, even if I don't say it correctly sometimes."

"I hope you didn't try to pressure her about the divorce, or say anything negative regarding Daniel's character."

The aroma from the steak, onions, and mushrooms was overwhelming, causing Bishop's stomach to growl. He cut the meat into tiny pieces and drenched them with A1 Steak Sauce. Queen Esther looked down and nervously twisted her hands together.

"I may have suggested she should try to work on her marriage. When I told her that, she attacked me and became infuriated. She even cursed at me, Bishop, in the Lord's house. Then she threw Ezra in my face and how I've abandoned him."

"Hmm, sounds like the conversation deteriorated quickly." He speared a piece of steak and put it in his mouth.

"Is it so wrong of me to want one of my children to have a normal life?" she lamented as she waved her hands in the air. "Since Ezra's been gone, you take Ruth's side over mine, like you think it's my fault our son turned his back on his Christian and moral values. Homosexuality is an abomination in God's eyesight, and no one knows that better than you, Bishop."

"I think Ruth may have suggested in her own understated way that you can't throw stones at her, because you have your own cross to bear with Ezra. Sometimes I feel guilty that we didn't accept our son for who he is. I just want to make sure I remain active in one of our children's life." Bishop's voice choked.

The fork he held clattered to the desk. He hadn't seen Ezra since his son confessed his sexual preferences. Bishop and Queen Esther's treatment of their son was a sore point between them. She noticed the look of anguish on her husband's face. She rose from her chair, walked to the back of Bishop's chair, and entwined her arms around his shoulders.

"We know the Bible says homosexuality is a sin. You've been ordained to preach the word according to the Good Book, and we have to be strong, even if affects our children. There's something else you need to remind your daughter of; that marriage is until death do us part. You need to reinforce that theory to her."

Bishop put his fork on the table and turned his chair away from the table to face Queen Esther. She moved closer to her husband and tightened her grip around his shoulder as Bishop silently clutched his wife's midsection like a drowning man.

Chapter Twenty-one

Ruth sat on the passenger side of Alice's car, holding her body rigidly. Alice peered over her glasses as she drove slowly north on State Street.

"We're almost there," she said to Ruth. "Be on the lookout for a parking space."

Alice circled the block a couple of times, and fifteen minutes later, she parked the car across the street from the Pacific Garden Mission. The women looked both ways as they crossed the busy intersection and walked inside the shelter.

"Is there a man by the name of Ezra Clayton staying here?" Ruth asked the attendant at the front desk. Voices rose and fell from adjoining rooms. Alice looked around curiously.

A man, his hair in desperate need of trimming, and reeking like he hadn't bathed in years, walked over to Alice. "Did y'all say you're looking for Ezree?"

Alice answered, "Yes, we're looking for a man

named Ezra Clayton." She described her friend's brother to the indigent man while Ruth waited for the attendant to check the mission's records.

The attendant wore a nametag, which identified him as Mr. Duncan. He looked at Ruth tiredly and pushed his glasses up on the bridge of his nose. Paper was strewn haphazardly across his desk.

"Ezra stayed here up until a couple of months ago. He became ill and we had to transport him to Cook County Hospital. That's all the information I have."

Ruth took out a pen, and on a snippet of paper, wrote down the date Ezra was sent to the hospital. Alice tried to dislodge herself away from the homeless man, because his breath was wreaking havoc on her stomach.

"Ronnie, leave the lady alone," Mr. Duncan ordered the man.

"Aw, Mr. D, I'm just tryna help da ladies." He wore a one-piece, dingy gold uniform, which looked like it hadn't seen a washing machine in years. His hair stood up like wires on his head, ala Don King.

"Can I help the next person in line?" Mr. Duncan asked.

Ruth walked away from the front desk, turned to face Ronnie, and said anxiously, "What can you tell me about Ezra?"

"We calls Ezree the music preacher man. That man sho can talk up God, and he can sang and play the piana." Ronnie began pantomiming like he was shouting in church. He stopped abruptly, lowered his voice, and whispered to the women,

"He ain't doin' too hot." His voice dropped another octave. "He got the virus." He made a slashing motion across his neck.

"Do you know if he's still in the hospital?" Ruth asked Ronnie.

"If he ain't there, he's at the hospice near the County. That's where they take 'em when they kick 'em out the hospital."

Ruth and Alice pushed a five-dollar bill into Ronnie's hand. He whistled as he walked away and headed down the hallway.

"We might as well go. Where to now?" Alice asked Ruth as they walked out of the shelter.

"Let's go home so I can call the hospital. Maybe we can go there in the morning."

"That sounds like a plan." Alice unlocked the car door once they had made their way back to the car.

The following morning, Ruth, Naomi, and Sarah sat in the kitchen finishing breakfast. Naomi planned to return to school on Sunday, but she and her mother hadn't talked in much detail about the separation. Ruth felt this was as good a time as any to talk to her youngest child.

"Are you two still hungry? Do you want something else to eat?" Ruth asked, as she put the eggs and bacon back into the refrigerator.

"I'm fine," Sarah and Naomi chimed together.

"So, what do y'all have planned for today?" Ruth asked her daughters.

"I'm going to chill out. I checked a stack of books out the library, so I plan to read," Sarah proclaimed. "I need some down time away from the children."

"I need to study for finals and get my braids done," Naomi said. She poured a glass of orange juice and gulped it down greedily. "Daddy called, he wants to take me and Sarah out to dinner this evening. I won't go if you don't want me to, Mom."

"Of course I want you girls to have dinner with your father. The problems your dad and I are experiencing are ours alone."

"But it feels weird to me that you and Daddy aren't living together." Naomi's voice dropped. She looked helplessly at her mother.

"I know the situation between me and your Dad is hard on you, your sister and brother, but in time, things will get better. Is there anything you want to ask me about me and your Father?" Ruth folded her hands on the table.

"Um, I do. Why is Daddy gone?" Naomi asked. "I don't want to upset you or anything."

Sarah and Naomi looked at their mother expectantly. Ruth chewed her bottom lip and sighed. "I've always believed honesty is the best policy when dealing with family matters, although some things are private between a man and wife. But I will try and answer your question as best as I can. Your dad wants his freedom because he's not in love with me anymore."

Naomi's lips trembled. "What do you mean Daddy doesn't love you anymore?"

"I mean people change sometimes." Ruth looked entreatingly between Sarah and Naomi. "Couples grow apart or may not share the same interest any longer. That doesn't mean we'll ever stop loving you, your sister, and brother." She stroked Naomi's quivering hand.

"Why can't things stay the same, Momma?" Naomi whined. "Can't you and Daddy stay together? It's not our fault y'all grew apart, and it's not fair that we have to suffer too. Granny Queen says it's your duty as a wife and mother to keep our family together."

Ruth felt a tendril of anger that her mother was so vocal about her feelings regarding the state of Ruth's marriage to Naomi. She took a deep breath and said, "Life doesn't always go the way you want, Naomi. We all have to deal with dilemmas we don't want to from time to time. Your grandmother has her own opinion of how life should be. But I have to do what's best for all of us, and that's what I plan to do."

"Naomi, I don't think Mom has control of the situation. After all, Daddy hasn't come back home yet," Sarah said, gently patting her sister's arm.

She pulled away from Sarah. "Granny Queen says if Momma asked Daddy to come back he would. It's Momma's fault that Daddy is gone. She told him to leave and he did," she said, stubbornly. "I'm going to ask him to come home. Maybe he'll come back if I beg him." Her eyes filled with tears. She looked down at the table.

Sarah and Ruth looked at each other helplessly and shook their heads.

"Naomi, your Dad loves you. Our divorce isn't going to change that. Regardless as to whether your Father and I live together or not, we'll always be your parents, and we'll always be there for you." She stood, walked over to Naomi and hugged her. "I want you to go to dinner with your father and have a good time. Will you do that for me?"

Naomi used the heel of her hand and wiped away a tear from her eye. "I'll try, but I sure wish you and Daddy would get back together." She hugged her mother's neck tightly.

Ruth's voice sounded muffled, "I know you do baby girl, but as I just told you, life doesn't always go as planned. No matter what happens between me and your daddy, I know in my heart, we'll both be there for you." Ruth held out her hand and beckoned to Sarah to join her and Naomi. The three women huddled together sharing a group hug.

Chapter Twenty-two

Sarah washed the breakfast dishes. Naomi's best friend, Maya, arrived at the house at eleven o'clock to pick her up, and the two young ladies headed to the hair salon. Ruth went into the den to call the hospital to try and locate her brother. She called information to get the telephone number to Cook County Hospital and immediately dialed the number she was given. After being transferred many times to numerous departments, Ruth eventually learned that Ezra was staying at a hospice not far from the hospital as Ronnie at the shelter had stated.

She wrote the information on a pad next to the phone. She put so much pressure on the pencil she was holding, it snapped into two pieces. She slumped against the back of the sofa and a veil of depression filled her soul.

Life had been so simple some forty odd years ago. Alice had a crush on Ezra since kindergarten. Even back then, Alice was Queen Esther's first choice as a wife for her son. The Claytons and Cartwright's felt the union of their children would be a match made in heaven, and would strengthen the two churches.

Ezra was light skinned like his mother, and he had inherited her slight build. He wasn't tall, only medium in height, and he possessed all of Queen's features, except for his nose and eyes; they were Bishop's. He was a slim, handsome young man, and all the girls in and around the church vied for the attention of the young piano playing man.

Before ninth grade, he accepted his ministerial destiny and could quote scriptures better than his father. Bishop enrolled him in a secular school for post elementary education.

Like Ruth, he had attended a Christian elementary school. When Bishop allowed his son to attend Simeon High School, Ezra felt a heady sense of freedom. He began hanging out with non-Christian young men and experimenting with drugs and alcohol, and eventually sex.

By his junior year of school, Ezra and Bishop argued constantly, especially about what Ezra termed the hypocrisy in the church. Then one day, Ezra brought Martin Collins home for dinner. The young man appeared to have a calming influence on Ezra and he settled down somewhat.

Martin was short in stature, light-brown skinned, and pretty-boy handsome. He and Ezra bore a slight resemblance to each other. When Ruth and Alice met Martin, they both had schoolgirl crushes on the outspoken young man.

The two boys hung out together all the time.

Martin spent many nights at the Clayton home. Their families were unaware the boys had become lovers.

Martin considered himself bisexual, long before the term became popular, and he developed a fondness for Alice, much to Ruth's dismay.

Ruth remembered, like yesterday, the last argument Bishop and Ezra had. Their voices were so loud they filled the house like claps of thunder.

Bishop had just left Ruth's bedroom, admonishing the girls to stop giggling and to go to sleep. Then he went into Ezra's bedroom to check on the boys to tell them to go to bed because they had to rise early for church. What he found inside his son's bedroom stunned him. It rocked the very foundation of his spiritual being. He opened the door and found his son performing heinous acts on Martin's body.

"What's going on in here?" he roared as the boys drew apart.

Ezra clutched the sheet around his thin body. He looked ashamed. He stood and said defiantly, "I love Martin."

Martin looked frightened and flinched from Bishop's anger. He shook his head from side to side.

"Young man, get your clothes on. I'm taking you home immediately."

Queen Esther walked into the room. Her mouth drooped into an "O" when she saw the boys. She ran to Ezra and began beating him about the head and shoulders.

Bishop pulled her off Ezra and pushed her out the room. Martin hurriedly put his clothes on.

Ezra sat on the bed with tears streaming down his face.

"Ezra, I'm taking Martin home. Don't leave this room. When I come back, you and I are having a talk. You will not continue this, this, unnatural behavior. Do you understand me?"

Ezra refused to answer Bishop. He sat slumped on his bed. Ruth and Alice stood at her door listening to the outburst down the hallway.

"What do you think happened?" Alice whispered.

Ruth replied, "I don't know. It sounds like whatever Ezra did, he really messed up this time."

When Bishop pulled up in front of Martin's house, he turned to the backseat and said, "Son, you've abused our hospitality. I don't ever want to see you in or around our house again."

Martin glanced at Bishop sorrowfully, jumped out the car, and fled inside his home.

Bishop sat in the car, debating if he should go inside Martin's house and talk to his parents. He glanced at his watch. *It's much too late to bother people this time of the night. And what can I say to his mother and father anyway? Maybe this is a teen thing, and the boys are just experimenting or being rebellious. I'll give it time to blow over.* He never talked to Martin's parents. He had his hands full trying to save his own son's soul.

When Bishop returned home thirty minutes later, he hurried to Ezra's room, where he stayed up all night trying to reason with his son about the folly of his ways. The boy was unwavering in his belief that he loved Martin, and nothing his father said would change that. Queen Esther was so rattled by the incident that she'd taken a sedative and laid unconscious in her bed. Ruth and Alice didn't have a clue as to what had transpired.

For the first time in many years, Bishop didn't attend church service. He called the assistant pastor and informed him that a family emergency had arisen and that he would be absent that Sunday. He read Biblical scriptures to his son, trying to reason with him, and fell to his knees praying to the Lord to remove the demons that inhabited his son's body.

Nothing swayed Ezra. Not promises of punishment, or the loss of driving privileges. He confessed to Bishop that he always knew he was gay. He tearfully told him that he tried to fight his feelings because he didn't want to hurt his parents.

The following day, Bishop withdrew Ezra from Simeon High School, much against Ezra's counselor's better judgment. He enrolled his son at Hales Franciscan High School, hoping the monks could help stop the assault on his son's soul. Not his father's pleading and prayers, nor the good brother's stern discipline was a match for Ezra. He cut classes routinely and would meet up with Martin when his school day ended.

Queen Esther was mortified by her son's behavior, and she was terrified that church members would discover his secret. Ezra refused to go to church. His grade point average tumbled so abysmally that he failed to graduate with his class. Bishop, at Queen Esther's urging, asked him to leave the house when the letter arrived announcing that he wouldn't be graduating with his class.

Ruth was heartbroken by her brother's departure. Queen and Bishop decided to withhold the true circumstances of their son's leaving from their daughter. Ruth assumed that her mother was ashamed of Ezra's failure at school and that his actions caused her mother to hate her brother.

Martin and Ezra met one fall night, a few months after Ezra had been ousted from his home. Martin felt guilty for all the woes, which had befallen his friend. They sat on a bench in the park together near Martin's house.

"Ezra, I wish you could stay with me and my folks, but they don't know about our relationship. The grapevine has been busy, the church community is aware that you aren't living at home, and with your Father being a minister and all, my Mom and Dad are taking your parent's side." Martin looked miserable.

"Don't worry about me," Ezra replied, stroking Martin's hand. "I know how to take care of myself. I'll be fine. I found me a part time job at Mickey D's on 78th and Cottage Grove. I'll save my money and find somewhere to stay."

Martin and Ezra continued their relationship. Ezra, finding refuge on the streets, developed a serious drug addiction. He half-heartedly worked day labor jobs, earning just enough to feed his habit.

Ruth obeyed her father's warning that she no longer have any communication with Martin. What Ruth didn't know was that Martin continued to stay in touch with Alice. She felt a flicker of alarm when Alice called to inform her of the secret nuptials after her and Martin's Las Vegas honeymoon. By then Ruth had already heard rumors regarding her brother's sexuality. She tried to warn her friend that Martin may not be what he seemed, and how he was involved in Ezra's fall from grace that night at the Clayton's home many years ago. Alice's feelings were hurt, and she accused Ruth of being jealous, and for the first times in their lives, the women's friendship became strained.

By the couple's fifth year of marriage, Alice learned by accident one evening when she arrived early at Martin's office to meet him for dinner, that she was sharing him with Ezra. Only then was she able to piece together the story of what happened at the Clayton's house ten years prior.

She finally called Ruth in tears to make amends, and the two friends mended their relationship. Ruth was heartbroken after Alice provided her with details of her parent's callous treatment of her brother, whom she idolized.

As time passed, Ruth and Alice found solace in each other's company. Through tears and many conversations, they became believers in the saying, "that which doesn't kill you, will make you stronger," and tried to cling to the hope that God doesn't put more on you than you can bear. Through reading the Bible and praying together, they were able to accept Martin and Ezra's relationship for what it was. As Ruth struggled to accept her parents for being human and Daniel's roving eye, the two women's friendship deepened and became stronger. Ruth and Alice were closer than sisters. The two women had each other's backs; nothing and nobody came between their deep relationship.

Chapter Twenty-three

Ruth called the hospice and learned that Ezra was indeed a patient there. She told the attendant to inform her brother that she would see him later that afternoon. Then she called Alice and informed her that she had located her brother and asked her to go with her to see him.

Sarah was asleep in her bedroom. Ruth walked in and shook her awake. "I'm going out for a while with Alice. I should be back in a couple of hours."

"Okay, I'll see you later. I'm going to go to dinner with Dad and Naomi." Sarah rubbed her eyes and smiled at Ruth.

"That's good, baby. I hope you and Naomi have a good time with your Father."

As Ruth slipped on her coat, a car horn sounded outside. She looked out the window and saw Alice waving. She mouthed, "I'm on my way out." Ruth emerged from the house. There was purpose in her step as she walked to her friend's car.

She locked the door behind her after she got inside the vehicle.

As Alice pulled away from the curb, she asked Ruth, "What do you plan to accomplish by seeing Ezra?"

"At this point, I'm not really sure." She looked over at Alice and exhaled loudly. "I just know I have to see him. He's my brother, and my parents act like he doesn't exist. I have to make amends to him for not being there when he needed me."

"I hear you." She squeezed her friend's arm.

An hour later, Alice pulled into a parking space near the entrance of the hospice. Ruth and Alice quietly walked inside the red, brick building. Ruth winced, because she could feel and smell death lurking in the corners of the building. The pair walked to the information desk.

"What room is Ezra Clayton in?" Ruth anxiously asked the nurse. Her hands shook.

The nurse flipped the pages of a chart and answered, "He's in Room 208. You can take the stairs over there." She pointed to her right. "Make a left when you get to the second floor."

"Thank you," Ruth said.

Sympathy shone in the nurse's eyes. "You're welcome."

When they reached the second floor and passed the nurse's station, the attendant at the desk stopped the women. "Ladies, are you visiting a patient?" Alice and Ruth nodded.

"Would you wait here for a minute? I'll have the aide bring you a set of protective garments to put over your clothing. It's just a precaution."

"Sure," Ruth said.

After Alice and Ruth donned papers gowns, mitts, and masks, they walked down the hallway. Ruth couldn't help peeping into the open doors they passed. As they closed the gap to Ezra's room, her stomach felt as if it were twisted in a million knots. When they reached the door of his room, Ruth's knees bucked weakly. Her eyes were drawn to the figure in the bed. Ezra was asleep, and his intermittent breathing seemed extremely loud in the silent room.

He looked so thin, like a feather could knock him over, and since he hadn't ever been a big man, the weight loss was drastic. His illness had severely altered his appearance.

The small room smelled of bleach and other medicinal odors. Ezra lie on his left side, and he had an IV needle attached to his arm. She went to the bed and gently shook his shoulder. He opened his eyes and smiled when he saw his sister's face.

Her eyes glistened with tears. She bent over and gathered her brother's small frame into her arms.

Ezra cleared his throat a couple of times and said hoarsely, "What you doing here, little sis?"

She continued clutching his body. Her voice broke as she tried to joke. "Can't a sister just come by to see her big brother?"

"Hello, Ezra," Alice called from the chair near the door. Seeing her first love knocking at death's door ripped her heart in two.

"Looka here, the wind done blew in my two favorite women in the world. Alice Fay, come on over here and give me some love." Ezra lay tiredly back on the pillow. Alice walked over to the bed and hugged Ezra.

Ruth and Ezra talked quietly, while Alice sat silently in a chair on the other side of the bed watching them.

"How are the King and Queen?" Ezra asked Ruth chuckling, referring to their parents by his childhood names for them.

"They're fine. Daddy is supposed to be on a no salt, low calorie diet, and his blood pressure is a little high. But Queen keeps fixing his favorite dishes; food he shouldn't be eating. But overall, they're both doing well."

He nodded and closed his eyes. His lips looked dry and chapped. "How is your family doing? Danny I, II and III, the girls, and your grandchildren?"

"Would you like water or ice?" Alice asked him. She felt helpless, like she needed to do whatever she could to help Ezra. "I can go and try to find someone."

He nodded, and Alice went in search of a nurse or LPN.

"Danny and I are separated," Ruth admitted, looking down at her nails and the wedding band on the second finger of her left hand. It hurt her mouth to utter the five words.

"I'm sorry to hear that. You guys have been together forever. Don't tell me he finally got tired of our parents' interference?"

"No," she sighed. "It's more like he got tired of me. I've been put out to pasture for a younger model."

"I know that had to hurt," he said, swallowing hard. He licked his dry lips.

Alice returned to the room with ice chips. She handed the cup to Ruth, who held the cup up to Ezra's mouth.

"What has the doctor told you about your medical condition?" Ruth asked after she set the cup on the table near the bed.

"I shoulda been outta here a long time ago, but I keep defying the odds. My body tells me it won't be long now." He coughed and his thin body shook the bed. He covered his mouth as thin flecks of blood trickled from it.

Ruth wiped his face with a tissue. She realized her brother wasn't long for this world, and she felt like having a tantrum. She wanted to fall to the floor, kick her feet, and cry at the unfair curve ball life had thrown her idol and big brother. She could tell Ezra's strength was waning. He closed his eyes and drifted off to asleep.

"How much longer do you want to stay here?" Alice asked Ruth. Her voice cracked with emotion.

"Give me another ten minutes," Ruth answered. She didn't look at her friend. Her eyes were glued on her brother's face.

"I'll meet you outside," Alice said as she walked out of the room.

Before Ezra fell asleep, Ruth promised him she would come back the next day. She held her sibling's hand in her own, then caressed his cheek and departed.

Ruth stopped at the nurse's station again and asked the attendant for Ezra's doctor's name and telephone number. When she received the information, she put the slip of paper inside her purse and walked outside. Snow was falling. She found Alice huddled in the doorway of the building, smoking a cigarette. Her eyes were red and swollen. She inhaled deeply, dropped the cigarette to the ground with a guilty look on her face, like a child caught with their hand in the cookie jar. She stepped on the cancer stick.

"Are you ready to go?" Alice asked her. Ruth nodded she was.

The temperature had fallen below zero. Ruth and Alice shivered as they walked to the car.

"I thought you stopped smoking?" Ruth chided her friend as she fanned the air.

"I did, but I backslide when I'm stressed out. And chile, seeing Ezra looking so frail has definitely stressed me out."

"You and me both," Ruth admitted. "He looks bad, doesn't he?"

Alice nodded her head. "When was the last time you saw him?"

Ruth closed her eyes. "He called me at the beginning of the year, but I haven't seen him in about three years. He was working for the Salvation Army, one of those men you see ringing the bell outside of a department store. But you know Ezra, instead of ringing the bell, he played a little keyboard, which looked like something he'd gotten out of the garbage. He was playing Christmas carols with an upbeat jazz tempo at the K-Mart in Oak Lawn."

Alice laughed out loud. "That sounds like your brother." She frowned at Ruth. "You never told me that."

Ruth nodded in agreement. "You're right. But for the first time ever, Ezra was ashamed of how far he'd fallen. He said he was trying to get his life together and was off drugs. He asked me not to tell anyone about his plans in case he backslid. That's the only secret I've kept from you." She crossed her heart. "His clothes were tattered. I went inside K-Mart and bought him a warm jacket, socks, underwear, the works. Daniel would also see him from time to time, and he told me he'd give him money."

As the women sat in the car waiting for it to warm up, they sniffled and wiped tears from their eyes.

"I'm going to talk to his doctor tomorrow and find out what's going on. Alice, I've been thinking, and I'm pretty sure the Lord put it in my heart to bring Ezra home with me and take care of him."

"Are you sure about that, Ruth? You have so much going on in your life right now, like your unfinished business with Daniel. I just don't want you to bite off more than you can chew." She turned on the windshield wipers to clear the window of the light dusting of snow.

"What else can I do? He's my brother and he's

dying. My parents have treated him so shabby. Someone should do the right thing and try to make his last days on earth peaceful ones. You know my Mother isn't going to lift a finger."

"You work three days a week Ruth, how are you going to take care of your terminally ill brother and work? Let's not forget your participation on your multiple church committees and your number one priority, *a divorce*?" Alice drove slowly behind a salt truck.

"Jesus will work it out," she said, sagely. "I asked Sarah to move in with me. I'm pretty sure she'll help take care of Ezra. I also plan to call the city. There are some agencies that can help, maybe someone can come to the house the days I work."

"Hmm." Alice's eyes widened. "It sounds like you've given this idea a lot of thought. If there's anything I can do to help, let me know. When I saw him lying in that bed looking gaunt, and obviously in so much pain, I realized how much the Lord has blessed us. Even going through your divorce, you still have so much compared to your brother. Martin and I had long given up sex before he was even diagnosed with the virus. And it's only by the grace of God that I was spared, because it could be me lying in that bed." She brushed a tear from her cheek and then pressed her left turn signal to enter the expressway.

After Martin was diagnosed with AIDS, Ruth remembered the agonizing bi-yearly visits to Alice's physician for Alice to be tested. The two friends had always suspected Ezra infected Martin because of his street lifestyle, but in reality, they just didn't know.

Alice would shut down emotionally before her doctor visits, and there were many times Ruth feared for her friend's sanity. Every time the test results came back negative, they would sit together in Alice's car, grab each other's pinky fingers as they'd done as young girls, and thank the Lord for another good report.

Ruth and Alice alone knew the true circumstances behind Martin's demise. Ruth didn't even share the details with Daniel, even though he remarked at Martin's funeral that he was sure the man was gay. He'd heard rumors on the street.

"If anyone would've told me when we were younger that my first love would end up my husband's lover, I would've told them they were crazy," Alice would say.

"Amen," Ruth would reply.

As years elapsed, Martin began displaying symptoms of the disease that would claim his life, and he tested positive for HIV, which later developed into AIDS. When he informed Alice, the first person she called was Ruth, who showered her friend with kindness and compassion. Ruth was Alice's rock through Martin's illness and death. On his deathbed, Martin urged his wife to find Ezra and take care of him, if and when the time came.

"If Sarah won't help you take care of Ezra, which I know she will, then he can come to my house if you don't have any other options," Alice declared.

Ruth looked at Alice with a sad expression on her face. She said, "Thank you. Did I tell you Daniel is taking Sarah and Naomi out to dinner? I guess he's going to tell them his version of why the marriage went bad."

"If only I could be a fly on the wall," Alice laughed.

Chapter Twenty-four

The hostess led Sarah, Naomi, and Daniel to a booth at the Olive Garden restaurant in Chicago Ridge. The sisters sat together and Daniel sat opposite from them. The young lady handed them menus, which they quietly studied.

Daniel took a sip of cognac, which he ordered while the trio was waiting in the bar area for their table. After he set the glass down, he opened the menu.

"I think I'll have pasta and chicken," he declared. He closed the menu and set it on the table. "What are you girls having?"

Naomi rolled her eyes at him, "Daddy, we're women or ladies, not girls. Can we get appetizers?"

"Sure, whatever you want. Sarah, how are Josh and Maggie doing?"

"They're fine, Dad," Sarah replied. "They missed seeing you on Thanksgiving. DJ's son, Daniel III, has grown so much."

"I'll have to come by your place and see the kids one day," Daniel declared.

Naomi decided on a shrimp scampi entree, and minestrone soup for an appetizer. Sarah and Daniel passed on ordering an appetizer. They both selected pasta and chicken entrées. The waiter wrote their orders on his pad.

Before the waiter departed, Daniel asked him, "Would you bring me another cocktail?" He gestured toward his half empty glass.

Naomi looked at her father disapproving.

"I'll be back with your appetizer shortly," the waiter said to Naomi as he collected the menus.

As father and daughters waited for their meal, they chatted about trivial matters for a while.

Daniel took a deep breath and looked at his daughters. "I know your Mother has told you about our separation. I don't want you to think we're getting a divorce because of you guys or anything," he said, awkwardly. He put his glass on the red and white covered table.

"Yeah, Mama talked to us. She told us you don't want to be married anymore," Naomi said nastily as she cut her eyes at her father. She was dressed in denim jeans that Daniel felt were entirely too tight, and a black wool sweater.

Sarah wore jeans and a matching denim shirt. She shook her head warningly at her sister, which Naomi ignored.

How could Ruth be so stupid as to tell the children something like that? Daniel thought to himself. His eyes flashed with irritation. "It's not that cut and dry, Naomi. People divorce all the time, for all kinds of reasons. Your Mother and I are no different from anyone else."

"Mama is a minister's daughter," she retorted loudly, with her lips poked out like a small child, "so, that makes you and her different."

"Did Mom tell you about the kids' good grades?" Sarah interjected, hoping to defuse the situation. She didn't want things to get out of hand between her father and sister.

"I recall her mentioning something about them getting good report cards," he answered, gratefully. "Those are some smart kids you got, Sarah. How are your grades this semester, Naomi?"

"I don't know yet," she answered, belligerently. "I guess they're okay." She picked up a breadstick and spread butter on it. "Anyway, as I was saying, Mama is a minister's daughter, and it wouldn't look right for her to get a divorce. The church members will think Bishop can't even help his own family when they have problems."

Queen Esther is alive and kicking, long live the Queen. Daniel frowned as he stared at Naomi critically. "I think you need to concentrate on school and passing your classes. Let me and your Mother work out our own problems," he said, stubbornly.

Naomi sucked her teeth and rolled her eyes at Daniel. "I'm going to the washroom," she mumbled as she stood and stalked away from the table.

The waiter returned to the table and set the bowl of soup in front of Naomi's seat. When he departed, Daniel grumbled. "I swear, I don't understand why your sister can't be more like you."

Daniel and Sarah talked. Naomi didn't return to the table for twenty minutes. While she was gone, the waiter and a helper brought their meals.

Sarah dropped her head and said grace. Then she picked up her fork. "Naomi is upset. Dad, we all are. She's just a little bit more vocal about expressing herself."

"What about you, Princess, are you disappointed with your old man?"

Sarah cut her chicken into small pieces. "Of course I am. I don't understand what happened any better than Naomi does. But I do know the problem is yours and Mom's issue to work out. I just wish we could become one big happy family again." She looked at her father unhappily and put a forkful of food into her mouth.

Naomi returned to the table and sat down in her seat unceremoniously. She dug into her meal.

"How is Brian doing?" Daniel asked Sarah after he ingested a piece of chicken.

"He's fine. He's up for a promotion at work. I'm praying he gets it. The extra money will come in handy," Sarah replied.

"I love eating at the Olive Garden." Naomi had a smile on her face. "My food is excellent."

"I'm glad I was able to do something this evening that met with your approval," Daniel took another sip of his cognac.

"Ugh, I don't see how you can drink that stuff," Naomi commented to her father. "It tastes and smells horrible."

"And how would you know?" Daniel asked severely. "You haven't been going to parties and drinking at school have you?"

"Of course not." Her jaw dropped. She looked at her father like he had sprouted another head.

The waiter returned to the table after they finished eating. "Would anyone like dessert?" He asked.

"I'll have a slice of coconut cream pie," Naomi said. She moved away from the table and rubbed her stomach.

"Just coffee for me," Daniel requested.

"Coffee for me too." Sarah nodded her head and wiped her mouth with a napkin.

"How are you getting back to school?" Daniel asked Naomi.

"Like you care," she said, callously. She wore a bored expression on her face.

Daniel held up his hands. "Look, young lady, obviously I care or I wouldn't have asked you. Do you need a ride back to school? If not, okay. I know you're upset, but in time, I hope we can get past this. I'd like to maintain a friendly relationship with you, your sister, and brother." He picked up his glass and sipped.

Naomi stared at him wide-eyed. She burst into tears. The napkin on her lap fluttered to the floor as she galloped to the ladies room. Sarah shook her head at Daniel and followed her sister helplessly.

He watched his two daughters' hasty retreat. The restaurant became quiet as diners followed the ongoing saga.

Chapter Twenty-five

Ruth sat in her father's office at the church, thumbing though the worn pages of her Bible. She had arrived at the conclusion of the seven o'clock prayer meeting, hoping to catch Bishop and talk to him about her visit with Ezra.

She could hear the congregation singing, "God Be With You Until We Meet Again," signaling the service was at an end. Bishop, sweating profusely, walked into the room. His eyes brightened when he saw his daughter. "Ruthie, what are you doing here? Why didn't you come into the church and join us for the service?"

Ruth shifted her weight in the chair. "I wanted to talk to you, not attend the service. Daddy, I saw Ezra today," she blurted out.

Bishop removed his robe and dropped it in the corner of his office. The cleaning service would pick up that one and his other robes the next day. He unloosened his tie and cleared his throat.

"You did? How is he?" Bishop's voice cracked although he wore a stoic expression on his face.

She wiped the corner of her eyes and sighed, "He's dying, Daddy. He has AIDS. I'm going to see his doctor tomorrow. It's obvious to me, he doesn't have long to live . . ." her voice trailed off.

Bishop turned toward the window, his eyes filling with tears. His hands trembled. "I'm sorry to hear that." His voice sounded gruff.

Ruth stood, walked over to her father, and hugged him. Then they sat down.

"He looked bad, Daddy. It hurt to see my big brother looking that way." Ruth's eyes became saturated with tears.

He passed her his handkerchief so she could wipe her streaming eyes. "I can imagine it did."

Ruth took a deep breath, deciding one more time to give her parent's a chance to do the right thing. Although she knew her efforts would be futile. "I think you and Queen should bring him home to stay with you," Ruth proclaimed. She dabbed at her eyes. "It's not like he doesn't have anyone. He's your son and my brother; we can't just abandon him."

"I hear you, sweetie, but you know your Mother isn't going to go for that." His face flushed in embarrassment.

Ruth's eyes flashed angrily. "I don't understand you or Queen, Daddy. Why wouldn't a minister and his wife want to bring their dying son home?" She held her hand out as if begging her father to reconsider what he said.

"Your Mother made her mind up a long time ago about Ezra and his sexual orientation. And she's stubborn as a mule. Once she has her mind set on something, you know she doesn't change it." He stroked his beard.

"I know, but I don't understand why she's like that," Ruth complained. "The premise of Christianity is forgiveness and being Christ-like. Why can't she show that same compassion to her own son?"

"Deep down inside your Mother is a good person, but like all of us, she has her faults. She's simply unable to forgive easily. Her father was the same way. Reverend Grandberry was a strict, rigid person. He was obsessed with presenting a perfect façade to his membership. That's how your Mother was raised, and she's never deviated from that trait ever," Bishop tried to explain.

"How could you love someone, Daddy," Ruth probed, "who can't show love or forgiveness to their own children? How can you get up on the pulpit every Sunday and preach about compassion and forgiveness to your membership, if your own wife won't?" She nervously twisted the sodden handkerchief in her hands.

"Another doctrine of Christianity is one of not being judgmental. And that's how you sound to me; like you're judging your Mother and I. If only life was that simple, Ruthie. But you know that's not the case," Bishop said.

"I apologize if I sound like I'm judging you and Mother, that wasn't my intention. I'm just so frustrated with the whole predicament. If you and Mother won't bring your son home, then I will." Ruth stood up and put on her coat. "I'm so disappointed with your lack of action, Daddy. Ezra needs all of us. You have to know part of his problem has been Mother's treatment of him, and being disowned by the family."

Bishop stood and grabbed her arm. "Don't be hasty in your decision to bring your brother home. I ask that you pray and ask God for guidance. You have a divorce coming up in a few months, and the separation has been an adjustment for you. Don't try to take on another project that you know will bring grief to your mother."

She pulled away from her father and looked at him, her face dripped with loathing. She swallowed as if a rock were lodged in her throat.

"Ezra is my brother, and my house will always be open to him," she said as her voice throbbed with emotion.

Bishop opened his mouth, and then he shut it. Ruth walked out the room and closed the door behind her.

Chapter Twenty-six

After Ruth, Sarah and Naomi walked the length of the track inside Gate 24 of Union Station to Naomi's train, Ruth kissed her daughter good-bye. The temperature was chilly, and Naomi covered the lower portion of her face with her mitten-covered hands.

"I don't want you worrying about me and your Dad while you're at school. Will you promise me you'll do that?" Ruth asked her daughter as they stood outside the entrance of the train.

Naomi looked anxiously down the track. She removed two pieces of luggage from the push-cart. "I'll try not to worry," she replied. "But I can't promise that I won't. Mama, I know I'm going to fail all my classes this semester. I feel so depressed, like my world is a beach ball bouncing out of control."

Ruth nodded and stuck her hands in her coat pocket. "Trust me, Naomi, behind every dark cloud there's a silver lining. As the song goes, 'weeping endureth for a night, but joy comes in the morning.' Everything that happens in our live is for the best. Sometimes we don't see it that way when bad or unexpected things occur and life seems overwhelming, but I promise our lives will get better. Have I ever lied to you?" She tried to smile.

They stood in front of the doors of the Amtrak train. Ruth reached into her pocket and pulled out a check, which she stuffed into Naomi's hand.

"I want you to put everything that's happening between me and your Father out of your head and study hard so you can pass your final exams. Before you know it, Christmas break will be here and you'll be back home. Then we can talk some more. Call me when you get to the dorm," Ruth said to her daughter.

Naomi pecked her mother's cheek. "I will." She pulled the clothing bag onto her shoulder. "Bye, Mama." She turned and kissed her sister.

"Calm down. Try not to fret, and ace your tests. Bring us all A's when you come home," Sarah admonished her younger sibling.

She waved to her mother and sister as she boarded the train. Ruth and Sarah trudged slowly back to the gate. Ruth missed her baby already.

Puffs of smoke wafted from their mouths as the women sat in the vehicle. The inside of the car was frigidly cold. Sarah decided to drive home because Ruth had a headache. She started the engine and turned the heat on low as they waited for the car to warm up. Sarah pulled out of the parking space. As she drove home she gave her mother the details of their dinner with Daniel.

Ruth shook her head sadly. "I asked Naomi the day after you two had dinner with Daniel how the meal went, and she became closed mouthed. She just said everything was fine. I should've known she wasn't being truthful."

A few moments of silence elapsed between mother and daughter. Ruth turned to Sarah and said, "I'm thinking about bringing your Uncle Ezra home to stay with us. He doesn't have long to live, and I don't want him to be alone at the end."

"Mama, how unselfish of you," Sarah exclaimed. "Of course you know I'll help you out. I think Uncle Ezra is lucky to have a sister like you."

"Somehow I had a feeling you'd say that. Thank you. It breaks my heart to see him looking so worn out. He's wasting away to nothing." Ruth's voice broke.

"It's a shame that me Naomi and DJ didn't get to know him very well when we were younger," she remarked.

Ruth wiped the condensation off the window. "He was a dynamic musician in his day. Your uncle truly had a gift for making a piano or organ come to life. Bishop wanted him to succeed him in the ministry, but we all knew Ezra's heart lay in music."

"Hmmm, like Aunt Alice." Sarah mused. "Is that what caused the rift between him and Granny Queen?" Sarah asked. She was only a few blocks from their home. Traffic was light that Sunday evening and they made good time, although the snow began falling lightly.

"No." Ruth hadn't talked to her children about

her brother's lifestyle. "Your Uncle is gay, and that type of lifestyle doesn't sit too well with people when you're a minister's son and heir apparent to the church throne."

Sarah's eyes widened, although she kept them on the road in front on her. "Wow, knowing Granny Queen, that explains a lot. Have you talked to Uncle Ezra about staying with us yet?"

"No. I wanted to talk to his doctor first. That's another item on my to-do-list."

"Along with a million others, I imagine." Sarah commented.

"That's the truth," Ruth sighed. "Sometimes it scares me how much my life has changed since you're Father's been gone. I try to keep the faith that my life isn't under my control, but the Lord's."

"Shall I park your car in the garage?" Sarah asked as she paused at a stop sign at the corner of their block.

"You might as well. With the snow falling, I don't plan on leaving the house again tonight, unless an emergency arises," Ruth replied.

Sarah drove slowly down the alley. When she arrived at the house, she pressed the garage remote control unit. The garage door slid up in perfect symmetry. They exited the car and walked in the back door of the house.

Ruth fumbled in her purse for the key. She rubbed her hands together when they went inside the house. "It feels so warm and cozy in here. I hate Chicago winters," she said.

"Me too," Sarah echoed. She took hangers out of the closet and hung up their coats.

Ruth walked into the kitchen and filled a pot with water. "Sarah, I'm going to make cocoa, would you like some?" she called out to her daughter.

"Sure," Sarah called from the living room. "I'm going to call Brian to find out what time he's bringing the kids home."

When Sarah finished her call to Brian, she went into the kitchen and joined Ruth.

"Sarah, I wanted to thank you again for taking me up on my offer to stay here at the house with me." Ruth told her daughter.

"I should be thanking you," Sarah replied as she sat at the kitchen table. She picked up the cup and warmed her cold hands. "I think our living together will signal a new beginning for both of us. There's nothing in this life more precious than family. I've heard Bishop preach about where one door closes another one opens." Sarah raised her cup to toast her mother. "We're treading on new ground and life can only get better."

The women tapped their cups together. "Amen," Ruth exclaimed as her head swirled with thoughts of just how much her life had changed. She eagerly looked forward to a new chapter in her life and Ezra's presence in it.

Chapter Twenty-seven

Monday morning Ruth sat in the waiting room of Dr. McCoy's third floor office of Cook County Hospital. Though she thumbed through an outdated Time magazine, she really didn't see the print. Ruth kept a watchful eye on the nurse, hoping she'd tell her that she could see the doctor soon.

"Mrs. Wilcox, you can see the doctor now," the nurse announced fifteen minutes later. She walked Ruth down the hallway to his office. "The doctor will be with you in a few minutes."

"Thank you." Ruth made herself comfortable in a black leather chair in front of the doctor's messy desk. She took her date book out of her purse and perused it. She had an appointment with the lawyer Alice recommended after her meeting with Dr. McCoy.

Dr. McCoy looked harried as he walked into the room. He shook her hand and sat in his chair. "What can I do for you, Mrs. Wilcox?"

Ruth took at deep breath and stared at the kindly looking doctor. Silver wire-rimmed glasses sat on the edge of his nose, which seemed to magnify his droopy blue eyes.

"I'm here to talk about my brother, Ezra Clayton. You see, I'd like to bring him home and care for him."

"That's very commendable, as well as ambitious of you." The doctor pulled Ezra's file from the stack on his desk. "Let's see," he said, flipping through the pages. "Ezra was diagnosed as being HIV positive seven years ago. I've been his doctor for five years. After running a series of tests, the results came back that he was afflicted with AIDS. Before then, he was in and out of different medical facilities. I talked him into going to the County Hospital when his latest episodes occurred so we could keep track of the disease's progress. That way, I could treat him here and at the hospital. I have to be honest with you, Mrs. Wilcox, the final outcome isn't far off."

Ruth swallowed hard, trying to stifle the cry that wanted to tear from her throat. "How long does he have?" Her voice came out strangled.

"Hmm, I would estimate another six months to a year at best. Caring for AIDS patients in the last stage of the illness is a full time job. You'll need help, particularly toward the end. Are you comfortable with doing that?"

"Definitely, Dr. McCoy. I don't want my brother to die alone." Ruth's eyes shone with tears.

"He could stay here in the hospice, and you could visit him on a daily basis if you choose," he suggested.

"I thought about that," Ruth admitted, "but I feel he needs to be home with the people who love him. If not, when you get him stable again, he'll just end up back at the shelter. And I don't want his last days to be in a shelter or a hospice. So, please tell me what I need to do to bring my brother home?"

"I suggest you take a trip downtown to City Hall. Chicago has some excellent social service programs in place for AIDS victims." Dr. McCoy leaned back in his chair.

"Does the program cost the patient anything?" Ruth inquired.

"In Ezra's case, because AIDS is such a debilitating disease, he would be considered disabled. So the cost will be minimal for him. Another thing you should do is talk to the social workers at County Hospital." He removed a pad of paper from his desk drawer. "I'm going to give you the names of some of the people on staff there. They can help you cut through the red tape, so you'll have your documentation in order when you go to City Hall."

Ruth shook his hand at the conclusion of the conversation. "Thank you so much for your time and information, Dr. McCoy. I'll be in touch with you in a few days."

"Don't hesitate to call me here or at the hospital," he said after he presented her with his business card.

The lawyer that Alice had recommended was located downtown, not far from the hospital.

Twenty minutes later, Ruth had parked in a multi-level parking garage and was walking inside the attorney's building.

After she nervously sat in the waiting area for twenty minutes—feeling agitated and thumbing through a magazine wondering if she was doing the right thing by pulling the plug on her marriage so soon—the perky looking receptionist led her into Dafina Goodwin's office.

"Why don't you take Mrs. Wilcox's coat?" Dafina said to the receptionist.

"Sure, Ms. Goodwin." The young woman took Ruth's coat and hung it in the closet outside the lawyer's office.

Dafina's phone rang. She picked it up to take the call. She looked at her new potential client regretfully. Holding her hand over the receiver she mouthed, "I have to take this call. Give me five minutes."

Ruth nodded and walked to the window opposite the attorney's desk giving Dafina privacy. She peered outside and could see the waves swelling and receding in Lake Michigan. The day was dark and gloomy, and the weather forecast predicated snow showers.

The receptionist returned to the room with two cups of coffee on a tray. "Cream and sugar?" she asked. "Why don't you have a seat at the table?" She motioned toward the furniture with her head.

"Sugar only," Ruth answered.

The woman set the tray on a round table in the corner of the office and passed Ruth a cup, along with two packets of sugar.

Dafina hung up the telephone and walked over

to the table. "I apologize for the interruption. Sometimes it gets rather busy here." She held out her hand. "I'm pleased to meet you, Mrs. Wilcox."

"Hello, Ms. Goodwin," Ruth replied. "Alice has told me many good things about you." She stared at Dafina.

Dafina was dressed in a navy blue suit and white silk blouse. She wore her hair in a French twist, and her chocolate face appeared to have been made up professionally. She was tall, nearly six feet, and she wore navy low-heeled pumps on her long feet. She looked to be about thirty-five years old. On the second finger of her left hand was an enormous diamond ring, which glistened brightly.

Dafina took a sip of coffee. "I try to keep some meetings as informal as possible."

Ruth felt frumpy and she nervously ran her fingers through her hair. She was dressed in a black skirt and a beige turtleneck sweater.

Dafina set her cup on the table. "Why don't you tell me a little about yourself, Ruth? You don't mind if I call you by your first name, do you?" She smiled.

"No, not at all," Ruth answered. She blew lightly on the coffee.

Dafina uncapped an ink pen and set a yellow legal pad on the table in front of her. She looked up at Ruth expectantly and nodded her head encouraging Ruth to speak.

"Well, as you already know my name is Ruth Wilcox. Alice and I have been friends since elementary school. My husband has decided he wants a divorce. He asked me to initiate things, and here I am." Ruth's hands began shaking. She dropped them in her lap.

"How long have you been married?"

"Thirty-five years on December 31st," she answered, feeling miserable.

"Wow, that's a long time. Have you and your husband been experiencing martial problems?"

Ruth shook her head. "We've had some minor issues, but I didn't think we were divorce bound. I thought we could work them out, but obviously I was wrong. I believe there's another woman involved. When I confronted him with my suspicions, he denied it," she admitted painfully, clenching and unclenching her trembling hands.

"Unfortunately, I've seen many situations just like yours. Martial breakups are painful, but I try to do everything in my power to make my client's divorces as painless as possible," Dafina responded, trying to put Ruth at ease. She pretended she didn't see the tears on her potential client's cheeks.

"Do you have any children under eighteen, and are you employed?"

"Daniel and I have a daughter eighteen years old; she's in college. Actually, she's my oldest daughter's biological child. We adopted her once she was born and she doesn't know she's not our biological daughter. We'd like to keep that under wraps if possible. And I work as my father's secretary."

When Dafina heard the word adoption, she looked up at Ruth in surprise. "Is your husband currently paying your daughter's tuition? Do you think he'll have a problem continuing to do so?"

Ruth folded her hands on the table and nodded

her head. "I assume he'll continue, but I'm not one hundred percent sure. That will depend on how our assets will be divided, and whether or not he'll end up paying me spousal support."

"If you don't mind my asking," Dafina continued, "how did you two end up adopting your granddaughter?"

"No, I don't mind you asking. I don't know if Alice told you much about my background. My father is Reverend Isaiah Clayton, you may have heard of him. Our church is located in Chatham."

Dafina nodded. She picked up a pen and wrote on the pad. "Yes, I've certainly heard of your father and the temple. I've even attended a few of his services."

"My daughter, Sarah, was raped during her freshman year of high school. My family, of course, doesn't believe in abortions. But my Mother felt Sarah would be ostracized if she had a child in her teens, so I faked being pregnant. Daniel and I sent her to stay with a distant relative during her pregnancy. Lucky for us, my granddaughter resembles my husband, and not Sarah's attacker."

During the next hour, Dafina queried Ruth about her and Daniel's finances, assets, and bank accounts, and she noted the answers on the pad. "I think I have enough information to get started. That is, if you'd like to retain my services."

"Sure, that will be fine." Ruth reached in her purse and pulled out her checkbook. Dafina told Ruth her retainer fee and Ruth wrote out the check accordingly. Ruth handed her the check then she stood and put on her coat.

"Either myself or my secretary will call you if I need any further information."

"Thank you, Dafina." The two women shook hands.

As Ruth walked to the garage, she felt overwhelmed with burdens. So much had happened to her in such a short time. She could hardly believe she and Daniel were divorcing and that Ezra was dying. *How did life become so complicated so quickly? Hopefully all is quiet on the home front. I don't think I can endure another crisis.*

Chapter Twenty-eight

Later that evening after work, and verifying Lenora was having dinner with Felicia, Daniel walked into a tavern on Ashland Avenue. He spotted Fred and his cronies looking up at a television set. The set was turned to WGN, channel 9, and the Bulls were playing against Boston. The game was in the second quarter and the home team held onto a slim three-point lead over the Celtics.

"I didn't think you were going to make it," Fred said, nodding at Daniel. He eyes traveled back to the television screen.

"And why wouldn't I?" Daniel asked as he made himself comfortable in the chair across from Fred.

"Because of your new wife. Who else would I be talking 'bout?" Fred cackled like a hen.

Daniel felt mildly irritated by his brother's comments. He said, "The last time I checked, I was separated."

"Hey, at this point, it's all the same. You just exchanged one warden for another when you moved to Lenora's house. So, what's happening with you, little brother? How did dinner go wit'cha girls?" Fred asked. His eyes darted between Daniel and the television.

Bulls' guard Ron Harper missed an easy lay up. Paul Pierce pulled down the rebound and passed it to point guard Kenny Anderson. The Bulls raced down the court to get back on defense. Kenny Anderson passed the ball to Paul Pierce, who took it to the hole and slam-dunked the ball.

Daniel cursed. "I got money on this game. The Bulls better pick it up. And dinner went about as well as expected. I knew Naomi was going to give me grief, and she didn't disappoint me. Sarah was cool, as I figured she would be."

"Man, sometimes I think kids are more trouble than they're worth."

"How would you know? You don't have any type of relationship with yours. You only see them what, once or twice a year?"

Fred snorted. "That's enough for me. Shirley and Louise poisoned them against me when we split up, and things ain't been the same since then.

The two brother's eyes stayed glued to the television screen. They gave each other high fives as Scotty Pippen scored and tied the game.

Fred drained his can of beer. As he was motioning for the waitress to bring another round he said, "You paying for this round, Danny?"

Daniel laid a ten-dollar bill on the table. He glanced hesitantly at Fred, who was winking at a woman sitting a couple tables away from them.

The woman grinned at Fred, revealing her missing front teeth. He grimaced and turned his attention back to Daniel.

"I got a little distracted there, did you say something? What did I miss?"

"Naw, I hadn't said anything. Not that you would have heard me anyway." Daniel leaned towards Fred, his voice dropped to a whisper. "I've been thinking about getting some Viagra. Things were different when I was at home. Ruth and I hardly had sex. But now that I'm getting it on a regular basis and staying at Lenora's place and yours, I can hardly keep up with Lenora."

Fred laughed until tears streamed down his face. "Whew," he moaned. "Naw man, tell me it ain't so?"

There were a couple of men sitting a few tables away from Daniel and Fred. They peered at the brothers before turning back to the television screen.

"Do you think I'd joke about something like that?" Daniel hissed.

Fred stopped laughing when he saw how serious Daniel's demeanor was. "Hold up, now wait just a minute here, Danny. You don't want to be messing around with no stuff like that. I heard somewhere that it causes heart attacks. I don't care how good the sex is, it ain't worth dying over. However you handle you business with Lenora, that's the way nature planned it. Don't press your luck, bro." He chuckled. "Them research companies is always coming up with some new fangled idea to take people's money. Viagra is just a fad. Remember back in the day when people said Spanish fly got the ladies hot and made a man's nature rise? I ain't heard nothing 'bout the stuff since we were young studs."

"Yeah, I remember Spanish fly." Daniel's head bobbled up and down. "But I never tried it."

Fred warned him, "Don't let that young gal get you into some trouble your butt can't get you out of." He lit a Newport cigarette and exhaled a plume of smoke. "Where's the waitress when you need one? I want me another beer."

Chapter Twenty-nine

Dr. McCoy and Ruth met for two weeks non-stop, after Ruth finally convinced Ezra to come home and live with her the week before. It was a hard sell for Ruth—Ezra initially turned down her offer, saying he didn't want to be a burden to his sister. Eventually Ruth and Alice wore him down and Ezra agreed to the new living arrangements.

The doctor patiently instructed her on how to care for Ezra. Ruth played hooky from work and went to the hospice to observe the nurses care for the AIDS patients. Her heart went out to the men and women housed there, suffering the throes of the deadly disease.

When Ruth wasn't caring for Ezra, she talked, prayed, or read scripture to the patients who were amendable to her assistance. Dr. McCoy complimented Ruth for her tireless efforts and told her she should have been a nurse.

Alice went along with her to the hospice a couple of times. Two weeks before Christmas, Dr. McCoy pronounced Ezra's condition had stabilized enough to leave the hospice. He made arrangements for Ezra to be transported to Ruth's house by ambulance.

The doorbell sounded on the afternoon Ezra was scheduled to arrive at the Wilcox house. Ruth made a beeline for the door, expecting the EMT workers and Ezra. Instead, Alice stood there.

"I thought I'd be here with you when Ezra arrives," she said smiling at her friend.

"Come on in, and thanks for coming. I admit, I'm a little nervous."

After Alice removed her coat, Ruth laid it on her couch, and then they went into the third bedroom. It was the room Daniel used to occupy. Ruth had converted it for Ezra's stay.

Alice looked around approvingly. "It looks nice in here. You did a good job as usual."

"Thanks," Ruth replied, pulling on the ends of her hair. "I tried. With Sarah and the kids moving in over the past weekend, and Naomi coming home soon, I wanted to make sure everyone has his or her own space."

Ruth's eyes swept over the room one final time and then she and Alice left the room. "So, where is everyone going to be situated?" Alice asked, after they sat down in the den.

"Do you want something to eat or drink?" Ruth asked. Alice shook her head no. "Luckily, we had the attic remodeled a couple years ago. I wanted one big room like a loft, but Daniel had

the contractors partition the space into three bedrooms, and we put a bathroom up there. So, Sarah
and the children will stay there."

"Then that worked out well," Alice murmured
as the doorbell chimed.

"That must be Ezra." Ruth sprang from her
seat. Alice followed behind her.

Ruth opened the door. A red and white ambulance was parked in front of the house.

One of the EMT's tipped his hat. "Are you
Mrs. Wilcox?" Ruth nodded. "We have your
brother, Ezra Clayton, inside the ambulance. We
just wanted to make sure this was the right house.
Would you prop open the door please?"

"Sure," she replied. She stood to the side and
watched as the men brought her brother inside on
a stretcher. She directed the workers to the bedroom where Ezra was soon safely deposited into
the bed. Before they left, one of the men handed
her a bag containing his belongings.

As Ezra lay in the bed, his eyelids drooped and
he looked exhausted.

"Are you hungry?" Alice asked him, feeling
helpless, anxiously wringing her hands together.

"No, I'll eat something later." Ezra yawned.
"Right now, I'm tired and I just want to rest my
eyes for a little bit."

The women hovered on each side of the bed.
Ruth pulled a quilt over Ezra's shoulder and he
promptly fell asleep.

Ruth and Alice stole another look at him before
closing the door to the bedroom. They walked
back to the den and sat on the sofa, looking dejected.

Alice snapped her fingers. "I meant to ask you if Ezra needs clothing or anything like that. I'm going to Sears later on and I can pick up whatever he needs. That way, you won't have to go out."

Ruth went back into Ezra's bedroom and returned with his bag of belongings. In the bag was a freshly ironed change of clothing, which looked worn, along with underwear, socks, a pair of sneakers, and many vials of medication.

"It's a good thing you thought of his possibly needing clothing, Alice. Because if this is all he owns, then he definitely needs everything. Let me get my checkbook so I can give you a check."

Alice shook her head and waved her hand at Ruth. "Don't worry about paying for anything. I have this. Now, let's get some coffee, and maybe by the time we're finished, Ezra will be awake."

She was correct. By the time they finished their coffee and sampling the apple pie Ruth baked to welcome Ezra to her house, he had awakened. His voice sounded thin and reedy when he called out to Ruth. She and Alice went into his room.

"I don't think I've ever been to your house," he said breathing heavily, like he was experiencing shortness of breath. He sat on the side of the bed and smoothed his shirt down over his chest. "Where is the bathroom?"

"Can you make it, or would you like me to bring you a bedpan?" Ruth asked. She didn't want him to tax his strength anymore than necessary.

"No, today is actually one of my good days." Ezra tried to smile. He stood up on trembling legs. "Lead the way."

Ruth and Alice sat at the kitchen table and before long, Ezra joined them. The three sat at the table and talked after they finished lunch. All Ezra had an appetite for was tomato soup.

When they finished the meal, Ruth felt reassured seeing more color in Ezra's face. He turned the bowl up with shaky hands and slurped down the last drop of soup.

"I don't know the last time I had a home cooked meal," he remarked. Alice and Ruth chortled.

Ruth said, "Ezra, that was hardly a home cooked meal. It was more like Campbell's cooking. But if you want, we can fix you a real down home southern cooked meal."

"Cool. Did I see a piano in the living room when I came in?" he asked.

"You sure did. Do you still play?" Alice asked. She remembered the piano lessons she, Ruth, and Ezra shared as children.

"Believe it or not, I do. I guess you can say that I can still tickle the ivories. What about you, Allie? You still teaching?"

"I retired from working full time after Martin passed, but I still have a select few children I tutor and mentor," she answered.

"Allie, I just want to say I'm sorry about everything that happened," Ezra apologized. He rubbed the top of his head. "Sometimes I wish I could go back and relive my entire life over. I've made so many mistakes and hurt so many people."

"Shh, Ezra don't," Alice protested. She patted his arm. "There isn't a person on this earth who hasn't made a mistake that they wish they could go back and redo. I've accepted the high and low points of my life, and guess what, the good more than outweighs the bad."

"Thanks," he said, a smile spreading over his face. "I needed to hear that."

"Now, if you feel up to it, let's see if you remember Mr. Weaver's instructions from our piano lessons. As I ask my students, show me what you working with."

The women stood by Ezra's side as they walked with him slowly into the living room. Ruth's eyes misted with tears. *Everything's gonna be all right, I can feel it.*

Ezra and Alice sat together on the piano bench and practiced scales. When Alice attended Ruth's family functions, she always entertained them by playing the piano. When Ruth was home alone, she played scales or simple tunes. All of her children had taken piano lessons, but none of them proved to be musically inclined. Once a year, she had a serviceman come out to the house and tune the piano.

The tones emitting from the baby grand were haunting and beautiful. They played a short repertoire of gospel and show tunes until Ezra became tired. Alice helped him to the chair Daniel used to occupy. Coughing, he asked Ruth to bring him a glass of water.

While she was in the kitchen, the doorbell rang. "I'll get it," Alice called out.

Sarah, Maggie, and Josh were taking off their coats when Ruth returned to the living room. The children looked at Ezra curiously. Sarah walked over to her uncle. He stood up slowly.

"You must be Uncle Ezra, the prodigal son and

brother. I'm Sarah, Ruth's oldest daughter." She opened her arms, and Ezra hugged his niece.

"Hey, Nana." Maggie and Josh ran to Ruth and hugged her waist.

"Who is that?" Josh whispered. He looked shyly at the stranger in his grandma's house.

Ruth took her grandchildren by the hand and led them to her brother. "This is your great-uncle and my brother. You can call him Uncle Ezra. Ezra, these two are my grandchildren, Joshua and Magdalene, but we call them Maggie and Josh."

Ezra smiled at the children standing in front of him. He held out his hand. "Pleased to meet you. Sarah, you have some fine looking children. Do either of you play the piano?"

Josh and Maggie stared at their uncle with widened round eyes, and shook their heads no.

"Your Grandma tells me you're going to be living here with us. Maybe I can show you how to play while I'm here."

"That's fine with me," Sarah nodded. "Josh is only into basketball. He needs to broaden his horizons." The little girl shrugged sheepishly, "that's what Mommy says."

"Aw, Mom," Josh moaned, "playing the piano is for sissies."

Sarah took his face between her hands. "Don't ever let me hear you say that again, young man. Playing the piano is a gift just like basketball. There's more to life than sports. Do you understand me?"

The little boy, feeling chastised, nodded his head.

Some things never change. Ezra watched the exchange between mother and son amused. *They said the same thing when I was growing up.*

"Are you two hungry?" Ruth asked her grandchildren. "Let's go into the kitchen and see what's in the refrigerator for you to snack on."

Maggie rolled her eyes at her brother. As they walked to the kitchen, she whispered, "That was stupid what you said. Aunt Alice plays the piano, and she's not a sissy."

Josh looked at Maggie, superiorly. "Aunt Alice is a lady, and ladies can't be sissies. What do you know anyway?"

Maggie stuck her tongue out at her brother. "I know more than you."

"You two stop bickering," Ruth said, sternly. "Have a seat. I have apple pie and milk. Do you want some?"

They nodded their heads yes. Josh licked his lips and rubbed his tummy.

Chapter Thirty

Daniel had already left for work and Lenora was at her desk in her home office working on a spreadsheet when the door buzzer sounded.

"Who is it?" she asked, after pressing the talk button.

"It's me," Felicia answered. "Are you busy?"

"Yes, but you can come up anyway." Lenora pressed the button to admit her sister.

"What you doing?" Felicia asked, after she came in and removed her coat.

"I'm working on a profit and loss statement for one of my clients. He wants to expand his business, so I'm putting together some figures for him. What are you doing here? Aren't you working today?" She laid her glasses on the computer desk, and then she sat on the sofa next to Felicia.

"I left work early to go to the bank. Daddy called me this morning. Jamal was arrested last night. He was in a stolen car, and drugs were found in the vehicle. Daddy didn't have enough money to bail him out, so he called me."

"I'm glad he didn't call me," Lenora snorted. "Cause I would've told him no. And you shouldn't give him the money either. It's a different situation if he and Mama can't make ends meet, but bail money for Jamal? I don't think so."

"I disagree with you. He's our brother and we're in a position to help him, so we should." Felicia looked at Lenora disapprovingly.

"Neither one of our last names is Gates or Trump. I work hard for my money, and I'm not about to throw it away on our no good brother." Lenora's mouth tightened. She shook her head from side to side. She went into the kitchen and returned with two cans of Pepsi, and handed one to Felicia.

"I hear what you're saying, and that's your prerogative. But I'm going to help our family when I can, and one of them needs it now. And don't try to get all high and mighty with me. LaQuita told me you gave her five hundred dollars last week to buy clothes for Kente." Felicia took a sip of Pepsi.

"That's different," Lenora argued. "Kente is a baby, and LaQuita needs help 'cause Rashon has been a no show when it comes to supporting Kente. I feel if I can influence Quita, then Kente might have a better shot at life than our younger sister and brothers. Does Reggie know that you've been giving Daddy money on almost a monthly basis, when he calls us crying the broke blues and can't pay the rent?"

Felicia dropped her head guiltily. "No, I don't tell him all the time."

"Reggie's a good man, don't mess up your marriage over that boy's behavior."

"Trust me, I won't. I won't let it go that far. Still, I feel sorry for Mommy and Daddy. It's not like Daddy makes enough to support all of them. I think Mommy should work, but she won't. She says she has to take care of Kente," Felicia said.

"That's not true. Quita could get money from the state that would pay for childcare. Mommy just doesn't want to work. She wants to stay home and watch television all day. She can tell you word for word what happened on *Judge Judy*, *Judge Mathis*, and *the Jerry Springer show*. She's a couch potato wanna-be lawyer." Lenora laughed at her witticism.

Felicia frowned at her sister. "Mommy and Daddy don't know any better, Lenora. So, how can they teach our sister and brothers any better? I think it's our job to do what we can to help them."

"My job is to service my clients' accounts," she retorted. The conversation was starting to become heated.

"Don't turn your back on your family, Lenora. Remember, blood is thicker than water. You did some shady things to get where you are in life. This is me you're talking to." She pointed to her chest, "I know the real deal."

"I thought I asked you not to mention that again," Lenora snapped. She stood and walked to the window, with her arms folded across her chest.

"I'm sorry," Felicia sounded apologetic. She walked over to Lenora and hugged her. "I didn't mean to bring up that old stuff. But I still feel strongly that we have a moral obligation to do what we can for our family."

"You feel that way, Felicia, but I don't." Lenora sounded weary. "I need to get back to work. Can we continue this conversation another time?"

"Sure, give me a call. I didn't mean to upset you." Felicia walked out the door.

Lenora sighed and sat heavily on the sofa. *If it's not one thing it's another.* She lifted her legs off the floor onto the sofa and clasped her arms around her lower limbs.

She didn't allow herself to reflect on the past much. It was like a flame that drew her in with its brilliant colors. Then it burned her hand if she got too close.

When Lenora was fifteen, she was sexually abused by her biology teacher at school, whom she had a huge crush on. She was bitter at having opened herself up to him, revealing her inner most thoughts and then he betrayed her, snatching away one of her most precious gifts. A science teacher caught them in the act after school in Mr. Fraser's classroom. He was supposed to be tutoring Lenora. The science teacher ran straight to the principal's office, and all hell broke loose afterward. Mr. Gaines, Lenora's principal, didn't go into details about his request that Ernest and Glenda meet him at nine o'clock the following morning. They assumed their daughter had cut class or something of that nature.

Lenora was scared mute when she arrived

home from school that day. The thought of telling her parents what had transpired earlier that day terrified her, so she confided in Felicia, who spilled the beans to their parents.

After Ernest and Glenda left the meeting with Mr. Gaines and arrived back home, Ernest was so angry at the thought of his daughter being taken advantage of, that he threatened to get a gun from one of his friends and blow Mr. Fraser's balls off. Glenda had to plant her body in front of the door to restrain her husband from leaving the apartment.

Ernest, holding his hands up in surrender, promised his wife that he wouldn't do anything stupid. Fuming, he walked two blocks from their apartment and wandered into a local watering hole. His best buddy, Cornelius, sat on a bar stool, and Ernest told him what happened earlier that day. Cornelius advised his friend to look into filing a lawsuit against the City of Chicago.

A week later, Ernest retained the services of a legal firm whom Glenda found on the television. The lawyer assured them that their chances looked good for a large settlement.

Young Lenora felt torn prior to Mr. Fraser's attack on her person, or the incident as she called it. The young instructor surrendered to the police after the school completed an internal investigation two weeks after the incident occurred, rather than risk being arrested in front of his family. Lenora thought she would die from shame when she found out that the lawyer wanted her to testify against Mr. Fraser in court.

For a long time, she was haunted by the look

on Mr. Fraser's face from a picture in the newspaper, when he was led out his house with his
hands shackled behind his back. The paper ran a
picture of his wife, and in the photograph she
sobbed as if her heart was broken into tiny pieces.

Lenora felt wracked by guilt. She shut down
emotionally and lost ten pounds. Deep in her
heart, she was afraid that she might have sent her
teacher mixed signals and somehow the attack
was justified.

The lawyer was correct; the city settled the case
out of court for a tidy sum. But what Ernest didn't
realize was that the monies would be put into a
trust fund for Lenora. She, nor her parents, would
have access to the money until she turned eighteen
years old. The settlement also had a provision stating a portion of the money was to be reserved for
secondary education expenses for Lenora. Ernest
was given a small stipend, as his daughter's care-
giver, but the amount wasn't anywhere near what
he envisioned. Another stipulation of the ruling
was that Lenora undergo psychological counseling.

Ernest was beside himself with anger, and
Glenda feared he'd burst a blood vessel. The vein
on the side of his head throbbed uncontrollably
and his face turned purple with rage. He assumed incorrectly that the settlement would be
paid directly to him. He had planned on using the
money to improve the quality of his family's life.
After the notoriety the Johnson's suffered, Ernest
prayed for the day when they could leave the city
and start life anew.

When Lenora reached eighteen, she assumed
control over her settlement and decided part of it

should be spent on Felicia for her to attend a cosmetology school. Both sisters were successful with
their career choices. Felicia and Reggie owned a
successful hair styling salon on the south side of
Chicago.

*I don't know why she had to bring up all that old
stuff,* Leonora thought. *I know she's trying to make
me feel bad about Daddy and his second set of out-of-
control children, but it's not happening. Daddy would
have made me get up on the witness stand and relive
Mr. Fraser violating me. It's my money and I'll spend
it the way I see fit. And Daniel will never know the
truth about my past, under any circumstances.*

She walked back to the computer, put on her
glasses, and finished the spreadsheet she was
working on.

"Yes, Maxine, what is it?" Daniel held the telephone receiver to his ear. The departmental secretary's voice sounded animated as though
something out of the ordinary had occurred.

"There's a man here at my desk. He says he has
something for you," she whispered into the receiver.

"Okay, I'll be there in a minute." He hung up
the phone and walked to the front of the building.

A thin man wearing a navy blue parka sat on
the edge of a wooden chair in the waiting area.
He hopped up when Daniel walked into the area.

"Are you Daniel Wilcox, Senior?" the man
asked.

"I am. And you are?" Daniel replied.

"This is for you." The man thrust an envelope into Daniel's hand and departed.

Daniel scanned the papers. It was a petition to the courts from Ruth's lawyer dissolving the marriage of Daniel and Ruth Wilcox. He swore softly. *Did she have to serve me at work?*

"Is everything alright, Mr. Wilcox?" Maxine inquired, questioningly. Tiny glasses dangled on a gold chain, which rested against her chest. She wore a beige wool suit and a gold blouse.

"No, everything is fine. Thanks for calling me."

He walked back to his office and threw the papers on his desk. He closed his eyes and leaned back in his chair. Then he scooped up the papers and perused them carefully.

Ruth wanted full possession of the house, and for him to continue paying Naomi's tuition. She was also asking for spousal support for five years. *That woman is trying to break me.* He pounded on the desk.

He had hoped that he wouldn't have to retain legal counsel. Why should they give a lot of money to lawyers anyway? But based on the petition he held in his hands, he would have to rethink his strategy. He picked up the telephone and dialed his former house telephone number.

"Hello?" Ruth answered. Daniel could hear laughing in the background.

"Ruthie, I just got served with divorce papers at work. I thought we agreed to wait until after Christmas to get things started." Daniel didn't mince words and got straight to the point.

"Oh, Daniel," Ruth said. Ezra, Sarah, and Alice

sitting at the kitchen table looked at her. She put her hand over the receiver of the telephone, and said to them, "I'm going to take this call in the bedroom." Once she walked inside the room, she said to Daniel, "I'm sorry you're upset. But the more I thought about our situation, I didn't see any reason to wait. I want to put this behind me and get on with my life." Her voice was filled with false bravado, because inside, she felt like she was dying.

"Couldn't you have discussed your decision with me first? Do you know how embarrassed I felt getting the papers at work, of all places?"

"That was my lawyer's call. Anyway, I don't know where you're staying, Daniel."

"You could've called Fred's place. That's where I am most of the time."

"And the other times?" she couldn't resist asking.

"That's beside the point. I thought we agreed not to spend money unnecessarily on lawyers. What are you trying to do, break me?"

"Of course not." What Ruth really wanted was for him to feel the hurt she felt, and she knew the way to really get his attention was by hitting him where it hurt, in the wallet. She shifted her weight from one leg to the other. "Do what you feel you have to, Daniel. And any further questions you have, please have your lawyer contact mine." She hung up the telephone and went back into the living room to join her family.

Daniel was furious as he slammed the telephone down. *Why should I continue to pay Naomi's tuition alone? Ruth is just trying to get back at me. I*

bet Queen put her up to this. Well, forget that, I have
some rights too.

After spending the next couple of minutes fuming, Daniel picked up the telephone and called Richard White, one of his coworkers.

"Hey man, you busy? I know you and your old lady got a divorce a couple years ago. I need the name of the lawyer you used."

"Why do you need a lawyer? Is your son getting a divorce?" Richard asked, interestedly.

"No. Me and Ruth are getting a divorce. And the reason why isn't open for discussion. Just give me his name and number please." Daniel scrawled a name and number on his notepad. "I'll holla at you later." Then he picked up the telephone and called the attorney.

When he arrived at Lenora's later that evening, he was still in a foul mood. He didn't notice how pale she looked and how quiet she was. She had gone out to pick up Chinese food before Daniel arrived. Both were unusually silent. Though they weren't officially living together, Daniel was at her apartment ninety percent of the time.

Lenora went into the kitchen to fix plates. A few minutes later she called Daniel to come to the kitchen to eat. They supped quietly.

Finally he asked her, "How was your day?"

"It was okay," she replied, lackadaisically. "Felicia stopped by after lunch."

"How is she doing?" he asked, spearing a peapod with his fork.

"Actually, we had a little tiff. Jamal was arrested last night and she gave Daddy money to get him out of jail. I told her that I disagreed with her doing so." Leonora pushed food around on her plate.

"What did he do?"

"That fool was in a stolen car and drugs were found inside it. Felicia swore he didn't know the drugs were there, but I don't believe him. Those twins are magnets for trouble. They always have been since they were children."

"Humph, I can't say that I'm surprised. They seemed a little out of control on Thanksgiving," Daniel replied after he took a sip of water.

"That was the highlight of my day. So Danny, when do I get to meet your children?" She looked at him hard. "You aren't ashamed of me or anything?" Her fork hovered in the air above her plate.

"Um, I don't think now is a good time. Ruth served me with papers today, so I'd prefer to wait until after the divorce is granted."

"Say what?" Lenora's mouth dropped open. She tried unsuccessfully to suppress a smile. "Where did she serve you?"

"At work, of all places," Daniel complained. He dropped his fork in his plate and wiped his mouth with his napkin.

"That was a tacky way to do things," Lenora said, but secretly she was happy by the new turn of events. It seemed her dreams were finally coming true.

Daniel explained Ruth's demands and how he planned to fight them. He omitted the truth of Naomi's paternity; feeling he owed his family that much loyalty.

"What Ruth is asking for seems about right. Although I don't know about spousal support if she's working," Lenora commented.

"That's what I think too, but we'll see. I have an appointment with an attorney Thursday. One of my coworkers recommended him, so I'll see what he says."

Lenora stood, walked over to Daniel, and sat in his lap. "Are you still hungry, lover boy? She leaned over and kissed his lips while unfastening his shirt. She took his hands and placed them on her breasts. He caressed one, then the other. She stood and took his hand and led him to the bedroom like he was a little boy.

He couldn't take his eyes off her swaying buttocks. They seemed to beckon him, saying, *come on, Daddy*.

Chapter Thirty-one

Naomi decided that for the holidays, she would ride home from school with another SIU student who resided in her dorm. She didn't call Ruth and tell her of the change in her travel plans, deciding to surprise her family. When she turned her key in the lock and pushed the door open, voices sounded from the front of the house.

A tall, decorated pine Christmas tree stood near the window, and gifts lay scattered underneath it. Multicolored lights blinked, twinkling merrily. Gold and red ornaments were placed lovingly on the branches. Donny Hathaway's signature song, "This Christmas," played softly from the CD player. The room felt warm and cozy.

She looked at the chair her father usually occupied, half expecting to see him sitting there. She dropped her bags on the foyer floor and tiptoed into the kitchen. She wore a big grin on her face as she shouted, "Surprise!"

Footsteps sounded from above. Josh and Maggie ran down the attic stairs.

Ruth rose from her chair. Her face lit up like a candle when she saw her youngest child. She walked over to Naomi and clasped her tightly. Sarah did likewise. Josh and Maggie eagerly pulled on the sleeves of her jacket.

Ezra watched the hearty greetings from his chair at the table. He cracked pecans and put the meat from the shells inside of a bowl.

Ruth took Naomi by the arm and pulled her over to the table. "This is your Uncle Ezra. As I told you, he's staying with us now."

"It's nice to meet you," Naomi murmured, shyly.

"So, you're the baby girl Ruth has told me so much about?" Ezra wiped his hands on a dishtowel. He stood and shook Naomi's hand.

"Come see our rooms," Josh and Maggie urged their aunt. The three went upstairs.

"You have a fine looking family," Ezra observed. "Your baby kind of reminds me of Queen around the eyes."

"You may be on to something, Uncky." Sarah smiled. She turned and stirred the chili that was simmering in a pot on the stove. "By my estimation, dinner will be ready in another half an hour."

After Naomi returned downstairs from the attic, she and Ruth carried her bags into Naomi's bedroom. Though they both were supposed to be unpacking suitcases, only Ruth removed clothing from the bags while Naomi lay sprawled on the bed.

"I need my braids redone," she remarked, scratching her scalp. Her eyes rolled upward, and she complained crossly. "The house doesn't feel like home anymore, so many things have changed."

"Change is good, my child. Life doesn't ever stay the same."

Naomi pushed a braid off her forehead and wrinkled her nose. "I know, but Sarah and the kids are here. Daddy is gone, and your brother is staying here. How come we didn't know him before you and Daddy broke up? And how come he's so thin? Is he sick or something?"

Ruth closed the closet door and sat on the bed next to Naomi. She held up her hand. "Let's see, which question should I answer first? Sarah needs help with the kids, and I need help taking care of your Uncle, so your sister and I are helping each other. Ezra has been estranged from the family since he was a teenager, that's the reason you haven't met him. Yes, Ezra is sick, he's dying. I feel guilty about everything that has happened to him in his life, so I invited him to stay here until . . ." Her voice deepened. "As long as he wants. I hope you will get to know your Uncle. He was my idol when I was growing up."

"What's wrong with him?"

"He has AIDS."

Naomi's eyes grew round as plates. She whispered, "Is he gay or something?"

Ruth nodded. "Yes, but that's not the only way a person can contract AIDS."

"Wow. Why is he staying here with you and not with Bishop and Queen?"

"Your Grandparents and Uncle still haven't resolved their differences from long ago. I'm praying they will before it's too late."

"I find it hard to believe they wouldn't take in their own child under the circumstances," Naomi cried. She thought Bishop was God, and she listened to him before she listened to Daniel.

"Ministers are human too. I've invited Bishop and Queen over for Christmas, but I haven't gotten a response yet. I hope they will come. And I don't want you treating Ezra like he's a leper or something. He's my brother, your Uncle, and I want him to have peace of mind before he goes home."

Naomi nodded. "That chili smells good. I'm going to go see if it's ready to eat."

Ruth smiled as she stood. "I'll finish putting your clothes away. Go on back to the kitchen and spend some time getting to know your Uncle."

Chapter Thirty-two

At four o'clock in the evening at the police station on Twelfth and State Streets, the officer opened the jail cell door. "Jamal Johnson, you're free to go."

Jamal sneered at the cop as he walked out. "I told you my peoples would be here to get me out."

Ernest and Felicia stood as he walked into the waiting area.

"Boy, have you lost your darn mind?" Ernest roared. He grabbed Jamal by the ear and dragged him out of the station. Onlookers snickered at the sight.

A clerk remarked, "Amen. More parents need to get physical with their out-of-control children."

"Ouch, Pops!" Jamal yelled, rubbing his ear. "Did you have to do that?" He pulled away from his father.

"Boy, I'll take you back in that station and beat

your behind til you can't sit down. Do you hear me?"

"Whatever, I ain't did nothing. I was just riding in the car."

"Shh," Felicia warned, as she took long strides to keep up with her father and brother. "Don't discuss what happened on the police's front steps. Wait until we get in the car."

The wind gusts were high off Lake Michigan. The tail of Felicia's coat flapped outward as she walked quickly to her car. The wind brought tears to her eyes. Jamal stuck his hands in his jacket pocket. She and Ernest got in the front seat, and Jamal slid in the back.

"I don't have money to keep bailing you out of jail, Jamal. You're going to have to pick it up," Felicia said.

"Keep messing up and you're going to end up out at the prison in Joliet," Ernest warned. He turned around, and his eyes flashed daggers at his son.

"How many times do I gotta tell you what happened ain't my fault. I didn't know Saquan stole that car and there was drugs in it," Jamal stated.

"The next time you get picked up, Jamal, you're going to stay there. I've bailed you out of jail four times over the past two years. I can't keep doing this. Maybe it's time for you to face the music, do some time, and take responsibility for your own actions." Felicia glanced at him through the rearview mirror.

"Humph," Jamal snorted. "I didn't ask you to get me out the joint. If you didn't want to be bothered, then you shouldn't have come."

Ernest balled his fist, reared back, and punched his son in the mouth. "Watch yourself, boy," he warned.

Blood trickled from the corner of Jamal's mouth. He wiped it away with the sleeve of his jacket. He didn't say another word, he just turned and looked out the window.

At Lenora's apartment the following morning, the couple wasn't aware of all the drama that had occurred at the police station the previous day. Daniel lay in the bed, nestled next to Lenora, snoring lightly.

After waking up, Lenora moved Daniel's arm and padded to the bathroom. Once she arrived there, Lenora looked at herself in the mirror. Her face glowed softly with love. Lenora opened the medicine cabinet and pulled out her birth control pills like she did every morning. The case was empty. *Oops, I'll have to get a refill tomorrow.*

She turned off the light and returned to bed, snuggling up closely to Daniel's warm body. She put his arm across her chest.

When Daniel awakened that morning, his body ached all over. Sometimes he wished Lenora wasn't so adventurous when it came to sex. She had bought a copy of the book, *The Kama Sutra*, last week, and wanted them to try every position. *Maybe I need to see Dr. Burns and see if I can get a prescription for Viagra. That girl is wearing me out. I wish I could tell her we don't have to do all that experimental stuff, and that a quickie at night would suit me just fine.*

Daniel rose from the bed in his birthday suit and headed to the bathroom to shower. The warm pulsating jet stream from the hot shower massaged his sore muscles. After he finished bathing, Daniel got dressed. He could smell the aroma of sausage and eggs flowing from the kitchen. It was too bad Lenora couldn't cook, but he had to give her props for trying. She continued on her cooking quest as if to prove to him she could throw down as good as Ruth.

Sometimes, his mouth salivated just thinking about his wife's crisp, golden brown pork chops smothered in gravy with mashed potatoes. Those were the days.

When he walked into the kitchen, Lenora pecked his cheek and handed him a mug of coffee, which he could smell was too strong. Her robe hung loose around her body. Daniel smiled and thought, *Yeah, I'm going to make an appointment with Dr. Burns today*.

When Lenora bent over to remove a pan from the bottom cabinet, Daniel's groin stiffened with longing. He looked down at his lap and thought, *down boy*.

Lenora was left at loose ends after Daniel left for his job. She was caught up on her business projects. The couple had a dinner date planned for later that evening. So after loading the dishwasher, she sat at the table and wrote out a shopping list. Christmas was right around the corner and she hadn't bought a single gift.

Lenora picked up the cordless phone and dialed the telephone number to Felicia's hair salon. She hadn't talked to her sister again yesterday to find out what happened when they bailed Jamal out of jail.

"What's up?" Felicia sounded distracted after she and Lenora exchanged greetings.

"Not too much. I decided to take the day off and I'm going to Oakbrook Mall and do some shopping later. Why don't you come with me? How did it go with Jamal yesterday?"

"Not good," Felicia sighed, deeply. "He was charged with grand theft auto and possession with intent to distribute."

Lenora whistled. "Dang, there must've been a ton of drugs in that car."

"It doesn't look good for Jamal. We may have to hire a real attorney for him instead of using a public defender. You don't happen to know a good criminal lawyer, do you?"

Lenora's face reddened. She was glad her sister couldn't see her face, because Felicia could always tell when she was lying. The telltale blush gave her away. One of Lenora's clients was a lawyer, but it was her policy never to mix business with her personal life.

She lied, "No, I don't. But I can surf the net for you or check the yellow pages. How are Mom and Dad taking it?"

Felicia told her that Ernest popped Jamal in the mouth in the police station. "When we got home, Daddy beat his butt like he was a ten-year-old child. Girl, he made him get his thick belt. You know I'm not down with corporal punishment, it's the same as violence."

"See the problem is Jamal isn't a child, he's almost a man. I think Daddy should've beaten his behind a long time ago, then maybe he wouldn't be in the predicament he's in today."

"Anyway, I've got to find an attorney, so I can't go to the mall with you as much as I'd like to. I'll talk to you later. If you come up with a lawyer, call me back, but in the meantime I'm going to see what I can do."

Lenora glanced guiltily at her computer. *I know I told her I'd look for a lawyer, but I don't feel like dealing with family drama right now. Felicia is competent, and I know she'll find someone.* She resumed working on her shopping list, then showered and bundled up warmly against the cold wind to hit the shops.

Chapter Thirty-three

Ruth sat in the chair in front of her father's desk with her legs crossed daintily. She had just finished taking dictation and flipped the pad shut.

She looked at Bishop and asked, "Is that all, Daddy?"

He removed his glasses and wiped them with his handkerchief. "How's your brother doing?"

"I guess he's doing as well as can be expected. Some days he's weak as a newborn kitten and can't keep his food down. Then other days, he feels pretty good. It's been nice having him stay with me and Sarah."

"I'm glad to hear that."

"So, when are you and Queen coming to see him?"

"I don't know." Bishop stroked the cover of his worn Bible.

"You and Queen need to make your peace with

him before it's too late," she decreed. She stood and walked back to her desk.

She began typing a letter. The telephone rang, and the shrill tone shattered her concentration. Ruth picked it up.

"Mommy, you need to come home. I went to check on Uncle Ezra to give him his medicine and I couldn't wake him up!" Naomi's voice rose hysterically.

"Calm down. When did that happen?"

"About ten minutes ago." Naomi gripped the cordless phone tightly. She looked down at Ezra fearfully.

"Is Sarah there?"

"No, she hasn't come home from work. Mommy, I don't know what to do."

"Okay, calm down, Naomi. Call 911. I'm going to call Ezra's doctor. I'm on my way home. Call me on my cell phone when the ambulance gets there. Can you do that?"

"I'm scared," she whimpered. She held the phone like she was clinging to a life raft. "What if he dies?"

"Naomi, you can do this. Hang up and call 911." The terrified young woman followed her mother's instructions.

Ruth pulled open her desk drawer and found Dr. McCoy's business card with his telephone number on it. "Is the doctor available?" she asked the nurse. "This is Ruth Wilcox, there's an emergency at my house. My brother, Ezra Clayton, has become ill." Her voice rose hysterically as she fought to regain her composure.

"Hold one minute ma'am. The doctor is with a patient. Let me get him for you."

Eons seemed to elapse. Finally Ruth heard Dr. McCoy's voice ask tensely, "Ruth, what's happened?"

"I'm not at home. My youngest child called to say Ezra became unconscious," she wailed. "I told her to call 911 for am ambulance."

"Which hospital is located closest to your house?"

"Uh, I think Little Company of Mary."

"Then that's where they'll probably take him. Why don't you go there now and I'll call the hospital with details about Ezra's condition. We'll take it from there. I'll talk to you later."

"Okay. I'll do that." Ruth's hands trembled as she hung up the telephone.

Bishop came out of his office clad in his coat. He took one look at Ruth and knew something unforeseen had occurred. "What's wrong? Is one of the children ill?"

Ruth still had her hand on the phone. "No, it's Ezra. Naomi called and said she couldn't wake him. I told her to call 911. I just got off the phone with his doctor."

Bishop grabbed her coat and tossed it to her. "Let's go," he said.

The church was located about ten minutes from Ruth's house. When she called home to see if the ambulance had arrived, Naomi tearfully informed her mother it hadn't yet. Ruth glanced at her father and told Naomi that she was on the way home.

When they arrived at her house, total chaos ensued inside.

The EMT was arguing with Naomi. "Does he have AIDS? We aren't equipped to deal with an AIDS case."

Bishop's eyes darted to his son's still form. "Are you saying you won't take him to the hospital?"

"We can't, sir, not without proper equipment. We should've been told his status before we arrived here."

"Bishop, what can we do?" Naomi screamed in terror.

Bishop scooped up his son in his arms. Ezra's sharp bones protruded into his chest. He felt light as a feather. Tears sprung to Bishop's eyes.

"Ruth, get me a blanket. We'll take him ourselves." He turned toward the EMTs, disgust flaring in his eyes. "Your company will be hearing from me."

Ruth quickly removed a blanket from the linen closet. She helped Bishop wrapped his son inside the woolen cloth like he'd done when Ezra was a baby. Bishop held his son in his arms as he and Ruth rushed outside. He laid Ezra gently on the backseat.

"Take him to Little Company of Mary Hospital. His doctor said he'd call the hospital with instructions," Ruth told Bishop.

Fifteen minutes later, the hospital staff met them at the entrance with a stretcher. Bishop sat in the waiting room, while Ruth went to talk to the attending emergency room doctor.

Bishop covered his face, tears flowed from his eyes. He sobbed quietly. *My God, what have I done? That's my boy in there. My oldest child, and I abandoned him. Please forgive me, Lord.* He wiped his eyes and clasped his hands together. His mouth moved silently as he prayed for Ezra's recovery.

It seemed like an eternity had elapsed before Ruth returned from talking to the doctor. When she saw her father, his face looked ashen. His head was lowered as he read his Bible. He stood up when he saw her.

"How is he?" he asked.

She rubbed her eyes. "The doctor thinks he'll be okay. He's conscious now." She looked up and saw Sarah, Naomi, and the children walking into the emergency room.

"Thank God you and Bishop came to the house," Sarah said, after she hugged her mother and grandfather. "Is Uncky alright?" Her eyes flitted to the closed double doors.

"The doctor said he's weak," Ruth answered, "and that he'll probably pull through this episode. His white cell count dropped again. The doctor here on staff is talking to Dr. McCoy at the County. I think they're going to adjust his medication. The doctor wants to keep him overnight. I'm going to stay here until they move him into a room."

"Can we see Uncle Ezra?" Maggie asked. Her arms were clasped around Ruth's waist.

"Not today, sweetie." She patted her granddaughter's head. "You can see him when he comes home tomorrow."

Bishop pulled a few dollars out his pocket. "Naomi, why don't you take the little ones to get a snack out of the vending machine?" He handed her the money.

"Sure, Bishop." She took Maggie and Josh's hand, and they walked down the corridor together.

"You don't have to stay, Bishop. Sarah and I can take care of things from here," Ruth said to her father, tersely.

"No, I don't mind. I'll stick around for a while. Do you think I'll have a chance to see Ezra?"

"I'm sure you'll be able to after they get him settled. It may take some time though. Don't you have a speaking engagement at First Bible Church this evening?"

"I'm going to stay here for a while. Ezra's health is more important to me than a speaking engagement. I'm going outside to call your Mother. I'll be back."

Ruth watched her father's retreating back. She closed her eyes and looked up. *Maybe this is the breakthrough I've been praying for.*

Bishop walked outside the hospital. He called home and Queen Esther answered after the first ring. He explained to her that Ezra was ill. "Why don't you come to the hospital and see him? We're at Little Company of Mary's on west 95th Street."

"No, not now, Bishop. I think you should come home now. What if you run into some church members? We need to sit down and talk about how we should handle Ezra's illness."

"There's nothing to discuss, Esther. I'm staying here until Ezra is moved to a room. I wish you would come and see him. I don't think he has long on this earth. You need to make your peace with our son."

Queen's voice rose sharply. "Bishop, I said not today. The revival is tonight, and you're on the program. I've laid your clothes out. You need to come home and prepare for your big night."

"I suggest you call Henry and tell him a family emergency came up and that I have to cancel my engagement."

She moved the telephone away from her ear and glared at it. When she returned it to her ear, she said quietly but forcefully, "I think you're making a mistake, Bishop. Tonight will be a good opportunity for you to announce your mayoral campaign. I didn't tell you, but Reverend Simmons and I called the media and set up interviews. All the major television stations are going to be at the church."

"If I'm making a mistake—and I don't feel that I am—then the Lord will forgive me. I'll get around to announcing my intentions when the time is right. Esther, I'll see you later." Bishop clicked off the telephone and shook his head. He walked back to the waiting room.

Ezra wasn't moved to a room until eight o'clock that night, four hours after Bishop had brought him to the hospital. His complexion wasn't as dark and he was breathing easier. An IV was attached to his arm. He lay asleep on a white pillow inside an oxygen tent. When Ruth walked out of his room, Bishop had returned to the waiting room.

"Bishop, I'm going home with Sarah now. I had planned on spending the night here, but Ezra told me to go home. I called Alice and she wants to stay with him. She's on her way," Ruth said.

"I'll wait until she gets here," Bishop replied. "I promise." He kissed his daughter goodnight.

"Ezra's in Room 511. I'll talk to you later, Daddy." Ruth, Sarah, Naomi, and the children gathered their things and left.

Bishop picked up his coat from the empty seat next to his and headed to Ezra's room. He pushed the door open. As Ezra lay in the bed, he watched his son's fragile chest rise and fall, and tears filled his eyes once again. He walked and sat in the chair next to his son's side. He dropped his head and prayed.

Lord, although I try hard, I know at times I haven't always been your good and faithful servant. You showed me that today. How could I turn my back on my own child? Ruth was right when she stated forgiveness is one of your most profound doctrines. I had no right to judge my son for his shortcomings. I know Queen doesn't want Ezra to stay at our home, but that's where he should be. But Lord, I promise with all my fiber and being, that I will do right by my boy, no matter how much time he has left on this earth. Father, give Ezra the strength to fight his illness. And bless Ruth for opening her heart and home to her brother. Give this family strength for what lies ahead, Lord. Show us the way. These blessings I ask in Your son's name and for his sake. Amen.

When he opened his eyes, Alice was standing in the doorway. She walked into the room and looked at Ezra, who was still asleep. Then she walked over to Bishop and hugged him.

"I swear being in the hospital brings back so many memories of Martin . . ." Her voice trailed off.

"I know it does," Bishop intoned, hugging her. "Are you sure you're up to staying with Ezra? I feel like I should be here."

She took off her coat and hung it in the closet. "No, I promised Martin before he passed away that I would do what I could for Ezra. Even though Martin loved me in his own way, Ezra was his heart."

"You're a better person than myself and Queen," Bishop said, in a strangled voice. "God knows I hate seeing my boy like this. I had such high hopes for Ezra when he was born. He had the world by the tail."

"We all did," Alice said sympathetically. "But we have to deal with the challenges life throws our way and try not to let them get us off track. Don't beat yourself up too badly Bishop, with what could have or should have been. Let's just make a pact that we'll do right by Ezra while he's still with us."

"Amen, sister. When he awakens, tell him I'll be back to see him here, or at Ruth's after church tomorrow."

The smile on Alice's face was so wide that it seemed to stretch from ear to ear. "I think that'll be the best medicine in the world for him." She hugged Bishop tightly.

Chapter Thirty-four

Ezra cleared his throat and recoiled as he pulled at the needle in his arm. He peered around the room. Alice's arms were clasped around her chest. She had nodded off on the chair next to his bed.

"Hey, girl, what's up?" His voice sounded scratchy as he looked up at Alice.

She opened her eyes and said, "You're awake. Boy, you scared the life out of us yesterday."

"Where's Ruth?"

She told him, "Ruth went home after you were admitted yesterday. I pulled sleeping-in duties. Seems your getting sick is the only way I can get you to spend the night with me."

The nurse came into the room with a technician wearing latex gloves, pushing a tray of instruments. "Good morning, Mr. Clayton. We need to take your vitals."

"I'll be outside." Alice walked out the door and went outside to the hallway to use the pay phone to call Ruth. There were signs posted around the hospital asking visitors not to use cell phones in the building because it would interfere with cardiac patients who had pacemaker implants.

When she returned to the room, Ezra was lying in the bed with his eyes shut. He opened them and smiled weakly at Alice. "Now you know I couldn't check out without telling you how much I appreciate everything you've done for me, Alice. If only we could turn back the hands of time," he said.

"Ezra, you're like my brother and I love you. Of course I'll help Ruth take care of you. If life had been different, perhaps you would've been my husband. If we had combined my family's church and the temple, we would be overseeing a mega church today." The two old friends laughed together.

"When Martin became ill, I refused to care for him, and I put him in a nursing home. As his condition worsened, I felt guilty about not caring for him. As time elapsed, I managed to work through my feelings, and Martin made me promise on his deathbed that I'd take care of you when the time came," she added.

"How difficult it must be for you, caring for your dead husband's lover." His eyebrows rose ironically.

"What makes it easier for me is that his lover is that sweet boy I had my first crush on." She sat on the side of the bed and took his thin hands in her own.

"I'm sorry, Allie." Ezra's eyes shone with tears. "I wish things had turned out different for you, Martin, and me. Please forgive me," he begged.

"When Martin told me about you and the relationship he shared with you, I wanted to scratch his eyes out and then yours. I had to experience a huge spiritual growth to even stay in the same room with him. On his dying bed, he begged me to forgive him. He thought it was his fault you have the disease."

"One of the worse days of my life was when he told me he was HIV positive. And that was the last time we were intimate. And I thanked God every time my tests results came back clean, at least for a little while," he told her.

"I'm not going to lie to you, Ezra." Alice shook her head up and down. She closed her eyes, opened them took a deep breath and continued. "I wanted to kill myself. "Sometimes I don't see how I made it through the ordeal and continued living my life. Ruth stood by my side. Every time I wanted to end my life and give up, she talked me out of it. You know it's too bad Bishop has a thing about only male members of the family inheriting the church, because she has been going to a theological seminary off and on for the past few years and would make a darn good minister."

Ezra's eyebrow rose sardonically. "Speaking of Bishop, did I see him at the hospital last night? I thought I must've dreamed that. Whew what a dream," he said, trying to kid her to mask his feelings. He wanted to believe Bishop had come through for him.

"It wasn't a dream. Your father was here. He said he was coming back to see you today."

"Will wonders never cease?" Ezra's thin face crinkled into a huge smile.

"Actually, Ruth and Bishop brought you to the hospital. Ruth said there was some kind of mix-up with the ambulance workers."

"I bet Queen made Bishop burn his clothes when he got home." Ezra laughed and broke into a coughing fit.

Alice stood up and poured water into a paper cup. She held the cup to his lips. He drank greedily.

"Let's not overdo it. Why don't you rest? We'll have time to talk again," she said.

Ezra nodded. He fell against the pillows and went back to sleep.

At the Clayton's house, Bishop and Queen sat in the kitchen eating breakfast. Queen had been glaring at her husband off and on all morning. She was still upset about him changing his plans the night before.

"Would you pour me some more coffee, dear?" Bishop asked without looking up as he turned the page of the Chicago Tribune Newspaper.

Queen wanted to say, *get it your own darn self*, but she stood up and snatched the cup off the table. When she set it down next to him, coffee sloshed on the side.

"What do you have planned today?" she asked in a malicious tone of voice. "Are you going to the temple?"

He looked up at his wife with a grievous expression on his face. "No, actually I'm going back to the hospital. That is if Ezra hasn't been released already. If he has, then I'm going to see him at Ruth's house."

Queen snapped her mouth shut. Then she opened it and said, "What are you doing, Bishop? I thought we agreed years ago to step back and let Ezra lead his ungodly life. He'd go his way and we'd go ours."

"He's dying, Esther. Our only son is dying. Ruth was right to go get him and bring him to her house. He should be with family. You should be caring for him, not his sister."

Queen's eyes flashed with anger. She held her hand out pleadingly to Bishop as her voice rose sharply. "Have you forgotten he has AIDS? We can't have him bringing that mess here or to the church. If Ruth wants to expose her family to that filthy disease, then that's her business. Ezra can't come here under any circumstances."

"But he's sick, Esther." Bishop's voice cracked. "I held our son in my arms, and he felt like a bag of bones. That's when it hit me that he's dying. I won't have it on my conscious that I turned my back on him during his last days. You need to re-think your position. You carried him in your belly for nine months. For God's sake, don't you care? Do you even want to see him?"

She stared at him wordlessly. Then she stood, shook her head no, and walked into the bedroom and slammed the door. Bishop looked toward their bedroom with a concerned look in his eyes.

After he finished drinking his coffee, he put the cup in the sink. Bishop called the hospital, where a nurse informed him that Ezra had been released. He put on his coat and left to go to the hospital.

As Bishop drove to the hospital, his heart was hampered with thoughts of Queen's refusal to see Ezra and his son's overall health. He was disappointed with Queen's stance and he almost felt something akin to anger at her. All he could do was pray she'd eventually come around. He also felt conflicted about his mayoral run. Maybe he needed to let the dream go and help Ruth take care of his son. But he knew if he dropped out of the election, Queen would be impossible to live with.

He was still taken aback by his son's appearance. Ezra was a mere shell of his former self. He was only fifty-seven years old, and he looked like a man in his seventies. *Lord, show me the way,* he prayed.

When he walked into Ezra's hospital room, Ruth was placing his possessions inside a plastic bag and Alice had headed for home. He walked to Ezra's bedside and shook his hand.

"Hi, son," he said cheerfully, like his seeing Ezra was an everyday occurrence.

Ezra gripped Bishop's hand feebly. "I was telling Allie I thought I'd dreamed you were here yesterday, but she set me straight. I appreciate you coming to see me, Dad."

"I'm just glad I was able to help yesterday." Bishop turned to Ruth. "Why don't you go on home or to church? I'll make sure he gets to your house safely. I want to talk to his doctor before he leaves the hospital."

"Are you sure, Bishop? I can stay and take him home. It's no problem."

"No, you run along. I'll take care of him."

Ruth cheesed like a child opening his or her favorite present on Christmas morning. "Okay. I may stop by the church on my way home. I have some correspondence I need to send out. You have the key to my house in case I'm not home when you get there. Just let yourself in." Ruth left, waving good-bye to Ezra.

Bishop helped his son get dressed as the doctor walked into the room. "And you are?" He looked at Bishop curiously. Ezra's medical chart was tucked under his arm.

"I'm Ezra's father, Reverend Isaiah Clayton. I'd like to talk to you alone if you have the time."

"Pleased to meet you, Reverend. Sure, follow me," the doctor replied.

The men walked outside the room. The doctor asked Bishop, "What can I do for you?"

"My son looks so emaciated. Are you sure you're doing the right thing by sending him home? Is there anything else you can do for him? I can pay your fee, whatever it is, money is no object." Bishop glanced inside Ezra's room.

Dr. Richard shifted Ezra's chart from one hand to the other. "I understand your concerns Reverend, but due to their weakened immune system, AIDS patients are subject to health crises quite often. I talked to Dr. McCoy, Ezra's primary physician, and made adjustments to your son's medications. That's really all we can do at this point; monitor him and send him home."

Bishop nodded at the physician's words. "Are my daughter and her family in any danger having a person afflicted with AIDS living in the house?"

"Forget the myths you've heard about spreading AIDS." Dr. Richard continued. "Your family is fine. You know what your daughter is doing is commendable. You must be proud of her." The doctor looked down at his watch. "If you don't have any further questions, I'm late for a meeting. I would suggest you talk to Dr. McCoy at the County Hospital since he's your son's primary physician and he can discuss his medical history with you in greater detail."

"Thank you for your time. I'll do that."

The men shook hands. The doctor rushed down the hall to the elevator and Bishop returned to Ezra's room. He opened the drawer next to the bed and removed a small bag with Ezra's belongings. Then the men walked slowly down the hall to the nurse's station. The nurse handed Bishop a vial of medicine with instructions. Bishop left the hospital to bring his car to the front of the building while an orderly wheeled Ezra out of the hospital.

As he drove Ezra to Ruth's house, Bishop decided to bow out of the election. He didn't relish telling Queen his decision. But it just felt right to him doing whatever he could to help his daughter take care of his son. Though the text of Bishop's sermon was done for Sunday, he decided to rewrite it and change his topic to compassion. It wasn't lost on him that God had given him a second chance to make things right with his son. And he felt driven to obey the biding from his Father above.

Bishop peeped at Ezra who sat next to him. His body lay slumped over the seat and his head rocked backward and forward like a bobble head doll. His breathing was sonorous. He'd dozed off during the short ride to his sister's house. Bishop felt a gush of warmness in his heart at the sight of his son and felt he was making the correct decision.

When he pulled his midnight blue Lincoln Town car in front of Ruth's house, the door flew open. When he and Ezra walked inside the door, Ruth hovered at the threshold waiting for them.

"Are you okay?" she asked her brother, patting his forehead. "You look tired."

"I feel a little worn out," Ezra admitted. "I thought you were going to work," he asked her accusingly.

"I changed my mind," she replied. She then led Ezra to his room, tucked him into bed, and gave him a dose of medicine. She walked back into the kitchen, where Bishop sat at the table reading pamphlets he'd collected from the hospital regarding the AIDS disease.

"I want to thank you for your help yesterday, Bishop. You driving me home and taking Ezra to the hospital was a lifesaver. I don't know what I would've done otherwise." She sat down in the chair across from her father.

Bishop looked at her with a stern expression on his face. He pointed his finger at her. "Don't ever thank me for taking care of one of my children. What did you think I was going to do, nothing? Just walk away?"

"I don't know what I thought. I'm just glad you were here. Did you talk to the doctor?"

"Yes, I did. He explained to me that Ezra's

episode was a normal reaction due to his immune system and suggested I call Dr. McCoy. I'm going to do that tomorrow and talk to him more about AIDS in general, and what we can expect when Ezra comes to the end of his journey. Just seeing what happened yesterday tells me that it won't be easy. Are you sure you're up for the task?" Bishop's eyes emitted concern.

"Daddy, haven't you told me my entire life that through God all things are possible? And with Sarah and Alice's help, I can do it. My goal is to help my brother make the transition from this life to the next. Did Ezra tell you we've been reading the Bible at night?" Her eyes shone with pride.

"He mentioned it before he conked out on me in the car. I have to admit I'm surprised. What lit the fire under you, Ruth? It seems like just yesterday you were mourning your husband's leaving. Now, you look like a woman on a mission."

She smiled sagely. "I realize you can't make a person stay with, nor love you, if their heart isn't in it. Daniel will always be my husband in my heart. I love him and I always will. He's the father of my children. We've had good times and bad. Leaving me is something he feels compelled to do. But I have to go on with my life."

Bishop looked at her with admiration. *Maybe Queen and I didn't do such a bad job raising our children after all.*

Ruth folded her hands primly on the table, like a schoolgirl. "Ezra and I have been talking about his coming to church one Sunday. Spiritually, I think it'll do him good. I know Queen won't be happy with him being there. But he's going to come whether you approve or not, Daddy." She had a steely glint in her eyes, like she was ready to do battle for her brother.

"You're right. Your mother won't agree or understand. But I think that's a great idea. Let me know when he plans to come; I have some things I need to say to my son from the pulpit."

"You aren't going to embarrass him, or throw him out of church or something like that?" she asked her father, uneasily.

"Of course not, Ruth." Bishop touched his chest. "I can't believe you're asking me that question. My feelings are hurt," he teased her.

"Just checking." Ruth smiled. She stood and hugged her father's neck.

Chapter Thirty-five

Christmas would fall on Sunday and the Wilcox clan planned to attend church and feed the homeless at the temple on Christmas day. So Ruth decided to prepare the holiday meal for her family on Christmas Eve. DJ and his family weren't able to secure leave so soon after their Thanksgiving visit, but he promised to call her bright and early on Christmas morning.

Ruth opened the white oven door and pulled out the rack containing the huge stuffed turkey. She peeled a tiny corner of the aluminum foil back to check the bird. The aromas floating through the house were enough to make one's mouth water.

Sarah, Ruth, and Naomi stayed up late the night before cooking and cleaning the house. Ruth baked a red velvet cake and ten potato pies. Everyone, including the family's pickiest eater, Queen, swore they had never tasted pies as appetizing as the ones Ruth baked. The cake sat under a green-stained glass cake plate and cover, and the pies on tin pans on the dining room table.

Naomi wandered into the kitchen, clutching her cell phone. "Mama, Daddy's on the phone. He wants to know if it will be okay for him to stop by today and bring his gifts."

Ruth was stirring the pot of greens. She paused. "Sure, tell him that's no problem."

Naomi put the phone to her ear. "Daddy, Mama said okay. We'll see you later."

"What did you buy your Dad for Christmas?" Ruth asked. "You did remember to buy him something, didn't you?"

"Oops, I forgot," Naomi lied. She never had any intention of buying her father a gift.

"Look in the back of my closet. I picked up a couple of turtleneck sweaters for him just in case you forgot to buy him a gift. Wrap them up and you can say they're from you, Josh, and Maggie."

"Do I have to?" she grumbled. She paused in the doorway of the kitchen.

"Yes, you do. Now get to it, girl," Ruth instructed her daughter sternly.

Sarah walked into the kitchen. "What's wrong with her?" she asked, pointing to Naomi's retreating back. Her sister had attitude in her step.

"I guess she didn't want to give your father a Christmas gift. I gave her money specifically to buy him a present and she didn't. Luckily, I picked up some sweaters for him. They can be from Naomi and your kids."

"Thanks, but I already bought him two gifts, one from me and one from my children. Do you need help with anything?" Sarah walked to the pantry and removed an apron from a hook and fastened it around her waist.

"Why don't you make the punch? Alice and your Father will be over later." Ruth glanced at the butcher-block clock on the wall. "Later is coming quickly," she exclaimed.

Sarah took two cans of Hawaiian Punch, a can of pineapple juice, and other ingredients from the cabinet to prepare the punch. She poured the contents of the cans into the bowl and mixed the ingredients together.

Brian brought Josh and Maggie home an hour later. They spent the majority of the day visiting their father and his family. They were excited when they returned home with huge bags of unopened gifts.

"Look, Nana." Maggie ran into the kitchen and showed her new doll to Ruth. "My daddy and Grandma Peggy bought me an *Addie*, an American Girl doll. Daddy said me and Josh could open one present and this is the one I chose."

Brian walked into the kitchen. "Merry Christmas, Mother Ruth." He kissed his ex-mother-in-law's cheek.

Brian was a dark skinned man. He wore his dark hair in a fade haircut. His physique was average. Brian was pleasant looking and usually wore a big smile on his face. He was dressed in dark trousers and a red Nehru collared shirt.

"Hello, son. Happy holidays to you too. I hope you thanked your daddy and Grandma for the gifts," Ruth remarked to her grandchildren.

Josh and Maggie nodded and skipped back into the living room. Ruth resumed boiling water to prepare the gravy.

The doorbell sounded. Naomi yelled from her bedroom, "I'll get it."

Naomi, dressed in a black skirt with a red and green sweater, raced to the door to find Alice clutching the collar of her coat around her neck, trying to ward off the cold. Naomi hugged her godmother after she walked inside the house.

Alice strode into the kitchen carrying a cake container. She set it on the table and kissed Ruth's cheek. "I made a German chocolate cake. I hope that's okay." She sniffed as she stuffed her gloves inside her coat pocket. "It smells wonderful in here. I can hardly wait to eat. Is dinner almost ready? Is your daddy still here, Maggie?"

"Yes, he's in the living room talking to Mama," Maggie answered rocking her doll in her arms.

"Tell him that I need him to bring some bags out of my car for me." She handed Maggie her key ring.

Ruth replied to Alice's initial question to her as she stirred the gravy, "Give me another hour and the food will be ready. Now you know you didn't have to spend all that money on the kids."

Alice laid her sable coat over her arm. "You tell me the same thing every year, and I respond with the same answer. Your family is my family, and I'll spend my money as I darn well please. How is Ezra feeling today?" She took the matching fur hat off her head and pulled her twisties loose.

"He's doing okay. He said something about

you and him playing duets after dinner." Ruth reached up in the cabinet for the flour.

"Our performance is his gift to the family. He didn't have much money and he wouldn't take any from me. Do you need help in here?"

"Of course I do. Go hang up your coat. I have extra aprons in the pantry."

Sarah put the Temptations Christmas CD into the CD player. Soon the house was festive with Christmas cheer. She prepared appetizers and everyone munched on the snacks. Josh and Maggie kept running to the lit Christmas tree, counting gifts with their names on the tags underneath.

Ezra sat in Daniel's lounging chair with his legs outstretched on the ottoman. His color was clearer, and his eyes looked brighter. He was dressed in gray slacks, a white shirt, and navy sweater; gifts Ruth had given him for Christmas. He still looked painfully thin. He felt as though he'd been given a longer lease on life, and he was tickled pink to spend the holidays with his family and friends. He hoped Bishop and Queen would join them for dinner, although Ruth advised him not to get his hopes up.

The doorbell seemed to ring non-stop with family and friends eager to share holiday cheer. The meal was done, and Ruth stood in her bedroom changing her clothes. Alice had talked her into going on a shopping spree, so she'd updated her wardrobe. Ruth held fast to a tiny hope that if Daniel saw her looking her best he might want to come back home.

Once she finished dressing, the family would open a few gifts, leaving the remainder for the next morning, so Josh and Maggie could exclaim over all the goodies Santa Claus had brought them.

Maggie's hair was styled in Shirley Temple curls. The fat ringlets bounced on her head as she ran into Ruth's room. The little girl was dressed in a red velvet dress and black Mary Jane patent leather shoes and white tights.

"Guess who's here, Nana?" She held her hands behind her back.

"Give me a clue?" Ruth hoped her parents were in the living room.

"Granddaddy and Uncle Fred, and they brought a lot of presents." Her expression became serious. "Granddaddy said Santa Claus left me and Josh lots of presents at his new house." She took her grandmother's hand. "Hurry, Nana, come and see."

"I'll be out in a minute." The little girl scampered out of the room and back into the living room.

Ruth smoothed her green velour dress and screwed black onyx earrings into her ears. She was pleased with her looks. She had managed to lose a few pounds between work and caring for Ezra. She'd also begun taking Estroven after visiting her gynecologist a month ago, and the medication had helped diminish her hot flashes somewhat. She twirled a curl on the side of her face and sprayed her body with Estee Lauder cologne. Lastly, she took a deep breath and went into the living room.

Daniel was in a dark blue suit, a red shirt, and blue and red paisley suspenders, sitting on the sofa talking to Ezra. He hopped up out of his seat when she entered the room.

"Merry Christmas, Ruth." He pecked her cheek.

Ruth blushed like a new bride. "Merry Christmas to you too, Danny. How's life treating you?"

A loud knock sounded at the front door. Brian stood and said, "I'll get it."

Bishop walked inside, laden with gifts. "There's more stuff in the car. Brian, would you give me a hand?"

Everyone greeted Bishop as he laid the gifts under the tree. He walked over to Ezra. "How you doing, son? You look good today. Daniel, Fred, Merry Christmas." He clasped their hands.

"I feel great," Ezra proclaimed. "Being here with Ruth and her family has been the best medicine in the world for me." He looked toward the door. "Where's Queen?"

"She didn't feel well today. She sends everyone her love." Bishop had tried his best to coax Queen to come with him to dinner, but she refused.

"That's too bad," Ezra observed. "She's going to miss out on a good time."

"I'll be right back," Bishop promised. "I still have more presents in the car. C'mon, Brian."

"Danny and Fred, if you aren't doing anything later, you're welcome to join us for dinner," Ruth said to her husband and brother-in-law.

"Thank you, Ruth, that's generous of you. I think we will," Daniel said. He was feeling nostalgic being home and around his grandchildren, whom he still hadn't made time to visit.

Fred nodded his head enthusiastically, took his

shades off his nose, and put them inside his jacket pocket.

Ruth, Sarah, and Alice set the food out on the table. Naomi prepared glasses of punch for everyone. Before long, the family stood in the dining room with bowed heads and linked hands as Bishop said grace.

"Lord, we thank you for all of the many blessings you've bestowed upon us this year. What an honor to be gathered today to celebrate your only son's birthday. Lord, I want to thank you for sending my son home, and allowing him to be with us today. What a great present for all of us. Lord, we thank you for the cooks who have so graciously prepared our holiday meal. These blessings we ask in your son's name. Amen. Let's eat!"

Bowls and platters of food were passed around the table, and everyone ate to their heart's content. When they finished with the meal, Alice and Ezra rose from their chairs, walked to the piano, and began playing everyone's favorite Christmas carols.

To everyone's amazement, except Alice, Ezra sang or hummed a few bars of the tunes. His voice had diminished somewhat over the years, and his melodious, tenor voice was a little reedy, but still powerful.

When they finished their musical selections, everyone stood up and clapped loudly. Maggie and Josh looked up from the floor where they sat Indian-style. Their mouths dropped into an "O," and their eyes widened in awe at their uncle's talent.

Bishop sat at the dining room table alone. He covered his face and wept loudly. Everyone was surprised, because no one had ever heard him cry.

Ezra looked toward the dining room and quietly walked over to his father. He bent and put his arms around Bishop's heaving shoulders. Bishop looked up and grabbed Ezra in a big hug. Father and son stayed that way for quite some time.

"Forgive me, son," he repeated over and over, as if the words were a litany.

There wasn't a dry eye in the house. Ruth sat on a loveseat in the living room. She clutched her upper body and rocked back and forward in her seat whispering, "Another miracle has occurred today. Thank you, Jesus."

After everyone calmed down, Daniel asked Naomi to get his and Fred's coats. He told her they had another engagement. She frowned at him accusingly. The way her father said *engagement* piqued her interest.

Daniel walked across the room, bent down, and whispered in Ruth's ear, "Thanks for inviting us today. You're a good woman, Ruth."

She nodded her head. "No problem, Daniel. You're still our children's Father. I don't think it hurts for us to gather as a family from time to time."

"Ezra, it's been good seeing you again." Daniel held out his hand. "I'll be back to see you."

"Alright, man." Ezra chatted with him as he walked them to the door.

After Daniel and Fred left, Ruth dejectedly rose from her seat and began stuffing torn wrapping paper inside a garbage bag.

Chapter Thirty-six

Fred didn't waste a minute lighting a cigarette once he and Daniel were inside the car. His hands shook like he was afflicted with palsy.

"Did you see Ezra? Man, he looked bad. You don't think he done went and got that virus, do you?" He turned to look at Daniel.

"Hmmm, I don't know. From the way he looks, I'd say it's a possibility." Daniel pulled into traffic. He pushed his jacket sleeve up and glanced down at his watch. He had stayed longer at Ruth's than he had planned to. "Lenora is going to have a fit." But he wasn't worried because he had a special gift for her, and he'd bet his bottom dollar she wouldn't stay mad at him for long.

"Do you think it was safe for us to eat dinner with Ezra and touch him? I ain't trying to go out like that. AIDS is a foul disease." Fred inhaled the Newport. He rolled the window down slightly and exhaled.

"I'm sure having dinner with him was okay. You know you can't get AIDS by being around somebody. It's from the exchange of body fluids. Are you going to Lenora's with me, or you want me to drop you off at your lady's house?"

"I told you Janet is out of town. I'm gonna hang out wit'cha tonight. I tell you, seeing Ezra looking like a skeleton is enough to make a brother go buy some condoms." Fred turned the radio on.

Traffic was sparse and Daniel arrived at Lenora's apartment in record time. She was hosting the holiday for her family. He felt her place was too small for everyone to fit into comfortably, but it wasn't his space being invaded, so he wisely kept his mouth shut.

As Fred and Daniel exited the elevator, they could hear music blasting from down the hall.

"It sounds like the party is going on in there." Fred's mood perked up. He could hardly wait to meet Lenora's folks. Daniel had told him so much about them.

When Daniel pushed the door open, rap lyrics attacked his ears, and the pungent scent of alcohol hit his nose. Lenora's family stared at him curiously. Everyone was quiet, which was unusual for the Johnson clan. Normally, you couldn't get a word in edgewise, because everyone talked over each other. Ernest smirked at him from his seat; Daniel's lounging chair.

"Hey, baby." Lenora walked over to him unsteadily, snapping her fingers to the beat of the music.

Daniel leaned over and kissed her lips. "What's

up? Why is everyone so quiet? Did someone die?" Lenora helped him slip his jacket off and hung it in the closet.

"Why are you so late getting back?" she asked, her voice slurring. "Did you sneak and get a little nooky from the wifey?"

Lenora's family listened with bated breath. Fred intervened and asked Daniel if it was okay for him to get a beer from the refrigerator. Daniel replied, "That's cool."

Fred grabbed a can, popped open the lid, and took a huge gulp. Then he looked at Daniel and shook his head warningly, as if to say, *don't discuss what happened in front of her folks.*

"Let's talk in the bedroom." Daniel took Lenora's hand and rushed her out of the living room. She stumbled and he reached out his arms and caught her body. He closed the door behind them.

When he turned the light on, they found LaQuita and Rashon nestled under the mint green comforter.

"Are you crazy? Get your behinds out of my bed." Lenora's arms flailed toward the surprised couple.

LaQuita grabbed her clothes from off the floor and jumped out of the bed, covering her chest with a Kelly green blouse. Rashon reached for his jeans. As they ran into the bathroom, LaQuita mumbled, "Sorry," to her sister.

Lenora tumbled onto the bed. Daniel sat beside her. "What's going on?" he asked. Lenora covered her eyes with her hands.

"LaQuita and Rashon are obviously in heat. I

guess they saw the bed and couldn't stay away from each other." She glared at LaQuita and Rashon as they slid against the wall, tiptoeing out of the bathroom.

Lenora began sobbing and hiccupping. Daniel went into the bathroom and returned with a cup of water. She snatched the cup from him and placed it on the nightstand.

"I guess once you got around *your real family* you couldn't tear yourself away from them. And you didn't even bother to call me the whole time you were gone. How could you treat me so callously, Danny? I thought I meant more to you." She looked up at him with wide puppy dog moistened eyes.

"Come on, Nora, it wasn't nothing like that. I just hadn't seen my grandchildren in a while and I missed them. Fred and I decided to stay and have dinner with my other family. But you know you're my real family, baby. I also wanted to spend some time with Naomi, to make up for our dinner the last time she was here. But it didn't do no good, she's her mother's child. You know I couldn't wait until I got back home with my baby." He kissed her cheek, trying to soothe her sensitive feelings.

Lenora pushed him away from her. Her mind was still in a drunken haze. "When you left this morning and didn't call, I thought you didn't want to be with me anymore. Danny, you didn't even give me a Christmas present."

He lifted her from the bed and they walked to the dresser where his belongings were stored. "I was going to wait until New Year's Eve to give you this." He rummaged through the drawer and handed her a small, black velvet box.

Lenora nervously smoothed her hair down and felt embarrassed by her outburst. "Is this what I think it is?" She looked at the box in his hand.

He handed her the box. "Well, open it and find out."

Lenora opened the lid and found a marquis engagement ring that appeared to be at least a two carat ring nestled inside the tiny box. "Danny!" She jumped up and down and stared at the ring in disbelief. She opened and closed her eyes, as if she were afraid the ring would dissipate into thin air. "Gosh Danny, were you going to propose to me? Oh, my God."

He pulled the knee of his left pants leg and knelt down on one knee. "Lenora Renee Johnson, will you give me the honor of becoming my wife when my divorce is granted?"

She reached down and tenderly stroked Daniel's face. He stood and she put her hands on both sides of his face. She kissed his lips over and over. "Yes, boo, of course I'll marry you."

Daniel slid the ring on her finger. She stretched her arm out and smiled as she admired the gleaming precious stone on her finger.

"Let's go show everybody." She grabbed Daniel by the waist and led him out the bedroom. "Hey, look everybody! Guess what I got for Christmas?" she yelled, holding up her hand.

Felicia and Glenda ran over to Lenora and hugged her. Fred made a slashing motion across his neck. Daniel ignored him.

Ernest, with his arms folded across his chest, said to Daniel in a sardonic tone of voice, "Ain't you already married? How you gonna marry my Noree?"

"My divorce will be coming through soon. It won't be a problem," Daniel replied, smoothly. His hand rested on Lenora's neck.

"I can hardly wait to help you plan your wedding," Felicia gushed. She peeped at her husband. "Me and Reggie only went to City Hall."

Jamal went over to Lenora and grabbed her by the hand. "Is that stone real, old man?" he asked Daniel.

"I told you before, my name is Mr. Wilcox. And yeah, it's real. Nothing but the best for my lady." His face beamed like a hundred watt bulb.

Fred stuck his finger in his throat and made gagging noises.

Chapter Thirty-seven

Bishop returned home a little after nine o'clock that night laden with gifts and food Ruth and the family had sent home with him for Queen. He found his wife in bed with curlers in her head and a mud mask on her face. She didn't acknowledge his presence when he entered the room. She couldn't tear her eyes away from the television. *It's A Wonderful Life* was airing for the millionth time.

"Are you feeling better, Dear?" Bishop asked as he took off his tie and hung it in the metal rack inside the closet. "Everyone missed you and said to tell you hello."

"Humph," Queen replied, "I doubt that." She looked at her husband. "Did Ruth send dinner for me?"

"She sure did. The cake is scrumptious. Esther, I need to talk to you. I'd like you to keep an open mind, although I know what I'm going to tell you will upset you." Bishop sat down on the bed and slipped his shoes off.

Queen cut her eyes between Bishop and the television set. He picked the remote up from the bed and muted the sound from the set. His eyes darted to the Bible lying on the nightstand and back to his wife. He reached over and took his wife's hand.

"Esther, I'm not going to run for mayor. I have a much deeper calling."

Queen stiffened, snatched her hand out of Bishop's hand, and folded her arms across her chest. Her lips jutted out like a truculent child. "Please don't tell me you're not running because of Ezra?" She rolled her eyes at him.

"Actually, yes, he's the reason why I can't run. Ezra is our son, our firstborn. And I want to spend as much time as he has left with him. I refuse to abandon him, Esther. You can do what you want but that's my decision and I'm not going to change it." He tried to grab her hand, but she pulled away from him.

"I'm so disappointed in you, Bishop. To drop out of the race and encourage Ezra in this horror he's brought on the family is crazy." She had an ugly grimace on her face. "If I weren't such a religious woman, I'd leave you." She got out of the bed. "Mr. Clayton, I'm sleeping in the other bedroom tonight. And I'll continue to sleep there until you come to your senses." She glared at Bishop, turned on her heels, and stomped out the room. The elderly couple continued in a state of siege for nearly two weeks until what Ruth swore was a miraculous breakthrough occurred.

*   *   *

The sanctuary was hushed as Bishop made his way to the pulpit the second Sunday after the Christmas and New Year holidays. When he made it to the dais, Bishop preached a rousing sermon with Ruth in mind about the Good Samaritan. He also reiterated the importance of forgiveness among Christians. Queen didn't utter many Amens during her husband's dialogue as she usually did. She just paged through her Bible as he spoke, refusing to meet his eyes. When he finished his message, Bishop wiped his brow and sipped from the glass of water that sat on the lectern.

"I want to take some of you members on a journey back in time today," Bishop said. "The old timers here at the church will know whom I'm speaking of. As for my newer temple members, you're in for a special treat today. Sometimes it takes trials and tribulations for us, as people, parents, sisters or brothers, to understand what is near and dear to our hearts.

"Like many people, I've been guilty of being opinionated and judgmental, even though the Lord said, 'let he who is without sin cast the first stone.' Yes, even some of us who wear the black robe can lose sight of our basic human principals. We become older and set in our ways. Church, I lost sight of what was near and dear to me. Let's just say I was hardheaded. The Lord works in mysterious ways. It took me some time to grasp his message, but I'm a fast learner. For those who don't know him, I'd like you to meet my son, Ezra Clayton. Son, please come up to the pulpit."

Heads swiveled toward the back of the church. Ezra looked thin, but his eyes were shining. There was pep in his footsteps. He felt a sense of belonging, like he'd never left the temple.

Ruth walked on one side of her brother and Alice on the other. Their hands were tightly clasped together. The congregation clapped politely. Ezra and Alice took a seat on the organ bench. He flexed his fingers and began playing warm-up scales. Then his hands moved across the keyboard producing heart wrenching, emotional notes.

Ruth took the microphone from the stand in front of the choir and brought it over to the organ, holding it near Ezra's mouth.

He strummed a few more notes across the keyboard before speaking. "Giving honor to my Father above, and to the one on earth, I'd like to say there is no place like home. There's a saying, you can't go back home, but I'm here to tell you today the devil is a liar. With God, all things are possible." Ezra played a few more poignant riffs. The church became galvanized with the spirit waving their hands in the air and yelling heartfelt Amen.

"When my way seemed dim and I was lost, Jesus stepped in right on time. He brought my sister, Ruth, to me. God put it on her heart to take care of a sinner lost in the world. I love you, my sister," Ezra said.

Ruth's hand trembled slightly. She put her arm around her brother's shoulders.

"I have a testimony this morning, church. From the age of thirteen to eighteen, I was the youth musician for the young adult choir at this very church. And some things you learn in life, you never forget. Can I get a witness? Bear with me, church," Ezra continued speaking as he played the organ softly.

The church applauded. Hardy shouts of Hallelujah resonated throughout the church. Bishop stood on his feet, waving his handkerchief at Ezra.

"I want to sing you a song this morning. Throughout my journey of life, through the bumps and bruises, this hymn has been my testimony. When I lost my way and thought I couldn't find my way back, this simple song sustained me." He played the first verse of, "Amazing Grace."

The choir swayed in their seats and sang background to Ezra's lead. The tones from the organ, along with his voice, sounded pure and mellow. The congregation stood on their feet, clapping and stomping. Sisters moved to the aisle of the great sanctuary, filled with the Holy Ghost. Women shouted in tongues. The presence of the Lord was felt in the temple that morning.

Ezra played the organ like the true maestro that he was. When he repeated the word *lost*, over and over, and then held the note, Ruth wanted to lift the edges of her dress and shout, giving praise to God for his goodness.

As sweat continued to pour off Ezra's brow, and his strength flagged, Alice took over playing the organ. Without missing a beat, her hands crisscrossed the keys in an upbeat tempo and everyone clapped or stomped. Hands flew rapidly as tambourines bounced in the air. The drummer and guitarist kept beat with Alice.

The aisles were clogged with members of Jubilee Temple praising the Holy Ghost with dance and shouting. The members of the deacon board and the mothers of the church marched one-by-one to the organ and shook Ezra's hand, welcoming him home.

A wailing noise rose from the second row of the center pew. Those members not quite as overcome by the spirit as others turned their heads to see where the sound was coming from.

The melody emanating from the organ stopped abruptly and silence fell over the sanctuary as Queen rose from her seat. Her arms were stretched above her head, raised in supplication. She swayed back and forth on her heels. She moved to her left, inching out of the row, and she ran to the organ. Tears streamed down her face as she reached for her boy. Ezra stood and she clasped her son to her breast. The sounds from their mouths were loud and guttural.

"Forgive me, son. I was wrong," Queen sobbed. She looked at Ezra sorrowfully through tearstained eyes. "I'm so sorry."

Ezra pulled away from Queen and shushed her. He put a finger on his lips. "Everything is all right, Mother. Nothing matters but here and now. I just give praises to the Lord that we could come here today and put our differences aside and become a family again." His eyes were glistened with tears. "No matter where I was over the years, I never stopped loving or thinking about my family. There's no place like home."

Queen said, "I was so wrong about so many things. If you want, you can come back to your home. Son, I'm so sorry. Lord, please forgive me."

"We'll talk about it later, Mom." He pulled her into his arms.

The congregation erupted into cheers and clapped for five minutes without stopping. Bishop walked over to his wife and son and engulfed them in his arms.

Alice could barely see the organ keys. She was so overcome with sentiment. Sarah, Naomi, Maggie, and Josh walked down the main aisle and joined their family in the pulpit.

Ruth walked to the lectern, put the microphone back into its stand, and adjusted it. She waved her hands in the air.

"Isn't God good? Praise God, from who all blessings flow. I don't know about you, church, but I feel life is too short to hold grudges against our loved ones. You know it's that old devil trying to keep us from His blessings. If you have a mother, father, sister, brother, spouse, or child at church with you today, turn and hug them. Show appreciation for your loved ones while they are still here on earth," Ruth said.

Alice played the opening chords of the song, "There's A Sweet Spirit In This Place." The spirit of love and the Lord filled the church.

Finally, the Clayton family had reunited.

Chapter Thirty-eight

Nearly ten months to the day that Daniel walked out of the house on Prairie Avenue, the estranged Wilcox's sat on opposite sides of a courtroom on the fifth floor of the Daley Plaza building, waiting for their marriage to be officially dissolved. Ruth sat in a chair on the witness stand answering questions from her lawyer. She looked anywhere but at Daniel. Bishop and Queen smiled encouragingly at their daughter while Sarah gave her mother the thumbs up sign.

The judge awarded Ruth sole possession of the house. Bishop had provided her with the funds needed to buy out Daniel's share. Daniel gratefully accepted the money since the judge ordered him to pay her spousal support for two years. He was beside himself with anger. He was also responsible for half of Naomi's college tuition. So his plans to retire in a couple of years were put on the back burner.

After Ruth took a seat next to her attorney, Daniel took his turn on the witness stand. An hour later, the judge solemnly granted the Wilcox's a divorce.

As Daniel strolled from the courtroom, he shook his head regretfully at Ruth. Her lips trembled and unshed tears stood in her eyes. He didn't speak to his daughter or ex-in-laws.

Ruth felt profoundly discouraged at the impersonal manner in which her marriage ended. Sarah noted the sorrowful expression on her mother's face. She tucked Ruth's arm inside her own and said, "Let's go home."

With their heads held high, mother and daughter walked out of the courthouse, Bishop and Queen Esther trailing behind them.

Daniel sat in his Mustang, and removed his wedding band from the fourth finger of his left hand and flexed his fingers. He dropped it in the glove compartment and rubbed the indentation the ring had left. Then he started the car and drove to the south side. His cell phone chirped.

"Are you finally free?" Lenora asked him. She held her breath waiting for his answer.

Daniel could sense the strain in her voice. "Yes, I am," he replied, soberly.

"So, can we get married tomorrow as planned?" Lenora asked him hopefully as she stroked her swollen abdomen.

"Yes, we still have a date for tomorrow." Daniel thought it was ironic that he would be returning to the same building where his divorce was just granted to marry Lenora. The bride-to-be wanted her first child born in wedlock. The baby was due any day so her plans for a lavish wedding was scrapped.

"Hurry home, baby," she urged him.

"I'll be there as soon as I can." Daniel disconnected the call and dialed Fred's number. "Are you set for tomorrow? Did you pick up your tuxedo? And don't be late, I'm counting on you to be my best man tomorrow," he chided his brother.

"Naw, I ain't went to get it yet. I ain't superstitious or nothing, but this whole marriage thing is weird. I was your best man when you married Ruth, and you want me to do it again for you and Lenora. Ain't that bad luck or something?"

"You need to just chill out," Daniel fussed. "And no, it's not bad luck. You're my only blood relative outside of my kids. You know I couldn't tell my children I was getting hitched so soon after the divorce. If I get married a hundred times, I expect you to be there at my side."

"I don't understand why we gotta wear tuxes. We're only going to City Hall. That don't make no sense to me," Fred proclaimed. He lifted his ponytail and rubbed the back of his neck.

"Because Lenora wants us to. She's pregnant and I'm going to do everything in my power to make her happy, that's why. Not to mention she's due to give birth any day, and we'd prefer to be married before the baby is born," Daniel said through gritted teeth. "I just hope she doesn't go into labor tonight."

Daniel peeked out his rearview mirror and put on his turn signal and switched lanes. He needed to move over to the right lane of the Dan Ryan Expressway to exit at 99th Street and Halsted Avenue. He figured he might as well go to Evergreen Plaza to pick up his own tuxedo.

"I'm on my way to pick up my tux. You want me to pick up yours while I'm there?"

"Yeah, why don't you go ahead and get mine too. Say, I figured me and the fellows would take you out tonight for a bachelor party, and then you can crash at my place."

"Uh, Fred, I'm gonna pass on the party tonight. Since Lenora is so close to her due date, I need to stick around. I'm going to spend the night here with her."

"Man, I tell you," Fred growled, pounding on the kitchen table, "it seems like that gal got your nose wide open and then some. And I don't like it. I don't remember you hanging on to Ruth's dress tail when she had your children. Plus, I thought you didn't want any more kids? What happened? She tricked you, didn't she? Let's see, she said something like she forgot to take the pill, didn't she? One minute you're talking about how you don't want to be tied down. Then you get a divorce one day, and get married the very next day, and you have a child on the way."

Daniel's cheeks turned red. He was angry with his brother. No one could get away with talking to him that way except Fred. He steered his car into a parking spot and turned off the car.

"Just lay off me, Fred. I have a lot riding on tomorrow. My future is at stake here. I love Nora, and that's all there is to it. If you have a problem with me getting married again, then maybe you should step down as my best man." Daniel had gotten himself worked up into a tizzy.

"Now hold on just a minute. This is me talking, your brother. I got your back," Fred retorted angrily, as he sucked his teeth. "We've always been able to talk to each other about any and everything. I hope that ain't gonna change because you're hitching up with Lenora. But you have to admit everything has happened fast. I just have a feeling it won't be as easy to get out of this marriage, if it turns out to be a mistake, like it was with Ruth." He backed down, and a conciliatory note crept into his voice. "Just calm down."

"Are you gonna stand up with me tomorrow or not?"

"Sure." Fred realized his brother was gone, and that he was sprung. "I'll talk to you later. You go ahead and finish your running around." He hung up the telephone and shook his head wearily from side to side.

Fred's eyes darted to one of his upper kitchen cabinets. He stood, walked over to the cabinet, and pulled out a fifth of whiskey. He twisted off the cap and guzzled some down. When he finished imbibing the dark liquor, he sat back down at the table.

Whenever he happened to be around Lenora, his demeanor was one of amicability. But deep down inside, he realized he never really cared for her. He wasn't convinced she had his brother's best interest at heart as he knew Ruth had.

Daniel angrily closed his cell phone and drove

to the mall and parked his car. Not only was he picking up the tuxedos, but he planned to pick up a prescription for Viagra at Walgreen's Drugstore. Daniel had paid a visit to his primary care physician nearly a year ago and the prescription was about to expire before he could have it filled. As he stared at the little brown bottle he held in his hand, Daniel's mind wandered back to his visit with his primary care physician months ago.

Months ago as Daniel sat in the room waiting his turn to see the physician, his stomach felt riddled with anxiety. He knew Dr. Burns had the test results from his annual physical that he had taken two weeks ago. He hoped the results weren't bad.

"Daniel Wilcox, the doctor can see you now," a nurse, clad in blue scrubs announced as she stood near the opened door holding his file.

Dr. Burns was on the telephone when Daniel entered the room after knocking on the door. The doctor beckoned at him to have a seat.

After he finished his call, he opened Daniel's chart and perused it again. "Daniel, you're what, fifty-seven now?"

"No doc, I'm fifty-eight."

"Hmm. I have your lab results back. Your pressure is good and your cholesterol level is a little higher than normal, but it's nothing to be alarmed about. You just need to watch what you eat more carefully. Have you been following the diet I gave you a few months ago?"

"I've been trying, but I've been eating out a lot

lately. That should be changing soon." He told Dr. Burns about his impeding divorce, and his soon to be new wife and baby.

"I understand there have been changes in your life, but you still have to monitor your health and do as I instruct you."

"Uh, say doc, I was wondering if you'd give me a prescription for Viagra?" Daniel asked, wiggling in his seat like a little boy.

"What for?" Dr. Burns peered at him narrowly. "Your prostate is fine. You haven't had any impotency issues that you haven't discussed with me, have you?"

"Well, sometimes," Daniel hemmed and hawed, "I just can't go as many rounds as I used to."

"Pardon me?" Dr. Burns asked with a probing expression on his face.

Daniel lowered his voice and leaned forward in the chair. "I used to be like Ali in the ring, I could go round for round, pound for pound. Now, I'm lucky if I can go two rounds. And I have a young filly instead of an old mare at home. I have to please her, you know what I mean?"

"So, what you're saying is that you can't maintain as many erections as you could in the past, is that it?"

"Yeah," Daniel answered, looking relieved. He relaxed in the seat.

"You know what, I see this all the time since Viagra debuted on the market. Men come in here looking for a miracle to reclaim their youth." Daniel looked impatient, but he gave Dr. Burns his undivided attention.

"I personally think at your age, and any age for that matter, you need a woman who'll stick by you through thick and thin. Someone who will be there for you when the going gets rough, whether you can perform or not, and take care of you when you're sick. Can you truthfully say this new woman will do those things for you, Daniel?"

"I hear you, doc, and I know what you're saying. Yes, I think she'll be there for me." Even as he responded to the question, doubts crept into Daniel's mind. Ruth was the woman the doctor was describing. Lenora, on the other hand, was uncharted territory.

Dr. Burns continued. "We always hear about females being in menopause, but we hear very little about the male counterpart which I call midlife crises. Studies prove it exists. My grandmother, God rest her soul, used to have a saying that I didn't quite understand when I was younger. Now the meaning is crystal clear. And it went something like this, there's no fool like an old fool. Do you get my drift?"

Daniel looked Dr. Burns dead in the eyes. "Sure I do, but that doesn't apply to me. I found a lady I want to make mine, and that's what I'm gonna do. I just need a little help from you to keep the home fires burning. Do you get *my* drift?"

"I don't think you need Viagra, Daniel. You're in relatively good shape for your age. I know you exercise, and if you just watch your food intake, you should live many years without any serious problems."

"I hear you, doctor, but I beg to differ. I'd at

least like to try it. If you don't give me a prescription, then I can find another way to get it."

Dr. Burns reared back in his chair and laughed. "If I didn't know better, I'd say you're trying to blackmail me. Okay, against my better judgment, I'll give you a prescription. Maybe I'd better have my administrative assistant prepare a waiver for you to sign."

Daniel waved his hand in the air impatiently, and gripped the arms of the chair. "If that's what it takes, then bring it on."

After Daniel picked up the prescription, he stopped at the florist. Lenora had ordered a bouquet and boutonniere for the wedding ceremony. The flowers hadn't been prepared yet, so Daniel put a twenty dollar bill on the counter and made arrangements to have them delivered to Lenora's house.

When he returned to the car, he unscrewed the vial of pills and poured a couple into his hand. Then he dropped them back inside the bottle and screwed the top on. Daniel put the vial in the glove box. *The man who created these babies should be given a Nobel Peace Prize award. These pills will ensure mankind will continue to get his mack on. I swear it's the greatest invention since the car. I'd love to try one now, but Dr. Burns said to take it four hours before having sex.* He put the pills back in the bottle and dropped them into the glove compartment. Taking those pills would ensure that Lenora wouldn't ever leave him.

Dr. Pryor, Lenora's obstetrician, cautioned the

couple to refrain from sexual activity until after the baby was born. So once she was given the green light to resume relations after her six-week checkup, Daniel planned to give her the ride of her life.

When he arrived home, Lenora was in the bed asleep. She hadn't had a full night's sleep for months. Her face was drawn and her mouth drooped open slackly. Lenora's nose had spread from one side of her face to the other it seemed. She also had a dark rash on her neck.

Pregnancy didn't fill her with the glow that other pregnant women had. Privately, Fred called his sister-in-law-to-be the Goodyear Blimp.

Baby Damon kicked, and he kicked hard all the time. Lenora had an ultra sound test done during her sixth month of pregnancy, so the couple already knew the baby's gender.

She wore a loose fitting sleeveless smock, which bunched across her stomach. Daniel stood by the bed for a minute, watching her stomach rise and fall. She was so huge that he thought her abdomen looked like a couple of oversized watermelons had taken up residence inside her midsection.

Her wedding gown was hanging on the closet door. Daniel paused to stare at it. He hadn't seen such a large quantity of material in his life. The ivory colored tulle and satin gown was sleeveless with an empire waist and crisscross straps. Beaded organza flowers adorned the skirt and short train, with a satin ribbon around the midsection. Daniel turned and left the room. He went into the kitchen and got a beer out of the refrigerator. Then he returned to the living room, picked up the remote, and turned the television to the White Sox baseball game.

Finally, a couple of hours later, Lenora awakened. "Danny, would you bring me a glass of milk?" she called weakly from the bedroom.

"Sure, give me a minute." He walked into the kitchen after one of the White Sox players hit a home run and poured Lenora a cup of milk. Then Daniel went into the bedroom and sat on the side of the bed. "How are you feeling?" he asked, after he handed her the milk. Daniel stroked her belly. "That's my son in there," he boasted.

After she drank the milk, Lenora lay on her side caressing her tummy while Daniel massaged her back. She pushed tendrils of limp hair off her forehead.

"Not too bad. I talked to Felicia while you were gone. She and Reggie are spending the night with us."

"Why?"

"So she can help me get ready tomorrow. It was either her or Mama, and I felt she was the lesser of the two evils," Lenora joked. She gasped as a pain shot through her abdomen.

Daniel had turned to go back to the living room. He paused. "Are you sure you're feeling okay?"

"Yes, Damon kicked like he was punting a football that time." Lenora tried to smile through gritted teeth. The doorbell sounded. "That's probably Felicia," she said.

Daniel left to answer the door. *If I had known Felicia and Reggie were spending the night, my brother-in-law to be and I could have gone to the club with Fred.*

Chapter Thirty-nine

On the morning of Daniel and Lenora's wedding, September 13, 1999, a fine mist of rain sprinkled from the sky. Then the sun peeked from the clouds and shone brightly. Daniel had rented a limousine to chauffeur him, Lenora, and now Felicia and Reggie to City Hall. The white Lincoln Town Car stretch limousine was scheduled to arrive at noon. The Johnson family, including Lenora's aunts and their families, planned to attend the ceremony.

Fred, looking hung over had stopped by Lenora's apartment at 6:00 that morning grumbling, to pick up his tuxedo. Daniel asked him if he wanted to ride downtown with everyone else. Fred politely declined, explaining a buddy was parked outside and he was going to take him back home.

The chauffeur arrived at eleven-fifteen, and buzzed to say that he was waiting downstairs from the lobby. Felicia and Lenora were still holed up in the bedroom. Daniel had spent an uncomfortable night on the futon in Lenora's office. Reggie slept on the sofa bed in the living room, while Felicia bunked with Lenora.

Finally, Lenora and Felicia exited the bedroom. Daniel pasted a big smile on his face, trying to mask his anxiety. Lenora didn't look well at all. She clutched her back and moaned softly.

"Are you sure you're feeling well? We can always do this another day." Daniel commented solicitously as he rubbed Lenora's back.

She reached up and pushed back the circle of baby's breath that slid slightly down her forehead. "Oh no, we're not putting our plans off. Come on, boo, let's get married."

He took her swollen hands, and Felicia gave her the beautiful pink rose bouquet.

"Just think," Lenora remarked complacently as they walked out the door, "when we return this afternoon, we'll be husband and wife. I can hardly wait."

Shortly after exiting the apartment and getting into the long vehicle, the driver pulled the car in front of the Daley Plaza Building. As Daniel and Lenora got out of the vehicle, they noticed Fred and the Johnson clan standing in front of the building.

Felicia handed Lenora her bouquet and everyone entered the courthouse. "What's wrong, baby, you don't look too hot?" Glenda asked as she straightened Lenora's train. "You're not in labor are you?"

Daniel looked down at her and up at her mother.

"Well, I've been having a few pains all morning," Lenora admitted, "but I'm fine."

Daniel helped his bride-to-be sit on the wooden bench in the hall outside the courtroom as they waited their turn with the judge. Kente ran up and down the long hallway yelling just to hear his voice echo off the walls. LaQuita kept chasing him back to their seats.

Lenora's energy level flagged even more during the short wait. She kept wincing from pain. Finally, the bailiff announced, "Wilcox and Johnson."

Daniel helped Lenora stand. She waddled into the courtroom. The judge asked, "Miss, are you sure you're all right?"

"Your Honor, could you hurry things up? I think I'm in labor and I'd like to be married to my baby's daddy when I give birth." Lenora began breathing heavily, almost gasping.

The judge looked uneasy and instructed the bailiff to call 911. When he pronounced the couple man and wife, Lenora clutched her mid-section and moaned with pain. A gush of liquid ran down her legs and gathered beneath her feet.

"Oh my God, I think my water broke!" she shrieked. The EMTs rushed inside the courtroom in the nick of time.

Kente, who'd been quiet until now, looked up at LaQuita and pointed to Lenora. "Mama, Tee-Tee made a booboo."

The sounds of sirens permeated the air as the ambulance sped to Northwestern Memorial Hospital. Daniel held Lenora's hand as she moaned and squirmed.

"Mister, your wife is definitely in labor. We might have to deliver the baby here in the ambulance," the EMT calmly informed Daniel.

The father-to-be felt squeamish. His stomach contents promptly dislodged from his mouth.

Two hours after the ambulance pulled in front of the emergency room, Damon made his appearance.

Daniel walked down the hall to tell his new in-laws and Fred that Lenora and Damon were doing fine, and that they could see both of them shortly. LaQuita and Rashon left to take Kente home. The rest of the family remained.

"Brother Wilcox, is that you?"

Daniel looked up to see the president of the Missionary Board of the temple standing in front of him, clutching a Bible in her hand. He eyed her wonderingly.

"Yes. I don't remember your name, but I know you're a member of the temple."

"Right, I'm Queen's best friend, Edna, but everyone calls me Mother Campbell." Her false teeth clicked in her mouth. She looked behind Daniel. "Is someone sick? Can I do something to help?"

"No, we have everything under control. Have a good day."

Annette didn't miss Daniel's awkward fidgeting and couldn't resist saying loud enough for Mother Campbell to hear, "Danny, who does Damon look like, you or Lenora?"

As Mother Campbell walked away, her back stiffened. She turned and scowled at Daniel before continuing down the hallway, shaking her head condemningly from side to side. When she arrived home, she sped to the telephone and called Queen, who in turn wasted no time in calling Ruth.

"Ruthie, I'm your mother and I have your best interest at heart, so I thought I should be the first to tell you some distressing news I learned not too long ago. Edna was at Northwestern Hospital this evening. Her sister, Mary, is ill. And guess who she ran into?" The older woman's voice dropped noticeably.

"I'm sure you're going to tell me whether I want to know or not, Queen," Ruth replied, dryly. Thick knots of anxiety formed in her stomach.

"Daniel. He was there with a woman, who apparently just had his baby. Edna said everyone was dressed up like there was a wedding or something. Before she left the hospital, she checked with admissions, and sure enough, there was a Wilcox admitted, and she was in the maternity ward."

Tears sprung into Ruth's eyes. "Thanks for telling me, Mother. I was just getting ready to give Ezra his medicine. I'll call you back later."

"Tell Ezra I said hello. Hopefully, I'll see him at church tomorrow."

Ruth clicked the telephone off and dropped into the chair in the living room. *Daniel and I were just divorced yesterday and he got married today. That man has no respect for me or our children. I wonder why he didn't say anything, to Sarah at least. God, I guess you're telling me that my marriage is really over, and I that I do have to move on.*

Sarah walked into the room carrying a clothes-basket. She was headed to the basement to wash her and the children's clothes. She stopped in her tracks when she saw her mother crying. "Mama, what's wrong? Is Uncky feeling alright?"

Ruth debated with herself as to whether she should tell Sarah what Queen had told her. She felt vulnerable and related the details of her mother's call to her daughter.

"I don't believe it." Sarah dropped the basket on the floor and a few pieces of clothing slipped out of it. She sat heavily on the sofa. "What was Daddy thinking? Maybe Mother Campbell got it wrong. I don't think my father would do something like that without at least telling me," she said.

"You know what a snoop Mother Campbell is. Of course she went to Patient Information and got the scoop," Ruth said, bleakly. She stood. "I need to be alone for a while."

"Do you think I should call Daddy?" Sarah looked up at her mother with a devastated expression on her face. Her eyes begged for guidance.

Ruth shook her head helplessly. "I can't help you on that one, Sarah. You'll have to do what you feel best. Oh, would you give your uncle his medicine? I was just about to give it to him when mother called."

Sarah nodded. She was still stunned by her mother's announcement.

Ruth walked to her bedroom slowly, like she was weighed down with a sack of stones. She fell across the bed and cried her heart out.

Sarah stepped over the clothing that lay on the floor and hurried to Ezra's bedroom to give him his medicine. Then the young woman returned to the kitchen. Her hands trembled and became moist as she picked up the cordless phone. She dialed her father's cell phone number. The telephone rang, and then Daniel's voice mail greeting came on, inviting the caller to leave a message.

"Daddy, it's me," Sarah's voice quivered with tension. "I just heard some unbelievable news, and I need to talk to you. Call me as soon as you can, please."

Chapter Forty

Daniel sat in Lenora's room cradling his new son in his arms. *God, Josh, Maggie, and D III have an uncle younger than they are.* Damon wiggled in his arms and peeped into his father's eyes. The baby's mouth gaped widely as he yawned and then Damon's body went slack.

He weighed in at a little over nine pounds. Damon's features were his mother's. His slanted eyes and nose proclaimed the baby his mother's child. Lenora had a hard time delivering her first child, and the doctor almost had to perform a cesarean section.

The new mother lay in the bed asleep. Daniel looked at her soiled wedding dress hanging in the closet. She wouldn't ever wear it again. He felt a vibration in his jacket pocket. It was his cell phone. Maybe Fred was calling him. Before the ambulance left for the hospital, he asked his brother to call him. He stood and put the baby back into the cot. He went into the washroom and checked the number. He swore quietly when he saw Ruth's telephone number.

"Danny, where are you? Is something wrong?" Lenora asked groggily from the adjoining room.

He dropped the cell phone guiltily back into his pocket. "No, I'm washing my hands. I'll be there in a minute." He wiped his clammy forehead with a moistened paper napkin.

When he returned to the room, he smoothed Lenora's hair off her face and kissed her forehead. "There aren't many men that can say they got married and became a father on the same day."

"I would have to say we definitely pushed it to the limit. But at least Damon has your name," Lenora sighed contently. "Have you told your other kids about me and the baby?" She sat up abruptly and grabbed her stomach, obviously in pain. "Ouch, that hurt."

"Not yet. But I plan to soon," he said. "The doctor says if all goes well, you'll be out of here tomorrow. I'm going to go home to change clothes and come back later. I'ma spend the night with you and Damon." He tried to hug her, but she pulled away from him.

"Are you sure that's why you're leaving?"

"Of course I'm sure, Lenora," he answered impatiently, waving his hand around. "It's our wedding day, don't start with that talk. I don't know why you think I'm messing around."

She turned over in the bed, facing the wall. "Fine, please yourself."

Daniel exited the room and took the elevator to

the ground floor. He went to the gift shop and bought three big blue helium balloons announcing *It's A Boy*, and a plant for Lenora. He instructed a candy striper to take the items to Room #203. "They're for Lenora Johnson, I mean Lenora Wilcox," he said to the candy striper.

The cashier, a young girl, looked at him questioningly and remarked, "You must be a newlywed. And I'd say from the balloons, a new father too. Double congratulations." She smiled.

"Thank you. I guess the tuxedo is a dead giveaway." He looked down at his clothing and laughed aloud.

As he left the building, he realized he hadn't driven downtown. Once the ambulance had arrived at the courthouse, he asked Fred to pay the limousine driver and tell him that his services were no longer required. *How am I going to get home? He* walked outside and stopped dead in his tracks like his eyes were playing tricks on him. Daniel did a double take. His eyes darted to the car parked at the curb. Sarah sat inside her Honda Civic. She tooted the horn loudly when she saw her father.

Daniel nervously walked over to his daughter's silver gray vehicle. Sarah reached over and opened the door.

"Do you need a ride?" she asked her father in a tightly measured tone of voice. Her cheeks were mottled a bright crimson color and her eyes flashed wariness.

He entered the car and turned to face his daughter. He noticed her red, swollen eyes. He nervously licked his lips.

"Sarah, what brings you here? Do you know someone sick in the hospital?"

She stared at her father accusingly. "I just want to know one thing. Is it true, Daddy?" Her eyes traveled the length of his body. "You're dressed in a tuxedo, so I'm assuming what I heard is true, that you did get married today. Still I had to come here and see you with my own eyes and hear your answer myself. Tell me, Daddy? Is it true you and your wife have a baby?" Her voice broke sharply like shards of glass. Sarah gripped the steering wheel tightly with both hands and held her breath waiting for her father to answer her question.

Daniel could see she was visibly shaken; her body quivered. He shook his head and waved his hands helplessly. "Uh, yeah, I got married this afternoon and my new wife had a baby this evening."

"When were you going to tell us your news, Daddy? Don't you think being married and having a new child is pretty drastic? So, all this time you told us that you weren't involved with another woman, you lied." Sarah's voice rose hysterically. "DJ told me he suspected that you were involved with someone else. But I didn't believe him and I defended you."

Daniel tried to pat Sarah's back, but she pulled violently away from him. "Now just calm down honey, I was going to eventually get around to telling you and your sister and brother. I wanted a little time to go by after the divorce. I though you all might think my remarrying was too soon." He looked at Sarah and shrugged his shoulders, trying to make her understand his point of view.

"You're right. Of course we'd think it was too soon for you to remarry, your doing so is proof that you were cheating on Mama." Sarah cut her tear-stained eyes narrowly at her father. "Dad, you've hurt us badly. Mama is at home right now crying her eyes out. You should've had enough common courtesy to at least tell us your plans. Can you imagine how Mama felt hearing the news from Granny Queen?"

"I understand that now," Daniel said, trying to apologize. "I just didn't expect to run into Edna Campbell at the hospital. I'm sure she called Queen, and of course, she blabbed the news to your mother."

Sarah's shoulders heaved uncontrollably. She moaned, "All these years, me and DJ heard whispers at church about your unfaithfulness to Mama. But she wouldn't have anyone speak against you, and she stuck by you through thick and thin. And then you don't have the decency to tell us you planned to get married. When were you going to introduce us to your new wife? Are you sure the baby is even yours?"

Daniel tried to control his temper. He answered with as much patience as he could muster. "Now you're hitting below the belt, Sarah. Of course I'm positive the baby is mine, and like I said, I planned to introduce you to Lenora. I was just waiting for a good time."

"What if Naomi had been home when Queen called Mama, and she overheard the conversation? She's at home this weekend from school. Do you ever think about anyone except yourself?

Right now I don't like you very much, Dad, and if I wasn't a Christian, I'd probably say worse. Get out of my car. I don't want to be around you right now." Sarah, with a shaking finger pointed to the door.

Daniel sighed heavily. "I don't know what else to say, except I'm sorry, Sarah. I realize now that I was wrong about not telling you what was going on with me. I hope in time you'll forgive me for not being truthful about my plans. But I won't apologize for being in love with another woman. You're my child and I ask you to respect that. If it wasn't for me, there wouldn't be a Sarah, DJ, or Naomi Wilcox."

"No, you're wrong, Daddy. If it wasn't for my mother, there wouldn't be any children. Go now before I say something that I'll regret. This conversation is over. Your behavior is disgusting." Sarah's tone was icy.

He held up his hands in surrender. "All right, I'm going. I'll give you time to cool off and I'll call you in a couple of weeks. Okay?" He got out of the car.

Sarah's eyes bucked wildly. She looked at her father like he was crazy. When he closed the door, she pulled away from the curb and into traffic rapidly. Her tires screeched loudly. She pushed tears away from her eyes with the back of her hand.

Daniel watched his daughter speed down the street with a heavy heart. He walked down the street and flagged a taxi. *Good and bad, that's how this day has turned out.*

Chapter Forty-one

As the latest storm in Ruth's life raged, she tried to pull herself together and maintain a semblance of control. Ruth rose from her bed and called out Sarah's name. Her daughter didn't answer. She walked to the living room and looked out the window. Sarah's car was gone. *Lord, I hope she didn't try to do something crazy like confront Daniel. There's now no chance that Daniel and I will ever reconcile. My husband, no ex-husband, married another woman before the ink was dry on our divorce decree. As* Ruth walked into the living room her body was stooped from facing adversity after adversity. Her problems seemed endless.

A few minutes later, Ezra walked into the room and saw Ruth standing motionlessly as she stared out the window. Her shoulders were bowed with despair and when she turned to face him, she looked miserable, like she'd lost everything she held near and dear. He called her name and gathered her body in a tight embrace, then the siblings sat on the couch. Ruth began sobbing again.

"What's wrong, Ruthie?" he asked once she had finished weeping. He pulled a tissue out of his pocket and handed it to his sister.

Ruth dabbed her eyes. "It's Daniel, he, he, he got married today, and his wife had a baby," she stuttered. She then covered her face with her hands.

"I'm sorry to hear that, little sis. I know despite everything that has happened between you and Daniel that you still love him, and you were hoping you two would get back together. I feel for you, Ruth. It's nothing worse in this world than loving someone who doesn't love you back."

"I shouldn't be dumping all of this on you, Ezra. I'm so ashamed. I feel so inadequate. Am I such a horrible person that Daniel couldn't tell me in person that he planned to remarry? Of maybe he felt like he wasn't obligated because we were separated. It just would've been the decent thing for him to do." Her eyes dropped to her lap. She shredded the tissue.

"Now, don't feel that way or beat up on yourself." Ezra took Ruth's hand. "Daniel had his own agenda. And it had nothing to do with you. Sometimes men search for something they think they want or can't have. I know that feeling too well."

Ruth whispered, "I wasn't a good wife. Daniel told me I always put the children's feelings over his. I promised him when Naomi went to college I'd try to do better, but I didn't. I should've worked harder to save my marriage. Instead, I pushed him into the arms of another woman." Fresh tears trekked down her face.

"You don't have a selfish bone in your body, Ruth." Ezra scolded Ruth, trying to comfort her. I may not have been around when your children were growing up, but I know if they needed you, that you were there for them. You did what a parent, especially a mother, was supposed to do." He rubbed her back.

"That's not exactly true." Ruth's head dropped with shame. "There's something I've been meaning to tell you, but I hadn't thought of a good way to say it. So I'll just say it." She took a deep breath and expelled it. "You see, I'm not Naomi's biological mother . . . Sarah is. She was sexually assaulted when she was a teenager. I felt strongly, regardless of the circumstance, that abortion was out of the question. Doing so would've been against everything we were taught as Christians. So when Sarah told me she thought she was pregnant, I faked being pregnant, and the rest, as they say, is history."

Ezra sensed his sister was suffering mightily, but on the other hand, she had finally vocalized some issues, and he knew it felt good for her to share her pain with someone. He didn't want to say anything to add to her anguish, so he chose his words carefully.

"What a terrible experience for Sarah to experience. My heart goes out to her. She's good people. Who am I to judge anyone, especially you? I know you and Daniel did what you thought was right at the time."

"The problem is," Ruth went on rubbing her eyes, "Daniel didn't want Sarah to have the baby at all. He wanted her to have an abortion. I over-ruled his request."

"And what did Sarah want?" Ezra asked gently. He turned to Ruth and lifted her chin.

"She was so traumatized that she didn't really voice an opinion. She said whatever Daniel and I decided, she would go along with it. Sarah was just a child herself, and we really didn't take her feelings into consideration," Ruth admitted. "Daniel was also adamant about Naomi being told that she was adopted when she got older."

Ezra's eyebrow rose questioningly. "And telling her would serve what purpose?"

"Nothing that made any sense to me." Ruth's stomach somersaulted and her breathing became rapid. "Daniel felt keeping secrets of that nature would lead to trouble and that eventually Naomi would learn the truth that I wasn't her mother. He also wanted to go to the police and report what happened to Sarah. Bishop, Queen, and I thought it should be handled privately among the family, and Daniel accused me of taking their side. God, I wish I could change the past. I don't ever want Naomi to learn that Sarah is really her mother."

One subject of the sister and brother's conversation, Sarah walked inside the front door and her heart bounced to her feet and back to her chest when she saw the dumbstruck expression on Naomi's face. The young lady stood just outside the entrance to the living room, which was visible from where Sarah stood in the foyer.

Naomi covered her mouth with her hand. Tracks of the tears on her face were telltale signs that she had been eavesdropping—unbeknownst to her mother and uncle—on their conversation. The back of the couch faced the entrance of the room. The two sisters stared mutely at each other. Ruth and Ezra looked over at Sarah and then Naomi. Ruth's eyes beheld her youngest child shaking her head in disbelief and clutching her stomach, moaning softly. The young woman's face was devoid of color.

"Oh my God, Naomi, were you standing here all this time listening to what I was saying to your Uncle?" Ruth asked in a shaky voice. She tried to stand, but her legs felt useless, like they were made of rubber.

Naomi stood in the doorway glaring at her mother and wiping tears from her face. Sarah hadn't moved from the front door.

When Ruth was finally able to stand, she walked over to Naomi and made a motion to pull her into her arms.

Naomi moved backward, forcibly away from Ruth. "You mean you're not my mother and Sarah is? You lied to me. I hate you." She tried to run out the front door, but Sarah stepped in front of her.

She took Naomi in her arms, and the young girl sagged against Sarah's body. Suddenly Ruth's oldest daughter's face looked older than her thirty-two years. Ruth stepped forward to join them.

"No, Mama," Sarah held a trembling hand up, "I'll talk to Naomi. It's my job. I want to tell my daughter what happened in my own way." They walked down the hallway to Naomi's bedroom together. Sarah closed the door.

Ruth's legs almost couldn't support her body. She held her hand out feebly and grasped the top of the sofa to maintain her balance. She looked as though she were about to faint. She swayed back and forth where she stood. Ezra stood and helped her sit down on the sofa.

"Oh Jesus, my life is falling apart right before my eyes." She looked upward and wailed, "Lord, help us. Ezra, what am I going to do?"

He gently took her chin in his hand. "You're going to have faith that your family will get through this crisis. And doing so will give you strength to weather the storm. You'll make it, and I'll be here with you. We'll get through this together." He left her in the living room with her hands covering her face weeping. Ezra shuffled slowly into the kitchen to call Alice.

After Alice answered the phone, Ezra sighed. "You need to come here as soon as you can. All heck has broke loose in this house."

"I'm on my way." Alice vowed.

Chapter Forty-two

Daniel tipped the cab driver two dollars after he pulled the taxi in front of Fred's apartment. He was so shaken by his conversation with Sarah that he didn't think to call Fred to see if he was at home. Daniel hoped his brother was there because he desperately needed someone to talk to. His cell phone rang. He looked at the caller ID. The number displayed was the hospital. It was Lenora. *She can wait*, he thought to himself.

Instead of walking jauntily up the stairway to the second floor as he usually did, Daniel's steps were measured and slow like an old man. He hesitantly knocked on Fred's door.

"Wha'cha doing here?" Fred greeted his brother after he had unlocked the door. "I'd thought you'd be at the hospital with Lenora."

Daniel went inside and sat on the sofa silently. Fred sat on the chair opposite his brother.

"What's wrong, man? Instead of looking like a

happy groom and new Daddy, you look like the
sky fell in."

"I swear I can't get away from that darn church
no matter how hard I try. You wouldn't believe
what has happened to me since Lenora had the
baby," Daniel complained.

"Try me," Fred urged his brother. "You want
something to drink?"

"Naw, I better pass since I'm going back to the
hospital after I leave here. One of the members of
the temple, Edna Campbell, just happened to be
at the hospital today. She saw me and came over
and spoke. And Annette, wanting to cause trouble, deliberately asked me if the baby looked like
me or Lenora while I was talking to Edna. You
know what happened next; that ole battle ax
called Queen, and told her she saw me, Queen
called Ruth, and you can imagine the rest."

Fred stood and walked into the kitchen to the
refrigerator and pulled out a can of Budweiser
beer. Then he walked back to the sofa and gave
Daniel his undivided attention. "That's deep," he
said, suppressing a snicker. "If only I coulda been
a fly on the wall when that conversation went
down."

"When I left the hospital, looking for a ride,
who should drive up but Sarah," Daniel continued. "We exchanged words. It wasn't pretty.
Today sure didn't turn out the way I thought it
would." He looked away from his brother and
out the window with a dazed look on his face.

Fred whistled aloud. He picked up the can of
beer and swallowed. When he finished, he put

the can back on the table, then he looked at Daniel and said, "You been through some stuff today haven't you, little brother?"

Daniel nodded his head. "You were right when you said I should've told Ruthie and the kids about the wedding and the baby," he admitted in a gruff tone of voice.

Daniel's cell phone rang again. It was Lenora. This time he flipped it open.

"Danny, where are you?" Lenora's shrill voice sounded loud in his ear.

"I'm at Fred's."

"I thought you said you were coming back to the hospital. Well, are you?"

"I'll be there, just a little later than I planned. A family emergency came up."

Fred went into his bedroom to give his brother some privacy.

"This is our wedding day and our son's birthday. Nothing should come before me and Damon on this day. What happened? Did your precious Ruth call and ask you to come over? Is she the emergency?" Lenora's voice indicated she didn't believe him.

Daniel could hear Damon crying in the background. "I don't have time to get into that now. Let's talk about this when I come back to the hospital. Take care of my son, I'll see you later." He closed the phone thoughtfully.

Fred came back inside the room. "So wha'cha gonna do, Dan?"

Daniel stroked his beard. "I don't know. This was supposed to be the happiest day of my life and now my life seems to be falling apart. I didn't think I would ever feel guilty about being happy, but I am. Sarah told me when Ruth found out about my marriage and the baby, she became hysterical."

Fred took a sip of his beer. "You know why, don't you? She still loves you. A blind man could see that from the way she acted on Christmas day. Man you shoulda at least told Sarah 'bout Lenora. You know she would've told Ruth, and you wouldn't be on the hot seat now."

"I said you were right. What more can I say? I messed up, okay?" Daniel said, impatiently. His cell phone sounded again. Ruth's number was on the caller ID this time. "I swear when it rains it pours. This is Ruth's number, but I'm not going to answer it because I don't feel like listening to her getting on my case."

"Maybe you should answer it, Dan." Fred said earnestly. "She knows by now that you're married, so she wouldn't be calling you unless it was an emergency."

The telephone stopped ringing and Lenora's taunts flashed through Daniel's mind. "Ruth and I are divorced. I've moved on, and she has to do the same."

"I've said it before and I'll say it again, you're making another mistake, Daniel. You know Ruth, and that she wouldn't call you if she didn't have any other choice. Maybe you should call her back."

Daniel looked at his brother with an annoyed expression on his face. His tone became confrontational. "This is my life, not yours. I'll call Ruth when I get around to it. Not before, and not because you told me to."

"Suit yourself, Dan. I have a date coming over soon, so why don't you run on back to see your wife and son. Do what you have to do." Fred stood up abruptly and strode to his bedroom.

Daniel could tell from his brother's stiff back, he wasn't happy with him any more than his other family members were right now. He stood and walked out the door, and took the bus to Lenora's apartment since Fred didn't own a car.

Daniel returned to Northwestern Memorial at eight o'clock that evening. He walked into Lenora's room. She and Damon were asleep. He remembered to bring her suitcase along with him. He put it inside the closet. He also stowed the box containing Damon's blue quilted car seat on the top shelf. When he finished his tasks, Daniel sat in the chair next to his wife's bed and sighed loudly.

Lenora stirred and looked up. She shaded her eyes with her hand. "Oh, I see you managed to make it back. I thought you'd forgotten about us. What was the first family's emergency?"

He stood up, walked over to the cot, and peeped at his son. "Aw Nora, don't be like that." Daniel walked back to the bed and kissed Lenora's cheek, then sat on the side of the bed and told her about his conversation with Sarah.

She listened to his tale with a bored look on her face. *If he thinks I feel sorry for him, or his other kids, then he's a fool. I'm sure Ruth is going to have one emergency after the other at home, and she'll call him all the time needing his help.* Her faced hardened like a piece of stone. *It's not going to happen. Daniel is mine and he's going to stay mine.*

"You should've told one of your kids about our engagement and the baby. What are Damon and I, your dirty little secret?"

"Of course not," Daniel denied vehemently. "We were engaged while I was still married, and I couldn't tell my kids that. Sarah was the only one still speaking to me at the time. Ruth has her hands full taking care of her sick brother. I just don't want to upset things now. Speaking of Ruth, she called me earlier. I'm going to go outside and call her back." He stood up.

"You just got here!" Lenora screamed. She shifted her body and cringed from pain. "You haven't even asked me how I'm feeling and now you're off calling your ex-wife. The woman you complained about like she was the plague. This is our wedding day. Don't go, Daniel, you can call her tomorrow."

He stared at her as if he were seeing her for the first time. She'd just had a baby; he knew she was hurting and her hormones were running amok, but there could also be an emergency at Ruth's house that he needed to be aware of.

Lenora glared at him, but he stood rooted to the spot. He hesitated and then sat back down. "You're right. Whatever has happened can wait until tomorrow. Now, why don't you get some rest, Nora? I'll be here until we go home tomorrow."

"That's another thing, Daniel. The apartment is

too small. We need to start looking for somewhere else to live. I was thinking the suburbs might be a good place to raise a child. Someplace like Lansing or Lynwood. I heard you can buy a home in those suburbs for far less money than you'd pay for in the city. What do you think?" She looked at him expectantly.

"I think we can talk about that when we get home. Damon isn't even a week old yet. It's not like he needs that much room. We'll come up with something when that time comes, although I don't plan to move out of Chicago. Did you forget I work for the City and that I'm required to live here?"

Her cat eyes seemed to glitter brightly. "There are ways to get around that. Surely, you don't believe everyone employed by Chicago actually lives in the City?"

Damon began whimpering. Then he yelled at full steam, demonstrating his lungs worked just fine. Daniel looked at Lenora helplessly.

"Do you want me to bring him to you?"

She looked at Daniel. "No, he's either wet or hungry. After raising three children, I know you know how to change a diaper and feed a baby. And since I'm not breastfeeding, you can take care of your child, Daddy." Lenora lay down in the bed and pulled the covers over her arms.

Daniel walked over to the cot. When his older children were born, he didn't take an active role in their care. He considered raising children a woman's job. The only times he tended to Sarah and DJ were when Ruth was away from home. He participated even less in Naomi's care.

He picked up Damon in his arms, admiring his newest child. *He's a big baby, bigger than my other children.* Tiny tufts of brown curly hair covered Damon's skull. His complexion was light like Lenora's. Daniel noticed the tips of his ears were a shade darker.

Damon scrunched up his face and yelled loudly. Daniel laid him back in his bed and checked along the corners of his diaper. He needed to be changed. Daniel looked around the room and spied a stack of disposable diapers on the counter. He walked over to them, took one and some wipes, then changed Damon's diaper. Once he was finished, the baby stared up at him.

Daniel stared down at his child, then he picked him up and sat in the chair and held Damon in his arms. The baby opened his eyes and cooed at his father. "That's my little man. You got some kind of timing boy, born on me and your mother's wedding day." Daniel grabbed the baby's hand and pressed it to his face. "One day when you're older, we going to have a talk about the sports teams in Chicago. We got the White Sox, the Cubs, the Bears, and my personal favorite, the Bulls. I'll have to tell you about how your mother and I met at the Bulls basketball game . . ."

Lenora listened to her husband bond with their son. She closed her eyes with a satisfied smile on her face.

Chapter Forty-three

Later that Saturday night tears streamed from Ruth's eyes as she paced back and forth outside Naomi's bedroom door. Ezra came out of his bedroom and forcibly took her by the arms and led her back to the living room.

"When they're ready, Sarah and Naomi will talk to you. Sarah has to tell her daughter what happened. Give her space, Ruth."

"What's happened is my fault," she wailed. "I should've kept my mouth shut. We made a pact years ago we'd never speak about what happened to Sarah, and what happens? I'm the one to tell all."

The doorbell sounded and Ezra stood up to open it. Alice rushed into the house. She sat on the sofa next to her friend and Ruth explained what happened.

Meanwhile, back in Naomi's bedroom, the young girl still sat unmoving on her bed. Sarah knelt before her daughter and took her cold hands in her own.

"Naomi, please listen to me," Sarah begged. "I know what you learned has been a terrible shock to you. I could see it on your face when I walked in the house. The family did what we thought was best years ago. We thought we were protecting you." It had taken time before Sarah finally persuaded Naomi to open up and tell her what she overheard her mother and Ezra talking about.

Naomi looked at Sarah with deadened eyes. "Who was it best for, Sarah? You? Mama? No, I mean my Grandmother, or my Great-Grandparents? Do you know how messed up it was for me to learn my birth was the result of a rape? I just can't bear it." Her trembling mouth snapped shut.

"Listen to me," Sarah urged Naomi. "Only two people really know what happened the night you were conceived. You're about to become the third. I planned to tell Mama and Daddy what really happened one day. Naomi, I wasn't raped." She felt lightheaded, like all the air was being sucked from her body.

Naomi looked at her incredulously. Her body shivered violently as her teeth chattered uncontrollably. "What do you mean you weren't raped?"

"I began experimenting with sex at an early age with Brian. He's your Father. Mama and Daddy were having marital problems at the time, and she was focused on making things right with Daddy. She kind of lost sight of me and my activities at the time. I'd started my period when I was twelve years old. I was very physically developed for my age, and Mama and I had already had the sex talk. Brian and I had known each other since we were children growing up together at the temple. We started sneaking and fooling around. One thing led to another, and I became pregnant."

"I heard Mama tell Uncle Ezra you were raped. You mean my Father isn't a rapist?" Naomi's voice sounded tiny. She leaned forward and stared at Sarah intently, like her life depended on her answer.

"Yes, that's exactly what I'm saying. That's the main reason why I didn't go away to college, so I could stay here and be with you."

Naomi's eyes narrowed. She tilted her head to the side. "You're not saying this to make me feel better, are you?" She held her breath.

"I swear by all that is holy, I'm telling you the truth. I never told Mama or Daddy the truth about what happened when you were conceived. I've always read a lot, and as a child, I had an overactive imagination. When I missed two periods, I figured out I was having a baby. So I made up a story about being attacked on the way home from school. By the time Mama found out that I was pregnant, it was months later and no one could verify the validity of my story. To add credence to my story, there was also a rapist loose in Chatham at the time, so that added more credibility to my story."

Naomi didn't reply for a while as her brain processed the new information Sarah had given her. Sarah sat on the floor at her feet, relieved that the truth had come out, but sad at the way Naomi had learned it.

"I always thought our family was perfect, especially because Bishop and our forefathers are ministers. From an early age, all Queen preached was how we had to always do the right thing and lead by example for the congregation. Now I'm finding out that we're no better than anybody else." Naomi shook her head from side to side.

"No one is better than anyone else, Nay-Nay. That's what I used to call you when you were born. Mama let me pick your name. I hated being a minister's granddaughter when I was a teenager. No one invited me to what I thought was the best parties because everyone knew my Grandfather was a big time Minister. He used to come to school sometimes and check on my grades. Since the church has a radio program on Sunday evenings, it seemed everyone in Chicago knew who my grandfather was. He was in high esteem with the other famous Chicago ministers at the time like Maceo Woods, Clay Evans, and others."

Naomi shook her head wearily from side to side. "Queen always made it seem like we were better than everyone else. I always thought being a Christian and part of a minister's family meant you didn't have any problems because you were doubly blessed. Remember Queen used to say because of Bishop and her father, we were guaranteed a place in heaven?"

Sarah's shoulders slumped with relief. Maybe Naomi was listening to her, and with God's help, she could get through to her daughter. She rose from the floor and sat on the bed next to Naomi. Then she took her hands in her own.

"I believe on judgment day when we face God, he'll see what's in our hearts and decide our fate according to our deeds and hopefully the good ones will outweigh the bad. We, as human beings, are imperfect. Some of us are going to screw up at times, or circumstances will arise that test our faith.

"And even when our way seems most dim, and we can't find our way to the light, God will step in and show us the way. I didn't always think that way, but as I became older and experienced more of life, I found that to be the case. I made a vow, after Mama and Daddy decided to adopt you, that I would try to be the best Christian I know how."

"So, does Brian know he's my father? And did he go along with the adoption thing too?" Naomi asked. She had a puzzled look on her face.

"Yes he knows the truth. But keep in mind we were just children when you were born. I was fourteen and he was fifteen. We were just glad the truth didn't come out then. But I knew that it would one day, I just didn't think it would be today," Sarah sighed, audibly.

This had been one of the most trying days in her life. First there was the news of Daniel's marriage and his new child, and now Naomi's crisis.

A tap sounded at the door. "I know that's Mama," Sarah said. "I think we should let her in so I can tell her the truth. What do you think?"

Naomi shook her head. "Not yet."

Sarah stood and opened the door. Ruth nearly collapsed as she stood in the doorway. "May I come in?" she asked.

"Give us a little more time," Sarah answered. She closed the door and leaned against the wall. "Naomi, I'm so sorry you had to learn the truth that way. I wish I could go back in time and relive that part of my life over. I hope in time you'll forgive me, and you'll continue to consider me as your big sister. Mama has raised you and we can't take that from her."

"I feel strange." Naomi rubbed her arms briskly, like she was experiencing a chill. "Like I'm trapped in a maze and I don't know where or who I am. Yesterday, I was Naomi Wilcox, the daughter of Daniel and Ruth, who got a divorce. Today, I find out that I'm really their granddaughter, and that you and Brian are my parents. My mind is sagging in the middle. All this information, and all that has happened since I went to college, is too much for me to comprehend. Daddy left Mama, and later I find out we have a gay Uncle we never knew about because Bishop and Queen disowned him. My life is so weird right now." She began sobbing.

Sarah sat on the bed and held her daughter in her arms as she cried.

Eventually Ruth returned from outside the bedroom door to the living room when she realized Sarah and Naomi were still talking. She sat unmoving in her chair. Alice, who'd arrived thirty minutes ago, had given up trying to talk to her.

Ezra wasn't feeling well, so he had retired to his bedroom.

"How is Ezra doing?" Alice asked Ruth. She looked troubled. "He looks like he's losing more weight."

Ruth glanced toward the doorway and said distractedly, "He hasn't been doing well lately. I wish I had called you this afternoon and came to your house to see you instead of dumping on my brother. Then none of this would've happened. Naomi never would've overheard us talking." She began wringing her shaking hands together.

"When is Ezra's next doctor's appointment?" Alice asked, trying to distract Ruth from her troubles.

"Tuesday. I can see that he's fading. But he's still trying to comfort me while my life is falling apart," Ruth moaned.

She told Alice about Queen's telephone call around three o'clock that afternoon and Daniel's new bundle of joy.

"So, Daniel got married again? I'm surprised. I would've thought he would just play the field, instead it sounds like he got played." Alice nodded. "I bet you anything he married a younger woman. These young women today are twenty times more aggressive than we used to be. Danny's goose is cooked. He'll wish in time he had stayed with you. Bet on it!"

A grimace flitted across Ruth's face. "My brain knows what you're saying is probably right." She put her hand on her chest. "But my heart doesn't realize it yet. It hurts me to know I've been discarded like yesterday's news."

"In time you'll sigh with relief. Daniel is going to have his hands full," Alice predicted. "You watch and see what I tell you."

The women turned to face the hallway as they heard the door to Naomi's bedroom open.

Chapter Forty-four

Ruth nearly passed out like she'd been given a reprieve when Sarah and Naomi walked into the living room. She noticed that Sarah and Naomi's eyes were red. Naomi shot her mother a weak smile, and Ruth was so relieved that she nearly fell out of her chair. Sarah, on the other hand, looked serious as a heart attack.

Alice stood. "I can see that the three of you need to talk. I'm going to check on Ezra before I go home. I know whatever has happened today, that you three can resolve it." She squeezed Ruth's arm and walked to Ezra's room.

"Naomi, I'm so sorry you overheard me. I would cut out my tongue before I'd intentionally hurt you," Ruth apologized. "I had some distressing news, and it loosened my tongue."

"I'm still upset, Mama. But Sarah explained to me what happened. She needs to tell you something though." Naomi sat on the sofa next to Ruth who hugged her.

Sarah sat on the chair opposite Ruth and Naomi. She raked her fingers through her hair. "I don't know where to start." She fell silent. Then she began her tale again for her mother, the same information she had told Naomi earlier.

Ruth's mouth fell open several times. She wanted to interrupt her daughter, but held her peace.

When Sarah finished speaking, Ruth was stunned. Who would have thought that Sarah and Brian would've kept such an inconceivable secret for so long? She could see that Sarah, too, was suffering. Her eyes bore deeply into Ruth's. Ruth was speechless and the room became silent.

Naomi sat with her face downcast, periodically looking between her sister and mother.

What Sarah omitted deliberately from the story she told Ruth and Naomi, was that she had told Queen the truth about the circumstances of her baby's conception, and her grandmother advised her to use the rape story. Queen explained to her how Bishop, Ruth, and Daniel would have a hard time accepting her willingness to have sexual relations with a boy at such a young age. Queen told her granddaughter no one else needed to know, and that it would remain their secret.

The relationship between Ruth and her mother was just beginning to mend, mainly because Queen now visited Ezra on a regular basis. And Sarah knew if she divulged the truth of the events from eighteen years ago, it might cause a rift between them that might never be repaired.

"I hate you went through all of that alone," Ruth said to Sarah. She sounded heartbroken. "You should've told me what really happened."

"I thought if I told you and Daddy what really happened, that Daddy might've made me give the baby up for adoption. Though I was young at the time, I still wanted my daughter to grow up with me. I know what I did was wrong, and I ask the Lord everyday to forgive me for my sins."

Ruth nodded. "You're probably right. Daniel probably would've made those demands and more. But whatever happens to you, Naomi, or DJ, I want you to be honest with me, and tell me about your predicaments. I believe we're strong enough of a family to face them. Maybe we weren't as strong years ago, but our faith in the Lord has been strengthened, and we can sustain any obstacles thrown our way."

"I promise I won't keep any major secrets from you from now on," Sarah vowed. Naomi nodded.

"I imagine that caused a strain between you and Brian?" Ruth inquired.

"It sure did," Sarah admitted. "He's always felt we should tell everyone the truth, including Naomi. But as I told Naomi, you're her mother. You raised her, and that will never change."

A warm glow suffused Ruth's body, and she felt a sense of relief. "Naomi, what do you want? I'd like to think I'm a big enough person to share you with your biological mother. Of course, no one has to know but the immediate family." She held her breath.

Naomi rose from the sofa and she turned to Ruth. "Can't this family for once just be honest? Do whatever you want. I'm going to bed." She walked angrily to her bedroom and slammed the door.

"This is terrible. I feel so helpless." Ruth shook her head sadly. She looked at Sarah. "What do you want to do?"

"I think we need to sleep on it. I don't know what to do at this point. Naomi indicated we should just keep doing what we've been doing all along, and now it looks like she's changed her mind. Teenagers—they're so fickle, and Naomi has always been high strung. Her emotions are probably see-sawing right now—and she doesn't know what she wants. The true circumstances of her birth have probably shocked her to say the least. Emotionally, I don't know if she's up to going back to school just yet. Maybe one of us should call the school Monday and request a leave of absence. Let's give her a little time to see how she feels and take it from there. I feel we should play things by ear for now."

"Did you tell her about Daniel's marriage and baby?" Ruth asked. Sorrow blanketed her eyes.

"No. I thought that was a conversation for another day. Maybe we should talk to her old therapist, the one she saw a few years ago when she was experiencing self-esteem issues. Between the parentage issue, Daddy's remarrying, and his having another child so soon, she's going to have a lot to cope with at one time." Sarah shivered with fatigue. She yawned. "I'm tired myself. I'm going to bed. Tomorrow is another day and it'll give us a fresh perspective on things. We can discuss them in the morning."

"I'm so exhausted that I can barely think straight myself. I'll call Dr. Ryan tomorrow or after we see how Naomi feels in the morning. Don't be too hard on yourself, Sarah. You were a child faced with an adult situation." She stood and took her in her arms. "Weeping endures for a night, but joy comes in the morning. We, as a family, are going to have our joy."

"I hope so, Mama. God knows I do." Sarah walked upstairs to her room.

Ruth checked the telephone caller ID and saw that Daniel had called her back. His consciousness got the best of him and he was finally able to escape from Lenora after she was given a dosage of pain medicine. After she finally went to sleep, Daniel crept outside the hospital and called his ex-wife. Ruth knew that if Daniel hadn't just got married that day, she wouldn't have called him to give him a heads up on the latest events. But she realized forlornly that she had been relegated to her ex-husband from a legal standpoint, but not in her heart. All of her talk about moving on with lives was just that, talk.

Until today, she had held out a faint hope that one day they would be reunited. She wiped away a tear from the corner of her eye and turned off the lamp in the living room. Before she called it a day, she stopped to check on Ezra.

When she passed Naomi's room, she raised her hand as if to knock on the door, then quickly dropped it and walked into her own room.

After she showered and put on her nightclothes, she wrapped her hair. With her hands clasped together, and on bended knees, Ruth said her prayers. When she was finished, she rubbed her eyes and reached for her Bible from the night-stand. She opened it and turned to the 27th Psalm, the Fifth Verse. *For in the time of trouble he shall hide me in his pavilion; in the secret place of his tabernacle he shall hide me; he shall set me high on a rock.*

Chapter Forty-five

Lenora wrapped Damon in a sea blue cotton receiving blanket and sat him in the carrier, which lay on the hospital bed. Daniel had gone to the parking lot to bring the car around to the front of the hospital. A nurse and orderly walked into the room with a wheelchair. Lenora picked up the carrier, sat down on the chair, and the orderly rolled Lenora down the long winding hallway. She held the white plastic carrier with navy blue quilting on her lap. Damon was snuggled inside with a pacifier in his mouth. When they walked outside the building, Lenora pointed to Daniel's car. Daniel got out of the vehicle and opened the back passenger door. The nurse walked over to the car to verify and check on a clipboard that the car seat complied with state regulations.

Daniel fastened Damon securely in the back seat of the car inside the car seat. He noticed Lenora frowning as she lifted her legs inside the vehicle.

"What's wrong? Are your stitches itching?" he asked her.

She turned around to look at Damon. She pulled the blanket off his face. "No, my stitches aren't hurting, don't you dare jinx me." She looked around the interior of the car. "This Mustang is too small. It was fine for just the two of us to ride in, but maybe you should think about trading it in for something bigger. A sports car is hardly a family vehicle."

He put the key in the ignition and turned on the car. "That ain't happening. I'm not trading this baby in for anything. I've worked too hard, tons of overtime hours, to pay for my black beauty. If you feel we need a family car, then trade in your Toyota Celica for a mini-van. That makes more sense anyway. After all, the baby will be with you most of the time."

"We'll discuss it later," she said, sweetly. *He isn't going to drive a chick magnet while I get stuck with a miniature bus. This car has to go.* Daniel's license plate read BGDADY1.

"Did I tell you that Mama is coming to stay with us for a few days? She's going to help me take care of Damon. That's what I meant when I said the apartment is too small. We're going to constantly be on top of each other."

"I can always go stay with Fred for a few days," Daniel offered and peered at his wife and back at the road.

Lenora cut her eyes at him. "If you don't want my mother to stay with us, then you can take care of Damon yourself." She looked out the window. Her lips were pursed together like she'd sucked on a lemon.

"I was just kidding," he said, cajolingly. He reached over and patted Lenora's knee. "Of course I'm grateful Glenda will be staying with us. I know this is your first baby and you need your mother's help. Chill out."

Lenora's head swiveled on her neck as she turned to look at him. She sucked her teeth and pushed his hand away from her leg.

"Do we need to stop at a store? Is there anything we need to pick up before we go home?" he asked.

"No, I called Felicia and she's going shopping for me. The rest of the family will be over later."

He sighed aloud as he gunned the car's motor. Damon's body twisted in the car seat.

Lenora glowered at Daniel. "Do you have to make so much noise?"

He whispered softly, "Couldn't your people wait for a few days before coming over? It would be nice if we had some time to ourselves."

Damon whimpered from the back seat. Lenora leaned over and put his pacifier back in his mouth. "No, today is fine. They're my family and this is a big event for us. It's not my fault you're ashamed of me and Damon," she said, trying to make Daniel feel guilty. "You won't have to lift a finger to do anything. My aunts are bringing dinner and meals for us to freeze. So you don't have to cook for a while. Let's enjoy the pampering while we can, because when Mama goes home, we're going to be on our own."

"I guess it's okay. Your brothers aren't coming, are they? Maybe LaQuita will stay home too."

"Daniel, I don't believe you said that." Lenora's voice broke up and she sounded like her feelings were hurt. "Of course my brothers and sisters are coming to welcome the new arrival to our family."

"Then I guess I'll have to grin and bear it. Maybe I'll call Fred and see if he wants to stop by. He's not too hot on kids though." He turned to back the car into a parking space in front of their apartment.

He took the baby out of the car seat while Lenora slowly maneuvered her body out of the car.

Glenda opened the door before Daniel could insert the key in the lock. She took Damon from her son-in-law's arms, sat him on the sofa, and removed the blue blanket to examine her new grandchild.

"Mom!" Lenora said, surprised to see her mother already at the apartment. She carefully walked over to the sofa and sat down next to her mother. "We didn't expect you until later. What are you doing here?"

"Felicia gave me her spare key last night. So I thought I'd come over early this morning and surprise you and make sure the apartment was clean. Sure enough, it was a little messy. I straightened up a bit while I was waiting for you to come home. You don't mind, do you?"

"Of course not. Thank you."

"Me and your Daddy came over this morning and put up the baby bed. Say Lenora, do you mind if LaQuita and Kente stay here with us too?"

"Whatever for? This place is too small for all of us as it is." She shook her head warningly at her mother.

"That's what I told her, but I thought I'd check with you anyway." Glenda turned her attention back to her new grandson.

Daniel walked into the room. "Check on what?" he asked Glenda.

"Nothing," Lenora answered, quickly. "Daniel, did you see the baby's room yet? Maybe we should go take a peep?"

"I think Ernest did a good job of setting up the baby bed. Although you need to show him what wall you want him to put it on." Glenda interjected.

"No, I haven't been in the nursery yet. Let's go take a look." Daniel and Lenora walked to the room. They gave Ernest their approval regarding his work so far. Daniel stayed in the room to instruct his father-in-law where to place the crib. Lenora walked back to the living room and sat gingerly on the couch.

"I don't understand why Daniel hadn't already set up the baby's room weeks ago. When did he plan on doing it? You were due any day. Are you going to breastfeed Damon?" Glenda rocked the infant in her arms.

"No. Felicia should be here any minute with formula. I brought a couple of cans with me from the hospital." Lenora said with a frown on her face as she tried to sit in a comfortable position. "Isn't he the cutest baby you've ever seen?"

Glenda counted on her fingers. "He's the seventh cutest baby I've seen after you, your brothers and sisters, and Kente," she teased Lenora.

Glenda and her daughter laughed together

loudly. The doorbell sounded. Daniel walked out of the bedroom. "I'll get it."

Felicia and Reggie stood at the door. Ten minutes later, Lenora's sisters, brothers, and nephew arrived.

Daniel proudly presented the men with cigars, encircled with blue ribbons.

"Can me and Jabari have one, Mr. Wilcox?" Jamal asked as the men began lighting the cigars.

Ernest replied, after he puffed the Cuban cigar. "This is a special occasion, give 'em one just this time."

"You guys need to go out on the patio and smoke," Lenora ordered the men. Her hands were on her hips. "I don't want you smoking those stinking things in my house around the baby and smelling up my house."

"Did you bring your camera?" Glenda asked Felicia.

"Of course I did. Reggie, would you get the camera out the bag for me? Give Jabari the key to the car so he can bring the bags inside." She bent down and cooed at her nephew. She took him from Glenda's arms. "He's so adorable," she proclaimed, smoothing one of his red curls, which refused to lie down.

"See, that's what I'm talking 'bout," Lenora said to Felicia. "Can you believe Mama had the nerve to say Damon wasn't the cutest baby she's ever seen?"

"I want to take a few pictures of you, Daniel, and the baby. You're not too tired, are you?" she asked Lenora as Reggie handed her the camera.

"Just hurry up. My stomach is starting to hurt

again. I need to take more painkillers. Daniel!" she yelled, "come in here. Felicia wants to take pictures of us with the baby."

Daniel and Ernest came out of the second bedroom, which had been converted from Lenora's office to the nursery. Lenora and Daniel sat on the sofa. She held Damon as Felicia took many pictures of the new family.

Felicia said to Daniel, "You need to buy a camcorder, that way you can record every event of Damon's life."

"That's a good idea," he said. "I'll have to check one out."

"Those Sony ones are sweet," Reggie added. "I want to get one myself."

"I'm going to lay down now," Lenora said. She held Damon towards his father.

Glenda stood up and hurried over to her daughter. "No, give him to me. I want to spend some more time getting to know my new grandson. Felicia, go and help your sister get settled in bed. Ernest and Daniel, you two need to finish up the nursery. Quita, you and the boys go in the kitchen and fix sandwiches." She walked over to the chair by the window. She laid Damon on her chest, sniffed and exhaled. "I love that baby smell." She kissed his tiny hand.

Kente's eyes were wide as marbles. "Ganny, baby." He pointed at Damon. He stood at his grandmother's side, enthralled by the newest family member.

Felicia went into the bedroom with Lenora. She took a pink gown out of the drawer and handed it to her sister. Lenora moved cautiously on the bed.

Felicia unpacked Lenora's suitcase and took Damon's belongings to the nursery. When she returned to the room, Lenora had changed clothes and was lying under the bedspread.

"I have to hand it to you, Lenora, you've made big time changes in your life last year and this year. You married the man of your dreams and had a baby to cement the marriage, all on the same day. You go, girl." She smiled as she sat on the end of the bed.

"You know me, when I want something, I go for it," Lenora said, smugly.

"May heaven help whoever gets in your way," Felicia couldn't help adding.

Lenora's chin was propped on her fist. "You and Reggie should have a child. That way, our kids could grow up together. I hate to admit it, but I got a little nervous watching Kente with Damon."

"You know you wrong," Felicia laughed. "We'll have some influence over Kente's upbringing. You act like we have a juvenile delinquent in the making."

"Humph," Lenora snorted, "there's no telling how he's going to turn out with LaQuita and Rashon as his parents. But I'm serious about what I said. I think you and Reggie should have a baby. You're so good with children, and you'd be a natural."

Felicia sighed. "If only it were that easy. I've been trying to get pregnant since last year with no luck. I have an appointment with a fertility specialist next week. So keep your fingers crossed."

"I didn't know that," Lenora exclaimed, sitting

up quickly. Her face became clouded with pain. "Why didn't you say something?"

"Girl, you know Reggie likes to keep our business between us. But after seeing Damon, it made me realize how much I really want to have my husband's baby. Then my life will be complete."

Daniel walked into the room carrying the baby. "I thought you might be missing this little fellow." He handed the baby to Lenora. "Glenda wants to know if you need anything."

"No, not now. But you can bring the bassinet in here. Are you and Daddy almost done with the nursery?" She cuddled Damon in her arms.

"Yeah, give us another half hour and we should be finished. We just need to setup the changing table and re-arrange the bed and dresser. Oh yeah, I still need to assemble the toy chest. It's a good thing I painted the room a few months ago. Well, holler if you need something," Daniel said, turning to go back into the nursery.

Lenora wiggled her finger for him to come over. She kissed his lips. "Thank you for giving me my beautiful son. I love you, boo."

He lifted his eyebrows lecherously. "It was my pleasure pretty lady."

"You two are sickening," Felicia said, rolling her eyes at the couple. "Still, I envy you. Was childbirth horrible? Do you want to have more kids?"

"Girl, childbirth was a cross between the worst tooth and tummy ache you could possibly imagine. Still it was worth it." She laid the baby by her side. Her voice dropped to a whisper. "Don't tell anyone this, but I've decided to get it over with, having children I mean. When the doctor gives me the green light to resume sex, I'm going to try and get pregnant again. Maybe by that time, you'll be pregnant too."

Felicia's eyes widened. "Lenora, you're simply scandalous. Why do I have a feeling you haven't discussed your plan with Daniel?"

Lenora smirked wickedly at her sister. "There are some things a man doesn't need to know. This is one of them."

Daniel walked into the room carrying the bassinet. "You need to get some rest, Lenora. Don't overdo it."

She stretched her arms upward and cringed with pain. "You're right. I'm going to do just that. Put Damon in the bassinet and turn off the light on your way out."

Felicia stood. "I'll be back later." She and Daniel left the bedroom to join the family members in the kitchen.

Chapter Forty-six

The Sunday following Daniel's wedding, a spiritually, and physically weary Ruth stood in front of Naomi's bedroom. Her face looked wizened, and she felt wracked with indecision. She knocked on the door. Neither of her daughters answered. Ruth twisted the knob, pushed the door, and walked inside the room.

Sarah lay huddled on the left side of the bed. Naomi was burrowed beneath her body. Sarah stirred. She looked up and saw Ruth. She smiled and put her finger to her lips. She removed Naomi's arm from around her waist and rose from the bed. Sarah and Ruth walked into the kitchen.

After Sarah sat at the table, Ruth handed her a cup of coffee. Ruth sat in the chair across from her daughter. "Are you going to church today?" she asked.

"I think I'm going to stay home." Sarah took a sip of coffee. "I checked on Uncky earlier. I have a feeling this isn't going to be one of his good days. I also want to talk to Naomi some more. I called Brian last night, and he's going to come over and try to talk to her."

"Has Naomi been up this morning? How is she feeling? I know what you told her was a lot for her to grasp. I feel like her finding out is my fault. Please forgive me for opening my mouth, Sarah." Ruth's face showed that she was clearly frustrated.

"Mama, we just have to have faith that in the long run everything will work out for the best. I overheard Naomi crying last night when I came downstairs for a glass of water around one o'clock this morning. I went to her room to try and comfort her, and I ended up spending the rest of the night with her."

Ruth felt a coil of jealousy spiral in her heart. In the past, whenever her youngest child was troubled about something, she always came to Ruth with her problems. What was going to happen now? Did Sarah want to take her place as Naomi's mother?

Sarah saw a glimpse of the green-eyed monster cross Ruth's face. She set the cup on the table and took her mother's hand. "No, I'm not trying to replace you, Mama. Not that I could anyway. You're truly an amazing woman. What I really want is for Naomi to feel good about herself. I think if Brian talks to her, that will help ease the situation. I told her emphatically last night that you're her mother. You've earned the right to that title. But I still need to work on reassuring her that all of us will get through this."

Ruth felt a rush of relief surge through her body. "I agree with everything you've said. I just feel so useless. Once we get through this disaster, then we'll have to tell her about Daniel. I wish he had been honest with you all up front. DJ is going to have a fit, and Naomi won't be too far behind him."

"Well, I let him have it," she said, harshly. "I went to the hospital after you told me the news." Sarah dropped her eyes to the table. Then she looked up at Ruth, agony spewing from her eyes. "I feel like Daddy has lost his mind."

"I suppose if he's starting another family, then his bride must be fairly young," Ruth said with a melancholy tone in her voice.

"It wouldn't surprise me to find out that Daddy's wife is much younger than he is. What about you? Are you going to church today, Mama?"

"I think so. Unless you need me to do something . . ."

"I can hold down the fort until you return." Sarah smiled and stood up. "Go get your spiritual food, and bring home leftovers for me."

"I will."

The cordless telephone rang. Ruth snatched it off the table and glanced at the Caller ID unit. "It's your father," Ruth said to Sarah after she answered the telephone. "I'll take it in my room." She plodded down the hallway to her bedroom and placed the telephone to her ear.

"How are you feeling today, Daniel? I hear congratulations are in order. What did you have, a son or daughter?" she asked him.

"Thanks Ruth, we have a son," Daniel said. He

felt relieved that Ruth hadn't blessed him out. "We named him Damon. And before you get on my case about keeping my plans so hush-hush, I admit, I should've told the kids what was going on. I hope it hasn't caused too much of a problem."

"You're right. You should've said something to them. But that wasn't the reason I called." Ruth explained the latest emergency.

Daniel listened intently as he ex-wife spoke. Then Damon began crying in the background. "Hold on a minute, Ruth. I'm going to take the baby's bottle into the bedroom to Lenora."

So that's his wife's name. Her spirits sunk lower than an ebb tide. She could tell by the way his voice seemed to caress Lenora's name that he truly loved his wife.

Daniel didn't return for ten minutes. Ruth held the phone to her ear impatiently before hanging up. It promptly rang again.

"I'm sorry about that interruption. You mean to tell me, Sarah and Brian lied about Sarah being raped? I'll be doggone," Daniel said, incredulity was overt in his voice.

"Yes, apparently that's exactly what happened. But we should feel blessed that our child wasn't molested. I just feel bad that she didn't confide in me the truth about the circumstances of her pregnancy. Maybe we could've handled the situation differently."

"They were so young back then. Neither of them were thinking straight, and I'm sure they were scared of facing the consequences of their actions. Sarah was barely fourteen," he said. "Though I don't know what we could've done differently. Still, you're right. It's a relief to find out Sarah wasn't raped. But, she should've told us the truth. How is Naomi taking the news?"

Ruth told him, "Not too good. And we haven't told her about your marriage and baby yet. I have a feeling she won't be going back to school this semester. Too much has happened for her to concentrate on studying."

"You're probably right. Do you think I should tell her myself?" he asked.

"Danny!" Lenora called from the bedroom, loud enough for Ruth to hear. "Would you help me to the bathroom?"

"Ruth, I'm going to have to call you back. Why don't you and Sarah discuss how I should handle breaking the news to Naomi, and I'll call you back today or tomorrow. You can let me know if you think I should tell Naomi, or if one of you should."

"I think you should definitely call DJ, and soon," Ruth suggested.

"Yeah, I will," he replied. He sounded distracted. "I'll call you back."

Ruth clicked off the cordless phone and walked into Ezra's room. The television was turned to a religious channel. The choir was singing, "On Christ The Solid Rock I Stand." The soaring three-part harmony sounded majestic. "How are you feeling today, brother?"

"Poorly," Ezra replied. His hands shook slightly.

Ruth looked at her brother anxiously. "Do you need to go to the hospital?"

"No, I don't feel that bad. Are you going to the temple?"

"I don't know." She pushed the ends of her hair under the scarf on her head. "I was thinking about going to church with Alice."

"Are you avoiding Queen?"

"Hmm, that's a thought. I truly don't feel like listening to her questions."

"She called earlier. She's going to bring me dinner after church, so you might want to stay out for a while. How is Miss Naomi feeling this morning?" Ezra coughed.

"I haven't talked to her yet. I pray in time she'll be fine."

"Sure she will. Like you said, she just needs some time to adjust to everything that has happened."

"Well, I'm going to get ready for church. I'll see you when I get back." She bent down and felt Ezra's forehead. "You feel warm, like you have a fever. Are you sure you don't need me to stay home with you?"

"Go on to church, sister. Sarah and Naomi will be here with me. We'll be fine."

"Okay." Ruth went back to her room. She dialed Alice's telephone number. "How about I pick you up for church this morning, and we go to your church instead of mine?" she asked her friend after she answered the phone.

"Sure. That's no problem.

Good. I'll meet you at your house in an hour."

Chapter Forty-seven

Damon's ear splitting wails raised a ruckus in the Wilcox household, so Daniel went into the bedroom, picked up his son, fed him a bottle of milk, and burped him. Then he changed his diaper, laid him in his bassinet, and put the pacifier in his mouth. Damon curled up in a fetal position and went back to sleep.

Lenora held the remote control in her hand and kept continuously changing the channel. She looked bored and glanced at Daniel, who sat in the chair next to the bed.

"Who were you talking to on your cell phone? Fred?"

"No, that was Ruth."

"Well what did she want? You would at least think she'd have the courtesy not to call you today. After all, technically we're still on our honeymoon," she complained.

"There was an emergency at her house and she wanted to talk to me about it. Trust me, Nora,

Ruth wouldn't call me unless she didn't have any other choice."

Now he's defending her. "So what happened that she needed to call you?" Lenora scratched her tummy.

Daniel explained how Naomi overheard Ruth and Ezra talking about the truth of Naomi's conception.

"What's the big deal? What do you mean by she learned the truth?"

Daniel explained how Sarah became pregnant at age fourteen, and how he and Ruth had adopted Naomi.

"You church people have more drama going on in your lives than us poor sinners," Lenora joked. "So you and Ruth perpetrated a lie and your youngest daughter is really your granddaughter?" Her eyebrows curved upward as she tried to suppress a snicker.

"Yeah, that's the case. And I know finding out the truth was a shock for Naomi."

"Why did Ruth need to call you? What are you going to do about it? Like Ruth and your daughter, you were a conspirator during the deception too."

"Ruth and Sarah think Naomi might need to go back into therapy. I pay Naomi's medical bills, and Ruth wanted to make sure the visits are covered by my insurance."

"You mean your daughter is crazy?" Lenora's eyes widened.

"No, of course not. Don't say that, Nora," Daniel scolded his wife. "She was in therapy a few years ago, and Ruth and I found out that Naomi, like a lot of teenaged girls, had self-esteem issues. Or at least that's what her therapist said. She's a little overweight, but she's still a pretty girl."

A vision of a young girl with a butterball figure popped into Lenora's head. She stifled a laugh. "It sounds like Ruth and Sarah have things under control. Why did they need to talk to you?"

"For one thing, she's still my daughter, and she still doesn't know about you and Damon. Ruth wanted to know if they should tell her, or if I would do it."

Lenora nodded. "What are you going to do?"

"I'm going to think about it and weigh my options."

She said, "Coward. Maybe when I'm back on my feet, we can invite your daughters over here so they can meet me and Damon."

"That's a good idea," Daniel replied, sweating. "I'm going into the living room to think."

"I'm going back to sleep." Lenora turned over in the bed.

When he went into the living room, Glenda was sitting on the sofa watching television. The cocktail table was messy—a plate, utensils, and food was spilt on it. Daniel had almost forgotten that his mother-in-law was still at the condo.

"Do you want to watch something? I can go in the room with Lenora," Glenda said gathering up the items on the table.

"No, you go ahead, Glenda. I need to make a phone call anyway." *Nora is right, there's no privacy in the house anywhere. I guess I'll go into the nursery and call Fred.*

"What's up, Daddy O? How are your bride

and Damon doing?" Fred asked, after he answered the phone.

Daniel could hear the television blasting in the background. Fred asked his brother to hold on a minute so he could turn the TV down.

"They're fine," Daniel answered when Fred returned to the telephone. "What's happening with you?"

"Nothing much. I'm just chillin'."

"How come you haven't been over to see your newest nephew yet?" Daniel didn't admit it, but it bothered him that his brother didn't make an effort to welcome his new arrival.

"I'll get over there soon. I just been tied up. Dan, he can't even talk or walk yet. He ain't going nowhere anytime soon. I'll be by there as soon I can to see him."

"I need to talk to you. Are you going to be home for a while?"

"You mean Lenora gave you permission to leave?" Fred asked, sardonically.

"Don't start that mess. I really need to run some things by you."

"Well, I'll be around until later this evening. On your way over, why don't you stop and pick up some chicken from Harold's."

"Okay, give me an hour and I'll be there."

"Later, man." *What has Daniel gotten himself into now?* Fred picked up the remote control and changed the station to an action and adventure movie.

Daniel arrived at Fred's house forty-five minutes later.

"You musta had a bug up your behind to get

here so fast. Wife and baby too much for ya?"
Fred took the bag of chicken from Daniel. "Um,
that smells good. Did you remember to bring
some beer?"

"Yeah, Fred, I picked up a six pack of beer,"
Daniel replied with a deadpan look on his face.

Fred tilted his head to the side and pointed to
Daniel. "Ya nose look bigger. Ms. Nora got it wide
open?" He spread his hands a few apart after he
set the bag on the kitchen table.

"Oh, you got jokes, huh?" He threw a can of
beer at Fred who caught it easily.

Fred looked down at his watch. "I thought
you'd be on lockdown at less for another week.
Did you bring a picture of the little rug rat
wit'cha?"

Daniel pulled a picture of Damon out of his
wallet. Reggie had printed out photographs from
his digital camera. Daniel handed the picture to
his brother.

Fred scrutinized the picture carefully. "He's
definitely Lenora's child. The jury is still out on
you."

"Don't start with that kind of talk. You know
that boy is mine," Daniel replied hotly. "Sarah
had the nerve to suggest the same thing."

After he helped himself to two chicken breasts
coated with hot sauce and catsup and fries, Fred
pushed the container towards Daniel.

"I guess I should tell you another emergency
came up last night. Ruth was babbling to Ezra
and she accidentally let it slip that Naomi is
Sarah's child."

Fred's mouth dropped open. "Say what? You

picked a good day to get married. I wonder if that's a message from God that He ain't happy with you dumping the minister's daughter."

"Stop fooling around, Fred," Daniel warned his brother, holding his hand out. "As it turned out, Sarah didn't really get raped. All these years of having everyone believe that's what really happened, Sarah was pregnant by Brian the whole time."

"Now that's deep stuff, but it's a good thing. My stomach still gets tied in knots all these years later at the thought of Sarah or any female in our family being violated." Fred scooped cole slaw inside his mouth with a plastic fork.

"But there's something about this new story that bothers me. How would Sarah at fourteen years old know to come up with a story like that?"

"What do you mean? Do you think Ruth was involved in whatever went down?" Fred asked, shaking his head. "I don't see Ruth going along with something like that."

"No, of course not. Ruth could never lie very well, even if her life depended on it."

"So what'cha saying?"

"I don't know for sure what happened, but I have my suspicions. Even though you didn't ask, Lenora and the baby are doing fine. Glenda is staying with us for a week and it's driving me crazy."

"Didn't Queen stay with y'all when Ruth had Sarah? I don't get it. What's the big deal?" Fred turned up the bottle of beer and gulped it down.

"I haven't really warmed up to my in-laws yet.

I'm trying though. Other than Felicia and Reggie, everyone else seems crazy as bedbugs."

Fred shook his head. *This don't sound good at all. That girl is just messing with his head.* "The Johnson's is just ghetto like me. What's the big deal?" Fred tried to josh with his brother.

"For one thing, those twin brothers of hers; they're nothing but junior gang bangers, especially Jamal. The other one, I always forget his name, is okay. The first time they came over for dinner after Nora and I hooked up, someone ripped me off—took fifty dollars from my stash in the bedroom. And they only got that much cause that was all I had in the house at the time. And I told you how the little sister, LaQuita, and her baby's daddy were in our bed. They were going at it like jackrabbits. Man, I ain't never seen a family act the way they do."

Fred laughed, then swallowed the wrong way. After he cleared his throat, he said, "Dude, you been spoiled. You done got used to them hoity-toity Claytons. You needed to come back to earth anyway. Most people ain't like Bishop and Queen."

"I hear you. Pass me one of those chicken wings," Daniel said, dubiously. "Ernest is always making snide remarks about the difference in me and Lenora's age. Glenda is okay, but she talks too much. And she's been hogging the television in the living room. It's a big screen model, I just bought it a month ago, and I can't even watch it."

Fred sucked a chicken bone and waved it in the air dismissively. "You know her peoples go with the territory. Lenora's who you wanted to be with, and she brought baggage with her, just like with Ruth. Although them church women can beat Glenda and her sisters hands down in the kitchen."

"I'm still worried about the twins. Jamal got arrested a couple of weeks ago. He was riding in a stolen car, and wouldn't you know it, there was dope in the car."

"Well, you ain't gotta worry 'bout him. The law will probably lock him down anyway."

"I guess you're right. Her people just give me the heebie-jeebies."

Fred pointed his white plastic fork at Daniel. "They ain't just Lenora's people no more, they Damon's folks too."

"Yeah, you're right. I hadn't thought about it that way." Daniel wiped his hands on the hot sauce stained napkin and took another swig of beer.

Chapter Forty-eight

It was midday Sunday. Sarah was wearing khaki pants and a white blouse. She sat on the floor with her legs crossed Indian style, next to Naomi's pink striped canopied bed. Naomi lay on the bed on her side facing the wall. Sarah asked Naomi twice if she wanted to talk to Brian and was disturbed by the young woman's lackadaisical response. She stood up and rubbed her hands on her hips. "I'll be in the kitchen if you feel like talking later."

Sarah walked to the kitchen and prepared a bowl of soup for Ezra. When she took it to his bedroom, her uncle didn't appear to have much of an appetite. "Just leave it on the tray. I'll eat later." He turned over in the bed and went back to sleep.

Ruth called later that afternoon to inform Sarah she was going to lunch with Alice and that she'd be home later.

Around three o'clock that afternoon, Brian brought Josh and Maggie home after the children spent the weekend with their father. After greeting the children, Sarah gave them permission to go upstairs to play their Nintendo game after they changed their clothes.

When Brian arrived, Sarah was seasoning chicken to prepare for dinner.

"So, how is she dealing with the news?" he asked as his eyes darted toward the hallway off the kitchen toward Naomi's room. The door was closed.

She shrugged her shoulders. "I thought she was doing fairly well until this morning. She's been quiet and has stayed in her room most of the day. Maybe you can talk to her."

"What do you want me to say to her, especially if she's in a bad mood? Maybe we should give her a little more time to adjust to the news?" Brian asked, optimistically. He didn't relish the idea of talking to Naomi. "Is it okay if I get some water?"

"Sure," Sarah replied. "There's bottled water in the fridge." She dusted the chicken parts with flour. "And I don't know what you should say to her. Play it by ear. Ask her if she has any questions."

"This is really a bad situation. I wish your mother had kept her mouth shut." He unscrewed the top off the bottle, turned it up, and drank from it like a man trekking through the hot desert.

"What's done is done, and we can't change what happened in the past. We just have to deal with it. Why don't you go talk to Naomi? I'll come in her room after I put the chicken on."

"How about I wait until you're done?" Brian asked. He tossed the bottle in the recycling bin.

At that moment, they heard the door to Naomi's room open. She walked into the kitchen dressed in blue and yellow floral cotton pajamas and a white robe.

"Oh, I didn't know he was here," Naomi said, glaring at Brian.

"Uh, how are you feeling this morning, Naomi?" he asked, nervously.

She folded her arms across her chest and rolled her eyes at him. "How do you think I'm doing?" She opened the refrigerator and took an apple from the bottom bin.

"I guess you're a little upset, or maybe the correct word would be unsettled?" He squirmed in his seat. He felt a trickle of sweat drip from his armpits.

Naomi took a paring knife out of the cutlery drawer. "Yeah, maybe unsettled would be the better term." She turned and walked down the hallway.

"Way to go," Sarah said sarcastically as she put a pot of water on the stove to boil corn in. "You couldn't think of anything more profound to say than that?"

"She took me by surprise. I wasn't expecting her to walk in here. And you're right, she is in a foul mood. I think we should hold off talking to her for another day or two at least. Since she's in such a bad mood, I don't know what we'd accomplish now."

"Don't try and weasel out of this, Brian. Communicating with her during this time is important."

He shook his head disagreeing. "I think we should wait, Sarah. Naomi obviously isn't up to talking just yet. When she's ready, let me know and I'll come back over. I have a few errands to run. I'm going to tell the kids good-bye." He stood and squeezed Sarah's arm as he walked up the attic stairs.

Sarah shook her head at her ex-husband's departure. She glanced at the clock on the wall. Bishop and Queen were due to come over later, and judging by the time, probably in another hour or so. She turned the burners down on the stove and picked up the telephone to call her grandmother.

The telephone sounded in the Clayton house. Queen was ladling chicken soup from a pot on her stove into a Tupperware container. "Bishop, would you answer the telephone? My hands are full. If that's for you, don't talk long. We're going to Ruth's house. I told Ezra I'd fix dinner for him today."

"Give me a minute," Bishop called from the study. His hand covered the telephone speaker. He put the receiver back up to his ear. "Sarah, I'll probably be at your house in thirty minutes. I'll talk to you later."

He sat at his desk with his hands covering his face in a daze. Sarah had relayed what happened at the Wilcox house yesterday. He was perturbed when he learned about the false rape accusation. He wondered if his wife had anything to do with the wildly concocted rape story, because he couldn't imagine Sarah coming up with it on her own. *No, she wouldn't do something like that. I know my Queen is capable of many things, but falsely accusing another person of such an atrocious crime, she wouldn't stoop that low.* Still, Bishop had doubts and his forehead was furrowed with concern.

He remembered how he had to call one of the deacon's of the church, a member of the Chicago Police Department, to physically restrain Daniel and Fred from taking their illegal firearms and leaving the house to hunt for Sarah's attacker. Bishop sympathized with Daniel and felt his pain. Still, he felt cooler heads needed to prevail.

Queen walked into the room. She had on a light jacket over a sleeveless red and pink dress. "Come on, Bishop. Ezra is waiting."

He stood, walked over to his wife, and took her hands in his. He led her to the sofa. He told her what happened at Ruth's the previous evening. As she listened to his story, her face blanched flour white. Bishop stared probingly at his wife, suspicion sweeping from his pores. He groaned and shook his head. Queen's expression verified that her handy work was indeed stamped all over Sarah's deception. Her eyes dropped to the floor. Queen stroked her throat nervously as she cleared her voice.

"Isn't it a blessing that our Sarah wasn't raped? It would've been a horrible stigma for Naomi and Sarah to bear. Don't you think?" She gave her husband a bright, but false smile. Red dots of color appeared on her cheeks, like they were painted on with a makeup brush.

"Oh, Esther," Bishop muttered, as he glanced upward. *God in heaven, sometimes this woman tries my patience.*

Queen rose from the sofa and walked to Bishop's desk. Her hands trembled violently as she pushed papers around on his desk. Though her head was lowered, she peeked up at Bishop. Her heart plunged to her feet. He looked upset, and the vein in his neck throbbed ominously.

I hope Sarah didn't say anything to Ruth about my part in what happened. Shoot, I was only trying to protect the family. Any woman would have done what I did. The only problem is, Ruth won't understand. If Sarah said anything, I'm dead meat, Queen thought morosely.

"Queen Esther Grandberry Clayton, get your behind back on this sofa," Bishop roared.

She opened her mouth to reply, and then thought she'd better not. On quaking legs, she walked to the sofa and sat a foot away from Bishop.

"Now Bishop, calm down. You don't want your pressure to go up," she said, weakly.

"Forget my pressure. Please tell me you didn't have anything to do with Sarah's lies."

Queen folded her arms across her chest defensively. Her voice rose shrilly. "I did what I had to do to preserve our family's honor."

Bishop held his hand up. "That's a bunch of manure, my dear. I could understand if you said you did it for Sarah. But to sit and say your

actions were for our family's honor is unaccept-
able. Queen, you're the wife of a minister, and
your father was a minister. You better than anyone knows that lying always comes back to haunt
you. You reap what you sow."

"I know what I did was wrong in theory Bishop,
but my intentions were good. I was concerned
about Sarah. She was just a child." She tried to de-
fend herself. "What would you have me do, let
Daniel and his uncouth brother kill someone?"

Though it was difficult for him, Bishop managed to get a hold of his emotions. "Queen, it
wasn't your decision to make. Do you understand that? It was Daniel and Ruth's decision.
Not yours or mine."

"What you're saying is sort of true. But Sarah is
my grandchild!" she shouted. "I love her with all
my heart. Of course I was concerned about her
predicament when Sarah told me she and Brian
were having sex and she thought she was pregnant. That's why I supported Ruth adopting Naomi.
I made what I thought was the right choice at the
time, and if I had to do it over, I'd do it again."

Bishop shook his head sadly. "I love you, Esther. We were married by your father in the house
of the Lord before witnesses. But I swear, woman,
if you pull one more stunt like that, I don't know
what I'm going to do. I'm going to say this one
last time, and I mean it. Stay out of our children's
business. Do you understand me?" He pointed his
finger in Queen's face. He simmered with rage.

She had never seen her husband so upset before in all their years of marriage. She nodded her

head meekly. "Do you think Sarah said anything to Ruth about my part in this?" she asked, fearfully.

"Knowing Sarah, I doubt it. But you better pray on your knees every night that Ruth doesn't figure out your part in this. Because if she does, and she decides to cut you off, there will be nothing I can do."

"I hope Sarah doesn't tell Ruth that I advised her to lie. For the first time in many years, Ruth and I have been getting along better. I just hope I haven't jeopardized our relationship. I've come to realize how I've been a horrible mother to my children. And I love them, Bishop, I really do." Queen's eyes filled with tears.

"I know that. But do they? You know the right thing would be for you to tell Ruth yourself your part in what happened, and let the chips fall where they may. That would be the Christian thing to do. I know you mean well, even if you don't always show it."

Her shoulders shook as she bit back a sob. "I just hope the children realize it."

She looked like a wounded bird to Bishop. He felt an urge to put his arms around his wife and comfort her, but he stood his ground.

Queen was a proud, stubborn woman. One had to really get close to her to get a glimpse of the complex woman that made up her psyche. Despite her shortcomings, she was generous, helpful, and sharp as a tack. Bishop called her a study in contradiction. He loved her as deeply as she loved him.

Bishop put a stern expression on his face. "Let's go to Ruth's house. Didn't you tell Ezra you'd bring him dinner?" He stood and held out his arm to her.

Chapter Forty-nine

Ruth, Bishop, and Queen accompanied Ezra to the hospital the following week for his doctor appointment.

Bishop kept peeping at Ezra through his rear-view mirror. His son lay limply against the back seat. His head was thrown back and his eyes were closed. His breathing sounded awfully shallow to Bishop.

"Would you turn on some music?" Ezra gasped. "I'd like to hear me some old time gospel tunes like Mahalia Jackson."

Bishop obliged his son and put the CD into the compact disc player.

"That's what I'm talking about." Ezra nodded his head.

Tendrils of fear wrapped around Ruth's heart like an octopus. She knew, even without talking to the doctor, what time it was. Since Ezra came to stay with her, the siblings had stripped themselves of all pretensions, allowing their inner selves to be seen by each other.

She had only allowed three people to see and hear what was in her heart, and that was Bishop, Alice, and Daniel. Ezra became the fourth. She swayed in her seat to the tempo of the music.

Lord, I ask that you please don't take my brother away from me so soon. I understand if that's your will, I have no choice but to accept it. Give me strength, Lord. Let me lean on you. Father in heaven I pray. She blinked hard to hold back the tears that wanted to surge from her eyes.

Ezra watched his sister struggle for composure. His strength was ebbing quicker than he liked. He reached over and grabbed her hand. Queen pressed her hand tightly against her mouth.

Forty minutes later the family arrived at Cook County Hospital and sat together solemnly in the waiting room until Ezra's name was called.

After Ezra's examination and while Bishop helped his son get dressed, the nurse informed Ruth and Queen they could go into the doctor's office. Bishop walked with Ezra back to the waiting room and joined the women in the office. Fifteen minutes later Dr. McCoy walked inside the room, where a somber Clayton family awaited him. They all knew in their hearts what he was going to say.

"Ezra is fading, isn't he?" Ruth asked soberly as her teeth chattered like she was naked in a snowstorm.

The doctor folded his hands in a triangle. His eyes roamed the room. His patient's family's sadness permeated the room. "Truthfully, he's lasted longer than I would have ever predicted. I think he's been running on sheer willpower for so long, and it's now time for him to rest."

A moan escaped Queen's lips. Her body weaved in the hard wooden chair.

Bishop grabbed his wife and daughter's hands. "How long?" he asked, in a flat voice.

"He's near the end of his journey. I'd predict a week or two. Although I'm not a betting man."

Queen looked at the doctor. He thought her face was wrinkled with sorrow. "Then we'll do what we can to ease his trip home," she half said and moaned. She stood and pulled her jacket around her shoulders.

"If you'd like, I can call the hospice and see if they have room for Ezra there. He'll need nursing care round-the-clock. There isn't much we can do for him at this point, except make his last days comfortable," Dr. McCoy suggested, kindly.

"That won't be necessary—bringing him to the hospice. He's our flesh and blood, and we'll tend to him," Bishop declared as he placed his straw boater hat on his head. "Good day, Dr. McCoy." He could barely support Queen and Ruth's weight as they walked out of the office.

How sad, Dr. McCoy mused as he closed Ezra's chart. He was touched by his patient's family's strength, and yes, faith. So many of the men and women he had treated over the years didn't fair as well. A great majority of them were buried in potter's field, unclaimed by ashamed, uncaring, and sometimes, unforgiving relatives. He'd heard many tales from the men at the homeless shelter and the hospital talk of a musical minister named Ezree.

The physician thought Ezra was a fine man. *Good for him. May the Lord have mercy on his soul.* Dr. McCoy pressed the call button on his phone. "Leona, send in my next patient."

Queen, Ruth, and Bishop looked miserable as the minister drove from the hospital. Only Ezra felt at peace.

"The doctor suggested you should go to a hospice, son. That's an option if you'd prefer to do that. Although I told him we'll take care of you at home." Bishop took his eyes off the road and peered at Ezra as he stopped at a red light.

"Personally, I'd rather die at home. But I could go to the hospice if my care becomes too much for you all to handle," he said.

"Don't talk like that, Ezra," Queen scolded him as she wiped a tear from the corner of her eye.

"I'm just trying to keep it real. It's inevitable I'm going home, and this old weak body says it won't be long." He sat back and closed his eyes.

Queen and Ruth began sniffing.

"Come on now, Esther and Ruth. We'll make it," Bishop said gruffly as he cleared his throat. A fine mist veiled his eyes.

Ezra struggled to sit upright in his seat. "I wanted to tell all of you that it's a miracle from God that we were able to put our differences aside and I'm grateful we had this time together." He voice sounded thin as though he was experiencing shortness of breath. "I'm really tired now. Wake me when we get home."

Ruth and Queen continued to sob quietly. Before long, Bishop pulled up in front of Ruth's house. He exited the car, picked up Ezra in his arms, then walked inside and laid him in the bed.

Ruth and Queen sat glumly at the kitchen table. Bishop walked into the room and sat with them.

"Anybody want coffee or anything?" Ruth asked as her fingers tapped lightly on the tabletop.

"No," Bishop and Queen said in unison.

"I know your house is crowded right now, Ruth, but I think Queen and I should move here until, you know . . ." Bishop's voice trailed off.

"That's a good idea. You know I have room in the basement. Alice plans on staying here to help out also. Me and her could sleep down there, and you and Mother are welcome to stay in my room," Ruth offered.

"I'll move some things around on my calendar. Maybe take a short leave of absence from the church and together we can all do everything humanly possible to send your brother home," Bishop added.

Queen stood. "I guess we'll head to our house so we can prepare for our stay here. We'll be back tonight or in the morning. Can you handle things until then?"

"Yes, I can," Ruth sighed audibly.

"Thank you, Ruth. The Lord will bless you," Queen said. She squeezed her daughter's hand. "We'll see you later."

Later that day Ruth called Alice and brought her to date on Ezra's dire diagnosis. She promised she'd be over in a couple of hours and would stay for the duration. Ruth walked to her bedroom. The morning events had taken a toll on her energy level. She called a medical supply company and ordered the list of items Dr. McCoy instructed they get. Then she laid on the bed and fell asleep.

"Mama," Sarah shook Ruth awake. "There's a man at the door. He says he's from a medical supply store."

"Oh," Ruth looked at the clock, "I slept longer than I planned. Have him come in. I'll be right out."

"Sure. I'll have him take the stuff to Uncky's room." Sarah left out the room.

Ruth went into the bathroom and splashed water on her face. Her eyes were still red-rimmed from crying. She patted her face dry with a towel. She knew she had to pull herself together for Ezra's sake.

Ezra sat painfully hunched on the chair in the bedroom while the men set up a medical bed and oxygen tent. Ruth stood at the doorway, giving instructions. When the men were done setting up the equipment, she left the room to pay them.

Sarah helped Ezra back into bed. After she got him settled, he asked, "How is Nay-Nay?"

"Not too good," she said as she sat in the chair, waiting for Ruth to return. "I think anger has set in, and she's having a hard time trying to cope with everything she's learned."

"Give her time," he advised. He closed his eyes. "She's a Clayton and a Wilcox. That girl is made of strong stuff."

"I hope so," she murmured. Her face telegraphed waves of tension. Sarah looked so sad.

"The doctor says I don't have much time left," Ezra said, opening his eyes, looking at his niece. "So, I want to thank you, Sarah, for all you've done to take care of me. I'm so glad we had this little time together, to get to know each other."

"Uncky, I'm glad too. I just wish you had been around when we were growing up."

"All things in their time." Ezra tried to smile. Then his expression turned serious. "Ruth is going to need you after I'm gone. She's putting on a brave face, but I know my sister, she's hurting inside."

"You don't even have to ask," Sarah protested, shaking her head from side to side. "Mama has been there for me through thick and thin, and I'll do the same for her."

"I want you to encourage her to finish her studies. I think she'll make a great minister. In fact, I'm going to talk to Bishop about that before I check out. Times have changed, and women are just as capable as men of being spiritual leaders." His eyes glittered with pain and his voice weakened.

Sarah peeped at the clock, then back at her uncle. "I think it's time for a pain pill. I'll be right back." She stood and walked into the bathroom.

Ruth sat on the sofa in the living room. She could hear Ezra and Sarah's voices, though not clear enough to decipher what they were saying. She folded her arms around her body.

Lord, I guess you won't be performing any last

*minute miracles like sparing my brother's life. I guess
I'm just being selfish. I love my big brother so much. I
wish he could be here with us for the next twenty
years. But that isn't your will.*

She folded her hands together as tears streamed
from her eyes. *You brought Ezra home to us. Your doing
so was such a great gift. Lord, just give me the strength
I'm going to need to get Ezra ready to go home. Lord,
please give my entire family the peace and power to come
together as we send our son and brother into your loving arms. And Jesus, please help Naomi and Sarah as
they struggle to define their relationship.* Ruth wiped
her eyes with the hem of her skirt. She pushed her
hair off her face and went to Ezra's room.

He had fallen asleep. Sarah sat in the chair
watching the rise and fall of her uncle's chest.
When Ruth walked into the room, she rose and
hugged her mother.

"It hurts, Mama, it hurts so bad to see him like
this. I wish God had seen fit to spare Uncky."

"Me too," Ruth said, sadly. "Me too."

Chapter Fifty

After spending a week with the newlyweds caring for Damon, Ernest journeyed to Lenora's house to fetch Glenda. After her parents left, Lenora tended to Damon for exactly one day, and the outcome was disastrous.

When Daniel returned from work Monday evening, Lenora moaned and cried until Daniel requested a two-week paternity leave from work. As the week wore on, Lenora ran him so ragged that Daniel wished he were back at work.

The second morning of his baby duties, he arose wearily to give Damon his two o'clock feeding. As he sat in the rocking chair in the nursery and peered into his son's face, Daniel was amazed at how little his newest offspring resembled his siblings. Damon had his nose, but the rest of his features mirrored his mother's.

He changed Damon's diaper. When he finished, he slid into the bed next to Lenora. She glanced at him sleepily. "He's really a good baby," she murmured.

How would you know? I spend more time taking care of him than you do, careened through Daniel's mind. "Yeah, he's not too bad. Naomi cried a lot when she was a baby. Say Lenora, I wanted to talk to you about something. I don't know where or why the screw-up occurred regarding your getting pregnant, but I want you to know, just so there isn't any misunderstanding, that I don't want any more children. So whatever you got to do, get your plumbing tied or get on the pill; just do it. No more children, do you understand me?" He looked at his wife, absorbedly.

"Danny," Lenora whined. She scooted over and wrapped her arms around his neck. "You don't want Damon to grow up an only child, do you? His life would be more complete with siblings."

He gently removed her arms from around his neck. "He's not an only child. He has two sisters and a brother."

"You know what I mean. His siblings are old enough to be his parents. I meant sisters or brothers a few years younger than him."

"No, Lenora, I don't want any more children. I had planned to retire when Naomi graduates from college. Instead, now I have to cough up more college tuition. I don't know what you've cooked up in that pretty little head of yours, but if it involves having another baby, don't do it."

Lenora pouted prettily as she moved away from Daniel. "I don't understand why you have to pay Naomi's tuition anyway. Why don't your daughter and your ex-wife pay it?"

"For one thing, they can't afford it, and my doing so is stipulated in my divorce decree. I just didn't plan on starting over with the expenses of another child. Having Damon is really going to set me back."

"But he's worth it," she answered, smugly. "We'll be fine."

What she didn't tell him was that she still had money from her settlement, at least a couple of hundred thousand dollars. In order to avoid discussing the circumstances behind how she obtained the money, she pretended her past experience didn't exist, and she planned to keep things that way for the time being. Daniel's funds were theirs, and her money was hers.

"Uh, Nora, I'm going by Ruth's house today to talk to Naomi."

"Is that necessary?" Lenora frowned. "What I mean is, now that she knows you're really her grandfather, you don't have to be bothered with all that drama. Why can't Sarah and her husband handle the situation?"

"See, that's where you're wrong," he replied as he fluffed his pillow. "As far as the law is concerned, Naomi Wilcox is my child, and that's not going to change."

"Maybe it should, then it would free up some money."

"Forget it, Nora, it ain't gonna happen." Daniel gently pulled Lenora's body into his own spoon style. "I can't wait until the doctor gives you the green light to resume our private dances." He nuzzled the back of her neck.

"Hmm, me too." She turned and brushed her lips against Daniel's. She looked down at her husband's ballooning pajama bottoms. "Patience boo, our time is coming," she said, teasing him.

A week later, Lenora ventured out of the bedroom where she'd been residing the past couple of weeks. She decided it was time for her to try and establish a new routine with having a baby in the house. Daniel was away running errands.

She sat in the living room on the sofa dressed in a turquoise flowing gown reading the newspaper. Damon lay curled on his side in the fetal position on a yellow receiving blanket on the other end of the sofa. Lenora glanced at him and smiled. Her life was progressing nicely. In less than a year, she had married Daniel and solidified her position as the mother of his son.

Felicia had an appointment with a fertility specialist that afternoon and Lenora could hardly wait to hear the results. She was coming over later that evening to tighten up her hair. A blue bandana covered her mussed hair.

She turned the newspaper to the real estate section. Lenora's eyes quickly scanned up and down the columns. She was looking for a house to rent or buy. She picked up a pen off the cocktail table and placed check marks next to the homes she considered possibilities.

She still hadn't convinced Daniel to move out of the condo yet. He didn't want to move out of the city, but she wanted to move to the suburbs.

The only areas she would consider living in the city were Beverly, Hyde Park, or Bronzeville, but she knew Daniel would consider the million dollar plus houses in those communities out of their price range, although in reality the areas weren't.

Lenora owned her condo outright and she knew she wouldn't have a problem selling or renting it if push came to shove for additional funds for buying a new house. Lenora was in great shape financially. Daniel wasn't aware of his wife's net worth and Lenora couldn't tell him without some explaining about her past.

When she had attended junior college, the experience was an eye-opening one. She learned about investments and had put her settlement money into interest bearing accounts and bought stock on the advice of the financial planner she hired.

She was shrewd and lived modestly, so no one could readily estimate her financial worth. Ernest thought she'd gone through her money long ago. Only Felicia was privy to her secrets. Lenora made a good salary from her bookkeeping business. She planned to tell Daniel the truth about her financial status when the time was right. To appease his feelings about keeping her money situation from him, she might have to cough up money toward a house in the city if she couldn't change his mind about the suburbs.

Damon awakened and began to whine. Lenora took him in her arms and walked to the kitchen and took a bottle from the counter. She looked at the clock; Daniel should be returning home soon. She walked back into the living room where she fed Damon. She burped him, changed his diaper, and laid him back on the sofa.

Daniel walked inside the apartment carrying four shopping bags. "Hey, baby, you're out the bedroom. I'm shocked." He took the bags into the kitchen.

"Did you get formula?" she asked, as she picked up the newspaper and resumed reading.

"Of course I did. I can read a shopping list." He began putting groceries in the refrigerator and the pantry. When he finished, he walked into the living room and looked at Damon. "He's growing already." He sat in a chair. "What are you doing?"

"Reading the paper; looking for someplace for us to move. I know you've been avoiding the subject, but when Ma stayed with us, it was obvious this place is too little." Her hands swept around the room. "We need to start looking so we can move before the winter." She looked at Daniel hopefully.

"Okay, you've made your point." He held up his hands. "I need to warn you though, that I'm not in a position to take on a lot of debt until Naomi finishes school. Her tuition is going to cost me at least another thirty thousand dollars."

"You mean she isn't getting any type of financial aid?" Lenora asked, looking at him with an astonished expression on her face.

"No, her grades aren't that good. She finished her first year at Southern with a C average. And I don't see that changing anytime soon. School was never her strong suit. I was just glad she only failed one class."

"I still think Sarah and her husband should

kick in some money. Why can't the three of you split the cost?" Lenora grumbled. She looked back down at the newspaper and checked off another house.

"We already had that discussion. Anyway, what did you see in the paper?"

"I know you want to stay in Chicago, but I personally think we can get more square feet in the house for the money if we move to the burbs. Boo, there are all kinds of advantages to moving outside the city. The school systems are better, and most of all, the crime rates are lower. I know there are people who work for the city who live in the suburbs. People do it all the time."

"I'm sure there are, but I don't plan to be one of them. I'm trying to retire from CTA, not lose my job. Because the rules state if you work for the city, you must reside there. Do you want something to eat or drink?" Daniel walked to the kitchen and returned with a bag of pretzels and a soda.

"It will be expensive if we try to buy property in Chicago. Plus, there are only a few good areas to move to in the city."

Daniel picked up the remote and turned on the television, he muted the sound. "What do you mean by only a few good areas? What are you talking about?"

"I don't want Damon to grow up in the hood, giving him the opportunity to turn out like my brothers. If we have to stay in the city, then I don't see us living anywhere other than Hyde Park or Beverly."

He shook his head. "Uh, uh, those places are

out of the question. You're talking about spending at least a million dollars or more for those properties. I just told you, I don't have it like that, especially with a new baby and Naomi's school fees. I also have to pay alimony for a couple of years. Did you forget that? Since we're on the subject of money, are you going to keep working?"

Lenora looked up at Daniel and nodded her head. "Since I work from home, it won't be a problem for me to continue to do so. And we won't have to pay for childcare. When I need to consult with my clients in their offices, Mama, will keep Damon."

"You sound like you have everything figured out. But I'm not moving out of the city. There are other areas in Chicago we can check out. When I go back to work, I'll talk to some of my coworkers. I want to invite Naomi, Sarah, and her kids to dinner one day soon. Are you up to it?"

"Of course, Danny. It's time I met your children." Lenora stood and walked over to Daniel. She sat in his lap and snaked her tongue in his ear. They began kissing passionately.

She pulled away breathlessly. "Whoa, we have what, another three weeks? Then we can get this party started." She sulked dramatically. "Danny, I'd really rather stay in the suburbs. Here where we're staying now, Evergreen Park, is a suburb. Since we got married, haven't you been using my address for work anyway?"

He pulled her closer. "No, I'm still using Fred's like I did after me and Ruth separated. But I can't use it indefinitely."

"Why don't you ask Fred's landlord to put you on your brother's lease? That way you'll have a city address, and we can at least look in the sub-urbs. It's cheaper to buy property there. Won't you at least consider it?"

Daniel caressed Lenora's burgeoning breasts. "Yeah, I'll think about it. But if I get fired, you're going to have to support all of us." He gently pushed her off his lap. "I'm going to call Sarah."

She smiled. "You do that, and I'll continue to look in the newspaper for houses that we may want to move to." She knew she had him hooked. Her husband would move wherever she wanted.

Daniel walked into the kitchen and dialed Ruth's number. Sarah glanced at the Caller ID unit and answered the telephone.

"Hi, Daddy," she said, dryly. "What can I do for you?"

"How is everyone doing?"

"Okay."

"Um, I want to invite you, the kids, and Naomi over for dinner one day next week. I know I was wrong by not telling you kids what was going on in my life, but what's done is done. I just hope you can forgive me." Daniel rubbed his bald-head.

"You're right; what's done is done. We haven't told Naomi about you being married and your new bundle of joy yet. I still think the information would be better coming from you. Uncle Ezra isn't doing well and we've all been concentrating on his health issues. So now is not a good time for us to get together with your new family."

Darn it. I thought someone had told her by now. "Is Naomi home?" Daniel asked.

"Yes, hold on." Sarah yelled, "Naomi, telephone. It's Daddy. I'll talk to you later." She handed her sister the cordless phone.

"Hey, Daddy," Naomi said glumly.

Daniel sensed she was depressed. "If you aren't busy, I'd like to come by your mother's house later today and talk to you."

"You want to talk to me about what?" she asked. She assumed it was about Brian being her biological father.

"I'd rather not get into over the phone. Do you have a couple of hours for your old man? Ask your mother if it's okay for me to come and talk to you at six o'clock this evening." Daniel waited while she went to talk to Ruth.

She came back and said, "Mama said that's fine."

"I'll see you then. Bye." Daniel clicked off the phone.

When he returned to the living room, Lenora and Damon had vacated the room. He walked down the hallway and peeped into the master bedroom. His wife and baby boy lay fast asleep in the bed. Daniel walked back into the living room and nodded off in front of the television.

A few hours later, Daniel stood in front of the mirror in the foyer and pulled a White Sox cap down on his head. The downstairs buzzer sounded.

"I'll get it!" he yelled to Lenora. "I'm on my way out to see Naomi. I'll be back later." He opened the door to admit Felicia. They exchanged greetings as Daniel walked outside the door.

Felicia walked into her sister's bedroom carrying a large shopping bag in one hand. She flew over to the bassinet. She dropped the bag on the floor and lifted Damon in her arms.

"That's Tee Tee's baby. Isn't he a pretty little boy? Yeah, he's the handsomest baby in the world." She rubbed the skin under Damon's chin.

Lenora looked at her and Damon amused. "Is he the only person you see in this room?" she teased her sister.

"Oh, hey girl. How you doing?" Felicia looked up at Lenora and smiled.

"How does that old song go? I'm sitting on top of the world. Slowly but surely I'm bringing Daniel around to the idea of moving into a house. This condo is entirely too small." Lenora wrinkled her nose distastefully.

"You one scheming sista," Felicia said, holding Damon in her arms as she sat in the chair by the bed. "Just remember, Daniel is an old school player, so watch your step."

"Girl, please," Lenora held up her palms, "I got this." She pulled the gown down over her thighs. Lenora looked at the bag on the floor. "So, what did you buy me? I can hardly wait to hit the stores."

Felicia laid her nephew back inside the bassinet and picked up the bag. "I didn't buy you anything. I saw the cutest little Baby Phat outfits at Carson Pirie Scott, my favorite store, and I couldn't resist buying a couple for Damon and Kente." She reached inside the bag and laid the garments on the bed.

"These outfits are so cute." Lenora looked over at Damon. "See what Tee Tee bought you?" The baby chortled and kicked his legs. "How did your doctor visit go?" She laid the clothing on the bed.

Felicia sat on the edge of the bed. She looked downward and smoothed the coverlet. "It went okay. We discussed my medical history and the doctor thinks I'm a good candidate for an invitro procedure."

Lenora smiled happily. "That's good, isn't it?"

"Yes, it's good, but it's an expensive process. Not all of the cost is covered under our current medical plan. I have an idea on how to raise the funds, but I'll need your help." She looked up at Lenora.

"Well, what is it?"

"I don't know how much you know about invitro. It's a process by which a lab technician would merge my eggs with Reggie's sperm and inject it into my womb. Each time the procedure is done the cost is going to run many thousands of dollars. The doctor thinks we should try to harvest at least five samples."

Lenora whistled sharply. "That's not cheap. What do you want me to do?"

"Well, I was wondering if you'd consider refinancing the mortgage on the hair salon? We could use some of the equity from the building to fund the procedure. I'd like to use it and try the specialist's recommendation and go for the three to five treatments."

"How much do you already have saved?" she

asked. Using her feet, she pushed the bedspread toward the bottom of the bed.

"About five thousand dollars. You know normally we put our profits back into the company. Last year we expanded the building, adding a day spa, and I hired a masseuse. It's taken a minute, but I'm slowly but surely building up my clientele."

"What kind of odds has the doctor given you?" Lenora's thumb lay under her chin, and her middle finger was pressed against her right cheek.

"Seventy/thirty. Not perfect, but not terrible either. Reggie and I have decided if the procedure doesn't work, then we'll consider adopting. But I'd like to give us a fair shot at having our own baby first."

"I hear you," Lenora said. She felt a thrill of power, like she held her sister's fate in her hands. "Of course, let's go for it. Why don't you put some figures together, I'll look at them and we'll go from there."

Felicia reached into the shopping bag and removed a file. She handed it to her sister.

"You're serious aren't you?" Lenora looked at Felicia.

"I am. I'd love for Reggie and me to conceive a child together, but we've accepted that it might not happen."

Leonora set the papers on the nightstand. "I'll take a look at them later and I'll call you tomorrow."

"Thanks, sis." Felicia's body sagged with relief.

A foul odor permeated the air. The sisters

looked over at Damon. He waved his hands in the air.

"I'll change him," Felicia volunteered, pushing up her sleeves. "I might as well get some practice."

Chapter Fifty-one

Daniel noticed Bishop and Alice's cars parked on Ruth's street as he walked up the cement pathway leading to his former residence. He rang the doorbell. Naomi's face appeared briefly, peering out of the window. She unlocked the door.

When he walked into the house, the odor was so acrid, that it brought tears to his eyes. He looked toward the back of the house.

"Where is that smell coming from?" he asked Naomi. "It smells like something died in here."

Naomi shrugged her shoulders and rolled her eyes at her father's comments. "Uncle Ezra isn't doing well," she whispered. "We can go to the basement and talk."

The pair walked toward the kitchen. Daniel could hear Bishop's voice. "I'm going to go speak to everyone. I'll be downstairs in a minute."

The Clayton family looked bereft. Bishop and Queen looked elderly, and their appearance suggested they'd aged overnight.

Daniel offered his sympathies. "I'm sorry to hear Ezra isn't doing too well. If there's anything I can do, feel free to ask."

Queen gave him a wan smile and nodded.

"Thank you, Daniel." Bishop rose from his seat and shook his hand..

Daniel glimpsed Ruth exiting her bedroom. He walked down the hallway to meet her.

She nervously smoothed the edge of her apron down. "Hi, Danny. I guess you're here to talk to Naomi. She told me you were coming by."

"Yeah. I don't have a good feeling about this. I just hope the conversation goes well." He looked down at his feet.

"You'll be fine; just speak what's in your heart." Her first inclination was to join them, but she knew the situation was something he was going to have to deal with in his own way.

He headed to the lower level of the house and joined Naomi.

His youngest child sat on an old, peeling leather recliner. Her tapping feet betrayed her nervousness. Her moist hands were laced together. There was a catsup stain on her light blue denim shorts.

Daniel was dressed impeccably as always, in a white polo shirt, and deeply creased blue jeans. A new pair of K-Swiss sneakers enclosed his feet. His goatee had been freshly trimmed. He stopped at the barbershop before visiting Naomi.

He coughed and cleared his throat nervously. "Your mother told me what happened between Sarah and Brian. I was shocked, to say the least. But it showed me how things can work out for the better, even many years later. Brian isn't so bad. You could have had worst for a biological father." His eyes searched Naomi's face for some hint of how she was feeling, and he was amazed at how much she resembled Brian. It was plain as day how much she looked like her sire, and no one had ever noticed it before.

She glanced over at Daniel, obviously troubled by his comments. "I guess so, but I remember you saying Brian was a loser when he didn't have Sarah's child support money, Daddy. Or should I call you Granddaddy like the other kids? If my birth had been the result of a rape, did that mean you couldn't love me? Did you ever love me?"

A flash of annoyance crossed his face. He immediately tried to squelch it. "Look here, young lady, I'm your father, period. I have raised and loved you as I have my other children. I'm not always good at expressing how I feel sometimes, but yes, I love you. I'm not going to lie to you, Naomi. It hurt when Ruth told me what happened to your sister. Sarah and I have always shared a strong bond, one that me and DJ haven't been able to. I hope one day in the future, we'll have a chance to work on that.

"I thought Sarah should've had an abortion. She was too young to be having a baby, and I was sure having you would only bring her bad memories. I hated what happened to Sarah, but no, I didn't hate you. When you were born, I wasn't jumping cartwheels or nothing like that. I was sad over the circumstances of how you got here. Ruth, on the other hand, took one look at you and she fell in love with you. I don't think any of us suspected Sarah and Brian were having sex at such a young age. That's the God's honest truth, and I swear by it."

Naomi put her hand on her chin. "Well, thanks, Daddy, for at least being honest with me. I know I can depend on you to tell me the truth, even if it hurts."

Daniel stood up, went over to Naomi and hugged her. A sinking feeling grew in the pit of his stomach. The words she spoke were prophetic. He realized he was about to wound her even more. He sat back down on the sofa.

"I need to tell you something else, Naomi. It's good or bad news, depending on how you look at it. And I hope you'll keep an open mind."

"What is it, Daddy?" She looked at Daniel puzzled.

"Well, you know me and your mother have had problems over the past few years. And I admit I didn't handle things the right way. I had a special friend, her name is Lenora."

Naomi recoiled away from him. Her eyes bucked and she breathed heavily through her nostrils. "Why are you telling me this now, Daddy?" She tightened her arms defensively across her chest and glowered at him.

Daniel looked down. He was too ashamed to look at Naomi's face. "Well, I, there's just no other way to say it. Lenora means a great deal to me. Uh, me and her, we got married and we have a baby son." He peeped up at Naomi.

She stood so still that she might've been made of marble. She tried to speak, as tears gushed out of her eyes. "But, Daddy," she held out her hand, "you and Mama just got divorced. How can you be married to someone else and have a baby so soon?" Her face reddened, like she was being throttled. "Oh, my God. Daddy, you cheated on Mama!" Her voice rose in volume. She laughed and cried. "You're a cheater, Daddy, a low down dirty cheater." She stood and nearly fell as she raced up the stairs, still chanting cheater.

Daniel stood and made a move to follow her. But he was too embarrassed to go through the kitchen, because he'd have to face Ruth's family. He hit the wall in frustration.

He then sat back against the sofa to compose himself. Footsteps sounded on the wooden stairway. He hastily wiped his eyes before asking, "Naomi, is that you?" As his eyesight cleared, he saw that it was Ruth. "Oh, it's you." He sat down feeling deflated. "I guess you've come to gloat. Yeah, I messed up, and it just hit me how badly when Naomi went running up the stairs."

"Danny, do you realize how much your being married and having a baby is a shock to Naomi? The news was upsetting to me as well. I can hardly understand it myself, so how do you expect an eighteen-year-old child to get it? I'm going to call her therapist tomorrow and try to get her an appointment as soon as possible. It's sad to see over thirty years of marriage end the way ours did, but I don't wish you any harm. Because, mark my words, your day is coming, and what goes around, comes around." She turned and went back upstairs.

He then sat on the sofa in stunned silence for a

minute. Then he put on his White Sox cap, went upstairs, and let himself out the front door without saying a word to anyone.

Naomi had locked herself inside her bedroom and lay sprawled across the bed. *Grownups always say teenagers are screwed up, how we don't know anything, or haven't lived long enough to know about life. But I swear my family takes first place in being dysfunctional. They're liars and cheaters, and who knows what else. I always thought there wasn't any family in the world like the Claytons, and how I was proud to be a part of this family. Now I hate all of them, the Claytons and the Wilcox's. Both my families are totally screwed up.*

Ruth and Sarah knocked on Naomi's bedroom door, but she didn't answer.

"Perhaps we should give her time to adjust to everything—you and Brian being her biological parents, and now Daniel and his new wife, and baby. That's a lot for a young person to grasp. She's not in any shape to go back to school. As I said earlier, I think we need to consult with Dr. Ryan and see what she recommends." Ruth commented as they walked back to the kitchen.

But Sarah felt torn with indecision. She or someone should do what they could to ease Naomi's pain. "I'm going to call Brian," she announced. "It's time he took some responsibility for the situation. We created this predicament, so it's our job to clean it up."

Bishop and Queen sat at the kitchen table, taking in the going-ons around them. Bishop looked at Queen with an expression that silently entreated his wife to come clean with Ruth.

Instead, Queen bid a hasty retreat. "I'm going to check on Ezra."

"I'm going to call Dr. Ryan now and see what she thinks about the situation with Naomi. Maybe she'll be able to see her today." Ruth clutched Sarah's shoulders.

Ezra lay in his bed semi-conscious, dreaming. His life seemed to flash before his eyes. How proud Queen was of him when he began playing the piano by ear when he was five years old. Another pleasant memory for him was when Queen and Bishop brought Ruth home from the hospital. When Queen told him his new sister's name, he called her Baby Ruth, like the candy bar. He was enchanted with his infant sister from day one.

His life fast-forwarded to an unpleasant memory. One Sunday after the church evening service, he was alone in the men's bathroom. He heard the swinging outer door open. He turned to lock his stall door when Brother Peter, the church pianist, flung open the stall. He looked at Ezra and smiled, then unfastened his pants. When Ezra left the washroom, he had experienced his first taste of forbidden fruit. He had performed oral sex on another man, and the pianist did the same to him.

He wanted to talk to his father about what he was feeling, but Brother Peter forcibly insisted he couldn't tell anyone. He and the musician shared the secret for years, until another boy claimed the piano player had molested him. Bishop fired the man on the spot.

Ezra managed to suppress his feeling for men for a while, but he never forgot the experience. Bishop dropped hints when he was in eighth grade that it would please him and Queen if he and Alice married one day.

On his first day at high school, he met Martin, and his suppressed feelings for men came back to the forefront of his mind and heart.

One of Bishop's strongest philosophies was to teach a child God's word, and the child would not stray. As the years went by, despite his depressing plight, whenever Ezra had an opportunity, he sang and preached the word of God.

He and Martin continued to see each other, and whenever they met, Martin gave him money to survive on the streets. And Martin tried, from time to time, to encourage him to go to rehab, but he couldn't convince his lover to check himself in.

The day that Martin told him he was HIV positive, Ezra felt like the ground had dropped under his feet. Martin gave him an address and cash to get himself tested. But he shot up the money in his veins. Several years later, he went to a free clinic and tested HIV positive. The men continued to see each other until Martin became home bound.

During their last conversation before Martin passed, Martin promised his lover that he would make sure he was taken care of. He wasn't able to make good on that promise; he passed shortly afterward.

Ezra continued to eat at soup kitchens and sleep on and off at the Pacific Garden Mission until his condition worsened. He was waiting for the grim reaper to claim his life when Ruth and Alice walked into the hospice and his Baby Ruth gave him a new, albeit shortened, lease on life.

Queen gently patted Ezra's sunken cheeks. "Son, wake up. Please don't leave us, not yet." She sat beside the bed and held his hand.

An hour later, Bishop came into the room. He squeezed his wife's shoulder. "I'll sit with him now. What you need to do is talk to Ruth."

Queen stood wearily and stretched her arms. "I'll think about it." She walked out of the room.

Chapter Fifty-two

Ezra moaned and thrashed his head from side to side, as if he were in pain. His eyes opened. He looked over and saw Bishop dozing off in the chair next to the bed. He felt so tired, but there were some things he needed to say to his family before he closed his eyes for the last time. He tried to sit up, but fell weakly back onto the bed.

Bishop's eyes flew open. He looked at Ezra and smiled. He tried to swallow the lump in his throat. "You're awake. It's time for your medicine."

Ezra sat up and ingested the pill, droplets of water dripped from the cup and down his chin. Bishop dabbed at it with a towel. Ezra lay back in the bed and waited for the medication to take effect.

Twenty minutes later, he felt moderately better, and infused with a little strength. He turned and said to Bishop, "Daddy, I need to talk to you."

Bishop nodded. "Sure. Go ahead." He blinked his watery eyes rapidly.

"I don't want you to feel like it was your fault for the way my life has turned out. I accept full responsibility for my actions."

When Bishop heard Ezra say "Daddy," the word tugged a string of his heart. His children rarely called him that. Sometimes he missed being called by his parental title.

"No, son," he shook his head. "I was the one who handled the situation incorrectly. Instead of putting you out the house, I should've tried to talk to you more, or gotten professional help to assist you in working through your problems. Looking back in retrospect, I shouldn't have put you out of the house under any circumstances. Please forgive me."

"You give yourself too much credit, Daddy. Like a lot of young people, I was hell bent on doing what I wanted to do. There wasn't anything you could've said or done to change the course I charted for myself."

Bishop looked like a man haunted. "Did someone in the church do something to you to make you the way you are? I remember the scandal with that musician years ago. I've prayed to God that what happened to you wasn't related to anyone in the temple."

Ezra hesitated. "Yes, Dad. Someone did approach me. But don't blame him, that's old history. I realized later that he didn't make me do anything that I didn't want to. What happened wasn't your fault."

Bishop covered his face with his big hands and cried openly. "So many mistakes, so many things wrong."

"Now what is that you tell your church members? Doesn't it go something like, how we can't change the past that we just have to learn from it? I knew my destiny lie in the church in some form or fashion, and, Daddy, I'm proud that I've ministered to so many men. The churches and shelters that assisted the homeless and drug addicts allowed me to play the organ and sing. So I never turned away from the church and my teachings, I just went about it a different way."

"I know, and I want you to know I'm so proud of you and all your accomplishments. Son, I went to Pacific Garden Missions and shelters on the west side and talked to their staff people and made donations in your name. They all told me about the man they called the musical preacher. You don't know how hearing those words filled my heart with joy. God is good all the time, all the time God is good."

"Amen," Ezra replied. "I want you to think about something, Dad. And I want you to think about this as a father and not as a minister of one of the largest churches in Chicago. Can you do that?"

"I'll try with all my being. What is it?"

Ezra explained to his father how Ruth had attended seminary and was training to be a minister. "She's such a good person, and she's experienced firsthand, through me, you and Queen, life's lessons. I want you to give her a shot at working with you, Dad. Your rule about a male inheriting the temple applied in the old days, but times have changed. You're almost seventy-five years old. I know you want to spend some time with Queen, travel, and whatever else you two like to do."

Bishop looked thunderstruck, like he'd had an epiphany. "I never knew Ruth had aspirations to minister. Of course, we'll do something about it. Thank you son, for telling me. She never said a word to me."

Ezra had fallen asleep. His strength was failing rapidly, but he knew in his heart that God would allow him the few days he needed to complete his earthly business. A smile crossed his face.

Bishop walked out of the room and returned to the kitchen. He walked over to Ruth. She stood quickly. "Is Ezra all right?"

"He's sleeping. When all of this is done, we'll have to talk. Ezra has brought some things to light that I need to mediate on. I'm going into the living room. I need to pray."

Queen glanced down the hallway. She stood as if to follow Bishop, but instead turned to Ruth. "Can I talk to you?"

"Sure, Queen. We can talk in my bedroom," Ruth answered.

"Alice and I will hold down the fort," Sarah said, looking at her mother and grandmother wonderingly as they walked down the hall. "Take all the time you need."

Queen walked over to the window in the bedroom. She turned to face Ruth, who sat in the rocking chair. "Ruth, I owe you and Daniel an apology."

Ruth's eyebrow arched upward. "For what?"

"The thing with Sarah and Brian. I was the one who instructed Sarah to tell you and Daniel that she was assaulted. I don't have any excuse except I thought I was doing the right thing at the time."

"I figured out as much. There's no way in the world that Sarah could've concocted that story alone. I knew someone had to be coaching her. At first I thought it was Alice, but I knew she would've at least talked it over with me first."

Queen's shoulders heaved uncontrollably as tears trickled down her face. "I was wrong. I've always been bossy and wanted to do things my way. I've been thinking about why I'm the way I am. Probably because I was the only girl in my family, and with four brothers and a minister father, they spoiled me rotten. Bishop has spoiled me too. I hope one day you'll find it in your heart to forgive me, and I promise to keep my nose out of your business from here on out." After her confession, Queen looked humble, and turned back to the window.

Ruth looked at her mother disbelieving. *Could this really be the regal Queen speaking?* She stood, walked over to Queen, reached out her arms, and turned her mother's body towards her own.

"Mother, of course I forgive you. Through prayer and with Ezra's help, I realized you were only doing what you thought was best for Sarah and the family. But I'd appreciate it if you let me work out my own issues in the future. Even if I fail, it's my God given right to try and work it out. And with God on my side, I'll eventually get it right."

Queen embraced her daughter. She murmured

as she held Ruth in her arms, "You're so correct. Ruth, thank you for being so understanding. If our positions were reversed, I'm not sure if I could so graciously do the same. I'm working on changing my attitude somewhat." She giggled. "Ezra being home has taught me the virtue of being humble and how I can't control situations. Praise God. I promise, and you know it's going to be hard, that I'll do better in the future."

Mother and daughter stood with their arms entwined, then they walked out of the room.

Chapter Fifty-three

When Daniel returned home from his visit with Naomi, he wore a preoccupied expression on his face. He rushed to the bar and quickly poured himself a drink. He hadn't had any liquor since Damon was born. He downed the first drink and then fixed himself another one. Lenora walked out of the bedroom. Felicia had worked magic on her hair, giving her a perm and a facial. She looked close to her usual beautiful self.

"What's up, Boo? How did your visit with your daughter go? Are they amendable to having dinner with us?"

"No. They won't be coming here anytime time soon. I tried to talk rationally to Naomi, and I felt like I was doing a good job and that the conversation was going well. Then when I told her about you and Damon, the situation snowballed like a runaway train."

Lenora walked to him and led him to the sofa. She stroked his hand. "I'm sorry. Give them time, they'll come around." Secretly she was pleased. She and Damon were still the center of his life, and she didn't plan on the family rank changing anytime soon.

Damon made his presence known by crying in his shrill voice that Daniel said would wake up the dead. Lenora went into the bedroom and returned with the baby, a diaper, and the newspaper. She deposited Damon in his father's arms.

"Couldn't you have changed his diaper before you handed him to me?" he protested.

"You know where the diapers are; go ahead and change the baby. While you're doing that, I want to talk houses with you. I've seen a few ads in the paper that look promising."

Daniel grumbled, but he went ahead and changed his son's diaper. The baby looked up at his father and a smile crossed his face. Daniel hugged his boy. His heart was still burdened, and it still stung that Naomi called him a cheater. He kissed Damon's head and joined Lenora who sat at the dining room table leafing through the newspaper. Daniel took a seat opposite hers. He moved the gold and black silver floral arrangement from the center of the table and moved Damon on his shoulder so he could get a better look at what Lenora wanted to show him.

Leonora noted the morose expression on his face, so she decided to go easy on him.

"If we move out of here, what are you going to do with this place?" Daniel asked. He shifted the baby into his arms and tickled Damon's stomach. The infant began whimpering.

"I'm thinking about renting it to LaQuita. She

needs to be out on her own or she'll never grow up." Lenora turned to the real estate section.

"I don't know if that's such a good idea." Daniel stood and walked into the kitchen. He put a bottle in the microwave to heat.

"Why not?" she asked.

"Well, for one thing, your sister is only, what, sixteen or seventeen years old? She's too young for the responsibility of caring for a house."

"She declared her independence from our parents the day she turned sixteen. She'll be eighteen in a few weeks. And who do you think keeps Mama and Daddy's house clean?"

Truthfully, nobody, Daniel thought. He shook a few drops of milk on his arm. The bottle temperature was just right. He returned to the dining room, sat down, and put the nipple in Damon's mouth. The child looked up at him with droopy eyes and sucked greedily on the bottle.

"I think you're asking for trouble. What if the twins or Rashon, or other teenagers start hanging out here? The condo board will shuffle her out of here so fast she won't know what happened. Don't you still owe a mortgage on this place?"

"No," Lenora answered, haughtily. "I own it outright. I'm going to do some checking. But I think I can rent the place to Quita and get Felicia to co-sign on the lease for her. I want to look into getting Section 8 certification, but I need to make sure the condo board doesn't object. If that were to happen, I could get paid even more."

Daniel looked down at Damon who had fallen asleep. "I didn't know you owned the condo.

Why don't you sell it and we can use that money towards the down payment on the new house?"

"This is my first house, my first piece of real estate. I have nostalgic feelings about this place. I'd like to keep it in the family."

"Considering I can't contribute much, I guess it would make sense to at least try to generate income from it. That could help toward the mortgage at the new place. But your sister isn't working, so how is she going to be able to afford to pay rent?"

"Quita just got her GED last month. Felicia is going to bring her into the shop and start training her as a shampoo girl. And with her being away from the family and in her own place, she'll qualify for financial aid to pay for cosmetology school and section 8 housing. The government will pay daycare expenses. She'll still get a link card for groceries and a medical card. The tips she'll make in the shop will pay for her little incidentals."

Daniel looked at her admiringly. "Sounds like you have everything figured out. But how are you going to keep the twins away from LaQuita?"

"If Quita and Kente leave home, that'll give Daddy more time to concentrate on raising the boys. I think it might be too late for Jamal, but since Jabari shows a little bit more potential, perhaps it's not too late for him."

"With Ruth's brother being on his last leg, I probably won't be getting my portion of the money from the house for a couple of months. Can you wait until then?"

Lenora tried to keep a victorious expression off

her face. She knew she had Daniel exactly where she wanted him. "I can, but if I see a house that we both like, then I'd like to go ahead and get started. I didn't tell you about my financial situation because we weren't married then. But I got a settlement from the City when I was a teenager, and I've invested the money wisely. So you can just give me your share when it's available."

Daniel nodded his head. "Do you want to tell me how you got the money or what happened?" He was shocked that she had neglected to tell him about the money.

"That's a story for another day. We'll talk about it one day, just not today." She finger combed the edges of her hair. A sad look crossed her face as she turned back to the newspaper. She rose from the chair and took Damon to the nursery as Daniel pondered his good fortune. His young wife had money. *Wait 'til I tell Fred this.*

Chapter Fifty-four

Later that night while the rest of the family talked or napped, Ezra was dreaming again. He was aware, on some level, that his family and Alice were keeping vigil over him. He could hear their weeping, and he wished he had a little more time. He had made his peace with his parents and Alice.

Naomi had come to him earlier, but she was too overcome with pain of learning family truths that she just bawled uncontrollably, and Ruth had to escort her back to her bedroom. When Maggie and Josh came to say good-bye to their uncle, he waved to them as they stood in the doorway. He had talked to them a while ago about his going home. They were good kids and he knew they'd be fine.

Martin had been appearing in his dreams lately. He kept reassuring his friend that the suffering he felt would soon pass. He felt Martin's presence in the room was to help his conversion to the afterlife. But Ezra had one more task to do. He knew it was only a matter of time before Ruth came to him.

The last time Ezra attended Sunday services, he tore the church up playing the song "By and By." The words were a fitting tribute to his life at this moment in time.

Ezra moaned, opened his eyes, and closed them. *Thank you, Lord, for giving me the opportunity to make my peace with my family. I realize your sending me home was also a way to help Ruth get her life on track. Please give me the strength I need to talk to her one more time, and then I'll be ready to come home.*

"Ruth," he called. His voice sounded weak and rusty.

Ruth heard Ezra's call through the monitor she had set up in the kitchen. Only she and Alice were still awake. It was around two-thirty Saturday morning. Bishop and Queen were in her bedroom asleep. Sarah lay dozing in the bed with Naomi. Brian had taken Josh and Maggie home with him hours ago.

Alice looked at her friend. "Do you need me to come with you?"

"No, my sister. I've got to do this alone. Wake up the family. I have a feeling the end won't be long now."

Alice stood and hugged Ruth. "It's really fitting that you be with Ezra at the end. Send our brother home." The women hugged and wept.

Ruth walked heavily down the hallway. She knew Ezra's time had grown short. She wanted to hit the wall or drop to her knees and beg the Lord to spare her brother. Ezra's voice sounded in her head, telling her to remember the passage from Ecclesiastes, *to all things there is a season.* She rubbed her reddened eyes with the heels of her palms, then straightened her shoulders and walked into the bedroom.

His eyes glittered with pain. Ruth took a pill from the medicine vial and poured water into the paper cup. She walked and sat on the edge of the bed.

"No," Ezra said, shaking his head from side to side. "I want to think clearly while I talk to you."

Ruth set the pill and cup on the nightstand. Then she put hands over her face and cried. Ezra weakly stroked her back. "It's okay, Baby Ruth. Please don't cry. You'll have me crying in a minute, and we both know there's not a darn thing we can do to change the outcome of what's about to happen."

"Ezra, you don't have to be heroic with me. I know you're in pain, pain that I couldn't even imagine. I don't want to let you go, but I know your sorrows, trials, tribulations, and pain will be over soon. You'll be in our Father's house. A much better place than the one we inhabit now, and I'll see you there one day."

"See, that's what I'm talking 'bout." His voice became a little stronger. "Just get me some water. You know I have one more request to make of you, and you can't turn down a dying man."

Ruth nodded her head dejectedly and poured water from the pitcher on the nightstand. She helped her brother drink the cool liquid, set the cup back on the nightstand and sat on the side of the bed. "What is it, Ezra? You only have to ask, and you know I'll do it."

"Look in the top drawer."

She complied with his request. She quickly read the papers that she retrieved from the drawer. "Ezra, it's your funeral program." Her eyes widened with disbelief.

"Keep reading," he instructed her. He closed his eyes.

She dropped the paper on the bed. "You mean you want me to preach your eulogy? Ezra, I can't do it. Shouldn't Bishop be the one?"

"No, it's time for you to show Bishop and Queen what you're made of."

"It's too much. I don't know that I'll have the strength."

"You'll find it, and I want you to do something else for me." His body seemed to shrink. His breathing became more labored. "Preach, Ruth; spread God's word. It's what's in your heart. I talked to Daddy, not Bishop, and I asked him to support you. I think he will. Do it for me, and do it for you. Don't run away from our destiny. I love you, Baby Ruth."

His eyes glazed over. She reached over and grabbed his hand. He smiled at her, and then his head fell limply to the side.

"No!" Ruth wailed. She dropped to her knees, still holding her brother's hand. "Ezra, don't leave me!"

Bishop, Queen, and Alice rushed into the room when they heard Ruth's screams. Bishop took one look at his son and knew he had left this earthly place. Alice tried to take Queen in her arms, but she pushed her away and walked to the bed. She sat on the chair next to the bed and rocked back and forth in the seat as she wept, staring at her son's face.

Bishop lifted Ruth from the floor and led her to her bedroom. Alice followed him and ministered to her friend. Then Bishop went back to Ezra's room. He and Queen sat with their son another half hour. Then he called an ambulance and Ezra's doctor.

Friday afternoon at twelve o'clock, the temple opened the church doors to allow mourners to pay their last respects to Ezra Clayton. By eleven o'clock, a line had already formed around the corner of the building.

Queen had been in seclusion since Ezra's death. But she promised Bishop and Ruth that she would attend the funeral, though her heart wasn't in it.

When the limousine arrived to pick up the family for the wake, Queen was dressed in black from head to toe, and wore a long veil atop her head. Ruth snuggled in her mother's arms. The women wept together. Josh and Maggie were gathered in Sarah's arms. Alice kept a watchful eye on Ruth as she put her arm around Naomi's shoulders. Only Bishop seemed possessed of inner strength.

When the vehicle pulled up in front of the temple, the clan was astounded at all the people gathered in the front and on the sides of the large edifice.

"Where did all these people come from?" Naomi asked, wonderingly.

"Obviously Ezra knew more people than we could ever have imagined," Ruth answered, feeling proud of her brother.

The family marched somberly inside. They sat in the front row. The mortician had done a wonderful job preparing Ezra's remains. To the left of his coffin propped on top of the table was a collage of pictures depicting stages of his life.

Reverend Robinson, one of Bishop's associate pastors, walked toward the pew. He bent down and asked Bishop if he could open the church to the public. Bishop looked at his family and nodded his head yes.

For the next four hours, men, women, and children, entered and exited the church. The family's hands ached from shaking so many hands. Brian took the children outside intermittently. They still didn't quite comprehend what was going on. They thought Uncle Ezra was asleep.

Ruth looked around for Daniel, but he didn't show up. Fred stopped by and offered his condolences.

"I'm so sorry, Ruth. I know this has been a rough year for your family, but you've been hanging in there tough, girl. If you need me to do anything, you have my number." He kissed her cheek.

The Mother's Board prepared supper for the family. Mother Campbell told them not to worry, that they'd take care of the repast tomorrow.

After the viewing, and as the limousine drove the family back to Ruth's house, Bishop turned to his daughter and asked, "Do you want me and Queen to spend the night?"

"You don't have to unless you want. We'll be fine," Ruth replied.

"I think we'll stay with you tonight. Queen and I are going home to get our clothing for tomorrow. We'll be back later. I think today went well. Ezra was well respected."

"Yes, he was," Ruth said, sadly. She kissed her mother. "We'll see you later."

The next morning at ten o'clock, after Reverend Robinson finished praying, Ezra's funeral service was officially underway. Bishop sat in the pulpit beside Ruth, who's left knee didn't want to stop twitching. She leaned over and whispered to her father, "Maybe you should go sit with Mother. She looks lost." Queen was sitting in the front pew with her head bowed down.

Bishop glanced at his wife and squeezed Ruth's hand. "Okay. You'll be fine, I know you can do this." He got up, stepped down from the pulpit, and took his seat beside Queen. She rested her head on his shoulder.

Ruth stood, walked over to the podium, and adjusted the microphone. She pulled it close to her mouth. "Good morning church. I'd like to thank everyone for taking time out from your busy lives to be here with my family as we send my brother home. The program that you have in your hand is my brother's creation." The audience chuckled. "So, following along in your program, the choir will now perform an A and B selection."

Alice played the opening verse of the first song, "His Eyes Are On the Sparrow." The choir followed that song up with "Precious Lord Take My Hand."

Naomi, who wasn't returning to school until the following semester, in a halting, teary voice read her uncle's biography. Sarah thanked everyone for the cards and calls they'd received. Then Ruth asked members of the congregation to come to the podium and share any stories or experiences about Ezra. Quite a few people responded. Her heart soared with pleasure as she watched an older man, who she remembered from the homeless shelter, clad in mismatched worn but clean clothing, walk down the center aisle.

"My name is Robert Lee. I just wanna say that Ezree was a good man. I represent the fellas at the Pacific Garden Mission." He asked them to stand. To Ruth's amazement, the group of men took up nearly three rows near the back of the auditorium. "We came to know Ezree really well. He also told us never to give up hope. And we gonna try and do that." Robert looked embarrassed as he walked away from the pulpit. Ruth called his name, walked down the aisle to him, and shook his hand. *Ezra would be so proud.*

She stood once again before the microphone. "I'd like everyone to give Ezra a hand." The round of applause lasted almost five minutes. "When my big brother asked me to preach his eulogy, I told him I couldn't do it because his going home would be too fresh in my mind and weigh too heavily on my heart. I wouldn't be able to put aside my own sorrow to comfort someone else. But I promised him I would try, so here I am. If I breakdown and cry, just give me a moment to compose myself." Her voice broke, as she looked at the sea of faces that seemed to await her next move.

"When I think of my last conversations with my brother, the third chapter of Ecclesiastes comes to mind. He made me read that passage of scripture aloud every night. *'To every thing there is a season, and a time and purpose under the heaven: A time to be born, and a time to die.'* He told me to keep reading those verses, and in time his passing won't hurt so bad."

When she finished the eulogy, the church broke into a hearty round of applause. There wasn't a dry eye in the building. Bishop and Queen gazed at their daughter proudly.

"I'd like to now turn this portion of the service over to the morticians as they prepare Ezra for final viewing. The ushers will escort you to the front of the church." Her legs felt heavy as she walked from the pulpit and sat next to Queen. Mother Campbell brought Ruth a bottle of water. She thumped her on her back and said, "You did real good, sugar."

Ruth gulped down the water. "Thank you."

As the crowd took their last glimpse of Ezra, Ruth looked up to see Daniel walking to the coffin. Lenora trailed behind him holding Damon. Naomi gasped when she spied her father. When

Daniel walked over to pay his respect to the family, everyone held their breath. Ruth and Bishop stood.

She held out her hand and said, "Thank you for coming, Daniel. This must be your wife." She turned her attention to Lenora.

Lenora shook her head yes. "It's nice to meet you. I offer my condolences and Daniel's on the loss of your brother."

Ruth patted Daniel's arm. She leaned over and whispered in his ear, "It's all right. She's your wife and she has every right to be here with you. Ezra told me not to sweat the little things." She had a twinkle in her eye.

Daniel leaned forward and embraced Ruth. He mouthed, "Thank you."

Naomi rolled her eyes. She refused to acknowledge Lenora and Damon. DJ did likewise. Sarah, taking her cue from her mother, graciously greeted Lenora.

After the funeral service concluded, the family went to Burr Oak Cemetery, where other deceased family members were buried. Ruth felt better knowing she was leaving her brother in good company. Martin's grave was located not far from Ezra's.

After the burial, the limousine drove slowly out of the cemetery. The family sobbed loudly, beginning the healing process. Ruth turned to peep out the back window and she blew Ezra a kiss.

"I love you, my brother. I'll be back here often to talk to you. You're gone but not forgotten."

Chapter Fifty-five

The newlyweds had their first serious spat during their ride home from Ezra's service.

"It wasn't decent your coming to the funeral, Nora. It wasn't the right place to make a statement. You were plain wrong."

"Your precious Ruth didn't seem to have a problem with me being there. And how else was I going to meet your other children?"

"If you had given it time, the meeting would've eventually happened. Now you've probably set us back years," Daniel grumbled. He seethed with anger.

"Excuse me," Lenora snapped. "You sound like you're putting your first family ahead of me and Damon again. I won't have it, Danny. I'm your wife and I want the world to know it. Do you know how many years I had to stay on the down low, sneaking around with you? We'll, I'm out the closet now and there's no turning back. Get over it."

"You can be an evil witch at times, you know that."

"But you love me," she retorted. She leaned over and kissed his cheek.

A week later, Dr. Pryor gave Lenora the green light to resume sexual relations. Felicia was baby-sitting Damon for the weekend. Her fertility treatments had paid off. She was expecting a bundle of joy in the winter of the following year. The specialist warned her that there was a possibility she may be carrying twins. Felicia and Reggie were ecstatic.

After weeks of searching, Lenora selected a house in Park Forest as their new residence. Daniel agreed to use Fred's address for the time being. LaQuita and Kente were scheduled to move into the condo a week after they vacated the premises. Lenora had applied for a Section 8 certificate and was still waiting for the results.

Ernest was livid when he learned of Felicia and Lenora's plan. It seemed everyone benefited from Noree's money except him and Glenda.

Even though Ernest and Felicia had hired a competent lawyer, Jamal was sentenced to five years in jail. Lenora breathed a sigh of relief. She wouldn't have to worry about her incorrigible brother hanging around the condo. Jamal was stunned when the verdict came back. He broke down and cried like a baby before he was led off in handcuffs to Pontiac prison.

Daniel dropped his son off, along with a mountain of bags at Felicia's house. When he returned to the car, he opened the glove compartment and reached inside for the bottle of Viagra. He quickly unscrewed the top and popped a pill inside his mouth. He ran a couple of errands before heading home.

He whistled as he walked inside the building. *Yeah, once I take this medicine a couple of times, Nora will never leave me. Who's the man? I'm the man.*

He stuck out his chest like George Jefferson from the television sitcom. He knew Nora had something special planned for them. Before he could put his key in the lock, she opened the door dressed in her birthday suit. Daniel's tongue wagged as he admired her body. She practically tore his clothes off him. They kissed passionately, and then moved the party to the bedroom.

As many months elapsed after experiencing mind-blowing sex from taking the magic pills, Daniel's good fortune changed, and his moods became stymied in a perpetual state of confusion. His life became a continuation of the one he shared with Ruth. Lenora was always either working or taking care of the baby. Once again he felt neglected, except Lenora made sure his sexual needs were fulfilled.

Nine months after Daniel began taking Viagra, he and Lenora had just finished a tryst between the sheets. His heart began to beat rapidly and sweat poured off his face like water in a sieve.

Lenora turned to him and said, "Guess what, Danny? I think I'm pregnant again. The timing couldn't be more perfect. Me and Felicia's children will grow up together." Her eyes bucked and her expression became horror stricken. "Danny, are you okay? Speak to me. Boo?"

Daniel felt like a ton of steel lay embedded in

the middle of his chest. "Ah," was all he could manage to say. His body twitched and he lay still as foam poured from his mouth.

Lenora jumped from the bed. She rushed to the telephone and called 911. The ambulance arrived and rushed Daniel to St. Francis Hospital. Later, the doctor diagnosed Daniel as suffering a heart attack. Lenora frantically called Fred and asked him to come to the hospital. His girlfriend, Janet happened to be at his apartment and they broke speeding laws to rush to the suburb.

Fred went with Lenora to talk to the doctor, and when he asked what type of medication Daniel was taking, she shook her head helplessly.

Fred cleared his throat and said in a hoarse sounding voice, "My brother was taking Viagra. I warned him not to take that stuff. He didn't listen to me. And look where he is now."

When Daniel was released from the intensive care unit a few days later, Fred went to his brother's room. He shook his head sadly. "Boy, you done messed up all the way 'round. You tangled with that young filly, and roped her, and now look what happened. I tell you, bro, Ruth looks better and better each day. I told you those church girls make good wives. You shoulda stuck it out with her."

Daniel pointed toward the door with his good arm, motioning for Fred to leave. The relationship between the brothers had cooled somewhat. Fred didn't care for Lenora, and made no bones about making his feelings known. Daniel's attack was so severe that Lenora consulted with several attorneys. She had considered filing a lawsuit against the manufacturer of Viagra.

Daniel never fully recovered from his illness. By the time he completed physical therapy, his appearance was that of a man twice his age.

Felicia came over once a week and shaved his head. He still couldn't talk well, and he wrote her a note asking her to stop. It wasn't like he had anywhere to go.

Daniel stopped working and was put on permanent disability. Only Sarah came to visit him, and Lenora legally controlled his finances. He was able to communicate a little bit clearer and get around on his own, but his stamina never returned to its previous level. Daniel felt emasculated, and to add insult to injury, he couldn't get it up anymore.

Lenora gave birth to twin boys, David and Darnell and they howled all the time day and night. She hired Mrs. Lewis as their nanny/housekeeper, and began hitting the clubs with her new girlfriends, or so she said.

One Friday evening, Daniel sat in a lounge chair in his bedroom at the new house. His legs were weak and he could barely move. The remote control and a silver bell lay on a tray near the chair. The door opened and Tresor perfume announced Lenora had come into the room.

He looked up. His wife looked like a vision of sexiness as she stood near the television. Her feet were shod in stiletto heels, and fishnet stockings covered her legs. She wore a short, snug fitting, low-cut black dress, which covered her lush frame.

Her body had filled out after the birth of their sons.

She kissed Daniel's cheek. "Boo, I'm going out with the girls for a little while. It's Charisse's birthday. I should be back before too late. If you need anything, or help to the bathroom, ring your bell and Mrs. Lewis will come to assist you."

As he watched his wife sashay out of the room, a tear trickled down his left cheek. He finally understood what his doctor meant when he told him the story about no fool like an old fool. And yes, he could relate to Johnny Taylor's song, "It's Cheaper to Keep Her."

His nostrils flared. He clutched his stomach and moaned, "Aah." *I know Nora's cheating on me. Why didn't I hold on to the good woman I had?*

Chapter Fifty-six

Six months after Ezra's death, Ruth made good on her promise to her brother and returned to the classes at the seminary. She tackled her classes in earnest. Naomi returned to school for the fall semester. After Ezra's funeral, she resumed sessions with her therapist, but she still refused to talk to Daniel. DJ was of the same mind as his youngest sister.

Sarah extended the olive branch and met with Daniel and Lenora a few times for dinner. Later that year she and Brian reconciled, much to Maggie and Josh's glee. Sarah felt bad when she informed Ruth of her plans to move back into the apartment with Brian.

Ruth surprised her daughter by telling her that she and Brian could have the house. She and Alice planned to invest in an apartment building that had come up for sale in Chatham.

Naomi finally finished college after spending five years at Southern Illinois University. She was indecisive and kept changing her mind about what subject to major in. She finally decided to become a social worker. By the time she graduated, Naomi looked svelte after managing to shed a few pounds. She eventually came to terms with her family's convoluted history, and she now claims both Ruth and Sarah as her mothers.

On Ruth's last day at the seminary, she swore to Alice that she could feel Ezra's love surrounding her.

Following the graduation ceremony, Bishop proudly informed her with a twinkle in his eyes, "I have a position available for a minister at the temple. It's yours if you want it."

Ruth screeched happily, "Of course I do. When do you want me to start?" She grabbed Bishop's body and hugged him.

Queen, wearing a black pantsuit, looked at her husband and daughter and sighed contently. "It's a new day. Women can do whatever they want. Just think, Bishop, Ruth can be your successor."

After Ruth congratulated and accepted congratulations from her fellow graduates, the family traveled to Ruth's favorite restaurant for dinner. The Clayton and Wilcox family, through faith, love, and their unshaken belief in God, weathered the storms of life triumphantly.

READERS GROUP GUIDE

1. Do you feel Ruth could have done a better job balancing her time appropriately between her husband and her children, especially Naomi?

2. Did Daniel appear to want his cake and eat it too? Did he seem to love Lenora or was the emotion he felt infatuation? Did you feel he really overslept at Lenora's house, or did he use the situation as an opportunity to end his marriage to Ruth?

3. Was Queen too consumed with her duties as the First Lady of the temple to tend adequately to her children's needs?

4. Do you feel Ruth was correct in centering all of her attention on Naomi, or was she overcompensating for the attention she didn't receive from her own mother?

5. Do you feel now in the 21st century that society has softened their stance against gay people? Is the situation worse or better for

those who have come out and declared their sexual preference?

6. Should Sarah have gone along with the rape story that Queen cooked up?

7. From a financial standpoint, should Lenora have helped her parents/family more?

8. Bishop took his wife's side against his son's when he asked Ezra to leave the house. Could he have used other means to resolve the situation?

9. Are Bishop's views about women wearing pants and becoming ministers outdated?

10. Do you feel the Wilcox family was successful in maintaining their faith in God despite the many challenges they faced?

11. Do you feel the degree of closeness that Ruth and Alice shared was realistic in light of the relationship between Ezra and Martin?

12. Who was your favorite character and why?

13. Who was your least favorite character and why?

14. Did Ruth make the correct decision by putting Daniel out? Was she wrong to give up on so many years of marriage?

15. Ezra thought his illness was instrumental in bringing his family closer together. Do you agree with his assessment?

Coming Soon

Faith

By Michelle Larks

Prologue

Monet Caldwell inhaled loudly, held her breath, exhaled, then drew a deep cleansing breath. She smiled as she remembered her Lamaze exercises, and felt she was doing fine, even without her coach. Then her pretty smile faded abruptly because her situation at home, merely co-existing with her husband, Marcus, was not what she envisioned as a new bride twenty years ago when she imagined giving birth to their first child.

The gorgeous, petite, five feet two, formerly sized five, olive skin woman, with a mop of reddish blond curly hair, was upstairs in her bedroom sitting on the chaise lounge timing her contractions, while her dog, Mitzi, stood loyally at her feet. The only sound in the room was the ticking of a clock sitting on an oval table next to the chaise.

Monet's overnight suitcase sat upright next to the closet door. As she waited for the next contraction, her eyes roamed around the burgundy and gold striped bedroom. Matching borders were at the top of the walls inside the attached bathroom. Monet missed Marcus so much that her eyes became flooded with tears. She knew if she called him, he would come to her aid. But their marriage had been in a state of flux during her entire pregnancy, and somewhere deep within her soul, Monet wanted Marcus to come to her of his own volition.

A contraction poked Monet so hard that she moaned. She put one hand around her abdomen and massaged her temple with the other one. Mitzi stood at attention, her tongue waging as she cocked her head to the side, watching her mistress.

Monet picked up her mother's Bible, which was lying next to her on the chaise. She pressed the book next to her heart and prayed silently. *You told us that life wouldn't be easy, Lord, but I never imagined anything like this happening in my life.* She sighed. "Lord, keep me and my baby in your kind, loving arms. I know through your grace that we will both be fine. And when my labor of love has passed, I'll shout out your glory for bringing me through another valley along my journey of life. Because only you and Marcus know how long and hard I've prayed for a baby," she said aloud.

The contraction passed, and Monet couldn't keep a tiny grin off her face at the thought of her burly, chocolate colored bear of a husband. At six feet in height, his closely shorn hair was graying distinguishably at the temples, and much to Monet's delight, her handsome husband's face still took her breath away. Marcus was employed as a police detective, where he'd begun serving as a member of Chicago's finest shortly after the couple migrated to Chicago from a small town in Alabama over twenty years ago as newlyweds.

Forty-two-year-old Monet had two brothers, and forty-five-year-old Marcus had an older sister who lived in Texas. His parents were deceased. Monet's mother died instantly in a freak bus accident. The driver lost control of the vehicle and plowed into pedestrians crossing the street in the crosswalk. The accident occurred five years ago. After her mother's death, Monet's unmarried twin brothers, Derek and Duane, three years her junior, moved to Chicago from Alabama to be closer to their sibling. Monet's father had deserted the family when she was four years old. She had only fuzzy memories of the man she called Daddy.

Monet and Marcus met in middle school and became high school sweethearts. After Monet's graduation, she attended a small private college in Alabama and obtained a nursing degree. Her specialty was that of a neonatal nurse. The staff often said she had the *touch*. The Neonatal Care Unit boasted a high survival rate for its newborns. Many a night, if a parent wasn't at the hospital to see their child, Monet could be found providing the infant with a dose of TLC.

After graduating high school, Marcus joined the army where he served as a military police officer. His stint in the army ended when Monet graduated from college.

Monet glanced at the clock on the nightstand;

her contractions were close to twenty minutes apart. Her obstetrician, Dr. Armstrong, had instructed her to come to the hospital when the contractions were ten to fifteen minutes apart. For the most part, Monet had enjoyed an uneventful pregnancy, even though she had been categorized as a high risk patient due to her age.

Mitzi barked sharply as Monet stood up and waddled over and picked up her overnight bag. She clutched the suitcase in her hand and dropped her cell phone into the pocket of her maternity jeans. She clutched the banister tightly as she walked slowly down the stairs. Mitzi trotted beside her.

Then a contraction hit her so hard that she felt like someone had punched her in the back. She momentarily let go of the banister, dropped the suitcase, and fell forward. But like a ballerina, she managed to turn sideways. She tried to regain her balance as she slid down four stairs. Mitzi began barking loudly. Monet moaned as her water broke. She managed to pull her cell phone out of her pocket and dial 911.

Monet mumbled, "I need help. I'm in labor, and I fell down the stairs. Please send someone to help me." Then she passed out.

Chapter 1

Monet looked up and across the counter of the nurse's station desk as the sound of cracking bubblegum assaulted her eardrums.

"Ma'am, where is the maternity ward?" A stout, middle-aged woman with short twists in her head stood on the other side of the desk. She held a potted fern in one hand and several pink and purple balloons proclaiming, *It's a Girl* in her other one.

"Down the hall," Monet pointed the way with her ink pen, "and around the corner."

The woman shyly said, "Thank you." She walked down the hallway per Monet's directions.

Monet continued to make notations in the folders when the telephone rang. "St. Bernard's Hospital, this is Nurse Caldwell. How may I direct your call?" she answered.

"Hi, Nay-Nay." Nay-Nay was Marcus's pet name for his wife. "I know you're tired after pulling that double today. I wanted to know if you want me to pick you up from work?"

They lived in the community of Auburn on the southwest side of Chicago on the 3800 block of West 85th Street. Monet and Marcus worked in the community of Englewood, one of the most economically challenged areas on the south side of Chicago. When the pair moved from Alabama to the Windy City, they were young and idealistic and decided to work in communities where they could make the biggest impact in the lives of African Americans.

Marcus worked at the Seventh District Police Station on 63rd Street, and the hospital was located on 64th Street, so they worked less than five miles apart from each other.

"No, that's okay, honey; I'm good. I'm just about done here. This place has been like Union Station during Christmas travel all night," Monet joked, as she laid the folder in the to-be-filed pile.

"Hmm, that bad? I guess you're tired then. By the time you leave the hospital, it will be close to midnight. I can swing by and pick you up; that's no problem. You don't need to drive if you're that tired. We can come back to the hospital tomorrow to get your car," Marcus offered.

"Well, I am tired, but I can make it home," Monet replied. A smile crossed her face as she thought about her and Marcus's tryst between the sheets earlier that morning. Monet looked down at her stomach and thought, *maybe God has blessed us, and we made a baby this morning.*

"Okay, don't say I didn't offer to come get you.

I'll call you later. Love you, babe. Be careful," he said.

"I love you too, Marcus. I promise I'll be careful. You take care of yourself," she responded before ending the call.

After she had finished adding notation to the files, Monet stood up, stretched her body, and rubbed the lower portion of her back. As she smoothed down the top of her now wrinkled green scrubs that she'd worn to work that morning, Monet prayed that she had gotten pregnant and envisioned smoothing the top over a baby bump. She sat back down in the ergonomic chair and was putting the remaining folders in the tray to-be-filed when Dr. Edwards walked over to the desk.

"I realize that it's time for you to get off work, Nurse Caldwell, but I have an emergency." He glanced down at his still beeping pager. "Would you make sure this prescription gets filled for the patient in room 110?" Without waiting for Monet to reply, Dr. Edwards handed her a thick manila folder. "The prescription's inside the folder on top."

"Sure, Dr. Edwards." Monet stifled a yawn as she took the folder from him and laid it on the counter. She had just pulled a double, working the first and second shifts, and was tired. She knew that traffic would be lighter than normal at that time of the night on the Dan Ryan Expressway, and barring any accidents, she should be home in twenty minutes.

Monet asked a nurse's aide to take the

prescription to the pharmacy ASAP and to wait for it to be filled. After the young man departed, she removed her black leather purse from her bottom desk drawer and walked to the locker area. Several minutes later, she had put on her hooded spring jacket, locked her locker, and was headed home.

No matter how busy her day was, or how tired she felt, Monet always stopped by the neonatal ICU to look at the babies and would say a prayer for the newborns before leaving the hospital. Since she and Marcus had been unable to have children, she considered the babies in the nursery her own.

A smile slid across her face as she watched the different shades of babies. Some of the tiny faces were screwed up and crying, while others slept peacefully. Monet's tiredness was forgotten.

She bowed her head, closed her eyes, and said softly, "Lord, thank you for helping me to complete another day of work at St. Bernard's Hospital. Thank you for keeping me in my right mind as I cared for your children. Father, I beg you to take care of the innocent babies here in this hospital today, and all over the world in every hospital right now. Help their parents to do the best they can to love and take care of your precious children. God above, if it's in your will, please bless Marcus and me with children. These blessings I ask in your Son's name. Amen." Monet smiled at the babies and turned to walk to the elevator, which delivered her down to the first floor.

The temperature was mild for the fall season in Chicago in October. Halloween was next week,

and paper ghosts, goblins, and witches adorned
the pediatric ward and other areas of the hospital.

When Monet reached the hospital entrance,
David, the security guard, was seated at his post
at the main entrance. He asked Monet if she
wanted him to walk her to her car since it was
close to midnight.

"No." Monet shook her head. "I should be all
right."

"Well, I'll see you tomorrow, Mrs. Caldwell. Be
careful." He doffed his navy blue and white
striped brimmed hat at her.

"I'm off work tomorrow; I'll see you on Monday," Monet corrected David. "Have a nice weekend."

She walked out the door and traveled half a
block to the corner and turned left toward the
parking lot. She was filled with a buoyancy of
hopefulness. Monet had taken her temperature
that morning and discovered that she was ovulat-
ing. She and Marcus had made tender love before
she'd left for work that morning. Memories of the
couple's coming together caused merriment to
tug at the corners of her mouth.

When Monet entered the parking lot, she noticed the area was somewhat dim around her car
due to the nonfunctioning overhead light. She
frowned at the security camera which didn't appear to be functioning either. She hesitated, debating if she should go back to the hospital and
take Dave up on his invitation to escort her to her
car. *Stop being silly*, she chided herself. *You've
walked in this lot millions of times*. She then decided
to chance it since her car was no more than a few

feet away. Her hand shook slightly as she removed her key remote from her parka pocket.

Suddenly the hairs on the back of Monet's neck
stood at attention. She sensed someone behind her.
But before she could react, she was pushed from
behind. She fell hard, and became sprawled face
down on the ground, weight pinning down her
body. Monet was frozen, as a cloud of foul breath
invaded the back of her head.

Terror filled her soul. "Please let me go," she
moaned. "You can have my purse."

A sinister chuckle followed her pronouncement.
Then a male voice growled, "Did I say I wanted
your money? Now shut up!"

Monet felt her body being dragged into a
clump of tall bushes outside the parking lot area.
Please, Lord, don't forsake me, she prayed. She tried
to grab hold of the gold cross that always hung
around her neck, but her shaking fingers couldn't
grasp the chain.

Her attacker flipped her over like they were
gymnasts performing in a tournament, and pinned
her arms behind her back. Monet groaned and
squeezed her eyes shut. She had no desire to see
his face.

Her lips moved as she began silently reciting
the Twenty-Third Psalm. T*he Lord is my shepherd; I
shall not want. He maketh me to lie down in green pas-
tures; He leadeth me beside the still waters. He re-
storeth my soul; He leadeth me in the path of righteous
for His namesake. Yea, though I walk through the valley of death, I will fear no evil; for thou art with me;
they rod and staff they comfort me. Thou preparest a
table before me in the presence of my enemies; thou*

anointest my head with oil; my cup runneth over. Surely goodness and mercy shall follow me all the days of my life; and I will dwell in the house of the Lord forever.

She could feel the material from her scrub pants scrapping across her skin like sandpaper, as her attacker tore the garment from her body. After he had his way with her, his fist smashed into the side of Monet's head, rendering her unconscious. Then the deranged man hit her in the face over and over again.